I0522413

Acceptance

Rhobin Lee Courtright

A Wings ePress, Inc.
Fantasy Novel

**Wings ePress, Inc.**

Edited by: Leslie Hodges
Copy Edited by: Elizabeth Struble
Senior Editor: Elizabeth Struble
Executive Editor: Lorraine Stephens
Cover Artist: Robin Lee Courtright

All rights reserved

Names, characters and incidents depicted in this book are products of the author's imagination or are used fictitiously. Any resemblance to actual events, locales, organizations, or persons, living or dead, is entirely coincidental and beyond the intent of the author or the publisher.

No part of this book may be reproduced or transmitted in any form or by any means, electronic or mechanical, including photocopying, recording, or by any information storage and retrieval system, without permission in writing from the publisher.

Wings ePress Books
www.wingsepress.com

Copyright © 2005 by Rhobin Courtright
ISBN-13: 978-1-59088-606-9
ISBN-10: 1-59088-606-2

Published In the United States Of America

Wings ePress Inc.
3000 N. Rock Road
Newton, KS 67114

Dedication

For my sister Patty...
My confidant, supporter and cheerleader
§

One

Unobserved on a footpath high above the river valley, Kissre pushed wind-blown hair from her face and watched the wagons below her. The wind squalled down the valley's walls with a cold wail and the sting of icy air. It came at her from ever-changing angles, pushing her both forward and back, urging her to any direction. Ever obstinate, she remained immobile.

Her mother's caravan wove through the rutted path along the river's edge. The ox teams appeared cantankerous in the erratic wind. She recognized Jebe, the single outrider. He scouted the route, but for him, muck and mire created a more imminent danger than any covert observer.

Always dangerous, Seer Pass worsened at this time of year. Receding high spring waters allowed uncertain travel along the rocky track strewn with boulders dislodged from the gray cliffs by winter's ice.

Bother pulled against Kissre's rein-filled hand, signaling his restlessness. He stomped, digging a hoof into the gravelly soil, then shook his head with a spine-bouncing shiver that ran down his back. When she held him at a halt, he gave a deep, nostril-blowing snort, and heaved his sides in a sigh of resignation.

From Bother's offside Fudge yawned with a funny dog sound. Even sitting, his shaggy brown head reached well above her stirrup. Catching her gaze, he wagged his tail. Both animals reacted to her procrastination. A glance showed the lazy roan packhorse stood behind Bother with eyes closed, apparently asleep and unfazed by the wind.

Her eyes returned to the wagons. Naomi still employed Jebe as her guide. Kissre huffed her contempt. He rode ahead of the three wagons checking the terrain, but never looked up, never noticed anything above his restricted view.

Naomi and Tyna were down there: her mother and sister. The anticipated family reunion did not engender felicitous expectations. Only Tyna's plea in her last letter had brought Kissre this far. A visit put off for far too many months by the requirements of duty, plausible excuses, then sheer evasion.

"I'm a coward," she told Fudge. The huge walnut-brown dog rose to his feet. His lean Gazehound body stood poised to move, and his whip-like tail waved, oddly dissimilar from his shaggy coat. It hit Bother on the flank. The horse sidestepped from the buffeting with a low nicker of warning and a hind foot lifted in threat. Fudge's tongue lolled, smile-like, from a mouth hidden beneath an umber mustache.

Switching the reins to her left hand, she reached down to caress the wiry-fur muzzle. His rough tongue licked her hand. Grimacing, she wiped her hand on her leather-covered thigh. Bother snorted at her shifting, off-center weight, so she stroked his wheaten neck in apology.

"Facing an army in the field is easier than meeting my 'gifted' sister and Naomi." Thoughts of heading back into Kaereya flitted among possible alternatives. Bother sensed her indecision. She felt him tense through the saddle. His head bobbed and twisted, pulling at the bit. He wanted to go.

Kissre sighed and urged her horse down the steep embankment. No sense in putting off the inevitable.

~ * ~

Eldin stepped from where he hid in the shadows of the wagon, his withdrawal initiated by recognition of the huge buckskin horse. The rider was a known mercenary working for Kaereya. Unsure whether she would recognize him, he sought the safer route of concealment.

Watching the bay horse stop before Jebe, he listened as the caravan's leader told Kissre of her mother's death and Tyna's abandonment of the caravan. Kissre settled back in the saddle with a blatant expression of disbelief. Jebe stammered into more stories. Kissre asked something, but Eldin could not hear her.

"No!" Jebe's explosive negation burst through the air at nearly the same time Kissre's buckskin rose on his hind feet. Jebe's horse shied, and the man could not move fast enough to stay in the saddle. He fell with a loud splat in the mud. Kissre followed her advantage and leaped upon him, her falling weight forcing the wind in an audible whoosh from his large frame. Before Jebe could collect himself for a counterattack, one of Kissre's blades graced his throat. The few men working the caravan stopped their activity and watched, but like Eldin, none cared enough to interfere in the altercation, at least not with the huge dog on alert.

Eldin grinned. Jebe outweighed Kissre by several stones and stood a full head, maybe more, taller. A trained fighter, and once a captain in Kaereya's Royal Guard, Eldin thought he could take Kissre, but the cowardly blowhard she fought could not.

Kissre questioned Jebe thoroughly on his illegal acquisition of the caravan and demanded purchase payment. Jebe whined and cried, but Kissre pulled him to his feet, her knife biting into the flesh of his neck, and marched him to the main wagon. It appeared she knew where Jebe kept the strongbox.

Her appearance brought Eldin memories of a redheaded friend and an exile's longing for home. *Traitor.* He stopped his mind from going there and concentrated on this new development.

A Kaereyan agent riding through Seer Pass? To where, and for what?

Hooves pounded away, interrupting Eldin's thoughts. In his inattention, Kissre must have finished her business. Her horse moved off at a fast canter followed by her menacing dog. His glance followed her progress until the caravan's leader approached, throwing his arms up in anger and swearing,

Jebe sputtered in fury, his loose jowls shaking with his anger. "The bitch stole two years' profit. I'll kill her."

Eldin smiled. *Only if you hire someone to do it.* The man's smell would alert anyone to his presence. Huge, slovenly, and ungainly, the caravan leader continued his denunciation. The thought of him killing a mercenary like Kissre Pierce amused Eldin. Jebe's mismanagement of a profitable caravan, and his misjudgment of Eldin based on his short, slight build, revealed the man's perception.

"What did you owe her? I know her reputation. She would not steal from a traveling merchant."

"She claimed her sister's share."

"Tyna?"

"Yes. The caravan should have come to me when Naomi died. I did all the work. I made all the profit. Women!" Jebe shook his head.

"So you stole it?"

"No! Tyna gave it to me. She chose to stay in Cygna. She told me to take the caravan, wanted me to make her profits. Supposedly she stayed to open a market, but like all women, it was about a man."

"You cut your ties with her? When you had entry to Cygnese markets?" Eldin asked, unable to keep the incredulity from his voice.

"A mistake," Jebe said, seemingly abashed, "but I have the caravan now, free and clear." He spoke as if the lost market paid for his theft.

Eldin hid his amusement. Jebe disliked humor at his expense. "And Mistress Kissre is on her way to Cygna?"

"Yes. To visit her sister." Jebe swore. "May the witches strike such an unnatural, mannish woman dead."

After Jebe left to get the wagons moving, Eldin looked in the westerly direction the mercenary had taken. Kissre traveled to Cygna, the legendary land of magic and witches? His overlord, King Clement, desired the power of that magic. Was this Kissre's original destination, circumstance, or was Kaereya's King Warrick seeking an alliance with Cygna? An interesting development he could report. Whatever her purpose, it could work for him.

Within those supposedly impervious borders, Eldin knew discontent fermented. He helped keep the brew simmering as his liege ordered. It was easy. A word of dissatisfaction, a piece of gossip, an unexplained loss, bad luck, or other injury could twist opinion. If some accident befell an emissary from Kaereya, would not Cygna be held responsible? Conservative, reclusive Cygna, where strangers seldom found welcome?

Perhaps his hard-won contacts within Cygna could make a fitting welcome for this guest, this threat to Pertelon. His new liege would surely find this development of interest, a threat that needed elimination. King Clement hoped to pluck Cygna before even the witches knew of his tactic. Kissre and her Kaereyan influence could spoil that plan.

~ * ~

Riding from the caravan, Kissre took the track that led to Cygna. She gave a sour laugh at her earlier trepidation. The inevitable turned into a future eventuality. Her mother was dead. For Naomi's passing, she did not know what she felt, maybe an uncertain sorrow, but not grief. She would deal with it later, maybe. *Cygna. By the Holy One, what was Tyna thinking? Perhaps she had no choice? Perhaps the Cygnese witches coerced her?* Those disturbing thoughts drove Kissre onward.

One physical obstacle slowed Kissre's entry into Cygna. She knew the road twisted a few leagues along a swift river before coming to a shallow, but still dangerous, ford. Cygna never put out a welcome sign, let alone a bridge. Kissre chose an even more dangerous passageway, a shortcut remembered from a previous, hurried journey of departure long ago.

A path led off the road to a scenic waterfall. It was not hard to find, for even from the road, the roar of falling water reverberated. That path continued beneath the falls, and if still there, would cut the travel distance by many leagues. It had been years since she had traversed beneath the falls. Erosion might already have destroyed the way.

Dismounting, she found the path shrub-free, so knew either locals or travelers still used the passage. This close, the deafening noise of the water made all other sounds vanish. She walked the path first. Part of the rock ledge under the falls had given way, probably very recently. The breach was only a wide step's width. Kissre considered Bother's weight near the crumbling stone edge. She knelt on the damp mossy surface and looked over the edges. The supporting rock seemed secure. She straightened and looked around her. Spray from the cascade ran down the cliff's back forming shallow pools in depressions filling the ledge walkway. Rivulets from small, overflowing pools streamed toward the edge to join the downward torrent, but the floor held enough traction that hooves would not slide.

She led the blindfolded roan through the tunnel first with no trouble. She paced the horse so her gait would naturally span the broken ledge, except the beast stumbled as she neared the breech. Kissre slapped the animal's rear, making her jump forward across the break. Kissre made the jump at the same time, but one lashing rear hoof knocked a chunk of rock from the ledge. The roan panicked. Tugging on the lead, Kissre ran forward, forcing the mare to follow. On the other side, she tied the rangy horse to a tree and returned.

Bother easily followed her between the rocks that led to the short tunnel entrance. Fudge followed at the horse's heels. They emerged under the curtain of water and started across the ledge. Bother followed her calmly, stepping over the gap until one back hoof found only air. Startled, he stopped in mid-stride with his leg suspend in air. White lines appeared around his eyes, and his head popped up in alarm. His rear leg stretched back finding solid ground. Neighing, he backed in a rearing motion.

Kissre, pulled off her feet, hung onto the reins, and managed to grab a stirrup as she fell. Her scrabbling feet found no purchase on the slippery wet stone and her legs went off the edge into the void of missing stone. She hung there, dangling from two thick strands of rein leather and a stirrup. Below her water crashed on rocks, swirling and splashing in angry torrents. Releasing the reins, she tried with one hand to grab the stone, but her fingers failed to find purchase on the slippery edge and slid further into the abyss. She was suddenly jerked up as Bother backed from the edge. Quickly she threw her upper body on the ledge and let go of the stirrup. Beneath her stomach she felt the ledge vibrate with Bother's steps. He needed to get off the rock immediately.

"Jump, Bother, jump," she screamed over the roar of the water.

She heard him snort and screamed the command again. Piercing barks penetrated the rampaging fall of water. The rock vibrated as Bother charged forward. She closed her eyes and winced, waited for the ledge to give way, waited for one of Bother's huge hooves to graze her head as he jumped the missing section. No blow came.

She opened her eyes. "Follow, Fudge." The dog was quicker.

With some gyrating maneuvers, she pulled herself onto the ledge as crumbling rock widened the gap. Once upright, she glanced across the open space. Bother and Fudge had continued on, leaving her alone on the wrong side of the gap. That break now extended a considerable distance. Swearing, Kissre walked backward. Taking a deep breath, she started running and leaped at the opposite rock edge. One foot slid on landing. Her arm whirled, and she fell.

Landing on her knees, she thrust her body forward to splay along the rock. Beneath her, she felt a crumbling sensation that made her crawl, sprawl, and drag herself forward. Once safe on firm rock, she slowly rose to her feet. Shaking her head, she cursed—*all to save a few leagues.*

Emerging into the bright sunlight outside the tunnel, she found Fudge sat next to the grazing horses, waiting. His rough bark at the sight of her sounded like heckling, and his dangling tongue conveyed laughter at her appearance. She looked down at herself. Slime, mud, and mist droplets covered her. Her gaze rose to the dog.

"All right, it was a bad idea."

Fudge fell to the ground to roll in the grass, making grumbling noises. The two horses continued munching spring's first green blades of grass.

Inside her saddlebags, she found a cloth. A small pool near the falls provided wash water for her muddy hands. With the cloth she dried her hair and wiped her leathers clean. The short jack showed a few minor scuffs and a tear along one sleeve's seam, but the leggings fared less well. Sighing, she remounted and continued on the main road.

Entering the country of her birth brought no *déjà vu*, forbidding portent, nor sense of kinship. The earth still greened beneath the previous season's winter-browned stalks, the slow incline of the road stayed as twisted and rocky, and the budding leaves hung in a chartreuse lace against dark green firs.

The few people she passed seemed suspicious and belligerent at once, but unafraid. She put their reaction down to her outlander appearance. Cygnese women did not wear a mercenary's leather jack over trews and riding boots. They would not know the deep mist-purple color of the jack's soft, near immutable leather was the natural skin color from a wild ox found in the mountains south of the distant Zankiri Peninsula. The fawn leather trews, when not scuffed and scratched, were practical alternatives for a woman rider. The Cygnese would only see the foreign dress and short hair. The chin-length strands tended to tangle in wild loose curls and waves, a style even more unlike the fastidious, conservative local fashion.

With most of her weapons safely packed, except, of course, her boot knives, which had come in so handy with Jebe, Kissre felt her appearance largely unthreatening. Her dress might catch the natives' attention, but it was the glitter of gold at her ears and right brow that raised Cygna suspicions and widened their eyes, sending them scurrying away after a long look. Kissre supposed it just as well that the serpent-bird tattoo wrapping her right wrist and snarling down her hand remained hidden under gloves she had pulled on for warmth.

She had not traveled five furlongs beyond the border before two riders bore down on her, authority implied in the brown uniforms and superior attitudes. One lawman appeared much older than she, one much younger. Their small but rugged longhaired mountain ponies pulled up before Bother. It was absurd. Bother topped both shaggy gray beasts by at least five hands, maybe more.

She suspected them unfamiliar with warhorses, animals trained to dispose of small obstacles barring their rider's way. Squeezing her fingers gently, she backed Bother two steps. The roan packhorse pulled up close to her right leg before stopping. Fudge growled, and she warned him, "Out." His head swung toward her and then back to the officers. He sat in obedience. A prolonged yawn exposed a fine set of incisors before his long tongue wiped his muzzle and hung in a light pant.

"Officers?" Kissre asked and greeted in her pleasant tone.

"State your business in Cygna, sir!" The younger one spoke first, all self-appointed aggression.

Kissre stared at him, and when his hand clasped a small hilt, she decided escalating the provocation would get her nowhere. She rested her hands on her saddle's pommel. "Visiting. My sister. I was told she was in Sidih."

The man looked at her in not only obvious disbelief but also contempt. "You have relatives in Cygna?" Patent skepticism lined the words.

"Just so."

"Your name?" His voice added insult to the request.

Kissre straightened in the saddle at his tone and looked down on him from Bother's greater height with a look that worked well on new and recalcitrant recruits. Her fingers gave a subtle twitch on the reins, and Bother did his part. His head rose from his relaxed stance, his nostrils widened as if he smelled trouble. The young man's tension showed as his pony protested the sudden jerk of reins.

"Cygna does not easily welcome strangers, sir," the older officer said in a mollifying tone. Kissre turned to look at him. Obviously the senior officer, but she couldn't tell from any insignia on their uniforms. Kissre cursed Tyna silently. She considered abandoning her visit and returning to Kaereya but knew herself too stubborn to retreat before this hurdle.

"Tell your youngster," she said, looking at the senior officer as she nodded toward his companion, "that inflammatory gestures are a clear challenge to any mercenary. In response, I have restrained my mount from crushing his pony, my dog from ripping out his throat or hamstringing his animal. If that is not a sign of peaceful intent, I don't know what is." Exaggeration, but the youngster would miss the overstatement.

The older officer remained motionless, but she noticed humor glint in his eyes. The younger man's hands moved abruptly from his sword. He backed his pony out from under Bother's nose. Kissre relaxed back into the saddle, and Bother's head lowered with a soft snort of air.

"We still need your name, sir." The man was good, his voice conciliatory, but the attitude unyielding.

"Kissre Pierce. I am trying to find my sister Tyna. She brought a trade caravan in about a year ago, and it is mistress, not sir."

Both men startled at her comment and Kissre cursed under her breath at their assumption or insult. At that moment, the roan packhorse, with a quick toss of her rust head, bit Kissre's thigh. Cursing in crude soldiers' terms, Kissre snapped the ends of the lead rope over the mare's nose.

The roan snorted, threw her head up, and backed, pulling on the lead. Fudge rose to bark and nip at the packhorse's hocks. The surly animal bucked and kicked at Fudge before careening forward into Bother. Kissre jerked on the lead, grabbing the halter in a pain-inflicting action. The mare froze her attention on her pinched nose.

Kissre yelled at Fudge, but by then, his loud barks and spiral jumps had spooked the officer's mounts. The men had their hands full of shying ponies.

It took some moments to restore order.

Only Bother stood quiet, swishing his tail in annoyed impatience, his chin drawn to his chest, one foreleg pawing the ground. As the mare settled, Kissre released the halter's pressure and sat back in her saddle.

"My apologies, officers, for the disruption." Chagrin replaced her anger. She rubbed the spot afflicted by the bite just below her buttock. "I bought the nag before leaving Kaereya. She's a good beast with a few bad habits."

The older officer openly grinned, the younger was unreadable. "That's a fine vocabulary you have, Mistress Pierce. Sorry to have delayed your journey, but I think you no harm to Cygna. Just doing our duty, you understand. Good traveling."

In unison, the two twirled their mounts and cantered away.

With an exasperated look at Fudge, she said, "No welcome at all." Fudge barked one low woof she took for agreement.

~ * ~

After that, she encountered no problems. Entering an inn's courtyard that evening, the hostler refused to approach Bother. Dismounting, she released the girth on her saddle and tied the reins to the hitching post. Doing the same for the roan, she ordered Fudge to guard. The road had been a steep incline all day, and both horses were too tired to cause trouble, but precautions were in order.

Walking inside she massaged the roan's bite on her thigh, then stopped, realizing it looked like she rubbed her ass to the small group watching her. She ignored those eating at the establishment's tables as she entered. So many patrons spoke well for the food. Removing her gloves, she asked for a room. The bald man behind the desk looked wary, even frightened. His expression changed as she signed the register.

"Ahh, Mistress Kissre Pierce," he said, too loud. "We thought it might be you, but so close to the border, there is always some unease." The man turned out to be the inn's owner. He nodded to the patrons staring from all the tables in the room. "Captain Tyna's sister." His attention returned to her. "You must be proud to have such a Talent Adept in your family." Only her surprise at their knowledge stopped her blurting, in equal surprise, *'Captain'?*

Adept—the word triggered a memory of Naomi, packing and rushing, screaming to hurry. "No adept will test my baby. They are all witches! Witches!"

Witches or adepts, they flourished in this land, communicating with the ease of thought. That's why Naomi smuggled Tyna out in the first place—afraid the witches would take her baby from her.

The hostility all around faded into formal but accepting nods and the resumption of interrupted conversations.

"May my dog sleep in my room?" Kissre asked. The owner gave her every assurance while his eyes furtively scrutinized her tattoo.

"I'll look to my horses before I go upstairs." She handed over the coin payment for her room and stabling. It was an expensive extravagance, but she wanted to sleep in a bed. Besides, the suspicious country people might mistrust her camping along the road and draw crazy conclusions about her purpose.

The owner agreed and told her the dinner menu. She handed over more coins. "Two dinners. Give me a half a candlemark."

Easing past gawking villagers in the doorway, Kissre ignored the sound of multiple chairs scraping the wood floor and the movement at the windows and murmurs of, "Did you see…"

A few steps took her to Bother. She grabbed up his reins, and the hostler, who took the roan's lead, led her to the stable. Bother, his head bobbing above hers, nibbled her hair as they followed. She brushed his attentions away with affectionate irritation. 'Bothersome brute,' she complained. Inside the stable, the well-kept and deeply bedded stalls lined the center aisle. For Bother, the stalls looked on the small side.

The hostler spoke. "He's a Sunderlune, isn't he? Heard they got big, just never saw one up close." He ran an appreciative hand over Bother's rump.

"Actually, I was able to buy him because he is small for the breed, and of course, his color is off. The breeder wanted bays and blacks only."

"Well, buckskin or not, he's a beaut. Fine head, good eye, can see he's well made. Stall's a bit close for him, but I'll keep an eye he doesn't cast himself or get in any other trouble." He approached Bother's head and reached up to stroke the wheaten forehead where a small white streak stretched from between the eyes and down into the black of the muzzle. Bother lowered his head, permitting easier access. "Hey, he seems gentle enough."

"Once his girth is loosened, he is perfectly safe." Since the saddle remained on his back, the man backed off, saying he would see to the pack animal. Once she removed Bother's tack and seen both horses rubbed down, fed, and watered, she and Fudge returned for dinner.

From the owner's expression, she guessed a dog near the size of a native mountain pony unexpected. Luckily, Fudge was well trained. Heeling the dog when they entered the door, he sat as she stopped to drop her saddlebags. A startled waitress watched Fudge with frighten-lined eyes and pointed Kissre to her table.

As the owner approached the table with the two plates, Fudge rested his head on the tabletop and watched the man with entreating brown eyes. The innkeeper placed the plates on the table and reached a hesitant hand to stroke the soft but twisted and spiky brown fur on Fudge's head. Kissre smiled. At the open invitation, Fudge licked the hand and let his ridiculous tongue drape over his chin in a way that could only be called a smile. His nose nudged the hand into another stroke. Emboldened, the owner started talking to Fudge, who, true to form, put on his 'I'm wonderful' act. Kissre snorted softly.

"The second dinner is for Fudge. If you have an old plate he could eat from?"

"No need," he said lowering the plate to the floor, "he can use this one. Good boy, Fudge."

Fudge waited until the hands withdrew from the plate before delving into the food.

"He likes the house stew!" At the man's words, Fudge turned from bolting his dinner to bestow a grateful lick on the nose bent over him. The innkeeper sputtered, wiped his face, and grinned, slapping the dog's side in loud thumps. It was appalling how a dog could manipulate not only one but also a whole roomful of people. It allowed Kissre a chance to eat her dinner in peace. When a third plate of table scraps appeared for Fudge, she had to draw the line.

The damn animal gave her the same look of reproach as everyone else. "No really, he's fine," she reassured and commanded Fudge down. He huffed and groaned, even moaned, as he obeyed, but laid his head over one booted foot with a sigh. Another tankard of ale appeared on the table, which Kissre took her time to enjoy.

~ * ~

The unexpected hospitality at that first stop forecast her trip. As she traveled further into Cygna, the less alarm she engendered. Like magic, hostlers waited and approached only after watching her loosen the saddle girth. They would carefully remove Bother's saddle, take the reins, and lead both horses to the stable. Innkeepers welcomed Fudge. She knew her journey's progress reported by the damn adepts communicating between themselves. Overheard comments likened her to Captain Tyna. She smiled and made no comment such as, 'Yeah, like salt and vinegar. Both sting in an open wound, but it all ends there.'

The covert side-glances at her unusual appearance never ended but were at least, politely disguised. Word seemed to have spread about the tattoo, for she noticed people looking for it with appalled expectation as she removed her gloves.

Their fashion confounded her. Never had she seen a more conforming dress in a population. Men always wore a long coat over a tunic, which topped trews fitted into long boots. Women wore the same style tunic top over a long skirt and slippers. Clothes varied in fabric and dark color, usually brown or gray, but always the same cut. Their only extravagance seemed jewelry, which inevitably consisted of rings, at least one on each finger, usually more. Sometimes a color patch appeared on a sleeve, mostly solid blue, but sometimes striped in blue and red. Other than that, she occasionally saw a necklace or broach decorating a citizen, but rarely. Decidedly, no gold pierced any skin.

Used to anonymity and paying her own way, becoming the center of interest for so many made Kissre uneasy. A mercenary usually spawned fear and wariness; they seldom received any sort of privilege, especially on price. She did not imagine the eyes following her. They came to the roadside to watch her pass on the mountainous road to Sidih, the Cygnese capital.

Three days from Sidih, a small troop met her. From their manner, Kissre identified them as military men, not Talents. It hadn't taken long to realize the colored sleeve patches indicated Talent, or to learn 'nulls' were non-Talents, like her. These three were soldiers, also like her. While they initially seemed wary of a woman, in a short time introductory talk of the road, the weather, and her trip turned to anecdotes of other journeys, then of funny, stupid, or dangerous situations their business precipitated.

None of her company had ever fought outside Cygna, or even in anything other than border skirmishes. Her own tales of Pertelon, the Eastern Empire, the Doane Desert, and Kaereya openly delighted them. She knew they thought her a magnificent liar.

The sergeant, Tomel, and his two men were cheerful company. Tomel, noticing her guith on the roan, proclaimed himself a good tenor with a fondness for camp-side entertainment. Kissre played that evening. The small string instrument with its deep voice complimented her alto. Tomel proved himself as capable as he claimed, and the other men provided enthusiastic volume. Once they settled for the night, Kissre worked on the puzzle for the need of an escort—*to ensure her arrival or to protect the citizenry?* Tyna must be desperate for her visit.

Several leagues from Sidih she saw the city's legendary blue walls. Her guards proudly pointed out the great and ancient bulwarks. Cities always interested Kissre, which produced myriad questions. Each feature needed identification to her satisfaction. The five towers claimed names—Saints Marcu, Isa, Pippin, Farrand, and the Pointe, between which the great spires of the Cathedral Celestyn rose. She asked about the city gates, where they were, how many. How far beyond the walls had the city grown? From there, talk led to the city's defense strategy beyond that supplied by the military's adept squads.

Outside the city walls, small, well-constructed, bluestone houses, each a replica of the previous ones in style and tidiness, lined the rocky road. Kissre wondered how the inhabitants withstood the monotonous sameness, then thought of their consistency in dress.

Entering the city's gate, she sighed as her escorts became professional. One took the roan's lead line and fell in behind Bother; the others each took side positions. Bother looked like a hawk harried by sparrows and made her higher physical status the center of attention. Surrounded, her escort guided her in great civility through somber bluestone Sidih, whose inhabitants' quiet work stopped while they gaped. It spoke to Kissre of fear, distrust, and excessive suspicion.

They entered an iron gate surrounding a stone-walled compound with numerous foot soldiers. She still earned her share of stares, but from some of the soldiers, half-salutes also greeted her. She nodded in acknowledgment.

Inside the walls lay a residence much like all the rest in Sidih, only larger. Tyna stood on the steps of the portico. Her long, curly, fair hair formed a halo in the late afternoon sun. A handsome flaxen-haired man stood behind Tyna, his hand clasping her sister's arm. Both looked at Kissre, their faces set with different types of expectation. A small group stood near the bottom of the stairs. All wore sleeve badges, but these were striped in multiple colors.

No one rushed forward until she dismounted. She stood a moment, reins in hand, looking at her younger sister. "Hello, Tiny." The old childhood nickname came easily but felt uncomfortable.

The blond man holding Tyna released her arm, and Tyna rushed down the steps. She threw herself on Kissre, bringing memories of other impetuous childhood greetings. "Not so tiny anymore, Kiss. It's good to see you." It suddenly dawned on Kissre those gathered at the entrance were there to protect Tyna. They thought her intention to harm. Anger flared through her, but Kissre had long experience in banking her internal flares and kept her peace.

"Come in, come in," Tyna said, pulling on her arm.

"Ty, you know I've got to..."

Her escort riders had dismounted and moved away, but a man moved to Bother's head. Bother backed two steps, half rose on his hind feet, and squealed in angry warning. Kissre cursed herself for preoccupation and inattention. A strong shove pushed Tyna into the arms of the blond man who followed her. With a twisting turn, Kissre leaped back into the saddle. She curbed Bother hard, causing him to nearly sit on his haunches.

As her fingers released pressure on the reins, he immediately settled. Obedient to her, she could still feel his agitation through the saddle. A few quiet commands and his feet froze to the ground.

From atop the saddle, she lifted one side flap and loosened the girth. Uncertainty left Bother with a huge sigh. Kissre vaulted down and finished removing the saddle.

"He's safe now," she told the two soldiers who remained. Holding the saddle in one arm and rubbing Bother's neck with the other, she glanced at the group standing in horrified dismay around Tyna. Sure enough, Bother dropped his head to nip at a few blades of grass escaping the paving stone of the courtyard. Someone had already led the roan away.

"I'm sorry, it was my fault, the saddle was empty, and I failed to loosen his girth. He only did as trained." Her eyes caught Tyna's, who now stood encircled by those from the steps. "As I was saying, you know I need to tend my animals. Do you have a couple stalls free here, or would you feel safer if I took Bother to a hire stable?"

"I'll show her to the stables," a taller man said, his deep voice pleasant and filled with a subtle tenor of humor. He stood out because of his size and his darkness. Besides possessing black hair, he dressed in black—a raven of a man who wore no rings, only a sleeve patch.

They all had patches—multicolored patches—a coven of witches, then. A squad of Tyna's officers as Tomel had described. Kissre glanced at the raven man and then looked at Tyna.

"I can show her." In a querulous, command-filled voice, Tyna pushed through her protectors, throwing them an offended look.

Kissre knew messages were being traded that she would never hear. "You've got a dog, too. What's his name?" Tyna asked, putting a fist out for Fudge to smell. Masking her fear of Fudge succeeded as dismally as her emphatic pleasantness.

Taking a moment to pull Bother's head away from the flowers lining the courtyard allowed Kissre time to compose herself. The only thing worse than a private family reunion was a public one. She took a breath and released it. "Fudge. Sorry for the sideshow. I should have paid more attention."

The raven man stepped forward and took the saddle from her arm. "We knew of his peculiarity." His straight black brows dominated deep-set gray eyes and matched the thin linear mouth that seemed incapable of twisting into either smile or frown. Her eyes shifted from his intense gaze. She pulled Bother's reins through her free hand, bringing his head up. Kissre stroked his cheek.

"I should have been better prepared," Tyna said. "The stable is this way. No one pictured either animal as oversized; well, they said big, but any normal horse seems big when compared to a Cygnese pony. You didn't have these animals on your last visit." Tyna started down the paved lane leading to the utility yard behind the house. Her blond man stayed by her side. The raven walked a few feet behind.

An innocent but loaded remark. Kissre kept pace with her sister, Bother's hooves clopping in rhythm behind her. "No, I bought Bother as a two-year-old, just after my last visit. Nine months ago, a friend gave me Fudge. He is about a year old now. The roan I picked up leaving Kaereya."

"He's only a year? He is huge. I was surprised to hear you were inside Cygna."

"Yeah, me too," Kissre said.

Tyna gave her an indignant look but ignored the comment. "You've made good time. I had given up on a visit. It is hard to get a letter to someone with no address. You are staying, aren't you?"

"I've leave for a few sennight. I received your letter about seven months after you sent it. At the time, I had pressing duties that kept me in Kaereya. They've been at war, you know." She paused. "This was the last place I expected to find you."

Tyna spoke at the same time. "You were involved?" Her voice suggested she had no idea what mercenaries did and completely overshadowed Kissre's comment.

"I've worked for Aristo Aurelias, Duke of Lambere, in Kaereya this past year. He and his son-in-law led the attack on Pertelon's forces in Anatole. Anyway, I received a small injury and was unable to travel afterward. It took some time to find your caravan. Jebe told me about Naomi. I'm sorry, Ty."

Tyna gave her a look, and Kissre sighed. Every word out of her mouth was wrong, but not even to save Tyna's sensibilities would she pretend grief.

She saw the roan already stabled, and two men approached. One took Bother's reins while the other took the saddle from the raven man. Kissre watched the soldiers tend to Bother while she checked on the roan.

Satisfied, she picked up her saddlebags and smiled at Tyna, whose blond man still hovered protectively nearby. He stood about her height, with a face of tempting masculine symmetry. If his looks were not enough, startling blue eyes stared back at her. Kissre looked around her. The raven man had left. "This someone I should know?"

Tyna blushed beet-red, her look the same defiant expression used so often on Naomi. Tyna always got away with it. "My turn to apologize. I should have introduced you to my squad earlier."

"Forget it." Kissre removed her gloves. "Bother strained etiquette on both sides." She turned to the blond and extended her hand. "You must know our sisterly relationship had been somewhat taxed the last few years. My fault."

His mouth curled into a reluctant but wry smile. "Yes, I know. I also know your mother tried to keep Tyna out of Cygna, but as you have discovered, she is here, and of her own accord. I'm Kedriq, Tyna's husband." She noticed his gaze hovered on her tattoo before rising to her face. Kissre was too stunned to reply.

Two

"It's none of my business, Tyna." Kissre omitted that worry about her sister's situation drove her into Cygna, the last place she wished to go. "If you are content, fine, but if you are not, tell me. I will do everything I can to get you out of this country." She sat with a mug of hot cider. It lacked the spice and alcohol tang of the Kaereyan drink. Dinner had yet to be served, and hunger twisted her stomach.

After Kissre's silence at Kedriq's statement in the stable, Tyna had become a magpie, chattering inane conversations as she urged Kissre to the house. She gave Kissre time to clean off the road dirt in an upstairs bedroom. When Kissre came down, Tyna waited below, eyeing the scuffed leather trews she wore. How much did her sister think saddlebags held? She wore a clean, white, and well-made quilted tunic top. Tyna, in a traditional Cygna dress of dark blue that emphasized her delicacy, led her to a private sitting room. Once seated and served with the hot drink, Tyna explained her circumstance and how happy she was with it.

"You're absolutely sure?" Kissre asked, raising her brows. "You know Naomi wanted to save you from this?"

"She's your mother, too. Don't you feel anything?"

Seeing the sudden tear-sheen in Tyna's eyes, Kissre huffed softly and hoped her sister did not hear. "I feel many things, most are better not dredged up by either of us. I ask again, are you sure? There are ways to escape."

Tyna looked at her with sad, disappointed eyes for her failure, hell, failures. "Yes, I'm sure. What I have is far different from what mother foretold. Yes, I had a hard time at first, but things have changed, and I have a purpose here, people who depend on me. I love Kedriq."

"You're a Talent." Kissre said and took a sip of her drink before continuing. "I expect you feel like you belong here."

"I no longer have to hide what I am." Tyna's pouting defiance evaporated magically. She grinned with the pleasure of someone about to confound another. She had already done enough of that. Kissre waited.

"Plus, you are about to become an aunt." Tyna preened with pleasure.

"You don't say." Kissre laughed at her little sister, relieved Tyna had found a place to belong. As long as it was a free choice, Kissre had no trouble with it. "Well, for me, better an aunt than a mother. Congratulations. Perhaps this will help." She picked up a pouch she had brought from her saddlebags and plunked it on a table. The sound of clinking coins drew Tyna's interest.

"What's this?"

"Your share of the caravan, I imagine. Told you I'd seen Jebe."

Tyna bit her lip. "You know then. I thought he might have tried to hide it from you. What did you do to him?"

"Me? Nothing." Kissre shrugged. "Betrayal is hard to hide from a mercenary, but it wasn't my business. I doubt the caravan will last much longer under his guidance. Anyway, I only induced him to finalize his transition to owner."

A curious smile spread Tyna's lips, her disconcerted face surrounded and softened by loose honey-blonde curls. In a dismissive gesture, she flipped her hair behind her shoulders. She looked very dainty.

Different upbringing. Kissre tamped down that thought.

"How...never mind." Tyna picked up the bag. "It is disappointing to think so much work will be wasted so fast. Thank you for at least salvaging this."

Kissre nodded, feeling strangely content. With Naomi's absence, this might turn into a pleasant visit.

One of Tyna's squad, a young woman, knocked on the door and entered long enough to tell them dinner was ready. Kissre followed Tyna to the table. All present at her arrival waited there. Tyna made introductions. "You've met Kedriq. This is Meyer."

From habit, Kissre sized up each as Tyna introduced them. Meyer was short with corn-yellow straight hair, ruddy, compact, heavy, and defensive.

"Pelro." A sandman with fawn hair, tan skin, and blunt suspicious features who nonetheless nodded a welcome.

"And Silvie." Fairest of the fair, the woman who told them dinner was ready. With white-blonde, tight-curled hair, the petite, attractive woman looked as insubstantial as her soft descant voice.

"They are the lieutenants in my squad."

From their expressions, Kissre judged them unimpressed with their Captain's sister.

Tyna waved her hand toward the raven, who stood slightly apart from the tightly clustered lieutenants. "Dovel is Captain of another squad and a close friend. You will have to get used to Cygnese informality. Everyone knows everyone by their given name."

"Why? Doesn't it cause confusion?" Kissre asked.

Silvie answered. "Because if you've touched someone's mind, you know who they are, and using formality after that seems rude."

"Not everyone touches minds, though, do they?" Kissre asked with a raised brow.

"Well, nulls just follow suit," Meyer said.

Kissre smiled and looked at the other captain in the room. Dovel returned her assessment and remained inscrutable himself. The straight, stiff rods that served for brows seemed incapable of expression, but the deep-set gray eyes below and the harsh linear mouth conveyed a repressed humor. He topped her by a head's height, slouching in relaxation; he had clasped his hands behind his back. Standing straight, he would be much taller.

"You see before you the two types of people found in Cygna. I'm highland bred," Dovel said.

"All of Cygna is highland," Kissre said. "Bother now thinks his front feet shorter than his hind."

They laughed dutifully, but only the corners of Dovel's lips curved upward as if that was all the mobility his mouth provided.

He nodded to the blond-headed squad, and then her. "You're all lowlanders, short, blond, rash, and impulsive."

"Highlanders given extra height to see over the snowdrifts?" Tyna asked.

"But not extra flesh for warmth," Dovel added, mocking his lean length.

Kissre laughed. From the banter, it must have been a standing joke. "I've not been a lowlander for a long time, so I'll forgive your provocation, but I'd watch the others for retaliation."

Dovel's tip-corner smile appeared. "It doesn't matter. I'd hear their minds coming."

The ice broken, Tyna and Kedriq took the ends of the table. Tyna told Kissre where to sit. Everyone else knew their place.

"Where's your dog?" Dovel asked. His straight brows raised a fraction in interest. Clean-shaven, he wore his dark hair long in neat Cygnese fashion, braided, and tied at the back, but his hairline receded slightly from a widow's peak, and silver threaded each side. Of all those present, he seemed the most self-contained and at ease with himself.

"Fudge is in Bother's stall," Kissre said.

"Bother is a different name for a horse," Meyer said.

Kissre nodded. "Yes, but it fits."

"A warhorse?" Dovel asked.

"A Sunderlune heavy warhorse." She sensed disapproval and guessed it for anything from Sunderlune as she watched the two servers bring plates around for serving. Tyna's servants watched her with horrified interest and were not the only ones. Silvie could barely remove her gaze from Kissre's wrist. Kedriq watched, but his eyes rested on Tyna as often as herself. Meyer and Pelro kept their heads low, their eyes flicking upward in quick stares when anyone spoke.

"Roast squab, ma'am." She looked at the plate as the man placed it in front of her. Someone had arranged sliced, light tan meat and slivers of yellow and orange root vegetables in pretty whirls of dark sauce on the plate. It smelled appetizing, certainly better than camp fare.

"Your tattoo. It is very unusual."

Kissre looked at Dovel. He seemed a man undaunted by the unconventional. "In Cygna, yes."

"Why did you do such a thing to yourself?" Tyna asked. "You didn't have it on your last visit."

"It was given as a sign of accomplishment, a thank you, if you would, for services rendered."

"In Kaereya?" Tyna asked.

"No. In the east."

"The Eastern Empire?" Dovel asked.

"Yes, but Eastern Empire is a misnomer. Yes, there is an emperor, but he has little power, and there is no empire but a collection of royal houses called Senates. They rule over vast lands ceded them ages ago. Each Senate tries to keep their land under control and tries to prevent any other senate from conquering them. They use the Emperor's court to prevent overall mayhem. A convoluted governing system exists that seldom works particularly well. This is the mark of the House Aibhe."

"Did you like it there?" Silvie asked.

Kissre gritted her teeth. The voice was too child-like for a grown woman. "For a while, and I learned a lot, but eventually got homesick."

"It sounds like Sunderlune." The hard tone told Kedrick's opinion.

"In some ways it is, although I think Sunderlune's city governments treat their citizenry better." Kissre kept her voice carefully neutral.

"Did you buy your horse in Sunderlune? That was a remarkable performance this afternoon. We seldom use cavalry. Who trained him?" Dovel asked.

"I did. His training differs from that of a true warhorse. Actually, I have seldom been on the front line of battles. Usually, I do reconnaissance or surprise attacks. Bother knows my scent. His training prevents anyone from stealing him and leaving me stranded." Kissre took a bite of the roast squab. To her disappointment, it tasted like chicken. "He's strong and travels well."

"Why keep a warhorse if you don't use him in battle?" Pelro asked.

"He shows status because I'm a woman, and most soldiers have trouble dealing with that. A warhorse looks dangerous besides being something few mercenaries possess."

"The brute looked like it today." The angry dryness in Kedriq's tone surprised Kissre.

"He's only trained to prevent anyone but me from mounting him," she replied in a calm voice. "Ty and the soldiers who approached him remain alive, so there's your proof."

The clatter of dishes and utensils paused as diners arrested their movements. Kissre finished chewing her mouthful and took another during the elongated silence—probably silent only for her.

"What did you think of the meeting today?" Dovel asked, breaking the silence.

Tyna looked at him with a bemused look. "I think things are very precarious." She addressed her lieutenants. "Vitann says we will be sent to positions along the eastern border. Pertelon is moving troops."

"You will not be going," Kedriq said.

"And who will lead the squad?"

"We all know you can do so from here as easily as Guerestu."

"I will remain with my troops," Tyna said. "If you have issue with that, we will talk about it privately. I have already stated, several times, my presence will bolster the moral of the troops, no matter what my state of pregnancy."

"To hell with the troops," Pelro said. "They can be replaced, you can't."

"I thought squads fought by themselves," Kissre said. Her statement stopped the conversation.

"No," Tyna said after a brief lull. "Each adept squad guides several platoons of infantry. Our Talents help protect and direct them, but the troops do the actual fighting. With Pertelon's greater numbers, it is an alarming situation. I've been trying to convince Governor Vitann and the other statesmen that an Alliance with Kaereya would benefit our cause."

Kissre pursed her lips in thought after swallowing a tasty, but unfamiliar vegetable. She watched Pelro twirl his squab through the sauce before she spoke. "Alliance or no, it won't change much. Unfamiliar with your method of fighting, but I know Kaereya's and Pertelon's. If it comes to war, Pertelon will be fighting along two fronts, against two countries. King Clement lit a fire in Kaereya that I doubt he can extinguish. An alliance might help coordinate attacks or bolster defenses, but in the end, it all comes down to Pertelon's strength against the strength of its enemies." She shrugged. "Right now, Pertelon is stronger. Clement has five armies, each with larger soldier strengths than any of its neighbors' armies combined. However, protecting the extended lines in Kaeryean territory is difficult. They also have to protect their Eastern border. Attack armies usually take much higher casualties than defending armies. Whether Kaereya and Cygna align or not, it's a tossup who will win."

She tried Pelro's sauce swirl with a small chunk of bird and popped it in her mouth. The piquant sauce helped the tasteless meat. She took a sip of wine and tried not to make a face when she found it was only juice. *Tyna's pregnancy; what she endured, all endured? Oh hell.*

"So much for all my talk before the Dean's Cabinet," Tyna said in disgust.

"I'm not saying it wouldn't help. Only, knowing Cygna's historical position in these situations, it probably won't happen, so doesn't matter anyhow," Kissre said.

Dovel laughed. "That certainly clarified matters."

"Don't laugh. We will all pay soon enough. King Clement is a crafty devil. His genius is subversion, particularly softening a country up before he invades. He proved the strategy in the east, and it nearly worked in Kaereya."

"He can't do that in Cygna," Meyer said.

Kissre just prevented herself from snorting. "What? Unhappy nulls never run amuck?" The offensive remark brought more than affronted silence. She read anxiety, agitation, and fear in the faces around her. She had hit a nerve.

"Is that what he did in Kaereya?" Silvie asked. Her voice was as soft as her appearance and made Kissre wonder how this squad, even with Tyna's undoubtable Talent, could guide squads of soldiers.

"Yes. It was a long, well-planned attack. King Clement deals in deceit, treachery, and murder. He had gangs of men pillaging and killing as raiders inside Kaereya for twenty years. They made it look like insurrection and civil unrest. At least two Aristos were seduced into treason, the royal family murdered. His agents created enough chaos to undermine and nearly destroy Kaereya."

"You won," Meyer said.

"The battle, yes, with magic's help. Hard to imagine." She buttered a corner of bread torn from a roll as she spoke. "Of course, Kaereya has an exceptional navy, well-defended borders, and plenty of well-trained infantry, besides a much-loved living legend to rally around. None of that can be discounted." Placing the roll in her mouth, she chewed. They watched her with offended looks, and she wondered what table etiquette she violated. The waiters whisked away her empty plate.

"I thought Kaereyans didn't believe in magic? That they didn't have Talents? I thought they were all nulls," Silvie said. The dismissive little-girl voice sharpened.

"They believe now. Their magic is much like your own, people possessing unusual mind gifts. It just goes by a different name." A waiter placed a fruit berry pie before her. Silvie's comment intensified the first sour bite.

"The Aegis of Vere," Meyer said, nodding. "Some of our Talents in the south say they have felt him."

"The Aegis of Kaereya, now," Kissre amended.

Her remarks started a discussion on Talent in Kaereya. At their request, Kissre spoke of Kaereya's Aegis and his seer wife, of people tracked and murdered if believed to have magic-wielding ancestors, and of ancient sorceresses and prophecies.

"Sounds like a minor Earth Talent, a modest Time Talent, and probably a couple low-level Touch Talents," Meyer said, his heavy face with its square jaw set in speculation.

"Not witches?" Kissre asked.

"Adepts," Pelro corrected her in a touchy tone. "Adepts are trained to control their Talent."

"Wouldn't know. In Kaereya they're called witches," Kissre said in appreciation of his condescension. "Being a null, I never paid much attention to witch gifts." Across the table, behind Pelro, one of the waiters glanced at her and quickly swallowed a grin. Everyone else sat in hard silence. "Certainly you noticed?" She raised one innocent, inquiring eyebrow.

"You said earlier you were injured. Was that during a battle?" Tyna asked.

Kissre looked at her sister and read her defensive expression. Naomi had used the same look very successfully. Kissre felt heat flush her neck at having made such asinine and offensive remarks to her sister's friends.

"No. My employer deployed me as a bodyguard for his daughter. I injured myself trying to keep up with her. Had an accident in a muck hole called the Great Salt Marsh in Kaereya's Wessure Province. A place the Holy One surely forsook long ago. Landed on some kind of root. The damn thing went clear through my shoulder. Thought it had healed, but it broke open later." She twitched at the lie, but she had promised her employer not to mention to anyone the manner of her wound and expected that applied more in Cygna than in Kaereya.

"It must have festered," Meyer said. "Were you sick afterward?"

"For a while." Kissre took another bite of the pie, decided it was too good to waste over inconsequential drivel. Nothing could change her status and speaking freely of her lack poked a polite reminder to speak aloud.

"He's a Weaver Adept, so knows about wounds and health," Silvie said with obvious pride. "He will become a very good healer when our squad's duty is completed. He could look in your wound."

"Thanks, but it has now healed."

Silvie went on to explain all the various Talents at the table. "Tyna, of course, is overloaded with Talent—a Factor, Render, and Mapper Adept is most unusual. So is Dovel. He is one of the few quad-Talents. Chronos Talent is very rare."

Kissre smiled. "Exalted company, indeed." She listened with benign interest as talk swelled and dwindled about particular Talent types. She noticed Dovel remained silent. Sometimes she endured long intervals of silence and wondered what messages passed.

"Well, this has been very enjoyable," she said at last in one such quiet pause, surely interrupting someone. "But I think I'll make an early evening of it, for it's been a long journey, and I must check on Fudge and the horses before I retire."

"I'm off to bed myself, so I'll see you in the morning," Tyna said. She came around the table and rose on tiptoe to hug Kissre, placing a kiss on her cheek. The others rose, said their polite, 'So nice you're here, see you later,' comments, and let Kissre escape to retrieve her jack.

She went into the kitchen and asked for any table scraps. By the time they were gathered up, she knew the man's name, how long he had worked for Tyna and similar background information. "Thank you, Reg." Taking the plate, she said, "Fudge will enjoy this as much as I did." *More, since he didn't have to endure the table talk.*

At the stable, she let Fudge have the scraps, then picked up a brush and entered the roan's stall. Within a trice she had groomed and finished caring for the mare. The nag rewarded her with another nip. Kissre evaded the snapping teeth. "I know the feeling, old girl." She slapped its rump, tossed more hay into the rack, and closed the stall door.

In Bother's stall she took more time, there was more horse to curry and brush, and she finger-combed his black mane into neatness. He immediately shook his head, messing her efforts. Fudge sat in the doorway watching. She ordered Bother to lift his feet one by one, bracing each between her knees as she picked them clean, and cursed as Bother leaned on her while she worked.

A sound from Fudge drew her attention, looking under her arm from her bent over position, she saw in her upside-down view that Dovel stood next to Fudge, petting her dog and watching her. She finished her job and straightened. "Taking some night air?"

"I'm not so early to bed, and I don't think you are either."

"It has been a long day with a hard ride."

He laughed. His voice was a low pleasant tone between tenor and bass. "And you endured an even longer dinner. Most adepts don't realize when they are insulting a null, or when their conversation has become all mental give and take."

"Think I didn't realize that? Seems I gave some offense myself." She looked at the tall thin man rubbing Fudge's head. Fudge acted as if he had never felt a hand before, making throaty pleasure sounds. Older than herself, Dovel was more observant than the others; more approachable. Not beautiful handsome like Kedriq, but interesting in a hard, all lines and planes way. That he was here with a purpose, she didn't doubt. She'd noted his interest earlier. Mercenaries learned to read people, and took purposes very serious, especially those that didn't come around that frequently.

His smile smoothed away dinner's aftertaste. "Well, I'd say somewhat provoked. In a way of apology, I thought you might like to visit some of the entertainment found in Sidih at night. I noticed you had a guith strapped to your packhorse this afternoon. Perhaps you'd like to hear some of the local music?"

"Some of the local ale would be welcome, too." She threw several forks of hay in Bother's stall, ordered Fudge to stay. Dovel slid the stall door closed as she stepped out. Entering the house, they found the first floor empty. Kissre entered the kitchen and found Reg still working. After a short conversation, she left a message of her change in plans should anyone ask.

Sidih's night provided more variety than Kissre expected from the restrained Cygnese. People wore unusual dress, as if the darkness freed them, so more colorful clothing, often bordering on costumes including masks, paraded by.

Dovel snorted. "Spring Festival starts in a few days. The city always begins festivities early."

"Why the masks?"

"Mostly for fun. Masks do little good to disguise someone from a Talent. If you have Talent of even a minor level, another adept can recognize you. Most Nulls project so much emotion, so much inner turmoil, they give themselves away."

"Talents can detect which null is behind a mask?"

"If they try…"

"Don't they have laws or restrictions about entering someone's mind uninvited?"

"Yes." He looked at her. "For communication, both minds must agree, but in some instances the touch can be subliminal as well as forced. It's hard to catch or prove."

"What if you're a null?"

"Most nulls have some inkling of mental talent which opens them to adepts. Some nulls leak thoughts constantly."

"Is mine open to you?" Kissre gave him a side-glance as they negotiated the crowded walkway.

"No," he said, turning his head toward her. "You are completely closed. You haven't a trace of talent."

"Tyna got it all." She sighed in relief even as her gut clenched.

"Does it bother you?"

"Not anymore. I've lived with it for a long time."

"Twenty-two years. You're twenty-eight, aren't you?"

"How'd you know?"

"Simple addition. Tyna said you were six years older. She is obsessed about family. Says you are her last blood. That is why she has been so bristly over your visit. Kedriq said she's been upset about your absence since he first met her."

Kissre huffed. "Ty talks too much. I've been gone since she was ten. She hardly knows me. Besides, from what I know, Cygna is the wrong place to obsess about family."

He nodded. "Common knowledge we sometimes separate children from their parents, but things are changing. She worshiped you as a child."

Someone jostled Kissre as in passing. She moved closer to Dovel's side. "That will end. Today she saw me with grown-up eyes. She sees something very different from her memory—a null relative with embarrassing dress and manners. With Kedriq and a baby on the way, she's starting her own family." She made a circle gesture with her tattooed hand that waved away the past. "Her preoccupation with me will end naturally. It is just the result of Naomi's death and her dictums about comportment in life. Naomi was raised in a Kernite sect."

Dovel paused mid-stride. Kissre turned to look at him. "With all her caterwauling about family, she didn't mention that?"

"No. It explains a lot. They do place an emphasis on blood family."

A young man threw an object as he passed. Dovel reacted, stepping back and pulling Kissre with him. The thing hit and exploded on the wall next to them. Vile offal odors suffused the air with shouted epithets about Talent parasites.

Kissre did not hear. Her training had already taken over. A foot slowed the assailant. When he stumbled, he found Kissre's hand around his neck, his body slammed into the stone wall of a storefront, his arm twisted behind him in a merciless grip.

"Very bad hospitality," Kissre growled in the boy's ear. His face showed shock, fright, and pubescent signs of facial hair where it pressed up against the stone.

"Talent slut!"

Kissre pounded him against the wall once more. "Nasty mouth, too. What do you think you were doing?"

"Why don't you rape my mind and find out, adept bitch?"

Kissre swore in four languages. "Are you a simpleton? Have you looked at me? Do I look like an adept? Do you know the difficulty you are in?"

"You'll call the Talent law-keepers on me. "So what?" He struggled to get loose. Kissre raised his hand fractionally, and he groaned at the strain on his arm.

"No, dolt, right now, with me! I can break your arm most painfully. I can smash your head in quite easily. More to the point," she lifted her knee, and he cried out, "I can prevent your prospects of fatherhood. So keep a respectful tone—very respectful. Why did you try to ruin my evening?"

"On a dare, a bet." He was crying now. Kissre knew the pain he felt in his elbow and shoulder among other places.

"You've mistaken your prey. I'm just another null, and how you missed my foreign status, I don't know. Because I want to get on with my own pleasure, I'm going to let you go. Keep in mind, though, that I have an excellent memory for faces. If I see you around me, you'll regret it. My companion, who *is* a Talent, probably knows who you are, so don't be so stupid as to pull this stunt again."

"You're not Talent?"

"No." With a quick push, she released him and stepped back.

He looked at her with startled eyes. Free, he yelled, "Talent's whore," before running off.

Passersby, who had stopped to watch, moved on muttering.

"You should have turned him over to the peacekeepers."

"Just cause more delay. This some of the trouble that's not happening?"

Dovel sighed. "It is a particularly unflattering situation for the adept government." He sighed. "Or for Talents in general."

Thinking she had done enough talking, Kissre said, "Where's the music you've been bragging about?" Their conversation returned to mundane topics.

Dovel took her to several places. Most of the music was folk-based and very accomplished. She recognized some songs very similar to those she already knew and gave rousing and enthusiastic applause and whistles, drawing attention. Dovel remained unfazed by her behavior, even smiled at her. He seemed popular, night women giving him warm greetings. As they progressed through Sidih's taverns, Kissre found herself smirking at Dovel's discomfiture. She knew the women null, because even prostitutes wore badges on the sleeves of their clothing, and it was obvious they knew him. *So Dovel preferred nulls?*

Each alehouse differed. The brews excelled, alternating between light golden ciders and dark heavy ales. In between taverns, they walked the noisy streets, the crisp-cool air clearing their minds as they talked.

"It is always cool here at night," Dovel said, watching her chafe her arms. "It doesn't matter what time of year."

"I just need to acclimate. I've served in all four provinces of Kaereya, was based in Wessure, and fought in Easure. Both are warm and sunny much of the year. This is more like Norsure, although they get more fogs and mists than I've run into here."

"Cygna has its share of fogs and mists, but we are higher, and they burn off quicker. Here the winters are cold, nights freezing, but the days are quite warm. We get a lot of sun year-round in Sidih. Snowfall isn't as bad here as in the highlands." From the weather, they turned to Cygna's adepts.

She asked him about his striped arm patch. That was after six ales each.

"Stripes indicate multiple Talents."

"Let me guess. Red is for fire. Green is for grass." She laughed with inane drink humor.

Dovel looked down his straight nose at his patch in what appeared serious thought. "You're wrong. Blue is for Touch, the four crossbars say I am a Probe Adept. Red is for fire...er...energy."

"Then I was right." She cuffed him lightly on the arm as she crowed. "Probe is a type of Touch Talent? What do the four crossbars on Fire mean?"

"That I'm a Harness Adept. The green," he looked at her sternly, "is for Earth Talent. I'm a Mapper Adept."

"Then I was right again. Only three crossbars? And the single crossbar on the gray stripe?"

"Time Talent, a level one there or a Chronos Adept. Add it all up, and it makes me a squad Captain."

"So what's it all mean? You don't do the actual fighting."

"Don't tell a squad member that. They embrace a far different perception."

"Well? What's a Probe, Harness, Mapper, Chronos do?"

"Probe means I can enter any mind at will…"

"Except mine?"

"Except yours. Any mind with an iota of Touch Talent, which is almost everyone. Voids like you are a rarity. Harness means I can control energy fields. Most healers have to be Harness or Weavers. In my case, it helps hold the squad together."

"Meyer was a Weaver."

"With medical aspirations. Mapper means I can sense the typography of the land. And Chronos means I always know what time it is." He smiled, his lip corners tilting.

Kissre smiled back. "Very impressive. How come so many? They all seem very similar to me."

"They are all very similar. When Talents first started showing up ages ago, there were only two Talents, empathy and telekinetic. With time, each type began fragmenting. Every Talent is individual and varies in strength and ability. Naming them just sorts them so everyone has an idea of what you can do."

"So how's that help your platoons?"

"As Captain, I focus my squad's combined Talents. We tell the platoons what direction to take, where to strike, and when. We sense where the enemy is and keep our men out of trouble."

"Or commit them to annihilation when necessary?" She noticed Dovel didn't answer that question. "So how many squad members do you have?"

"Four. Adele, Wyn, Cath and Ulyss."

"And platoons?"

"We have eight, a total of about one-hundred men."

"That's a lot of men to guide. Do squads stay together forever?"

"No. Twenty years of service, then each member is moved off into a new service, although they always stay in close mental contact." He smiled but it was forced.

"You have aspirations, too?"

"I haven't allowed myself to make plans." He sounded so bleak Kissre decided not to follow the topic.

"Can I give you a warning?" She continued without waiting for permission. "Tyna's squad didn't think Cygna could be harmed by Pertelon subterfuge. Don't believe it. Cygna must have as many dissidents as any other country."

"We do. You saw it outside. The boy pulled the prank, but others, less obvious and more hostile, might well have goaded him into it. Such incidents have increased in the last few years. Tyna helped us put down a null uprising here in Sidih last fall. We thought the problem was taken care of. You are right to warn us of complacency, but I doubt our nulls would help Pertelon. At least, not the majority of them; they have suffered as much persecution from outsiders as Talents have." He pushed his flagon away.

"There's more," she said.

Dovel looked in question at her from under his brows.

"During the battle on Anatole Island, Pertelon used banned weapons."

She heard him suck his breath. "They would dare the Protectors?"

"Dare?" She scoffed. "Pertelon's King Clement doesn't believe in the Protectors, thinks it an old toddler-tale made by survivors of the Cataclysm Century." Kissre took a sip of her drink. "Who knows? He might be right. So far, his army has been unhindered by any intervention. I'm telling you, Dov, the situation is precarious. They have illegal weapons and aren't afraid to use them. Clement expected to have Kaereya by now. The Kaereyan Aegis taught him a lesson he won't forget. So now, he will come after weaker prey, one known to have an unusual weapon of its own. They'll come after the Cygnese witches. You are men short, adept squads or not. Once conquered, they will use your magic against Kaereya."

"Cygnese squads would not fight for Pertelon."

"They would if the lives of their family and friends were at stake." She read the reluctant agreement cross his face, but he held his comments. He probably could not talk if Cygna's Adept Council or Command meetings discussed such topics, at least, not with her, no matter how much he drank.

"Enough." His eyes slid to hers with his corner-tip smile. "We've covered adepts and the approaching war this evening. Now let's talk about you."

She shrugged. "Nothing to talk about, just a mercenary."

"You are most unusual looking in Cygna. You look native with your fair-hair coloring and features, yet your dress is exotically foreign, more mannish looking than accepted here. You wear a series of gold earrings and a brow hoop. The tattoo is already famous."

"Infamous."

"Yes. It all screams outlander."

"Too mannish an outlander for you?" Kissre watched the speculative twinkle appear in the gray eyes.

"I am known for eccentric tastes."

Three

During the night, Dovel felt a heavy body fall on his feet. Rolling over into the warmth already next to him, he raised his swimming head, gave up trying to think, and fell back into sleep. He woke when Adele flipped open his tent's flap, flooding the tent in the too-bright morning light. She gasped with a perceptible agitation and let the flap fall closed. Going immediately to Wyn, Cath, and Ulyss, his mind heard their questions and unhappy reactions—another null whore.

The weight holding down his feet sprang up into a giant brown bear. He rolled and pushed himself up to fight it off when a sleep-husky voice spoke next to him.

"Fudge! By the Holy One! How did you...?" Kissre looked at Dovel and laughed, as the great dog leaped on top of her and licked her face. She pushed him aside. "You forgot I was here!" He felt his face heat with her accurate accusation. "Hope you didn't forget everything about last night."

She stood, searched for her clothes, and began pulling them on as she found them among the bedding. Dovel watched.

"No, I remember all of the night, very well, now that I'm awake."

"That's good, or at least polite. Have I upset your squad? Or was that just a surprised gasp I heard? Hell, Tyna will...Well." She hesitated while she hopped, pulling on a boot, "will I see you again?"

"Do you want to?" Sudden visions of them together caused him to smile in anticipation. Chronos Talent didn't often provide foresight, so maybe it was just wishful thinking. Fudge started nosing him, and he petted the shaggy head and scratched behind the ears.

"While I'm here, yes. Most definitely." Kissre grinned and finished dressing. Running her hands through her unruly hair, she finger-combed the various colored strands altering from umber to sun-bleached cream, weaving them in careless unkempt curls. His breath caught.

Dovel rose and kissed her, running his hands down her back and pulling her hips against his. "We've been most indiscreet."

"It's no problem for me. Everyone here already thinks I'm a barbarian."

Dovel smiled. "You are, a most civilized and exotically enticing one, too. Will Tyna give you trouble?"

"Don't know why, I'm a big girl, unless she's worried about me contaminating you. From the looks of your squad member, you're in more trouble than me."

"Then I'll see you later tonight. Maybe dinner?"

"Come by and see what Tyna has planned." Kissre motioned Fudge to heel, and the dog immediately obeyed, his tail sweeping the floor in rapture. "You tracked me? Bad boy! You probably scared Sidih's citizenry to death."

The vision of Fudge hunting through Sidih horrified Dovel and filled him with unsuccessfully suppressed mirth. With a harassed, nasty look thrown at him, Kissre turned and left the tent, Fudge bounding at her heels.

His pants were barely on when Adele entered with a late breakfast. Well aware of the time, he took the hot cider, warm bread, and cheese before he turned away with a grin. She did not speak, but her gaze and mental aura were enough. Able to shield some but not all of his emotions from his squad, he knew they had shared some of what he had experienced last night. Explanations were unnecessary. They already knew all he would tell them, especially Adele, who knew his preferences. It was a warning to her to keep an emotional distance between them. She would not let it rest.

"A safe substitute for Captain Tyna?" His highlander lieutenant's brown eyes drilled holes in his back.

Dovel's mood turned sour with the direct hit. She knew it. Frowning as he opened his trunk and selected clothes, he said, "I'm headed for the baths." He should have taken Kissre to the house he had recently purchased. Returning to camp was just habit.

Washing and shaving, he recalled the night. Adele was right. She was very attuned to him, more so than he liked, but that was inevitable. Even touched by his emotions, she did not understand him. An attractive woman, she felt they should share their mental connectedness on a physical level. She did not understand his preference for nulls as partners nor how the forced intimacy with his squad rankled within him. Neither did she know how he hated the overwhelming bond Tyna had created by her untrained responses when she first came to Cygna, and the effects it inflicted on him. Adele always wanted more contact. He understood it somehow reaffirmed herself. He was just unwilling to supply it.

With Kissre, he had thought his actions candid enough. Kissre could not feel him at all, not even as much as most nulls. She was void. Touch so absent, not even a Probe Adept could penetrate her mind. When he met her yesterday, it was like seeing the invisible. Neither his squad nor Tyna's realized their antipathy toward Kissre was caused by the absence of mental touch. It diverted him. Kissre had made it perfectly clear she was willing, so he felt no guilt over their evening.

Except... he felt her now.

The realization penetrated the buzz lingering in his head from last night. Not mentally, but like a wisp of scent. He felt her move over the land and shook his head. No stray thoughts or errant feelings of hers registered in his mind. Still, he knew the exact moment she entered Tyna's house when the contact ended. How could he know this about a void? That discovery occupied him while he finished performing his morning ritual.

He had learned Kissre was a master of dissemblance. The wound she spoke of at dinner was far more severe than she had let on. The scar hid serious bone and muscle injury that had not finished healing. Appalled at her scars, he had mentally investigated her body while she dressed, amused she didn't feel a thing.

Taller than her sister, Kissre might not have the same facial beauty, but she was similar enough to Tyna to see the relationship. Her features were sharper, the nose straighter and thinner, the mouth less pouting but more generous in width, her prominent cheekbones and jawline too strong, the challenging look too bold for prettiness. Nonetheless, a compelling attraction lodged there. Her trim and muscular body, even though scarred, was perfect, her eyes spectacular. They changed from emerald to aquamarine with her mood, unlike any lowlander he had met.

Dovel chuckled. The boy last night might have mistaken Kissre for Tyna, but Kissre proved her difference in a most dramatic way. Never had he seen a woman react as fast as that, and very few men.

A small razor nick brought Dovel's thoughts back to the matter at hand. The direction his thoughts took was absurd.

~ * ~

First checking Bother, Kissre found him well tended and turned out to sun in a large paddock with an enormous pile of hay. The roan stood next to him, giving Kissre a moment's hesitation, but the mare had not come into season. She should have bought a gelding as a better companion for the stallion, but the mare was the best she could afford. Someone had given the horse a prissy-assed name she couldn't stomach, and she hadn't given any thought for a new name for the nippy nag except the roan.

"You're back."

Kissre turned, recognizing the childish voice. Silvie, thin and alabaster, the blue eyes huge in her round face, stood a short distance off and appeared offended by the barbarian sister. No good-morning welcome entered the woman's voice or vigilant regard.

"Silvie. Yes. As you can see."

"I thought you wanted an early night?"

Unapologetic, Kissre smiled. "So I did, but Dovel convinced me otherwise."

A sneering look of distaste covered the petite blonde's face. "Tyna is waiting for you in her sitting room. She expected you at breakfast."

At the mention of food, Kissre felt her stomach growl and realized she had probably missed a meal if Ty followed Naomi's dictums. She nodded at Silvie and walked into the house. The null servant Reg opened the door before she reached it.

"Captain Tyna waits in the sitting room. Would you like your breakfast brought in?" Giving the man a cheerful grin while betting Tyna hadn't authorized the offer, Kissre assented and headed for the mentioned room.

Tyna sat at her desk going over some papers and looked up as Kissre entered. She was alone. To her credit, Tyna didn't question her other than, "Enjoy your evening?"

"Yes, Dovel was very good company."

She watched Tyna swallow a remark and decided to behave herself. Ty wasn't Naomi. "Sidih was a more interesting place than I imagined it might be on my trip here. I thought the city extremely conservative, yet last night they acted rather merry and frivolous."

"They are very conservative. Spring Festival has pulled them out of their usual rut, but it won't last," Tyna said with a wry grin. "They don't like change, probably because they suffered so much of it in their early history when Talents first started emerging."

"You dress the part."

Tyna looked down at her dark blue clothing. "Well, it is comfortable, and finding other fashion is difficult. I imagine your appearance has rippled the waters. You know your mannish attire offends many Cygnese?"

Kissre gave an inner sigh. It seemed to offend her sister, too. "I've earned my share of disapproving looks, but it is typical Kennetsure attire for women and the dress of traders, as you very well know. Silvie said you were waiting on me?"

Before Tyna spoke, a knock on the door interrupted them with her breakfast's arrival. Kissre applied herself to the meal of eggs and sausage hash with enthusiasm. Tyna didn't look at her, only said, "We'll talk when you're finished." From her face, Kissre decided her manners disturbed her sister, but she couldn't figure out why. Her manners had been good enough to eat with the Court at Kaereya's Eternal Palace. As she shoved the last mouthful in, the servant appeared to take away the plate.

Tyna nodded to the man, and then looked at Kissre. "I was wondering if there was anywhere you would like to visit while you are here?"

"You can choose. I might like to see your army's camp if it is permitted. Are all your troops Cygnese or do they hire mercenaries, too?"

"Looking for a job?"

Kissre laughed. "No, I like my present one, thank you very much. Just, you asked. Other than that, maybe some musical diversions, or theater if available."

"Music?"

"Yes, or a play." Kissre disliked the skeptical look on Tyna's face. She took a deep breath and smiled.

"I wouldn't think Cygna's music to be much in your taste. It consists mostly of chorales, musical quartets, and solo entertainment at functions such as state dinners and parties."

Kissre pursed her lips in a wry smile. You don't take barbarian mercenaries to dinners and parties. "Well then, can you show me your army base?"

"I think that is possible," Tyna said in a tight-lipped smile as Kissre rose. "Kissre, I would enjoy your company at breakfast."

Kissre took the rebuke-invitation with an acknowledging smile and a safe platitude. When the time came for the camp visit, though, it wasn't Tyna but Kedriq who guided her.

"Where's Ty?" Kissre asked.

"Resting. She was feeling ill, and we did not think all the dust and commotion good. Not in her condition. I hope you don't mind."

"No, it gives me the chance to know my brother-in-law. Do we ride or walk?"

They walked over as senior officers requested Bother not enter the camp. She raised her brows but took no offense. It wasn't a far walk. She had made it that morning from Dovel's tent with no problem.

The camp extended around the city's entire south side between the fortress-like walls and the steep cliff dropping off from the outcropping holding the city. Taking a long look, Kissre realized that it was all man-made, the city's land carved and dug from the side of a mountain. The army base was broken into smaller camps, each centered with a large tent flying pennants, and encircled by neat rows of smaller tents.

Dovel joined them as they toured. Fudge bounded over to him, and Dovel rubbed the dog's head. "The banners identified squad headquarters," Kedriq said, pointing out Tyna's platoons. Kissre asked about how the command was structured and how each Captain and his squad operated within that arrangement. She was horrified.

"But how do you coordinate troop movements?"

"Each squad deploys their troops according to the Marshal's direction. We have three standing armies. One near Halli, this one, and the last in Guerestu, each has a Marshal as commander," Kedriq told her.

"But once deployed, how do you coordinate between your Marshal and the Captains? How do you react to the enemy's divergent tactics?"

"We didn't use to," Dovel said. Kissre heard the mortification in his voice. "The Captain's management of their troops was near sacrosanct before Tyna. The Marshal and his two commanders organized large-scale battles, usually of a defensive nature. For all else, the Captains are in charge. You forget we communicate with our Marshal by thought." He shrugged. "Tyna's Talent allows all the Captains and the Marshal to remain attuned."

Kedriq led them up a hill that looked out over the tented city below while Dovel talked. Kissre stopped and took in the view. She quickly estimated the army's strength with a couple more questions. She then asked, "Do you muster year-round, or is the army seasonal?"

"Seasonal. Our traditional enemy has been the Sunderlune city lords. Our enemies do little fighting in the winter as our snow-covered mountains keep them at bay. These camps have only been assembled in this past month. In an emergency, more can be drawn up after spring planting."

Kissre looked at Kedriq. "So far you've only fought border skirmishes? It's what, seventy years since your last war? Have you ever faced Pertelon's troops in battle?"

At his negative headshake, she looked away. Fear snaked through her gut on behalf of this country. "If I were your Marshal, I'd look for an attack at any time of year. This army ought to have relocated to Guerestu and been strategically deployed along your eastern border long ago."

Looking at her in offended dignity, Kedriq said, "We know how to fight our own battles."

She looked at her new brother. "I'm sure you do, but I doubt you know how to fight a Pertelon battle. I've fought them not only in Kaereya but also on its border with the Eastern Empire. Cygna is not prepared for what faces her." She huffed in disgust as both men assumed too-polite-to-argue expressions.

Neither Kedriq nor Dovel answered her. Kissre had found out much of what her curiosity deemed important. Dovel changed the topic to how ground troops in Kaereya were equipped and fought. Kissre, tired of struggling with touchy Cygnese temperaments, followed the change of topic. By the time that ended, so did the tour.

Walking back through the camp, Kissre noticed mercenaries, isolated into their own platoons, but obvious for-hires. It answered the question she had posed her sister. She didn't care much for their chances. Their recognition of her and greetings in troop jargon seemed to embarrass Kedriq. She suspected, though, it wasn't the idea that she was a mercenary as much as the fact she was null, and now a member of his family, that upset her new brother.

Dovel reappeared later in the day while Kissre groomed Bother and the roan. Singing to herself as she worked, she remained unaware of his presence until she heard a cord of guith strings. Startled, she dropped the brush she held.

She cursed him, and he grinned. "You scared the hell out of me!" Picking up her brush, she pointed at the instrument. "You just play cords?" He obediently fingered a folk song familiar from the night before and seemed surprised when she broke into the lyrics.

"You have a very good voice."

"Yeah, well, don't tell Tyna. She finds it impossible a barbarian like me knows or likes anything beyond weapons." She sighed as she rubbed the brush over Bother's rump. "Or else she doesn't want to be seen with me."

"Tyna's pregnancy has been difficult. She has been plagued with sickness and sleepiness she can't overcome during the afternoons and evenings."

"Oh? That account for her bad temper, too?"

"She also has the added burden that many adepts are dropping in on her mind to share her predicament, as they will probably never be in the same condition. Her squad spends more time with her to help keep intruders out of her mind. That's why I've been asked to take you to dinner."

"Dinner, huh? And this has nothing to do with me?"

His smile told her much. "She has wanted this visit very much. Anticipated and planned it since she learned of your presence inside Cygna's borders."

Kissre slapped Bother's shoulder, finishing his grooming while she listened. "Yeah, I know what you're telling me. One of those wish meets reality things."

"You could say that. I can tell you she loves you."

Untying the lead from the stanchion, she led Bother into his stall. "Well, I imagine that has become a struggle, too." She closed the bottom half of the door, and Bother stuck his head over the top for the carrot she held out. "And her squad?"

Dovel looked reluctant to answer.

"So they do hate me."

"Not hate. Nulls conspired at the murder of their former Captain. They probably would have died if Tyna had not bonded with them. Silvie even tried to commit suicide. They have a hard time relating to you."

She sighed. "They're not the first."

"You and your mother were estranged."

"Tyna tell you?" She asked with an oblique look.

"Indirectly. Do you and Tyna get along?"

Kissre hesitated before answering. "We have an uneasy affinity like the sun and the moon—better when only one of us appears at a time."

"She is not avoiding you—she is really feeling very ill. Her whole squad is."

"Another observation?"

"No, I feel some of what she feels."

Kissre laughed. "You feel what she does? That must be lots of fun."

"Anyone bonded to Tyna does, but not always, especially at certain times. It can be most...distracting."

"Why you like nulls?"

He looked taken aback. "How..."

"Observation."

"Your observations can be most annoying."

"But true. A mercenary's knack. Are you still going to take me to dinner?"

"You still want to go?"

"Yes—to everything. A repeat performance."

"Why? I mean..."

"No, I understand. I'll be leaving anyway. Why? I want to collect fond memories for the future." She smiled at the expression on his face. "Let me get cleaned up."

Dovel followed her into the house. The servants waited there with dinner already made. Dovel's face didn't change, but his eyes lost their sparkle, his mouth firmed a little.

"An evening in? We can share some music." At the renewed gleam in his eyes, she grinned and ran upstairs. She came down in a garment of Wessure fashion, made in an uncrushable fabric of gossamer fine wool and silk. The subdued but exquisite embroidery created glimmering reflections with movement. She brought her guith with her. Dovel took the instrument from her and admired the fine artisanship with its delicate decorative inlays.

Dinner was much less formal, and Kissre talked as much with the servers as with Dovel. She started her conversation with humiliating but funny stories of her encounters with foreign foods and customs. Once the server Reg learned the breadth of her travels, he became bold enough to ask questions about those lands. From the two servers' expressions, Kissre judged herself a new experience, and she swore a small smile hovered over even Dovel's near inanimate features.

"What did you do in the eastern empire?" Dovel asked.

"I was hired as a bodyguard for a traveler, ended up staying as a house factor."

"You liked it, then?"

"Loved it and learned a great deal."

"Like what?"

"Exercises; each House in the Eastern Empire has a distinct style. I learned those of the Aibhe House: fighting exercises, relaxing exercises, calming exercises. Movements meant to bring harmony to the mind, or victory to the warrior. I needed it. Women are marginally more accepted as soldiers there."

"Why did you come back?"

She laughed. "You'll laugh. It was too exotic. I craved ordinary things and the ways of my home. I wanted to taste plain bread, leek soup, and strawberry tarts."

"Of Cygna?" he asked, surprised.

"No, Kaereya. I spent my childhood in Vere. I love it there. It is my home."

"The two countries aren't that different, same basic language and culture. Once we were of the Vere. There are still back ways into the plateau."

"Probably why my mother settled there." At that point, Reg brought in dessert and two cups of a steaming hot drink. Kissre nearly groaned at the thought of juice but sighed with delight tasting the alcohol in the drink. She lifted her cup to Reg. He grinned and left.

Afterward, Dovel played and sang a few ballads and loves songs she had never heard. In return, she sang snippets of Kaereya's musical stories and the lyrical melodies of Kennetsure with their evocative imagery. While his face remained impassive, she smiled at the pleasure and surprise inherent in his eyes.

Later they took Fudge for a long, star-lit walk in the bright, quarter-moon night. Dovel threw a stick that Fudge joyfully retrieved.

Then, Fudge trailing, they went to her bedroom in the quiet house.

~ * ~

Very early the next morning, shushing each other's muffled laughter and Fudge's whine, they rose and escaped the house like unruly children. Bother and the roan, eager for a brisk run, carried them north of the city and onto a high plain frosted in white flowers. The horses' hooves drummed the ground, and Fudge's bass voice spurred their breakneck pace as he stretched his great lean length out into graceful, ground-eating strides. When they pulled up, the horses blew streams of vapor from their nostrils like the fire of fabled dragons.

This high above the city, the dawn's pink light streaked the night's last navy embrace. Kissre closed her eyes and faced the weak sun rising above the jagged peaks surrounding them. It gave little warmth but glazed the insides of her lids with distilled brilliance. Opening her eyes, she found Dovel's gaze on her and smiled. They waited in silence and watched the sun expose dark, shadow hidden Sidih below them.

Before they left, he pointed out several small lakes and the great birds gliding on them. "The swans migrate here each spring, usually at exactly this time, when we celebrate Spring Rites. The legend says as long as the black swans return each year, Cygna's magic will exist."

From a saddle pocket, Kissre pulled out a sight glass and looked. "They're mostly white."

"I know, but there are always black among them."

"Yes. I see one now." She watched a bird land in the water and then offered her glass to Dovel.

Shortly they started back. Both horses, with their breathing cadences returned to normal, remained willing, and needed to be held to slow loping canters back to the city. As they walked the steaming horses through the morning-activated city, the animals' ears twitched and swiveled as if listening to the quiet trivial talk exchanged between their riders.

"For someone who doesn't ride, Dov, you do it well," Kissre said.

"Before I became a squad leader, all I did was ride. I'll pay for this excursion, though." He fondly patted the roan's sweaty neck. "I've at last experienced the pleasure of a larger mount. I may never want to ride a pony again." He smiled. "The sores will be worth it. It was a glorious morning, Kiss. I wouldn't have missed it."

"It was." She yawned, took the reins in one hand, and relaxed into the saddle. "I seldom ride for the sheer joy of it."

"And you haven't missed breakfast." Dovel grinned at her.

"The house keeps strict rules?" Kissre asked.

"Tyna insists on it. Says her servants have enough to do without catering to the whims of adepts."

"Huh. You don't say. Good thing to know. I imagine I should inform Reg." She grinned at him.

"You have impressed the nulls of the house."

Kissre took no offense at the implication. It was true.

"Tomorrow is Spring Revel. Can I escort you?"

"You called them rites earlier. Is it long hours in the cathedral?"

"The priests bless the land tomorrow in Spring Rites at dawn, and we give thanks that the black swans have returned for another year. It's followed by music, dancing, eating, and drinking during the day."

Kissre's grin grew. "Kaereya has such a holiday. Their Spring Day is followed by Blessing Day, one of several double day celebrations. Only the mid-summer Sun Festival lasts longer—ten days."

"Spring Revel lasts a sennight. A time of entertainment, gaiety, and giving thanks for making it through the winter." Dovel said. He became effusive in his appeal. "It is the last holiday before autumn harvest. It is the signal for farmers to plant their fields, for shepherds to move their flocks into the mountains, for ponies to be bred, the end of winter hunting season, time for city folk to put away their winter clothes, for wives and servants to begin first cleaning, and the beginning of summer fishing and small game hunting. It is also the time to watch our borders, the beginning of warfare season. A time when outland traders are allowed into the country. It is our most important holiday, or at least the most avidly celebrated."

Kissre laughed. "Wouldn't miss it, then." They pulled to a halt at Tyna's stable. The inevitable troopers stationed at the house took the horses and Kissre ordered Fudge to stay with Bother.

Four

After the Squad Captains' daily meeting with the Northern Army's Marshal, Dovel visited the Assembly House's residential section. He searched for his old mentor within those halls and found her in the glassed garden room on the southern side, a sanctuary for ranking adept retirees. She sat small, wizened, and looking at nothing.

Zeba resided in the house-care section, her self-determination lost, sometimes unable to care for herself, and often not cognizant. Now she lived more in dreams than in reality. Her maid nodded as he approached, and he spoke to the old oracle.

Started from oblivion after several calls, Zeba's wrinkle-lined face looked at him a moment. Her pale eyes blinked before she said, "Dovel."

"Adept Zeba, may I sit with you?"

Gesturing to a seat, "You're always welcome. I have few visitors."

He faltered, looking around at the decrepit people in the conservatory. "The weather is warm today. Perhaps you would like to walk?" Her maid nodded at the invitation and left.

"That would be pleasant." She rose, still straight, but shorter and in need of support. He offered his arm, and she smiled and took it.

"It's been a long time since an attractive man has offered me his arm."

Once outside, he sought the grassy lawn surrounding the stone entrance walks. Her steps were short and shuffling.

"The sun is warmer today. It feels good," Zeba said, her face turned toward the sky.

"You're not a Fire Adept. Your Earth Talent lets you feel the earth's strengths. You should get out more often and renew yourself."

"The sun is as warm on the skin for Earth Talents and nulls as for Fire Talents. Besides, the earth here in Sidih has little strength left, none for wasting on an old woman. We have drawn it all away. You know that." She sighed. "Once the Earth Adepts found enough to make the Fountains of Power play. No more. There are only lifeless pools of water left."

"Don't tell that to the pike swimming in them. The land still grows good crops. There are fields of narcissus north of here. There is enough for simple healing."

She laughed. "There is no healing age, Dovel. I'm very old. I've been retired longer than you've been alive."

"Not quite that long. You would do better to get out. You are still capable of visiting your friends, of acting as a mentor, if you chose."

"My white hair and wrinkles scare the young away. And my reputation for being somewhat unstable, my frequent lapses into other frames of mind, haven't helped with the older adepts." She sighed. "I've enough touch left, though, to know you didn't come to speak of my health, but not enough for you to rely on my Touch Talent alone."

Dovel laughed at her humorous admission of inadequacy. "You remember I'm a strong Earth Talent?"

Zeba's brow wrinkled deeper in thought at his unusual beginning. "Yes, I remember. You are equally strong as a Fire Talent. Which is why your squad is composed of low-level Talents and a Latent Catalyst, far lower than those normally assigned any Captain. Your Talents carry the strength of your squad. Why do you mention this? Is there a problem with your Talent?"

"No. This has nothing to do with me."

"So?" Zeba said.

"A strange thing occurred, or at least I think it did. I felt it."

"There is a bench here, where I can catch my breath, and it is quiet." She lowered herself with his assistance and patted the stone seat next to her. "Tell me about it."

"I tracked someone."

She chuckled. "Of course you did. That's your Talent."

"This was more than just tracking, different. I wasn't trying to track her and should not have been able to."

Zeba remained quiet a moment. "So, you think you touched another Talent and bonded?"

"Maybe; yes, she must be, but it is implausible. I think I touched another Earth Talent. I had to have. How else could I bond with her?"

"Who?"

"Tyna's sister."

Zeba's light blue eyes widened, and her mind focused in perception. "Tyna, the new Captain? Yes, now I remember hearing about her sister, a barbarian null. How interesting. You've touched her?" At his hesitation, she added, "I see, most intimately, then. As I recall, you have a partiality for nulls. Tell me about her."

"How did you hear?"

"On good days, I can manage the Maze. I still have one or two friends who keep me informed. You must know the barbarian sister is a favorite topic. Is it true?"

"What?"

"The tattoo—a blue dragon?"

"She told me it was the bird-serpent of the Aibhe House of the Eastern Empire."

"So the answer is yes." A smile of relish crossed her face. "At last, I shall be able to contribute some gossip."

Dovel sat back. "This is serious."

She batted her eyelashes at him. "All is with the young. A well-traveled barbarian, tell me about her."

After Dovel finished his story, Zeba sat staring straight ahead, so quiet he thought she had fallen into her own visions. Finally, her eyes gazed at him with inquiry. "You say your Talent followed her, but that could be from a number of causes, or could be imagined. Have you been tested recently? Your own Talent might have changed."

"No. You know I don't like it."

She huffed. "With Orrthu in charge, few do...although some...if you had, a retesting might prove it, but that is impossible without a recent test for comparison. All Talents change with time, disposition, and illness; some grow, some diminish. Do you have any other proof of her supposed Talent?"

"None."

"Then what is your problem?"

"I needed to know if I should report my suspicions to the Talent Review Board."

Zeba considered. "Without more substantial proof, Orrthu would laugh at you. She only believes in testing and doesn't believe there is any Talent outside of Cygna."

"Kissre was born in Cygna," Dovel said, but Zeba did not seem to notice, lost in thought.

"It is rare that a null would be born from the same mother that produced such an adept as Tyna, but possible. You say she is a Touch void. That too is unusual. I knew a man once..." Her voice faded off, and she smiled in recognition at the emptiness before her and fell silent. Looking around, Dovel found the garden vacant. He waited. Finally, he touched her.

"Dovel, it's so good to see you." The look of surprised pleasure on her face did not faze him.

"I came to visit my favorite mentor. Can I help you back to your room, or would you like to continue your walk?"

Her bewildered face looked around the garden and then smiled at him. "I should like to continue if you would escort me?" Dovel readily agreed, but by the time they reached her room, she no longer knew who he was. Her maid met them and took Zeba's arm. He knew her days and her mental capacities came and went like this. It was just disappointing.

Walking through the blue granite buildings of the Assembly House complex, Dovel, along with others, stopped and sidestepped to the edge of the brick walk to allow Governor Vitann clear passage. A strong Talent from his own highland hamlet and a close friend of his grandmother, she had always shown an interest in Dovel's career, often acting as an unwanted mentor. She stopped in front of him, tall, steel gray, gaunt, and daunting. Dovel's gaze went to her Shield. Larig stood behind her, an armed and intimidating presence radiating the confidence his twin brother, Kedriq, lacked.

Dovel politely ducked his head once. A shiver ran down his neck and hid his disgust as Vitann tried to glean his mind. Vitann's surprise at her failure registered clearly, and he hoped he hid his own startled incredulity.

"What brings you to the Assembly House, Dovel?"

"I visited Adept Zeba in the retirement apartments."

Vitann's look measured him. "How is the venerable Oracle? Still lost in her visions?"

"Mostly. We had a brief conversation."

"Well, that is more than reported recently, although when lucid, the old gossip stays well informed. Oracles are so unstable. It is unfortunate. We need reliable prognostication right now." She nodded to him with another appraising look before she left. "You should be retested."

He stood and watched Vitann and her Shield disappear into the building at the end of the walk, still considering Vitann's inability to probe his mind. She was displeased with him. Her comment seemed a threat. He guessed news of his night had traveled beyond his squad. For him, privacy was the real void in Cygna. Finally turning, he took the longest route back to his camp.

It was clear that Kissre felt nothing of his mind. Once he realized he could sense her, first her presence, and after their second encounter, some fleeting emotions, he repeatedly tried to connect with her on any mental level. Nothing. The bond was one-sided. Kissre was Touch void. A reality possibly hiding a Talent, making it difficult to diagnose, but he suspected her not entirely null. He also knew reporting that suspicion could only lead to trouble.

Aspects of the situation disturbed him. The thinly concealed animosity between the sisters worried him. Tyna, with her unconscious air of superiority, held a desire to fix things, to fix Kissre. She wished to save her sister from her repulsive and dangerous lifestyle, to fit Kissre back into her family. Tyna seemed blind to the fact Kissre refused fixing, felt no need to be saved. In fact, Tyna's attitude abraded and offended her sister.

Kissre struck him as self-possessed, often repressed. In some ways, she was overly mature for her years, in some ways immature, but a person very capable of taking care of herself. She did not need her little sister's pity or help. On the other hand, jealousy, love, and hatred were a lethal combination and all tied together in Kissre. She knew it and exerted tremendous control over her responses.

She knew her sister's thoughts without mental intrusion. She saw in expressions and gestures what adepts learned through their Touch Talent. The verbal jabs at the first dinner were inconsequential pokes at contemptuous treatment. Only when away from Tyna and her squad did Kissre relax. She became comfortable enough to share herself. The problem was none of them understood the danger of the situation.

Whatever her motives, Kissre deserved credit. Perhaps staying away for such protracted periods was the safest thing Kissre did for Tyna's sake. He did not hold the right to intervene between them and felt separation was best for Tyna. It would be best for him, too. Thoughts of Kissre occupied too much of his time.

Kissre brought back his ambivalence about being an adept, which made him loath to report her. He felt his own squad's distaste for her and for his intimacy with her. Like Adele, they thought he used her, which was fine with them as long as he formed no lasting interest. Yet lately, his skill at veiling his mind from them had improved. Practice he supposed, so they did not know how his attitude was changing. That was good, for Kissre had no intention to stay in Cygna, and he did not want his disappointment broadcast when she left.

Adepts repulsed her. He was the first she had ever touched, partly from curiosity and easy availability, and then only because she realized he preferred nulls. By the time he reached his barracks, he still had not reached a decision. Law required that he report an unknown Talent, but it felt like a betrayal. He had time, though. Kissre would not leave within the next few days.

~ * ~

When Tyna left with Kedriq for a meeting, Kissre decided to take a nap and escape the squad who had stayed behind to wait. The lingering effects of her journey and the lateness of the last few nights had taken their toll. She was exhausted. It was mid-afternoon when she rose. Fudge rose from the floor beside the bed, whined, and licked her.

"All right, all right, I'll get up and take you for a run." She hustled down the back staircase and out through the kitchen. Fudge jump-trotted beside her in purposeful strides. With a pleasant greeting to the servants she passed, she rushed out the door and ran Fudge to the paddocks. Allowing him freedom to conduct his business, she roamed the adjacent grounds. Fudge chased after her, romped, jumped, and ran about her in huge circles. She laughed at his antics.

Commotion at the front finally drew her back to the house. Tyna had returned. She saw Kissre and motioned her forward, her face looking less welcoming for Fudge.

"Come in, I've bought you something." She grinned at Kissre. "The streets are full of people coming in for the Spring Revel."

"Find Bother, Fudge," Kissre commanded and watched him leave. She followed Tyna up the steps and into her sitting room. Tyna appeared happy and full of energy. Kissre perched in an overstuffed chair and waited. It didn't take long.

"I've been searching frantically for this." She handed Kissre a small box. Taking the box, Kissre opened it and looked at the contents. She recognized the amber pendant with its trapped insect as Naomi's with repulsed loathing. Tyna didn't notice. "I bought you some clothes to go with it," she said, opening another parcel and pulling out a traditional Cygnese outfit in deep gold. "Here, try it on."

"I'm sorry, but I can't accept this, Ty," Kissre said, cutting through Tyna's gaiety. She placed the lid back on the box and put it on a side table.

"Of course you can. Mother would have wanted you to have it."

"No, Ty, Naomi wouldn't. You do. I cannot accept it. I don't want it."

Tyna stilled, her full lips compressed, and a crease marred her forehead between her lowered brows. "Because you don't like it or because it was Mother's?"

"It makes no difference." Silence. Whatever her face held inflamed Tyna.

"How can you?" Tyna's voice rose in agitation. "How can you not even acknowledge your relationship? Not mourn her? Not even talk of her? How can you be so unfeeling? What is wrong with you? She was your mother, too!"

"Tyna, no. I don't want to talk about this." Kissre said in as level a voice as she could manage as she rose to her feet.

Tyna's voice rose. "But I want to! I want to know what caused you to hate her so! Hate me! What have I ever done to you?"

"I don't hate you, but I am leaving this room. Right now," Tyna moved as Kissre took a step, stood blocking her exit. Short of knocking her sister down, Kissre found herself trapped. Gritting her teeth, she looked into an expression hauntingly reminiscent of Naomi. Afraid, she backed away.

"You don't hate me? Then why do you come here looking like this," her hand waved to Kissre's hair, face, and attire. "Not even trying to wear something to make you appear less...less..."

"Coarse?" Heat surged through Kissre.

"Yes! Coarse, unfeminine," Tyna said with vehemence and dropped the Cygnese clothes she held. They fell to the floor in a disordered heap.

"Un-Talented?"

Tyna stopped, her face jolted at the never heard tone. "I never said that."

"You didn't have to."

"You could at least try to blend," Tyna said, lowering her voice, but her disgust evident.

"I am a mercenary and dress and act like what I am. What your Mother made me."

Tyna swore and turned away, then twirled back. "She didn't make you anything! You did! You behave like an uncivilized slut, free of responsibility, free to do whatever you want, whenever you want, because no one can read you. Then you bait adepts because of what they are, and everyone knows Dovel fantasizes..." Tyna stopped, her mouth still open.

"No, Tyna, don't stop," Kissre said, feeling her heart wrench, then swell and split.

"You're right, Kissre. No more of this." Tyna's gaze fell to her desk.

Kissre continued Tyna's topic. "You wanted me to know he fantasizes the null sister becomes the other, the untouchable, Talented one?"

Tyna turned away.

Kissre continued. "But you're wrong in one instance, Tyna. I don't bait adepts because they are, but because they see nulls as less." Kissre kept her sight concentrated on Tyna, her low voice a threat. Tyna looked at her in incipient denial. "And you know it's true, too, don't you, Ty? Because Naomi taught you to think like herself."

"No, I don't, not anymore. Kissre, stop." Tyna looked aside and bit her lower lip, just like when she was little and trying not to cry. "You were right. We should not do this. Please stop."

Watching panic crumple Tyna's face in misery, Kissre sensed her enemy's weakness, sensed she held the upper hand. Years of swallowed insult and contempt began boiling over her control. She returned her sister's earlier demeaning smile.

"Maybe it's time you learned the rest of the truth."

Alarm entered Tyna's face and Kissre's smile twisted in elation. At Tyna's sudden movement, she rushed the door ahead of her prey and turned the lock. The bolts clicked into place just in time. An instant later, the door reverberated with pounding fists. Beyond the iron hinged and banded oak planks, muffled voices shouted to Tyna. Kissre inspected the door and smiled. It was a well-made, heavy door.

"Enough, Kissre, say no more. You are right. We can only hurt each other," Tyna said. She backed away, her look not so scorning now.

Kissre ignored her, stalked her retreat. "Maybe it is time you grew up, learned what life is like for those who aren't cosseted, spoiled Talent brats. Yes, I am a coarse barbaric slut, but I didn't make me so."

Tyna backed a step.

"Guess who paid for your safety, paid for your food and your upkeep, paid all those years before Naomi bought the Caravan? Guess where she got the money to buy a caravan? What? Didn't you know how profitable soldiering could be? I didn't drink, gamble, or whore away every pay pack."

Tyna dodged behind her desk. Kissre leaned over it but went no further. Battle-trained reflexes held her, but unbearable heat consumed her. The kill was near. She sensed it, reveled in it—to hell with consequences.

"Can't guess?"

Tyna looked at her in defiant but ineffective bravado.

"Let me tell you." She allowed a knife's edge of silence. "Naomi sold her oldest daughter, the null one, to protect her *Talented* daughter. She sacrificed the common one to save the valuable one." The tightness in her chest exploded, bleeding the torment within.

"No, that's not true!" Tyna screamed, shocked, disbelieving, and provoked. "She said you were apprenticed. She paid for it."

"Yes, she did. She apprenticed her sixteen-year-old daughter to a mercenary, a man more than twice her age, plausibly to learn the trade. Except the payment went the other way. Lucky for me, he did teach me the soldiers' trade...eventually. Do you know, Tyna, do you have any idea what a young girl's first job as a mercenary's apprentice is? Don't shake your head. Don't try and deny it." Her words emerged low, slow, and soft.

"The thing is, Tyna, Naomi knew. Your beloved mother sold your sister into prostitution to save your precious self. I understand. She was newly widowed, desperate, didn't know what else to do. But as the resulting slut, I mind very much."

Tyna's streaming tears didn't faze Kissre. They released a savage delight that danced with the cadence of the drumming on the door and the chorus of voices on its other side. Tyna turned away.

"She made me feel it was my duty to protect you. For eight years my wages went to Naomi. Do you remember my last visit with you, on your eighteenth birthday? That's when Naomi told me, after I gifted you with the cloak that you laughed at as unfashionable. After taking my offering, she told me to keep my future wages. She didn't need them anymore. So think about that the next time your null sister embarrasses you." Tyna cringed.

She sneered at Tyna's back. "Think about that the next time you turn your back."

Barking erupted beyond the door. The background hammering ceased. The change jerked Kissre taut. A gaping dark precipice lay dizzily before her. Her mind tilted and swirled in the familiar after battle instant when the simultaneous realization of her survival and the cost collided. She stepped back. Tyna remained turned away, her harsh sobbing audible. Kissre felt ill. Never before had she unleashed her anger like this.

Tyna turned, looked at her with loathing. Tears shimmered in clear cascades across her cheeks, but she suppressed the aching sound behind trembling lips. Kissre closed her eyes, remembering her sister's pregnant state, opened them to recognize Tyna's hate and rejection.

She evaded the look by turning her head and taking a deep breath. "I think I've outworn my welcome." Catching her fingers threading through her hair, she lowered them and looked at the back of her hands. A blue serpent snarled back at her. "I apologize, Ty... Captain Pierce. It will be better if we don't see each other. I'll leave. Rest assured, I won't inflict my presence on you again." She turned and walked quietly to the door, unlocked, and opened it.

They all stood there, even Dovel, looking sick, disgusted. No doubt, they had heard it all. Fudge menaced them with a deep-throated rumble, his head down, teeth bared, and neck-ruff erect. Saying nothing, Kissre turned to the steps. Snapped fingers brought Fudge to heel as she left.

Cursing herself as everything Tyna had called her, she added contemptuous, sniveling, jealous, and bitchy snitch. While castigating herself, Kissre threw her few possessions into her saddlebags. Now her mouth was clamped shut. Too bad she hadn't thought of that simple measure earlier. None of this was Tyna's fault. Naomi's, yes. Holy One! The name pierced her with pain, and she gritted her teeth. And she had just taken all her loathing out on Tyna. One thing was clear, Tyna would never want to see her again, and better so.

Finished, she left down the back staircase, not wishing to reopen warfare by descending the front, and very sure no one wanted fond goodbyes. It took a trice to saddle Bother and pack the roan. Nobody disturbed her. Nobody came. She hoped she hadn't harmed Tyna or her baby with her unforgivable rampage.

She stopped as she put her foot into the stirrup. Anger reformed and refueled. Unforgivable; it worked both ways. Tyna had said unpardonable things. She saw Tyna's face, Naomi's face with that worth-measuring look that conveyed more than words. It hurt so bad her hands shook. She was used to swallowing acid, but this time it curdled in her gut and spread, burning its way through her heart and mind. It was no excuse for her behavior, but words, once said... She bowed her head against the saddle; bit her lip until she tasted blood. Her fists clenched the reins. She could neither forget nor forgive Tyna's words or repugnant look.

It was too much to bear, and she was too old to cry about such nonsense now. Swallowing her bitterness, she mounted Bother. Adults took different measures. Hers was escape and estrangement. From now on, she swore, she had no sister.

Chin firm, mouth set, she turned Bother and left the compound. The accusing looks every arm-badged person gave her set her resolve and lashed her with guilt. Shortly she reached the city gates.

Tomel, the sergeant who had escorted her into Sidih, stood talking with the guard. He approached her, and she obediently halted Bother. "Mistress Pierce, I've been requested to ask you not to leave, to return, if you please, to Captain Tyna's house."

"Am I detained?"

"No, Ma'am," Tomel said. "It was a request only. If I may say so, it is a little late in the day to start such a long journey."

"Now is as good a time as any. Thank you. Send thanks to Captain Tyna, but I think it best to leave now." She offered her hand to Tomel. "Thank you for your previous service, Tomel. I might wish for your clear tenor on my return trip."

"Then good journey, Mistress Pierce." Tomel took her extended hand, his eyes resting on the blue tracings. They shook once.

She nodded and opened a saddle pack, withdrew her gloves, and put them on. "Family visits, you know, should always be kept short and sweet." She grinned. It cost her, but Tomel took no notice. He grinned back.

"Goodbye, then, Kissre."

A side-glance caught furtive movement even as Fudge growled in warning. Swinging her head, she glimpsed activity in the rooftops lining the road. She yelled a warning to the people following her through the city's gate and wheeled Bother broadside to the stone archway for added protection. Searing pain pierced her thigh. Time slowed. She watched as people retreated to safety. Arrows pelted the cobbled ground, and gate guards ran forward from the screaming mob, knocking arrows as they knelt. Agony lanced her arm and side. She felt Bother go down in a sluggish, sinking motion, heard his anguished squeals and Fudge's frenzied barks as her vision faded.

~ * ~

"She won't come back." Tyna cried into Kedriq's shoulder. "I've ruined everything. I hurt her, called her terrible things. What she said, I did not want to believe, but I know them true. Kedriq, I've been such a fool. Thought I could fix everything. I kept pushing her, wishing her different, wanting her to be what I wanted. Instead, I drove her away."

Kedriq kept his arms around Tyna, crooning to her. "It's all right. It was a bad argument. Things got said. You must calm yourself."

Dovel watched, filled with bitter torment, his brows felt heavy with regret. The last scene repeated endlessly before his eyes. Kissre, under a tangible and alarming control, opened the door at last. Her eyes had measured Tyna's squad and him in one quick glance, read the truth of Tyna's accusation on his face. He felt it like a physical blow. The look she refused to give him told all.

Her departure with Fudge freed the squad to rush to Tyna. Their Captain's rolling mental turmoil, her anguish, hit all of them. Dovel had asked Reg, also a witness to the shouting confrontation within the locked chamber, the crazed squad, and the mad dog without, to bring hot drinks for Captain Tyna and her squad. He entered and sat in a chair, wishing he had set elsewhere when he sensed Kissre's lingering presence. At that moment, he hated everything to do with his Talent.

Kedriq tried to console Tyna, but a long time passed before she calmed enough to speak. Regret was uppermost in her mind, with a familiar urgent fix-it need. She broke from Kedriq and sat down. Whether from the pregnancy or the broken family relations, none of them had seen Tyna so vulnerable, so dependent, or so lost.

Reg entered with drinks for all, a concerned look on his face. As he placed the drink before her, Tyna, with an abstracted look, took the cup. "Reg, could you ask Kissre to come down? No, maybe I should go up. We should be private."

"No. We won't let you be private," Meyer said. "Not after what you felt during your last 'private' interlude. How did she threaten you?"

"Threaten?" Tyna said, her bewilderment evident. "She didn't threaten, just...It was her anger. It was so frightening...like it was eating her alive." Her head dropped into her hands. "Now so understandable, so justified."

"But, Captain Tyna," Reg said, looking a little perplexed. "Mistress Kissre is gone."

"A half-mark ago," Dovel said. "She's nearly to the city gate."

"How…" Tyna began to ask Dovel.

"One of my sergeants is at the gate. I have sent a message to him. He will ask her to return. If she is still too angry to come back, we will try again later. It is a long way to the border, Tyna."

He felt Tyna worm through his mind, find his sergeant, a platoon leader with Touch abilities so low he wasn't graded or badged. Dovel's mind, inexorably tied with Tyna and Tomel, felt the blow. He blanched and rose as Tyna screamed.

"Kissre!"

He felt the single word torn from either his or Tyna's throat, maybe both, but he was already out of the room and running down the walk. After that, it was hard to distinguish what he felt from what Tyna projected.

Thankfully, someone kept her at the house.

Five

Chaos reigned at the gate. Dovel heard Fudge's loud barking threats and growls, heard the crowd's cries of panic and the babble of outraged, frightened people milling just inside the gate. He pushed through the agitated mob. Adele's hand grasped his sleeve, then Ulyss tried to detain him. Brought by his alarm, they tried to protect him, pull him back. He brushed them off.

A platoon of archers skirmished beyond the scene of devastation. The roan and Bother lay in the road. The buckskin's head curled up with grunts and low squeals of pain as he tried to rise before dropping his head to the muddy pavers. His loud troubled breathing echoed through the discordant sounds filling the air.

Kissre lay twisted, back to the street, still in the saddle. Blood pooled around her. A crowd of men circled, trying to reach her. Fudge stood over Kissre, his muzzle curled back, fangs exposed. From recent experience, Dovel knew the fear the giant dog inspired. The lowered head, growls, and raised neck-ruff threatened would-be rescuers. His sudden charges, harsh barks, and snapping teeth created a circle of protection around his mistress.

Dovel ordered everyone back. As the men stopped threatening, Fudge trotted to Kissre and stood over her. He prodded her with his nose and whined, then resumed his protective stance. Dovel cautiously approached the downed horse and rider.

"Good-boy, Fudge," he said, projecting friendship at the dog, something he'd never done. Fudge watched him. A warning rumbled in his throat, and his neck-ruff rose. The eyes in the long shaggy head followed Dovel's approach. He brandished his fangs.

"Come, boy. Come, Fudge. We've got to help Kissre. Come now, you've done your job. Come, Fudge." Fudge's tail wagged once, and he whined a low piteous sound, but as Dovel approached nearer, the dog backed over Kissre with a renewed growl. Below the dog's stomach, a hand movement caught Dovel's glance.

"Kissre? Kissre!" He called in panic and relief, "Call Fudge off. Kissre can you hear me?" He felt other minds blend with his, his squad, Tyna, her squad, others. He projected to Kissre with all the sending power he could summon. There was no response.

Her hand moved to touch Fudge's knee with a weak touch. "Fudge...out."

She had heard him. Whether mental or vocal didn't matter. Fudge's reaction was immediate. The dog whined. He lowered his long whipcord length and curled up next to her.

Dovel warily reached Fudge. Someone handed him a rope, and with apologetic thoughts, he looped it through Fudge's collar and twice around his jaw. Fudge renewed his fight, twisting and turning, but three men were on him by then and trussed him immobile. He cast anxious, sad eyes at Dovel, piercing the squad leader with self-inflicted guilt. He stroked the dog's head and shoulder.

"Take him to the stables at my residence. Have him locked into one of the stalls."

One man nodded. It took two of them to load Fudge onto a cart that appeared through the crowd. By then Dovel's attention had turned to Kissre. They tried to pull her from underneath Bother.

"No! Don't move her!"

Dovel recognized Sergeant Tomel's voice.

"She took an arrow. Her leg's pinned to the saddle."

Someone from the crowd stepped forward, proclaiming himself a pony trainer. He wasn't much bigger than a pony. He stepped to Bother's head and stroked the animal's cheek. Bother's white-rimmed eyes rolled at the man. "Easy now, brute. Easy." He looked around the crowd. "Two of you, get ready to lift the woman. The rest of you push. Got to rock the brute here to his feet."

"Bother," Dovel said.

"Yeah, it is, but have to do it."

"No, his name's Bother." It seemed oddly important.

"Oh! Well, good enough."

"Dovel?" Kissre's weak voice called. He bent over her. She grasped his tunic with a bloodied glove. "Dovel…"

"You'll be all right, Kissre."

"Bother, take care of him for me. Do it quickly. Don't let him suffer." Tears flowed from the corners of her eyes back into her hair as Bother gave another pained squeal. "Promise."

"I promise." He wasn't sure she was aware of what was going on. Her eyes closed, and her hand fell away.

"Okay, let's try it," the small trainer said. He pulled Bother's head up, curling it back toward the huge body as he called to the horse. Other men heaved as Bother struggled and squealed. He rolled up, his hooves scraping and scrabbling for purchase, but he couldn't gain his feet. Giving up, he settled back on his side with a long and harsh strangled groan.

"Kill him and be done with it," one of the men said.

"Give him a minute," the trainer said. "If we can get him to his feet, it will be easier to remove her. You don't want to lift his dead weight." The man squatted next to Bother's head.

One horse ear twitched as the trainer talked to the downed animal. Dovel watched as with each labored breath Bother's side rose in pained measure. Time passed. The trainer kept up his soft encouragement. The low murmurs of bystanders formed an ominous wall around the hush hanging over the rescuers.

Of his own accord, Bother lifted his head. With a tremendous surge he tried to roll. Hands found purchase on shoulder, wither, saddle, and rump. The trainer pulled on the reins, lifting his head further. Dovel pulled on the stirrup.

With one heroic huff of wheezed air and a large gut-groan, Bother found his feet and rose. He stood, legs braced, head hanging, whinnying his agony in long soft waves of sound. A round of applause and cheers erupted from the spectators.

Kissre's body slumped over Bother, her blood running down both sides of the horse. A shaft emerged from her left arm. Another grisly wound pinned horse and rider on the right side. The arrow had broken in the fall. Its end lay exposed just below skin level, split and splintered. They applied a tourniquet above the wound and pulled her leg far enough from the saddle flap to cut the shaft. A mounted man took her before him on his pony and eased through the parting crowd toward the infirmary. Dovel didn't follow. He walked to the roan. The animal was dead.

Then he turned to the doomed Bother.

"Get him to the side of the road and put him out of his misery," someone advised. "The renders can handle him from there." Already two riders pulled the roan off the road with ropes attached to the dead horse's neck.

~ * ~

Finished with the report from Sergeant Tomel and other witnesses, Dovel, trailed by his squad, headed to where he knew Tyna and her squad gathered. Tyna's uncontrolled projections scourged his precarious composure. She had ruthlessly invaded minds to get visions of Kissre. He doubted anyone would report her.

Along the route, Ranor, Marshal of the Northern Army and Dovel's commander, joined him in the walk, followed shortly thereafter by other squad captains. With a silent groan, Dovel sensed an emergency command meeting developing. An entourage entered the infirmary and joined Tyna in a secluded waiting area. They perched on any available surface or leaned against walls, settling in to wait with Tyna. Dovel chose to lean against the doorjamb, half in, half out of the room, wanting to run, afraid to leave.

He looked at Tyna, her face drawn in worry, her uneasiness driving her into anxious activity. Whenever Kedriq failed to contain her distress, she paced the room.

Marshal Ranor, solid, blunt, and formal, asked Dovel for a report. That drew Tyna's distracted attention.

"Platoon Sergeant Tomel reported Mistress Pierce stopped to talk with him. He delivered a message for her to return, but she declined."

"I knew she would," Tyna said, trying to control her quavering voice, followed by a loud sniff. "No one is more stubborn than Kissre. When she looked at me as she did mother on that last visit, I knew she wouldn't return."

Dovel ignored Tyna's outburst. Everyone already felt her bruised emotions, her grieving sense of loss, impossible for her to restrain.

"He said she noticed something and that alerted his attention," Dovel said. "He saw a flash of color and motion where there shouldn't have been any. Then Kissre yelled a warning. She turned her horse to shield those at the gate just as the arrows flew. Tyna's projection brought nearby platoons to alert. By the time they arrived, Tomel had already brought down two of the assassins. There were no survivors."

"Why attack Kissre?" Tyna asked. "She isn't part of this at all."

"We believe you were the target," Kedriq said. "After your projection, the platoon believed they were defending you. Kissre's attack was a case of mistaken identity. She looks enough like her sister," he told Ranor. "We knew strong Adepts would be targeted if Cygna was infiltrated."

"Tyna's caravan friends might have known of her Talent," Silvie said.

"Jebe?" Tyna asked, distracted, her stab of hurt at her former friend's betrayal rippled through the room. "Kissre saw him on her trip here. She relieved him of a large sum of coins when she realized he had stolen my caravan."

"Jebe could have had you targeted because of that," Kedriq said. "He might have made dissident connections while here."

"Tomel brought down two?" Ranor asked with a contemplative frown. "We should have that young man tested. Those had to be either miraculous shots or Talent aimed."

Dovel agreed. "He said he just got a visual and shot two quick arrows, but Bother going down knocked him sideways, so he had little expectation of a hit, let alone two."

"He didn't stop arrows from hitting Kissre." Tyna swore, and her sniffs turned into uncontrolled sobs. Dovel looked up with a frown as Kedriq gave her a mental rebuke for her loss of control. Many others protested, hearing Kedriq's censure, some aloud.

"Who were they?" Tyna asked, forcefully composing herself. Dovel blinked and took a slow breath in relief as the mental pressure eased.

"We're not sure. They have not been identified, even through the Maze. Which leads us to believe they are not from Cygna."

"Jebe could have had Kissre targeted," Tyna said.

"Nonsense," Meyer said, sitting with arms braced on his knees, hands clasped in tight claws. "It's just more dissident nulls."

"Maybe, maybe not," Ranor said, negating Myer's belief. "Strategic Command has been expecting something like this. It is possible for agents to infiltrate the countryside, especially if they had help from dissidents."

The talk turned to means of keeping Tyna safe. A tall, blue-clad healer, his once black hair grayed and in disorder, entered and nodded to Marshal Ranor, interrupting the debriefing.

"Healer Bujyea," Ranor acknowledged the man. The healer shook the Marshal's hand, then gave his report to Tyna. Kissre would live, but she was very weak, had lost much blood. "A Weaver Adept helped me treat three wounds. The arrow piercing the upper arm also entered her side and struck a rib. The shaft did not, however, reach her heart or lungs. It is now a matter of time to heal."

"Can I see her?" Tyna asked. Bujyea nodded and turned to lead the way. Tyna looked at Dovel with a question in her eyes. Grateful for the silent offer, Dovel followed her.

Kissre's bed lay at the end of a long ward of empty beds. Her sun and earth hair seemed the only color amid the white bedding. Dovel watched Tyna approach. Standing by the bed, she pushed some unruly locks back from Kissre's high forehead.

"We seldom use this ward but under the circumstances and her foreignness, I felt it better," Bujyea said. "She has been reviving slowly and should come to her senses soon. Call her."

Dovel's lips firmed at the inherent insult to Kissre.

"Kiss," Tyna called repeatedly.

Kissre's eyes opened. For a moment, she did not focus on anything.

"I want to take her to my home. She can be taken care of there."

"That would not be advisable right now," Bujyea said. "Maybe when she has healed more."

As the healer spoke, Kissre's eyes focused on Tyna and widened in aversion. She struggled to move. Quickly exhausted, she closed her eyes. "No."

Her eyes opened with effort, cold in their composure, and locked on the healer. "I want to stay here. I can pay." She closed her eyes again.

Tyna gasped and cried. "Kissre, I'm sorry, forgive me. I didn't mean what I said..." She continued her apology as the healer nodded at Kedriq. He pulled his wife away. Halfway down the ward, Dovel felt Tyna give way to tears, and experienced her acute sense of loss, and the wailing thought that Kissre would never look on her as sister again.

As silence fell, Kissre opened her eyes and looked at Dovel with the same remote expression. "Did he suffer?" Her half-opened eyes searched his face.

"No. The roan was already dead."

She turned her head away, closed her eyes, attempting to hide tears. "Fudge?"

"He is safe. I will care for him until you can."

"Thank you." A heartbeat later, "I am obliged to you."

"Are you staying, Captain Dovel?"

At the healer's words, Kissre's lids flickered, but she said nothing. He nodded at the healer, who held Kissre's wrist. Laying her hand down, Bujyea brought a vial out of his pocket and pulled out the stopper. Kissre turned her head away, but the man's hand followed, and her next breath caught the vapors. She coughed and grimaced, but relaxed.

The healer sighed. "I had heard of a family riff. It is a sad situation. It will be better to keep them apart for now. I'll have a chair brought for you. If she wakes up, she will be groggy."

Dovel stood at the end of the bed, unaware of Bujyea leaving or the arrival of a chair until someone touched his sleeve. He thanked them, and they left. He quietly picked up the chair and placed it next to the bed. Sitting, he let his head fall forward into his hands.

During the night, a hand on his shoulder woke him. His lieutenant Ulyss stood next to him. Moonlight flooded through the window, accenting the snowy fabric covering the bed. After ascertaining the movement of the occupant's respiration, he turned his head to his lieutenant. In the shadowed face looking at him, only reflected moonlight glistened in the dark hollows where brown eyes normally dwelled. All else dissolved in the darkness.

He felt the concern filling his lieutenant. "You need to come rest."

"I'm resting here."

"We know you are not."

"Ulyss, as a favor, please—just go away."

Ulyss patted his shoulder, and he heard his steps fade away.

A new day's light woke him and ignited his mind with a vivid memory of the previous morning. Today was the first day of Spring Revel. Through the window he even heard the Rites taking place at the cathedral. The black swans were back on the high lakes, an event to celebrate.

A moan caught his attention. Kissre shifted in discomfort and opened her eyes. He offered her water. She sipped and let her head fall back onto the pillow.

"Do you mind me being here?" he asked, wrapping his fingers around her hand. The clasp was not returned.

"No. Do as you please."

While it wasn't what he wanted to hear, he was content. She fell asleep. During the coming and going of aides and healers, she slept.

A few times he walked about in aimless wandering. Unable to share the jubilation within the city, he soon retreated to her bedside.

His squad arrived with lamps and demanded he come rest. They told him how much time had passed. He refused. Another day's light streamed through the window before she woke. Though he sensed her tolerance, he knew something was missing and couldn't be replaced.

The healer's aide and his squad urged him to leave, something only a summons from the Assembly house achieved.

When he arrived, Cath and Ulyss trailed him, refusing to let him sink into despondency again. Zeba stood leaning on her cane with her maidservant in the main hall. She looked at him in concern, the pale blue eyes in her wrinkled face observant and intent. "Take me to her."

They made their way slowly as she explained. "The healer reported to the Talent Review Board yesterday. It was a good day for me, so I listened in the gallery. I remembered something you told me, so when no one else wanted to deal with a null, I volunteered to go. No one on the Adept Council believes, which is why Vitann agreed, and you found me waiting. They thought I did it as a favor for you. Poor Bujyea found his opinion dismissed—he only said she wasn't null. Everyone who has come near her says otherwise. Their inability to feel her causes their revulsion."

"Do you think...how long..." Dovel was unsure of how to frame his question.

"Will I be able to do it? I am focused, that always helps. Interest anchors the mind. Marshal Ranor pulled Tomel in for testing."

"That sounds serious."

Her face looked up at him. "How can you say so? Nothing has been detected or decided, and it may all come to nothing. What is clear, though, is Tyna has been adversely affected by this visit, and she affects every mind she touches. I," she said with droll pride and a hint of laughter, "volunteered to act as a conciliator. No one else wishes to talk with a barbarian. Once the sisters have reconciled,

I'm sure they will escort your Kissre out of the country with the enthusiasm of a fast country dance."

Kissre was propped in a sitting position with pillows. Her deep-shadowed eyes lethargic and huge in a sick-pale face watched their approach with apathy. Bandages bulged beneath the sleeve of her sleep smock. An aide removed a blood-tinged bowl of water as they arrived. Zeba teetered to the chair and sat with obvious frailty and relief but quickly gathered herself.

"Hello, Mistress Pierce. I'm Zeba, a mentor to Dovel many years ago. He brought me to visit. Would you mind talking with an old woman?"

"Why?" The voice barely reached whisper level.

"Because it seems you have limited the number of people willing to talk to you, and your healer thought you needed company to speed your recovery. He said you would speak to no one, not even him."

"I would rather not."

"I know. It is amazing what others expect one to put up with. How many are willing to intrude and make our choices for us, particularly when we find ourselves unable to do so. I run into it frequently." Zeba turned to Dovel and his squad. "Why don't all of you go away for a half-mark or so, while we chat?"

Zeba watched as Kissre's eyes followed the departing backs, then swiveled in suspicion to her. "What do you want?"

"Conversation," Zeba said. "I've also greatly reduced the number of people willing to chat with me. Different reason. Dovel felt we might get along. Have you no questions? Want no explanations?"

"My thoughts haven't progressed that far." The girl's eyes returned to Zeba's face. "You are an Adept."

"And you are a null, a complete Touch void, according to Dovel. "That is why the healer wants you to talk." One brow arched above the observant eyes. "He lacks the means to figure out how you feel otherwise," Zeba explained.

"He could always ask. What are you?"

"Do you never follow false trails?"

The flat green eyes blinked and looked away. "I'm a mercenary," she replied as if that explained everything.

"So Dovel told me, and so deliciously exotic looking for a native." That got her. Zeba watched the lips tighten.

"Not a native for a very long time."

"Yes, I can see it. I like the short hair. So trouble free and very attractive on you." Zeba reached out and picked up the right hand from where it lay on the bed. "I've heard about this, too," she said, holding the flaccid limb and examining the tattoo. "The Maze tumbled, enthralled and scandalized by it, for days. Do you mind?"

The hand in hers didn't move, and she smiled at the implied assent as she turned it over and back in frank inspection. From the shoulder down, incredibly fine blue lines twined on her arm, forming a scale-covered creature's body that twisted and writhed snake-like onto her hand between wing-like appendages. Its head, a combination of hawk and snake framed in ruffled feathers, screamed defiance from the back of the pale hand. "The maze?"

"What Talents call the method by which we talk mind to mind to mind throughout the country. Did it hurt?"

"Yes. You are a Touch?"

"I am a Sender Adept, which is a Touch Talent, and a Tracker Adept, which is an Earth Talent. But my strongest and most important talent was Time. Once I was an Oracle. I've been retired for many years. Oracles are historically very unstable Adepts." At Kissre's look, she added, "We tend to get lost in time." The brief interest faded. "Do you want to talk about what happened?"

"No."

"Not about the attack? Not about your sister? Not about Dovel?"

"Least about Captain Pierce or Dovel. The attack I remember moment by moment. I thought multiple talents were rare. Everybody I've met seems to have them."

"Multiple Talents are common among those with a single very strong talent. It seems unfair, doesn't it? But that is how it works."

"It makes no difference in my life, just curious."

Zeba lay the hand down and placed her own over it. "Well then, if I can tell you nothing, would you mind talking to me?

A petulant sigh escaped the bed-trapped patient. "Would you go away if I asked?"

"No. You've piqued my interest, and I've always been known for my curiosity and my persistence."

Another ragged sigh floated gently on the air. "What do you want to know?"

"Dovel says you are widely traveled—Sunderlune, Pertelon, Kaereya, even beyond Kaereya's Doane Desert and into the Eastern continent." She couldn't suppress the excitement that entered her voice. "He says you know about magic from the outlands. I wish to hear it all."

"Today?" Faint surprise and humor entered the lifeless voice.

Zeba laughed, a long-absent buoyancy entering her. "No, but maybe over the next few days? If you don't mind and feel up to it, that is. I've always wanted to travel, to see the world. I never shall now, except perhaps through your eyes."

Kissre gave a small shrug that brought a tinge of pain to her face. "Time weighs heavy here. Maybe you're right, talking will help it pass."

"Then tell me, how come you let someone hurt you for this? Did they force you?" She ran her finger over the blue tracings.

"No. It was an honor. The Aibhe House distinguished me with their mark of attainment. Few housemen receive the honor."

"Why?"

"I helped them in a dispute with another house."

Zeba patted the hand and told Kissre she would return tomorrow as Dovel and his lieutenants started walking down the otherwise empty ward. Zeba met him halfway but said nothing. What she believed was unbelievable, making a mockery of her boast of capability. No one would believe her.

Six

Dovel returned to Kissre's bedside the next morning. She didn't refuse his company but lay deathly still. The aide said they had made her stand and take a few steps on her good leg. Kissre rolled her eyes at their report but said nothing.

When the aide left, she asked, "How is Fudge?"

"Tearing my compound apart and frightening most of the troops stationed there. Some of them saw him protect you, and rumor is rampant."

Her eyes looked at him with the first spark of interest. He told her how hard it had been to rescue her. The mention of the rescue and her eyes deadened.

"He likes you. You will take care of him?"

"Of course. Until you are better, I promise."

"You mustn't let him get away with things." She told him a few commands to keep the dog in line. He didn't tell her that when finished terrorizing everyone with his wildness, the mangy animal lay by her bloody and damaged saddle, the remains of the baggage not crushed by the roan's death piled around it, and refused all enticement to move.

"Do they know the reason?"

"It is assumed an attack on Tyna. You were mistaken for her."

"Traveling?" Kissre scoffed.

"The assumption is Pertelon agents helped by dissident... citizens."

"Nulls. It's all right. I know what I am. Something is wrong with their logic." Kissre sighed. "I'm too tired to think on it."

"Plausible enough. Most wouldn't know that much about Tyna's habits and life. She was a trader before, and you dress similar to many traders."

"Is Captain Pierce all right?"

It was a loaded question. His emotional bond to her had disappeared, but he could guess the essence of the question. "Both she and her baby are fine and protected. Marshal Ranor put all her platoons on extra duty."

"Good."

"What are your plans?"

"To leave as soon as possible. It will be a month or more before I can work. I will need to send my employer an explanation for my continued absence and a resignation."

"I will help you in any way I can."

"Thank you. If you could help me write a letter to Aristo Aurelias and see it on its way, I'd be grateful."

He nodded. Two more days of perfunctory talk took Dovel to his composure's limit. Zeba continued to visit daily, her maid escorting her. His old mentor refused to talk to him about what she learned, fobbing him off with promises of later, a later he began to believe she would remember. He didn't need to hear her report, although he wanted to hear her views. The Ancient Oracle's vitality and focus told him much. She had a new excitement and interest in life. Kissre's stories she shared with a vivacity that told her avid interest in the other's travels and worldviews.

Kissre continued to fade, and Healer Bujyea became worried. "She should have made more progress by now, but we keep fighting infection and fevers. The wounds continue to seep. She eats little.

The apathy does not help. I think we should stop any visits that drain her more."

Later that day she fell into a deep sleep and wouldn't rouse.

~ * ~

"He cannot stay with her all the time," Adele said, "it is just guilt. He has always been too considerate." She paced the room, her face a pensive pout. "Like taking care of that damn dog."

Ulyss listened. He sat on the fireplace hearth with Fudge's head heavy in his lap. The forlorn dog had, at last, accepted his attention but remained indifferent. There was no use riling Adele with his own, different opinion. Right now, the emotions leaking from Dovel were enough to handle. They didn't need Adele's jealous whining lacing the fringes. All knew Adele thought Dovel belonged to her, even if he had only touched her physically once. How she reached that conclusion, he had never understood—unless it was because both she and Dovel were highlanders.

He cast a glance at Wyn and Cath. Both looked as unhappy as he felt, but of the Lieutenants, Adele held senior Talent. They knew Adele possessive of Dovel, but her regard was not returned. Dovel chose to be physically distant and sought as much mental distance as their bond allowed. All but Adele thought themself fortunate.

"We'll leave him for now. We know where he is, and there is no immediate duty for any of us," levelheaded Cath said. "We can stay sensitive to the situation without becoming intrusive."

"It's not good for him. Dovel needs a stable relationship, and this can lead nowhere," Adele said. Ulyss looked at Wyn, who shrugged. Adele took over as squad manager too often. "She was just using Dovel, anyway."

"I thought you said it was the other way around?" Wyn said. He always liked confrontation. Ulyss wished he'd held his comments as Adele rose to the bait.

"She's null! And look at her! An improper foreigner—barely a woman—he'll be the laughingstock of the company. Even Captain Tyna disapproves of her. Everyone felt that! If it continues, if she continues, I'll take it to the Adept Council as an unsuitable liaison.

They would never let a Talent of Dovel's ability remain in such a relationship."

"You'll do no such thing," Cath said, her mind filling with indignation. "Not everyone felt Tyna's distress, only those tied to her. The rest is just gossip. We'll let Dovel handle his own affairs. He likes his privacy. We all know it. We're lucky he accepts us, has made us his friends. None of us would be in a squad without his and Ulyss's Talent. So don't let a jealous tantrum ruin Dovel's life. We won't let you."

Cath only inflamed Adele. She screamed her answer, her mental outrage as unpleasant as the volume of her voice. "If Dovel treated us properly, we wouldn't have to protect him from Tyna's degenerate null sister! What could he possibly see in her?"

Ulyss cringed.

"I guess whatever he sees in the other nulls he sleeps with," Wyn said. "You should be careful how you speak of Captain Tyna's sister. You don't know the particulars, and everyone feels Captain Tyna's anguish over her sister's injury."

"I thank the Holy One every day Dovel doesn't treat us as some Captains treat their squads," Cath said before Adele could explode. "He treats us with respect, as equals. He'll come to us when he needs us."

Ulyss continued petting the brown dog. It was time to turn Adele's attention. "Hey Adele, you think I'd look good in a beard?" He pulled Fudge's head up and sunk his chin into the dog's topknot of wiry fur.

Wyn and Cath laughed, but Adele immediately catapulted into a lecture on proper behavior required of a Catalyst Talent.

~ * ~

Dovel dreaded his visit to Tyna. She stood silent, listening to the ominous report on Kissre's progress. She looked worn and tired.

"You have entry to Kissre's mind. You felt her pain. I know you did. I felt it through you. Let me enter."

"I've never had that type of entry, Tyna. I only felt trace emotions, then only randomly."

"Take me in. Emotions can be used. I can help her. Please let me."

"The bond has grown too weak, and it was only one way."

"Damn you!" she screamed. Kedriq laid a hand on her arm. At her continued insistence, and desperate himself, Dovel agreed and opened his thoughts to Tyna. When they failed to reach Kissre, Tyna railed at him for letting Kissre slip from him. "I could have helped her!" He had no reply.

Afterward, he walked to the Assembly House and told Zeba she could no longer visit, for there wasn't any need anyhow.

"Nonsense. Here," she gave him a small basket. "Take me to her." On the way, they stopped at Gregor's Mound, and Zeba ordered her maid to fill the basket with soil. "Homeopathy," she said to Dovel. "Infrequently used."

When they arrived, Kissre still slept. The aide shook her head in warning, "She won't wake."

Zeba ignored her. She walked to the bed and looked at Kissre for a long time. At last she picked up the blue-traced white hand and placed it in the basket. Her gnarled and wrinkled fingers filtered earth into the palm, then wrapped the long, smooth-skinned fingers around the soil and held them in place. Nothing magical happened. Kissre didn't wake. Her color didn't improve, but Zeba smiled.

Healer Bujyea entered and watched, his gaze as often on Zeba as Kissre. He stood, arms crossed with one hand lifted to his face, a finger curled over his pensive mouth as if to stop words escaping. Finally, he touched the wrist of Kissre's injured arm. He stood frowning.

"Not near enough, you old witch," he said at last. Giving Zeba a disgusted look, he lifted Kissre from the bed, turned, and walked away. The basket and dirt flipped to dust the white sheets with small clods of dirt. Zeba chuckled and followed the healer. Troubled and shocked, Dovel trailed them out of the ward and down the steps. A short trip took them to the small mound where Zeba's maid had dug the soil. A brick walk wreathed the grass hump extending an invitation for an endless circular journey.

The day was warm, and the mound, already sun-baked, had its edges just covered by lacy shadows from a nearby tree. The healer lay Kissre down, her bare back on the grass, her bed smock barely fulfilling modesty's duty. He looked up at the sun.

"It's warm enough. I have more patients to see, old woman. You wait with her."

"I'm sure Dovel will keep me company," Zeba said with a cheerful smile, her blue eyes sparkling through crinkles of skin.

Dovel took his first full breath in days. "It's true then? An Earth Talent?"

"Undoubtedly," she said to the healer's retreating back. "Of course, never tested because she is Touch void and appears null."

"How strong?"

"That I can't tell you, but perhaps substantial. It would take another type of Adept to tell. Perhaps an Assayer, but I don't know. Call one of your squad to bring her dog. He might help also."

Ulyss brought the tightly leashed dog. Once Fudge sensed Kissre, he dragged Dovel's lieutenant to her. Zeba talked with Ulyss, but his lieutenant sensed Dovel's mood and quickly departed. After standing sentential over his mistress, Fudge lay next to her. Zeba picked up the threads of conversation before Ulyss's arrival.

So it was to strange stares of every passerby that a woman slept in the warm sun, edged by a huge patch of brown fur, and watched by an aged adept known for her time madness, and a reticent squad Captain. They sat and talked on the grass of Gregor's Mound, then picnicked. Dovel found it a novel experience in eccentricity, a quality seldom found in Cygna.

Several candlemarks later the healer returned, demanded Dovel hold the shaggy monster back. Dovel took a two-handed grip on Fudge's collar and commanded, "Sit, stay." The healer wore an expression of wariness as he looked at the dog, mixed with a curious excitement over his experiment. Assured Dovel had a good grip on the dog, Bujyea finally moved to take Kissre's pulse, then picked her up, and told them to go home. He would see them tomorrow. He took his patient back through the infirmary's side door. Dovel held

Fudge's collar as he extended a hand to help Zeba rise, but the dog stood still, his eyes following the healer.

Zeba was quite taken with Fudge, who returned her affection with licks and low, muffled barks. "What a fine big fellow you are," she said in a light voice. "A pleasant day Dovel. I will have my maid bring me tomorrow. You will already be at the infirmary."

Dovel blinked but didn't question an Oracle. An urgent call brought Fudge, who had followed Zeba into the Assembly House, to heel. He grinned at the shrieks still emanating from inside the doors and headed back to his tent in the encampment. While his lieutenants stayed at his house, he wanted separation. Besides, the steady influx of farmer-soldiers demanded attention. Work would help him regain perspective. He chained Fudge to a stake set outside his tent. Before he could fall into his bed, Adele gave him a plate of food and insisted he eat before sleeping. He took the plate and curbed his inner anger at her following him. He sensed the others settling inside their tents, grumbling and as unhappy with Adele as he.

In the pre-dawn dark, a hand shook Dovel awake. Ulyss voice told him to go to the infirmary immediately, reiterating the serious plea in his mind. His eyes snapped open with a sense of dread that ensnared his chest in a tight grip. His squad, long patient with his desire for privacy, lost their induolgence and followed him. Within the city gates, his need became apparent.

The whole city buzzed in an angry tumult. People screamed and shouted from opened windows. The sound of slamming window sashes and shutters reverberated in endless repetition. Along the street excited dogs barked and rattled the fence slats they jumped against and from stables agitated ponies neighed and stamped in counterpoint. Above all, in the damp night air, the prolonged, reverberating howl of a demented demon sang. Crescendo and decrescendo the solo continued. Dovel, stunned, began to run.

He arrived out of breath at the infirmary's side door. Where the healer had disappeared that afternoon carrying Kissre, a huge, shaggy shadow sat with head thrown back in mournful disharmony.

A crowd had formed around the dog, several with large sticks, but no one dared approach, not after rumors of his behavior on the day of 'The Attack.' Shushing and cajoling did no good. Stones lay around the animal showing more drastic failed measures.

Healer Bujyea also stood at the door, his uncombed gray hair standing on end. With arms akimbo and displeasure lining his tired, frowning face, he waved Dovel forward. Dovel walked up to the dog. Fudge rose to a squat and gave him a quick lick of greeting, his front feet tapping the ground, and his tail swishing in rhythm. There was a communal and premature sigh of relief, both physical and mental, as the wail ended. Fudge, his greeting over, threw back his head in yet another long note of ear-piercing undulation.

"Out!" Dovel commanded as he unshackled the chain trailing from Fudge's collar. The discord stopped mid-note, and Fudge gave him a doleful look as applause started. Dovel wound the chain around the stake and extended it to Ulyss, who was laughing, having just removing his hands from over his ears. Ulyss took the chain.

"Fudge, heel," he commanded and went to the door. The healer with an abusive and indecent mutter to the dog, opened the portal, "This is against regulation."

"Do you prefer the alternative?" Dovel asked, his hand waving the dog forward. Fudge, ears pricked forward, bounded over the landing and up the stairs in three leaps. Dovel trudged after him.

Kissre had made it to the end of the ward before collapsing. Fudge whined his greeting, licking and dancing around her before she managed to grab hold of him. She buried her face in the rough and tousled fur. Dovel waited until she stopped crying, then picked her up and carried her back to bed.

Appeased, Fudge pranced down the ward at his side, tongue hanging in a cheery grin of accomplishment. Dovel's squad followed behind the dog. He put Kissre back in bed. She gave an almost smile as Fudge stuck his nose under her arm. Sleep immediately took Kissre, in a slumber far different from her previous sleep.

"You can leave him here." The healer's voice pulled him from his contemplation of Kissre's slumber, now not so peaceful and impervious. The healer placed a basin full of water next to Fudge. "Thought you might be thirsty after all of that crooning. You don't seem so dangerous now, but you are not to scare my healer aides." He ran his fingers through the unkempt head as Fudge slurped the offering. Done, Fudge groaned as he folded long bony legs to the floor. Bujyea looked at Dovel. "Thank you for coming. It was most unnerving, and everyone was intimidated by his reputation."

Before Dovel could answer, Tyna, wide-eyed, frantic pale, and trailed by her squad, ran up the ward. "Kissre, is she…"

"She's fine," Bujyea said. "Finally on the path to recovery."

"We heard Fudge. I thought…they say dogs howl when…I was afraid to touch your mind…" She stopped and gulped. Tears ran down her cheeks as she bit her lower lip and grasped Kedriq.

The healer patted her shoulder. "Take care of yourself. I'll take care of your sister. You all need to get out of here. First a dog, and now unrestricted visitors at all candlemarks." He sighed saying as he left, "I'll be called in for review."

Tyna stood and stared at Kissre long after the healer left. Kedriq remained at her side with his hand on her waist.

Fever soaked hair splayed over Kissre's pillow in dark strands, but a little color and tenacity showed in her translucent face.

"She talked to you?" Tyna asked.

"Not today."

"Before she took so ill…" Hope burned in Tyna's hazel-gold eyes.

"Not about anything personal."

"I have to let her go, don't I?"

"We both do."

"Did…do you love her?"

"You can't tell?"

"No, you've been very inviolable of late."

"Yes." His peripheral view caught Adele's start.

"Then I owe you an apology, for my words injured you."

"Not undeservedly. I just realized it too late."

She straightened and looked at him. "Thank you for that. What will you do?"

"Wait. Hope."

"I've been waiting for a long time. Hoping even longer."

"The infection has been lanced. Wait for it to heal."

Tyna nodded. She bent down and ran a diffident hand over Fudge, whose head rolled up, his long nose touching the cheek above him. For the first time, Tyna patted the dog's head in real affection. She rose and placed an arm around Kedriq as she left. Her squad fell in protectively behind her.

He looked at his own squad, waiting; friends, like Tyna's squad. They shared such on odd existence—partly mental through their bond—partly their culture. They couldn't enter his thoughts. One touch with Kissre and the bond restructured, or maybe it never diminished. Maybe it had been a measure of Kissre's weakness. Only he, Zeba, and Healer Bujyea believed in her Talent. He looked at her. After today, he guessed, at the very least an Earth gift of some power.

Maybe she was better out of such an existence. Kneeling, he caressed Fudge, who bestowed one slow lick on his hand before collapsing to his side. With his head in darkness under the bed, the dog emitted a deep sighing groan.

Jealous, Dovel said, "Let's go," and walked away.

~ * ~

The dog's howls woke Zeba. She envisioned the scene. Dovel would be there soon. She smiled when the terrible, outlandish sound stopped, restarted, and finally ended. Rumors of evil and demons abroad would run through the city and countryside with maniacal speed. The priests would be busy at the cathedral tomorrow. Not even explanations across the Maze would undo the stories floating around about tonight's event. Would this night earn a name too, like the day of 'The Attack'? She wondered if the title had been given the fight between the sisters or the one at the city's gate. It didn't matter. Legend brewed.

She should never have touched the girl, but how was she to have known? Such untrained generosity! Who could measure such a Talent? She could have killed Kissre in her debilitated state, nearly had, until her own memory responded. In the meantime, no caretaker had mentioned Zeba's remarkable healing, the strength and duration of her focus, her rejuvenation. None noticed she hadn't walked with a cane in days. That came from being invisible for so many years. Years spent in a half-dreaming, half-vacuous existence.

To her lasting shame, to hold that hand had become the core of her day. She had righted her wrong. Now she would find out how she could help Kissre. It put her in Dovel's dilemma, report or not? Most would believe Gregor's Mound healed Kissre, unwilling to believe any alternative. Maybe, given enough knowledge, the girl would choose as one wanted her to choose. Without touching Kissre, though, would the gift remain, or would she revert? Would she, or wouldn't she?

Dovel said he'd lost his bond. That could be from the many emotions affecting this situation. Not the least of which was Kissre's withdrawal from the world, her readiness, even willingness for her last journey. He didn't say how his other Talents were affected or how his own newfound strengths fared. Maybe he hadn't noticed. Now, all Zeba wanted was to remain, to see how these new stories played out. Excitement infused her with purpose.

~ * ~

From his attic window in his Lord's apartment, Eldin looked down on Bhatar Court, Pertelon's King Clement's primary residence. It was raining again, and the adjacent tower spires were obscured in a gray mist. It seemed like it always rained here. The dismal aspect was reflected in the room behind him. As the least of King Clement's wards, Aristo Uilleam Leavold's lodgings reflected his position at court.

"It's bad out," his new Master said, bounding into the room.

Without turning around to look at the young man, Eldin answered. "It certainly is."

From this height, on a clear day, he could make the thrusting mounds on the watery horizon that signified Kaereya. He refused to think about living there. For his circumstances, he had only himself to blame. In trying to improve his life, he had destroyed it. His plans, his stratagems to show his ability, all failed. Now he was the spy-servant, probable assassin for his chosen king—to this irrelevant boy.

"Cheer up, Eldin. You need not go out in it." Uilleam was cold and wet. He patted Eldin on the shoulder. His damp fingers left moist stains on the silk fabric that would remain.

Uilleam stood next to him, a silly grin covering his face. Eldin regarded his charge. Although older than King Warrick of Kaereya, Aristo Uilleam seemed boyish, a brown-haired young man with royal blood, tall and well made, but not much else; a cuckoo among the court's egrets. The grandson of the king before Clement, Uilleam provoked few concerns in Clement. The boy seldom drew anyone's interest except for the sports of baiting and ridicule.

Rumor claimed the idiot's winsome looks had won him some fair ladyloves, particularly among those more matronly and neglected at court. The same source sniggered and added, 'one had to be careful of the mindless tongue afterward.' Eldin guessed more than one chagrined Lady had found herself the butt of court humor.

When Eldin's agents failed in their Cygna effort, they had doomed him to this service. The king's first minister had condemned his efforts as useless. All his former assistance in Kaereya meant nothing. Hindsight showed he should not have reported Kissre Pierce's presence in Cygna, done less. He would be better off.

He looked at Uilleam, the oldest heir of the usurped King Leavold. At twenty-five, he was a child who loved the hunt, his horse, and all the castle dogs and cats—an idiot who idolized his younger brother.

Eldin grimaced. Uilleam loved even those who mocked and abused him. His ever-present grin indicated his unremitting good humor. His lanky, long hair lay tangled and twisted, sticking out in strange tufts, and he wore his haphazard, stained and mismatched clothing with unconcern. The wide-open innocence of his face marked him for torment. Uilleam had lost everything—all his family, except a brother who looked on him with shame, his titles, and lands, all of which made life meaningful.

It occurred to Eldin, with unusual insight, that he had earned this duty and felt his shame. This boy's life had been ripped from him, but Eldin had thrown his away. Once he had been a better man. His eyes wandered back to the window, seeking any sign of distant Kaereya, unwilling to admit how much he missed the rocky heights and the marshy insect-plagued islands. The rain hid it from him.

"Why are you sad, Eldin?"

"The weather has made me very introspective today, Uilleam." A glance showed a thought-twisted face was still trying to figure out his answer. "It doesn't matter. I've been a poor company of late. That is going to change. Get out of your wet clothes. I'll see if I can stoke up this choked fireplace. Have you seen Payden?"

"Paddy is out with all the squires, practicing on the arms field." His grin never faltered. "He beat me, and the arms master dismissed me. Paddy is very good with a sword."

"Yes, he is. Would you like to be?"

"I try."

"I know you do. Perhaps we should work on it."

"You'll help me?"

The surprised tone drew Eldin's gaze. "Why not? I am your man, aren't I?"

"King Clement said you were."

Eldin felt his involuntary reaction, his nostrils expanded, his jaw clenched. "Yes, he did."

"But unsworn for all of that."

"That is true." His thoughts slowed his words. "But easily rectified."

In a sudden decision, Eldin drew his own sword from its scabbard. Uilleam's eyes widened until white showed all around the brown-circled irises. He picked up Uilleam's dull and dirty sword from the floor where he had dropped it and handed it to the boy. He knelt before his simpleton master and raised the hilt of his sword before him.

"Aristo Leavold, I swear to you before the Holy One represented in my sword's hilt, to be your man, loyal to you until the Holy One claims my life forfeit."

"You're swearing to me? A new game?" The clear face showed the wary excitement court tormentors had taught Uilleam about 'new games.'

"Yes, my lord, but a serious game. I will not hurt you." Eldin looked up into the face, joyous in expectation. "If you accept me. This I must tell you, my reputation comes to you dishonored and sullied by my actions. I promise, though, to serve you with all the honor left to me."

"But you're sworn to King Clement. This game is no fun." The voice turned crestfallen.

"No, My Lord. King Clement never took my oath. I will be your liegeman. I swear to protect you, to see to your good and prosperity."

"Then, Sir Eldin...that's wrong, isn't it?" Uilleam's face screwed in thought. "It should be your surname, but I don't know it. I don't know the words either."

"Sir Innes. I accept your fealty and promise to be your good and loyal liege."

The smile returned. "Sir Innes, I accept your fealty and promise to be your good and loyal liege," he mimicked.

"Take up your sword, Uilleam, and touch my shoulders with the blade."

"Don't you have to kiss your hilt first?" Uilleam asked.

"I do so simultaneously."

Uilleam picked up the sword like he was going to cleave Eldin in half. "Gently," Eldin said in warning, "or you won't have a liegeman."

The sword swung down with alarming speed but only tapped the shoulder Eldin stiffened in response. He opened his tightly squeezed eyelids. Slowly the sword rose to swing over his head. "By the Holy One, I do so swear." Eldin kissed the polished quartz stone on his hilt.

His mind jerked. A fealty gift, he needed a gift. Even if Uilleam took this as a game, he did not. As Uilleam stepped back, Eldin removed the chain hidden by the silk ruffles extending above the jack he wore. He fingered the cloisonné enamel surface design showing the talisman dragon of Kaereya's Easure Province, unaware of his pensive expression.

He bowed his head and held out the small medallion. "Please accept this gift, My Liege, to represent my pledge to you."

The slight weight remained in his hand. He raised his head. The moronic grin was gone, and a strange expression rested in the clear blue eyes. Meeting Eldin's gaze, Uilleam grinned, this time in pleasure, and took the offering and placed it around his own neck. "A gift. You gave me a gift. Wait 'til I show Paddy."

"Uilleam," Eldin said, knowing the way of the court. "As your liegeman, I must tell you our game must be kept secret."

"Secret? Why?" Uilleam asked, his disappointment clear in his voice, but his gaze remained locked on his gift.

"My Lord, you do not want to make King Clement angry, do you?"

"No. He is not nice when he is angry." Uilleam's expression displayed his understanding.

"Our game might make King Clement angry, cause him worry. It is best if we keep my pledge between the two of us. Can you do that?"

Uilleam's tongue emerged as he thought. "A secret. Good. I like secrets. Even from Paddy?"

"Yes, even from Payden. Can you do it?"

"Yes. A secret between me and you. A secret from Paddy. A new game." Uilleam laughed in a familiar uncontrolled giggle.

"Go change your clothes, Uilleam, before you catch a chill."

"Can I keep your dragon on?"

"Yes, it would please me, but you must always wear it hidden, to keep our secret safe. It was my only possession of value, a symbol of my homeland, Easure of Kaereya. It was gifted to me from a good and loyal friend for protection. Now it will protect you."

~ * ~

Kissre woke to a lick and a whine. She turned her head and earned another lick. She laughed, a weak, effort-filled sound. "Down Fudge, down, boy."

"That's good to hear," a voice said from above her. She looked to see who spoke. The healer. He was tall and dark like Dovel, but his black hair was liberally streaked with gray. "You got up last night, we've screened your body, but all appears to be healing. So perhaps you can try today. The sooner you move, the faster you'll heal. Later we'll get you outside again."

"Again?"

"Yes, you spent several candlemarks flat on the ground yesterday."

"Flat on the ground? Here? In the Holy One's name, why?"

"Homeopathic healing. Earth Talents all heal faster when in contact with earth's strengths."

Kissre laughed outright at him, half-embarrassed by her weak effort. She wished she could put more derision in it. She petted Fudge.

"I thought animals weren't allowed here?"

"They aren't, but family is."

Later Zeba came, and she told the old lady the anecdote. Zeba laughed. "Image, and you void. It shows the fallibility of some of us."

"What do you want to hear today?"

"Oh, today, I think I'll switch the tables and tell you stories." She laughed at Kissre's wary look. "You've shared a lot of knowledge, stories, and folklore about the places you've traveled. I shall give you my knowledge of Cygna's stories."

Kissre snorted. "I might not want to hear them."

"Of course you do. You would not know so many unless the stories interested you. Besides, what else do you have to occupy your time?" Zeba's bony fingers rubbed Fudge's head, which had inexplicably inserted itself onto her lap. "Who walks Fudge?"

"Healer Bujyea took him out this morning."

"He hasn't been out since?"

"No."

"Well good. Look, here comes Dovel, and he has a crutch. Now you can take your dog out."

"Not unless I want to bare my backside before all of Cygna."

"I'm sure that would give you great pleasure, but here." Zeba swung an imperious hand at her maid. "I've had your trews cleaned and repaired, and your jack. The leatherworker was impressed. Very fine quality of rare leather, he said. Nearly cried at the tear but was able to repair it. Unfortunately, your under tunic was a total loss. My seamstress used it as a pattern for a new one. So get dressed." Zeba smiled in benign pleasure. "What's delaying you? Get out of that bed." She followed Kissre's gaze to Dovel. "For all's sake, Kissre, the man's already seen you in unmitigated splendor. A little more flesh won't make a bit of difference."

Dovel's lips tilted upward at the tips, and he said he'd wait by the door. Zeba laughed and prodded Kissre out of bed. Her maid helped Kissre stand and slip out of the sleeping smock.

"You have a very nice body, so muscular, so firm. I'm sure it is the envy of many."

Kissre threw her an offended look. "I assure you, despite whatever you may have heard through your Maze, my sluttish conquests are limited."

Zeba laughed. "Too bad for you. Try harder."

As Kissre finished dressing, Zeba waved a hand at her maid, who handed Kissre the crutch with murmured words on how to use it. The hopping gait and awkward movement tried Kissre's patience, and she lashed out at anyone who helped. The stairs were a struggle, but she made it, both thanking and cursing Dovel's hand that kept her upright. "I'll have to do this myself as you can't be here all the time."

"Until you find your feet, you'll need help," he answered.

Once outside at Gregor's Mound, Kissre sank to the ground, exhausted by the effort. Fudge ran, and urged on by Zeba's amused calls of encouragement, terrorized every passerby. The sun felt warm, and Zeba took a deep breath of the spring air. Tiring after a while, Fudge came and plopped down to roll in the grass, emitting dog grunts of pleasure. He settled, with his head close enough for Kissre to touch. Zeba ordered Dovel to help her down, then started talking about the wonderful weather and memories of other times she had sat here with someone special.

"I wager it wasn't in daylight," Dovel said.

"Not always, but I shan't tell you of those times."

"This some sort'a special place?" Kissre asked, not sounding particularly interested. Her eyes closed. "Holy One, it'll take me forever to get back in shape." Her panting breath separated her words.

"You weren't in that great a shape when you came," Dovel said.

"What do you mean by that?" Kissre asked, head rising from the grass, eyes glaring.

"You were already recovering from a wound. You talked about it, remember?"

Kissre huffed in disparagement. "Better shape 'n you."

"Gregor, the last Crucible, performed an Earth Calling here," Zeba said, interrupting them. "This is one of the few spots that still resonates with abundant earth strengths."

Zeba watched Kissre's eyes roll under her lids and smiled, knowing she couldn't feel it because she didn't know what she felt. Dovel sat next to Fudge's strung out body. His hand stroked the dog's side, and like Kissre, he seemed to enjoy the sun's warmth. Looking up, Zeba figured a few candlemarks of unfiltered sun remained before the tree's shadows overtook their spot. Twelve long paces away, people walked with purpose to the governmental complex. Their party drew strange looks as if they profaned the sacred spot.

Drowsy, Kissre asked, "So how'd he do that?"

"He prayed for it." She smiled as Kissre answered with a snorted laugh.

"To what? The great earth god?"

"No. Yes. The Holy One is everywhere."

Kissre huffed.

"You are not a believer?"

"Not since my first battle. It's better to believe in your own skill." Kissre yawned in the sun's heat, which formed drowsy calm around them.

"Neither did Gregor. Belief is hard for many, but need is a great teacher. Anyway, Gregor, being also a Factor Adept, called all Earth

Adepts into a united bond." Zeba continued unperturbed that her audience already drowsed. "They tied the energy the Crucible drew and transformed it, renewing the land." Zeba launched into the story in detail. It was not long before she finished. "Of course, his goal was to save the life of his son."

"She didn't hear you. She fell asleep," Dovel said when Zeba finished. The shade covered them.

"She heard enough," Zeba said.

"What do you see, old woman?"

"That you're walking a long, hard road."

He grunted at the turn of topic. "I know. Trust is difficult to restore, but I have to try."

"Do you know how?"

He smiled. "I hope so. I'm taking my cues from a dog."

~ * ~

With long strides Dovel took the infirmary's steps two at a time with Fudge pacing him. Bujyea had ordered that the dog and Dovel could now keep visitors' time. Fudge didn't seem to mind. Walking down the ward, Dovel slowed as he saw Kissre had company. Another Squad Captain, dark and tall also, but younger than himself and more akin in looks to Kedriq, sat by her bed. Captain Jycel smiled at him as he approached. Kissre, busy containing Fudge's enthusiastic greeting, caught his glance and smiled.

"Hello, Dovel."

Jycel's constant cheer always seemed suspect to Dovel.

"Maybe you can vouch for me, I was just introducing myself to your suspicious friend."

"What is your business, Jycel? Did Tyna send you?" Dovel asked, sensing Kissre's unease.

Jycel laughed. "Already asked and no. Governor Vitann asked me to deliver a message that came in a diplomatic courier's pouch. Performing a small flourish, he withdrew an envelope from his vest, which he handed to Kissre. "A slow and cumbersome method of communication, Mistress Pierce." He stressed the title.

Kissre looked at the inscription. "Yes," she said, breaking the wax seal, "but so private." She read the contents as Jycel chuckled. Finished, she looked at Dovel. "It is from His Grace, Aristo Aurelias, the duke of Lambere. My resignation has been refused. I am to await his arrival here. There is a diplomatic mission arriving from Kaereya. I am to act as personal security and aide for the mission's staff." The dismay reflected in her face echoed through her voice.

"Does it say when they arrive?"

"The protocol staff arrived yesterday with the dispatches," Jycel said with a smile. "You've missed Command sessions for a fortnight."

Dovel considered the younger man, always too confident, and smug with it. "I've been excused." He answered Jycel but looked at Kissre.

Without invitation, Jycel took the chair next to Kissre's bed. "Since you are still obligated to Aristo Aurelias, I can treat you as an ally. He will arrive at the beginning of Sixth-month with the Kaereyan Envoy Delegation."

"The papers aren't signed yet," Kissre said, leaning back. Fudge stood at the bedside, with his head across Kissre's lap, her hand in a constant slow stroke along the rough fur of his long neck.

"You became the curiosity of Command when this letter arrived. I assume, with your assignment to the envoy's mission, you will become even more involved in Cygnese politics. You are nearly an ally already."

"And you're ready to divulge state secrets?" Kissre said, her lips curling in a droll smile.

Dovel felt his lips twist in derisive disgust as he watched Jycel beguile Kissre with his well-known charm.

"Of course not, but you will need friends when you get out of here, and I think I'd like to be one." He smiled and made an elaborate gesture of leave-taking.

Kissre gave him a non-committal, "thank you." Her eyes followed the squad leader's exit in candid deliberation.

The hand never ceased its caressing motion. Dovel did not take the vacated chair.

"You've missed command meetings because of me?"

"Don't think on it Kissre. I won't lose my squad or even receive a reprimand."

"You've spent too much time here. Your squad must be in a near desperate state."

A polite dismissal. "They don't own me." He cringed when his words repeated Tyna's petulant and often-voiced complaint.

"I do not own Fudge, but he belongs to me as surely as my hand."

Dovel laughed. "Are you calling my squad members dogs?"

"No, just saying some bonds are so strong they cannot be broken."

"Like family?" He held his breath.

"Hard to break, but not impossible, if you're willing to bear the cost. Tyna wanted a family and never realized she and I never shared one. She's making her own. Once the baby is born, she'll forget about me."

Astounded at her answer, he pressed on. "You're still her sister."

"A meaningless state of circumstance. Believe me, she is better off without me. Why she feels loss, I don't know. The fault was mine. I lost my temper. Tell her so if you think it will make a difference." She turned her head away. "Enough, Dovel, I won't go back. The decision is made, and neither you nor Captain Pierce can change it. You don't have to hang around as an apology for any motive on your part. We both acted how we chose."

"I was a Talent. You should have suspected my motives."

A short, uncomfortable silence ensued. "I was curious, first time for everything. Not such a pure motive either, is it? It's over and done with."

"And?"

"We emerge friends."

She gave him a smile, but he couldn't read her emotions. They were there, just unclear. Not the answer he wanted, but better than the one for Tyna.

He changed the subject. "Security for a diplomatic mission implies confidence in your ability."

"For a mercenary?" At his look, she laughed. "Not all mercenaries are faithless nomads looking for the next conflict."

"I didn't mean to imply they were, but most are not entrusted with important official positions."

She handed him the paper still lying in her lap, and he read the inscription. "Colonel? In the Kaereyan Army?"

"Promotion after the last Kaereyan engagement." The hand stopped its motion, and horror lined her face. "A month, only a month to get back in shape." She closed her eyes.

"I'll help you," Dovel said.

Her eyes opened. "Thank you, but you will be busy with your squad and preparation for Cygna's upcoming conflict. If the Adept Council is talking with a Kaereyan envoy, it means they think war is inevitable."

"Maybe so, but I would like to learn your Aibhe exercises. You said we were friends. We can work together until my squad is posted."

"You going to learn sword usage, too?"

"Maybe." He smiled at her mocking tone. "I know enough, have read enough to know they are not just weapons exercises. Mind focus and concentration are things an adept could use. And a sword? Certainly an idea to shake up the Adept Council."

"I thought you already had techniques to develop concentration and focus?"

"Different. Never know what you'll learn from another perspective about the same problem." With ten more arguments, some specious and farcical, she laughed and finally agreed.

Seven

After Dovel left, taking Fudge with him, Kissre swung her legs off the bed and sat. Wooziness washed over her. It would pass. She had seen the wounds this morning when the aide changed the bandages. With Adept's help, they were well on the way to healing. Time to take control of herself. She'd been a timorous malingerer, discontent, and crying about her lot.

She rose to her feet, grimaced, and took a step. The leg held.

"Leaving? I don't recommend it."

She swiveled her head. "Hello, Healer. Been called back to duty."

"Not for a sennight or more. A few more days of rest and having someone take care of you wouldn't hurt."

"Should have known the news would be all over Sidih by now."

She pulled her clothes out of the cabinet and sat back on the bed to pull them on with slow and ginger care. As she rose to pull her trews over her hips, the healer said, "I guess that is answer enough. Listen. No strenuous exercise. Don't stay on that leg for an extended period of time. Eat right. Drink..."

"...plenty of liquids. Rest when I feel tired. Come back if I have any problems, see any redness or swelling."

"Rest even when you don't feel tired. You were a better patient when you were too weak to talk."

"I don't enjoy having Talents explore my body. It's healing now." Kissre grinned at the serious face regarding her. "I know the care drill, and I thank you for keeping me alive."

"I know. I've seen the scars. You are welcome."

"My point exactly. Anyway, I've received my orders. The envoy comes, and I need to contact the protocol staff. Whom do I pay?"

"It's been covered."

"By whom?" Her posture stiffened, and she stifled her belligerent tone.

"By Sidih's Mayor. Your actions saved citizens' lives."

She swore as she stretched her arm and shoulder to get her tunic on. He gave her a disgusted look, waited until she was dressed, then handed her the crutch. "Use it." She nodded, and he followed her to help her down the steps.

Dovel met them at the infirmary's side door. Kissre threw the healer an evil look. He grinned, nodded at Dovel, and closed the door behind her.

"Where are you going?" he asked.

"Call on the Protocol Staff. Find a room. Get information. Any ideas where I can find them?"

"I'll take you," he said in a resigned voice.

She looked at him.

"They're not too far away."

"You don't have to. You've done enough."

"My pleasure," he said with a smile. Her progress was slow, but she eventually entered apartments in the Assembly House complex. When they reached the door, she thanked Dovel and waited, watching his face.

He veiled whatever he felt, giving her his tilt-corner smile. "You're welcome. I'll bring Fudge." He left.

A staff member took one look at her and showed her to a chair. She gratefully accepted the offer and waited. When the mission's secretary entered the room after the announcement of her arrival, she recognized Napier Corbin, gauzy colorfully wraps floating about him.

"Colonel Kissre, it is so good to see you. No, stay seated." The black-skinned Kennetsurean offered her his hand. It clasped her own in its warm embrace, then held her cold fingers. "Are you all right? Are you sure you should be here?"

If her own outlander foreignness upset the Cygnese, she wondered at Kennetsurean Corbin's impact. "I received Aristo Aurelias' letter. Congratulations on your appointment as Secretary."

Corbin nodded and released her hand. "His Grace felt you would be of great assistance to our mission here. For my part, I was very grateful to learn I'd have you." He pulled a chair close to hers and eased his large frame into it.

Kissre laughed. "The help will all be on your side, I'm afraid. I've no uniform, few clothes, and no mount. Above which, I don't move too well."

"Right now, I need your knowledge and your mind, which appears to be somewhat functional, although leaving the infirmary so soon doesn't show the best judgment. For the rest, arrangements can be made. You will, of course, stay here."

"I hoped so, because I'm afraid you're right. My judgment might be somewhat off. I seem to be in desperate need of a bed."

She found herself shortly settled in a wonderfully comfortable bed and slept the moment she put her head down. At some point, a door opening woke her for a brief, senseless moment. The sound of claws clicked on the floor. A groan and a familiar dog scent registered. Kissre fell back into a deep slumber.

Late afternoon light filtered in the window and woke her. As she rose, Fudge whined for outdoors. Greetings met her, and servants jumped to open doors as she made her way through the apartment. Double doors at the back of the main rooms opened into a beautiful courtyard with a dry and silent fountain centerpiece. The yard was far too confined for a large dog, but a short walk led off the paved square to a gate hidden by shrubs. It was tricky, but Kissre managed to open it without landing on her butt. Outside and across a wide lawn skirted by a brick-paved access road, she found a well-tended wooded area. Benches scattered along the meandering walkways cut through the trees.

Once in the park, Kissre released Fudge from his heel command, and he joyously bounded away. He startled a rabbit from hiding and gave a short chase until the creature disappeared into the undergrowth. Hearing someone behind her, she twisted her head. Corbin came and joined her where she stood propped on her crutch.

"You don't look so death-like."

"It was a long walk, but I'll do better for having made it. Tomorrow I will be better yet."

"Do not push yourself. We will have dinner in our apartments tonight. Afterward, I would appreciate your insights on Cygna." He didn't wait for an answer. "Your healer sent over some medicines. I gave them to your maid. Aurelias sent more than a letter." She looked at him with a question in her raised brow.

He nodded his head back the way they had come. Kissre called Fudge to heel, and they started back. As they approached the road, Kissre halted, balancing on her crutch. A groom wearing a Kaereyan staff uniform stood with a horse. She knew the breed, Novere, had admired them in Kaereya.

The mare stood with her head erect and turned in their direction with her ears pricked forward. A white star blazed in her lilac-gray head, and intelligent, calm eyes assessed them. Her flaxen mane and tail hung to luxurious lengths, the tail nearly touching the ground. Both appeared in dramatic contrast to the gray body and black legs. Kissre knew the gray coat hairs were actually that rare color and not a mixture of white and black. She stood a little over sixteen hands, not as big as Bother.

Kissre felt a twinge and bit her lip. Liquid welled in her eyes. She blinked several times to clear her sight and cursed her weakness.

The mare's legs tensed as Fudge approached, becoming black pillars of threatening strength.

"The Aegis and his wife send you greetings and wish you to accept this token of their continued friendship. They heard about

Bother. Drew held great respect for that horse. He felt you would need another well-trained mount, which his wife, the seer, assured him, was perfectly true."

They'd heard about Bother? Someone had carried news quickly. Kissre limped up to the mare and ran her good hand down the silky neck. She swallowed hard. "This is extraordinarily kind and generous. What's her name?"

"Carillon."

Carillon nickered, hearing her name, then lowered her head to touch noses with Fudge. After a few heavy exchanges of scent, Fudge licked her nose, and Carillon's head popped up with a shaking motion, throwing her long mane into disorder.

"She's beautiful." She pulled on the halter to bring Carillon's head closer. Carillon jerked, tugging Kissre off balance. Both the groom and Corbin grabbed her to prevent her imminent fall.

"We need to go into dinner now," Corbin said. "Let her go back to her stable. You can get acquainted tomorrow."

Kissre stroked Carillon's head, stepped back at last, with regret, and motioned to the groom. She watched as he led the horse away. The mare's movement was perfect, legs tracking straight and true. A speck of excitement fluttered inside her.

Returning to her bedroom, Kissre found the armoire full. Her clothing that she'd left in Kaereya hung in neat array with her uniforms and many new pieces fashioned in Kaereyan styles. Things she'd secretly coveted but never bought, for where would a mercenary wear them? Someone had guessed her tastes well. Shoes and boots lined the Armoire's bottom. She raised her brows at the presumption of her compliance.

She laughed out loud catching the number motif skillfully hidden in a uniform's braid. Nine—her personal number, the number of order and the soul, threaded through not only the braid but also the fabric's weave. The positive aspects of the number eluded her character, but she was very familiar with the negative aspects— chaos, war, betrayal, lawlessness, and neglect. Picking up a sleeve, she inspected the work. She sighed, supposing she was orderly, but mental and spiritual attainment seemed foreign in concept. The obsession of her adoptive country brought an odd solace, a sense of belonging.

A cursory search proved the motif repeated in textile weaves and decorative touches throughout the wardrobe. She cursed. There were three elegant gowns included. Her brows rose in disbelief; *whatever for?* The rich brocades and velvets gowns were laden with pleats, tucks, semi-precious stones, pearls, embroidery, and lace, things she had never worn. Lace! She would be a laughingstock if she wore them. Thinking of Carillon, she smiled. They could have demanded much more, and she would have agreed.

Looking around the room, she found the imposing four-poster bed freshly made up, and her saddle packs and guith left in a neat pile under the window. Dovel must have had them delivered.

There was one thing she wanted. Off a door, on the far side of the room, she found an exquisitely appointed washroom. A wide smile of satisfaction spread across her face as hot water spurted from the tap, one of the few glories of Cygna. So few places had plumbing that worked, she'd be crazy not to take immediate and frequent advantage.

A female servant entered with towels and was distressed Kissre had started her own bath. "I am Fay, your assigned maid, ma'am. You must let me do these things for you." Kissre inspected the mousy-haired, hazel-eyed, petite, fine-boned, and attractive but not beautiful woman. She wore no badge.

"You're null?"

"Yes, ma'am."

"Don't look so downcast. So am I."

"I know, ma'am. Some guests prefer Talents. They like someone who anticipates their desires. If you do, it can be arranged."

"They couldn't anticipate my desires, or so I've been told. I'm not only null but also void." As Fay smiled, she said, "I've never had a maid. Always taken care of myself."

"You must have someone while here, ma'am. You are still too ill to properly care for yourself. It would be my pleasure to serve you."

"Then, thank you. You will do nicely." Kissre submitted reluctantly, but by the time Fay massaged her head to foot after her bath and rebound her wounds, Kissre welcomed her. When asked, Fay agreed to trim Kissre's hair. The cut was a credible job, much better than the hack job she usually performed on her locks. Some aspects of privileged hospitality, she decided, were to be thoroughly enjoyed.

~ * ~

Corbin filled her wine glass as she sank into the deep chair set before the fire.

"Is it safe to talk here?" he asked.

"Probably not, but I'm a null, and you probably are, too. They would have a hard time reading your mind, and from what I've been told, they can't read mine at all. Do you intend treachery?"

"No, but it is not a pleasant thought that someone could roam through your thoughts, and you remain unaware."

"It is illegal. Only a few Talents have a gift that strong. Besides, they save it for special occasions, and for your acute anticipation, they let you know it is going to happen first. Mostly they can feel emotional responses. As long as you keep yourself composed, they don't get much. I understand the envoy arrives soon."

"I am here to plan the accommodations and determine with the Cygnese the protocols for the talks. It is very difficult. They are a wondrously suspicious lot. Every suggestion for the smooth, orderly running of the meeting is cross-examined." Corbin sighed in an elaborate flourish. "I imagine we will debate everything to a standstill."

"This sounds like more than a war alliance."

"It is." He smiled with a cat's indefinable expression. "We are to begin general trade negotiations. There is some talk of relaxing the border restrictions, perhaps even establishing a joint force to guard the Seer Pass. We hope to establish reciprocal ambassadors. It is a remarkable change in attitude for so closed a society, and due, I'm told, to your sister's influence."

Something in his voice told her he knew that story. "Important enough to worry about a possible negative reaction from a distrustful and introverted people?"

"Yes. When we learned you had been attacked, it nearly ended the mission. Governor Vitann sent couriers to assure King Warrick you received superior care and that the whole episode had been a case of mistaken identity. His Grace Aurelias told King Warrick he knew nothing about any mission. He said you were only searching for your sister. Still, they took full advantage of the Governor's misconception."

"The Cygnese believe the assailants thought I was Captain Tyna."

"You sound doubtful."

"If it's true, the insurgents' reconnaissance failed dismally. They were all killed, so until more information comes to light, all is speculation."

"When we learned you in Cygna, your status as a native, and with such an important sister, it gave us hope for a diplomatic mission. Aristo Aurelias felt your visit a good first step." Corbin swirled the wine left in his glass. Its ruby color swirled black and dead in the room's candlelight. His face remained inertly calm.

Kissre snorted, feeling her equilibrium vanish at the disclosures about her journey. "His Grace is ever resourceful. I didn't even know where I was going, let alone suspected I'd end up in Cygna." She slumped in her chair, filled with a childish defiance. "I am no longer a native, and my sister and I have terminated a very strained relationship."

Corbin waved a negligent hand. "Makes no difference—it is the appearance that counts. You may be a citizen of Kaereya, but you have a look familiar to the Cygnese, no matter how foreign the costume. It makes you an acceptable, unthreatening member of the envoy's entourage."

Laughing, Kissre explained what acceptance her 'familiar foreignness' had earned so far.

"It doesn't matter. Your exotic familiarity broke the barrier, ignited curiosity among the masses. You have already established yourself as a presence. There is also a residual guilt at your injury during the attack, and your sacrifice of your beautiful Bother to save Cygnese citizens. Thanks to the assault happening at Spring Revel, the news was disseminated throughout the country. Compared to my foreignness, you become commonplace. I am a black desert vulture among swans." His laughter filled the silent room.

"The local swans are black, and you are much more colorful." Kissre looked at the brilliant blue and gold tunic over Kennetsurean style leather trews. "It's a long way from Kennetsure and its sunny hospitality."

"So it is, but the Cygnese, though reserved, are not lacking in respect. Let's talk about the antipathy between you and your sister."

"Captain Pierce."

Corbin gave her a look. "Exactly so. Answer me honestly, can you work in conjunction with her? She will, most likely, participate in the negotiations."

"Her presence will not affect my performance. I do not join in the negotiations. My task is to protect Kaereya's envoy and staff."

Napier raised his half-full glass to her. "Officially, your duties do not start until the envoy arrives. To our success." She raised her glass in salute.

~ * ~

Kissre entered the stables as the morning's sun began expanding over the mountains. A stable hand told her where her horse was stalled. She stood and talked to Carillon until the mare turned to face her. Taking off the sling holding her arm and abandoning her crutch, she took the mare out of the stall and groomed her in a get-to-know-you ritual. Searching the tack room, she recognized her saddle already perched on a rack. A skillful mend showed the hole patched, but an unalterable darker stain spread on the leather. Her fingers spread over the area in silent tribute. Her blood might be on the top, but it was Bother's below.

The saddle was not a good fit for the mare's narrower back, but extra saddle pads made it work. It took effort to mount and hoisting her leg across the saddle was agony. Tomorrow she would hire a saddle maker. Perhaps Fay or one of the other servants knew of a good one.

A slow walk several times around the paddock loosened her stiffness enough to put the mare through more vigorous paces. Carillon was like a dream, smooth and effortless, responding to the lightest touch with a floating gait. It must have been some time since the mare had been ridden for her energy needed controlling, though she was perfectly obedient. What struck Kissre most was the mare's daintiness for a horse of her size. A trait not expected in a heavier horse.

Returning to the stable, she slowly dismounted, angry to find her injured leg wouldn't support her. She hopped around as she took care of Carillon.

"That was an impressive performance."

Kissre turned to the voice as she led Carillon into her stall. "A mutual test. Jycel, isn't it?"

He nodded and gave a brief nod of his head. "I'd heard rumors of a new horse." He picked up her crutch and brought it to her. Kissre placed it under her good arm, and with a few final strokes down Carillon's dark pretty face, left.

Jycel kept to her slow pace. "I have heard, although it is strictly rumor, that you might be placed with an infantry group to see how we can best blend our two armies."

"There isn't an alliance yet."

"There will be. If this happens, I would like my platoons to be the ones you fight with on maneuvers."

"You're one of Captain Pierce's Captains, aren't you?"

He threw up his hands. "Don't hold that against me. My squad works independently of Tyna's. She only helps keep us all coordinated."

Kissre stopped. "From your voice, I'd guess you don't like Captain Pierce much."

"I find Captain Tyna," he stressed the name, "a charming person, and I appreciate her help, I just don't like any interference in my squad. Plus, she hogs the honor." His boyish grin took away the sting of his comment.

"Then why ask me this? I do not seek to harm Captain Pierce."

"That may be, but I've heard the stories, and anyone in contact with Tyna knows what she is feeling. You will have to be careful as many squad members hold you responsible for Tyna's recent distress. They near worship her, you know. But that is not why I ask."

He gave her another engaging smile that Kissre mistrusted. He sighed realizing it. "You want the truth. All right." He picked up her hand and brought her tattoo up to eye level, and Kissre just as quickly pulled free. He chuckled at her withdrawal. "I find you an intriguing person—attractive, exotic, intelligent, strong, and I want to get to know you better. Doing this will also give me a chance to snap my mental fingers in a childish way of comeuppance at some very deserving rivals, improve my squad's reputation and bring me to the attention of the Adept Council. There you have it."

Resuming her trek back to the apartment, Kissre told him, "The choice is probably not mine to make."

"But I'm sure your recommendation would go far in the selection."

"I don't know any squad well enough to confer recommendations."

"Then let me invite you to meet my squad. They and my platoon leaders are as eager for this as I am. Give yourself a chance to know us."

Kissre stopped and looked at Jycel. His dark hair and eyes, thin but well-built body, as well as his handsome features, probably allowed him to get away with far too much. While amused by his attention, she wasn't deceived by it.

She looked at the path yet to travel. "I will accept your invitation, but I'm not making any promise about a recommendation. Your help, though, in getting me back to the envoy's apartment in a seemly manner, might make me more sympathetic to your cause. I do not wish to crawl back." Jycel became practical immediately and rose a few points in Kissre's estimation.

~ * ~

"What do you think?" Kissre asked Corbin after she reported the conversation. They sat in a private antechamber off the main room.

"The suggestion for such a possible mingling of forces has not been officially made. It cannot be made until the envoy arrives. This might be in the minds of the Cygnese."

"They have a large land border and few troops to secure it. They will want Kaereyan infantry for their borders. Warrick might fancy a few Adept squads to keep check on Kaereya's watery borders."

"It is a wondrously effective means of communication." Corbin sat back in his chair, clasped hands raised to rest on his chest, face contemplative.

"But not something every Aristo would relish in Kaereya."

He shrugged and waved a negligent hand. "That is less of a problem than it was. With their acceptance of seers and the reemergence of the Aegis, the Aristos will accept other talents." He huffed a laugh. "Most are more interested in finding magic in their own family."

"That won't last. They still have issues with it here in Cygna."

"So they do, and maybe we can learn from their mistakes. I suggest you accept the invitation. It might provide you useful information and insight into their army structure that might help in the envoy's negotiations. Unless you want to go with Captain Dovel's?" At her expression, he said, "Sorry, I've been well informed on gossip and rumors."

"Then you must know my situation here..."

"...Is not as bad as you think. Cygnese supplement our servants, and they talk. My personal servant says the 'nulls' among them are excited by your presence. It seems their community sees in you the achievement and success denied their kind here."

"I'm just a mercenary who found a cushy job."

"Not at all. You are a ranking officer in the Kaereyan army. You'll have to live up to your reputation."

"I've no reputation in Cygna."

Corbin laughed at her. "You should know better," he chided. "Talk between soldiers extends beyond armies, borders, and nations. The mercenaries working for Cygna recognized you. Every null soldier in Cygna talks of you." He spread his arms wide, encompassing the chamber. "Even the men and women working here knew about all aspects of your career before you arrived in my apartment."

"I was on leave, and certainly not advertising for work."

"You were on leave and took a detailed reconnaissance of an army camp? Of the city and surrounding countryside? Captain Dovel reported the tour to his Regiment leader. He may not have read your mind, but he knew what you were doing. The prevalent assumption is Warrick sent you to 'explore' the situation before committing to an envoy. Their mistake has worked very well for our mission."

Kissre shrugged. "Training-induced impulses. How widespread was this speculation on my presence?"

"Wide enough to reinforce your doubt about the intended target of the attack. Any Pertelon agent working in Cygna would be instructed to get rid of you." Corbin rang a bell and asked the server to bring lunch. "Your work doesn't officially start until Aristo Aurelias crosses the border, so accept any opportunity you deem worthy of investigation. Wear this."

He tossed her a metal object. Kissre caught it and looked at the silver leaf insignia worn by an officer of King Warrick's Royal Guard. "Official status?"

"Definitely. You have joined the emissary's staff."

Her regard returned to Corbin. "The projected maneuvers are in Guerestu. It would leave you without security."

He waved a hand in dismissal. "We need no security here until the envoy arrives. Until Aristo Aurelias comes, you are free."

"When does he arrive?"

"Three sennight. You are to meet him in Seer Pass and act as a guide as well as security."

Eight

Kissre, wearing a Kaereyan officer's sash over the heavy blue uniform of a Kaereyan Royal Guardsman, rode Carillon to a Sidih tavern of Jycel's choice. He and his squad waited on the walk outside the tavern's entrance.

Before she reached them, Jycel strode forward followed by his squad. His lieutenants didn't look all that excited to meet her. Dismounting remained painful. Hands caught her as she swung her leg to the ground. Carillon stood rock still.

"You're lucky she doesn't have Bother's training, or you'd all be badly maimed." It was an exaggeration, but the irritating hands fell away, even though she stumbled on her stiff, sore leg. At Corbin's insistence, Healer Bujyea had seen her and declared her body healing, just used too much, too fast. "What about the limp?" Kissre had asked about the only thing that worried her.

"Infection settled in the bone and joint. Given time, it will heal."

A hostler from the tavern, an intrepid boy, ran forward and took Carillon's reins. "She'll be in the stable in the alley behind, ma'am. Where is your dog? Where's Fudge?"

At the boy's eager tone, Kissre raised her brows. "After his last escapade in Sidih, I thought it best to leave him behind." She pulled a cane from the scabbard attached to the saddle.

"Then he'll be following you here shortly? Like the first time you were in town?" Expectant pleasure spread on the young face.

"I don't think so." At the boy's disappointed look, she flipped him a Kaereyan silver piece.

He grabbed it out of the air. "Tell your server when you're getting ready to leave. I'll have Carillon ready for you, ma'am." She noted he already knew the name of her horse.

Jycel and his squad still stood nearby, watching her. "I can manage on my own," she said as Jycel put a hand on her elbow. "Introduce me to your squad, Jycel."

Jycel held open the door and grinned at her as she entered. "Prickly. Wait until we reach our room and get seated. We are delighted you accepted our invitation and have engaged a private room."

She raised one eyebrow at Jycel's comment, but it was probably an advisable extravagance. Her entrance evoked the usual, only now blatant, attention. The place seemed the gathering spot for the Cygnese army. Kissre guessed from the assorted looks sent her way, that her null status had a beneficial side. Knowing the reasons behind the expressions aimed at her was enough without hearing them, too. Those with scowls were Talents angered on Captain Tyna's behalf. Those with half-smiles were probably nulls. It suddenly struck her how hard a Talent might find such scrutiny. Maybe they had rules for themselves. Her hosts seemed unduly pleased at the interest.

Inside the private dining room, Kissre sank into a chair at one end of the table, held for her by one of Jycel's lieutenants, a stocky blond with full lips and the slightest of lisps. "I'm Maitiu," he said with a glance at her blue-traced wrist and hand.

She nodded as he took a seat to her right. "What's your Talent?" From his startled expression, it must have been the wrong question. "Sorry, but you must know I'm a null. The point of this dinner is to find a way, if there is one, of how to blend two different styles of command."

Maitiu looked to Jycel, who nodded from his place opposite Kissre. "I am a Sender," he said. At her continued look of interest, "My Talent allows me to place my thoughts in another's mind."

"Not take them?"

"Only surface thoughts. Jycel is the Probe here, only he could search your mind—"

"Not a void's." Jycel smiled. "You're unnerving my squad. They can't feel you."

The only woman squad member sat between Maitiu and Jycel. She smiled. "I am Cevoka, and I'm a Receiver-Screen. As a Receiver, I can only hear thoughts, but a Sender can relay thoughts to me." Cevoka was tall, dark, and skinny, looking like a blend of Jycel and Silvie. "As a screen, I find energy for Jycel's use."

"A Switch can control and direct surface energies for short times," Jycel said. "Which means I can use energies within a furlong of where I stand or pass it off to another Talent."

"Like wind?" Kissre asked.

"Any strong energy source, heat, wind, sound, light," Cevoka said with a look at Jycel. With his nod, she concentrated on the candle burning on the table. It suddenly smoked, the black smoke curling into uniform horizontal spirals. Kissre said nothing to the display but raised her brows in appreciation.

The remaining two men introduced themselves as Garod and Hew. Garod, short, heavy, and ashen colored, shared Cevoka's Talents. Hew, another highlander, was a Reader-Tracker. "Readers do exactly that. Read minds. Not without permission," Hew said as Kissre opened her mouth. She nodded. "A Tracker is an Earth Talent. It means I can follow almost anyone across the land."

"A void?"

"No. At least, not me—I follow mental tracks, and you don't leave any."

"Are there conditions under which you cannot track, besides a void?"

Hew nodded. "Some learn a hunter's stillness. They quiet their mind until it can't be felt. Luckily not many have that type of training."

She shrugged. "I'll probably never remember your Talents, neither will most Kaereyans." Immediately she responded to their affronted looks. "It's enough they will know you work as a team and that you are an invaluable asset to their battle movements. Mention of any mind talents will frighten them as witchcraft. Remember, this is a new concept to them. They are just coming to grips with the idea that 'magic' still exists in Kaereya. Your biggest challenge will be reassuring them you are not invading their minds."

Hew sputtered. "We don't—"

"Whoa!" Jycel said, throwing up his hands. "Let's eat dinner first before we ruin our appetites with your provoking details." Four waiters brought in prepared plates of roasted fowl surrounded by kale and white beans. Kissre decided foul must be the national dish. Surprisingly, they filled her glass with an excellent dry white wine.

"You have glass workers?" she asked, going to a neutral subject, holding the glass by its slender stem and inspecting the wine.

"On the Sunderlune border there are vast sand reserves and a long history of glass making," Maitiu said. "We have fine vineyards on our lower southeastern slopes, just below Guerestu. We needed glasses to appreciate the vintage properly."

"Probably why Pertelon wants your lands. I hear King Clement drinks prodigious amounts of wine. And you've never traded with Kaereya? They are mad for glass. I know Pertelon gets its wine from the eastern empire. Most of your crops are grown in your borderlands, aren't they?"

They worked to make the dinner pleasant, without the long silent stretches she had endured at Tyna's table, but what they had in common was interest in Kaereyan help. The conversation gravitated there, then to where and how she had fought. She found herself among a group of equestrians intrigued with Carillon, but proud of their own mountain breed whose long hair was harvested and woven into warm waterproof cloth. They bragged the ponies survived on meager mountain grass and could carry most large adult riders or the heaviest of pack loads.

"Even when your feet drag?" Kissre asked.

"At least no one needs a ladder to mount," Cevoka answered with a snippy grin. She and Maitiu talked as much as Jycel, but the other two members remained rather quiet, if from natural inclination or a distaste for the company, Kissre couldn't tell.

"Your last horse, did you buy him in Sunderlune?" Maitiu asked.

"Yes." She answered the distrust in his voice. "I worked in Sunderlune for a short while, and the opportunity came to purchase Bother. It was one of the good things I remember about the place."

"They certainly need good warhorses," Jycel said. "The cities are constantly battling one another, always skirmishing."

Kissre smiled. "The cities were too contentious for me to want to extend my stay."

"That's how we feel about all the outlands," Maitiu said. "Both our eastern and western borders are under constant attack from our land-hungry neighbors. Although, as you say, on the Sunderlune side, battles arise between rogue cities going against their chancellor."

"How much longer before you go to the Pertelon border?" Kissre asked.

"How did you know?" Cevoka asked, startled. "Command hasn't told the—"

"I noticed most of the camp gone. Have the platoons attached to your squad left already?" The squad shared a private look at her comment.

Jycel sat still for a moment, staring at her. "Dovel reported you were very observant. You are right. They have been deployed to the border. The Western Army in Halli is also on alert, as is the Eastern Army. It would be like some of the Sunderlune cities to take advantage of Pertelon's aggression."

"Pertelonese incursions?" Kissre asked.

"Yes," Maitiu said. "A few ambush raids. They escape back over the border."

"You have several sennight before Aristo Aurelias arrives. What's the chance we could go to the border? Show you how we work?" Jycel asked.

His companions seemed stunned, then jumped on the suggestion. Kissre let them talk her into accepting. As they prepared to leave the tavern, Jycel's squad acted as excited as children. Kissre, more familiar with the deadly aspects of their endeavor, kept her own counsel. She tallied her time. Five days out, a sennight in camp, and four days of hard riding to Seer Pass to join Aristo Aurelias before he entered Cygna. That left her a cushion of three days either way. As she left the tavern, Kissre's eyes roamed the crowd.

"Dovel's squad left for the border today," Jycel said, inserting his body between her wounded arm and a sure jostling from some of the heedless men weaving to the door. She gave him points for being as observant as he was handsome. His next words proved her deduction. "I thought you two had ended your relationship."

A sour laugh erupted from within her at her disappointment. "Doesn't mean I don't enjoy a view of his mulish face once in a while."

Jycel laughed.

~ * ~

Two days later, Kissre joined Jycel's squad wearing a light, leather-lined hauberk, plated leggings, and boot shields. A buckler, helmet, and sword filled scabbard were attached to her saddle, and the hilts of several knives showed on her sleeves and boots. Cursing her lack of a packhorse, she needed to wear what she could not carry in her bedroll and saddlebags. Her formidable appearance earned disconcerted expressions from her companions.

On Carillon she loomed over the squad on their gray mountain ponies for the trek to the Pertelon border. They followed the most direct path, a rough trail cut through rugged terrain. The squad's smug assurance of their ponies' superior agility in mountainous terrain amused Kissre, but she said nothing. She knew Carillon's capabilities.

Over her get-acquainted period with her new mount, Kissre looked forward to the ride. It provided her the opportunity to establish a trust bond with Carillon and let the horse become accustomed to Fudge flanking her side. After a few preliminary skirmishes, both dog and horse settled into an amicable agreement—Fudge wouldn't tease, and Carillon wouldn't kick. Carillon possessed far greater accuracy than Bother.

On the first day, they traversed beneath the extensive canopy of a vast conifer forest. Equine hooves fell soft and muted on deep mats of rusty needles, raising pungent resin scent to fill the air. They rode between gigantic tree trunks whose feathery branches spiraled to ethereal elevations. Glimpses of fleeing deer, squirrel, rabbits, and weasels caught her eye amid waves of triangular white flowers banked by ferns at every glade's edge. The chirps and warning calls of unseen birds occasionally broke the quiet. Several times she had to call Fudge back from a sure chase. Jycel told her to be wary, as mountain cats were known to be in the area. She thought he joked until they heard one yowl in the distance. It caught Fudge's attention, and Kissre called, distracting him from his alert stance.

Shortly after sunrise on the second day, they came to a small stream and followed a well-worn trail along its edge. All too soon, the easy descent changed. Now they traveled a rough track more appropriate for goats.

Carillon proved as sure-footed as the mountain ponies, denying her large and sturdy size. She planted her hooves with a dancer's precision on sheets of scree or precarious shelves of rock, and never balked at wetting her feet in icy creek water or sinking in mud to her fetlocks. Overall, the mare displayed an impeccable balance and temper.

Once, on a steep slope filled with loose gravel, Carillon hesitated. A gentle word of reassurance from Kissre caused her forward pricked ears to twitch backward, then forward. Carillon stepped forward to slip, skid, and plunge to firmer ground. Her willingness helped settle the ponies' more fractious inclinations into compliance. Their riders' attitude changed to near reverent envy, and Kissre learned to treasure her extraordinary gift.

They stopped in another forest for a midday meal, a place so different Kissre felt the alienness of it shiver over her skin. Only trees of gargantuan girth grew here. With her arms outstretched, she only encompassed a fraction of one tree's diameter. With no shrubs or undergrowth, it was a forest of unnatural quiet. The squad members talked more as they stopped to camp. Kissre, firmly informed her help wasn't needed, walked the cramps out of her bad leg on ground spongy with a deep layer of needles. Out of view of the camp, she started the movements of the Aibhe House Path of Focus.

"The food is almost ready," Cevoka said. Kissre turned to find the dark-haired lieutenant had followed her, unheard on the soft forest floor. Cevoka smiled and twirled, arms outspread, looking at the massive trunks rising into the heights. "This forest meanders throughout this southern region all the way to Guerestu and the Thou River."

"It's peaceful."

"Yes, it is, and ancient. Some birds, a few squirrels and other small rodents live here. Not much else besides the trees as they cut out too much light, and the soil is too poor and sour for most plants. But you are right. I would like to spend my afterlife somewhere so beautiful, quiet, and peaceful."

"It wouldn't bore you?"

Cevoka laughed and Kissre enjoyed the sound. "After spending so much time with other minds, I would like time to find myself."

"Is it uncomfortable?"

"Sometimes." Cevoka looked up at the boughs interlaced above them. "Sharing everything, knowing too well what someone else thinks or feels about me. Sometimes it's hard to distinguish my hurts, my jubilations, from someone else's. What is it like for you? I've never been around many nulls, and you are void. If I didn't see you, I wouldn't know you were there. Then you speak so calm and practical." Cevoka giggled. "If a person needed company in the afterlife, I'd choose you. You would give company without intrusion."

Kissre stared at her, sure she gaped.

"I've offended you, I'm sorry." Cevoka stretched out a hand in placation. "Really, please. I wish to know."

It took a minute's thought. "Uncertainty mostly, often loneliness. Awareness that, right or wrong, my choices are mine, and whether right or wrong, to make the best of it and take responsibility for the results."

Cevoka looked like she was considering the answer. "Responsible for your own actions. I've been told what to do all my life." Her gaze became quizzical. "What were you doing?"

"Exercises."

"For your leg?"

"Yes, but more for my temper. While in the East, I learned the movements. They not only increase strength and flexibility but also calm the mind and allow it to function in better ways."

"What ways?"

"They teach my body to move without thought, and my thoughts to flow without the impediment of emotion."

"Could you teach me?"

Kissre felt her mind twist then recalled Dovel had also asked. "Yes, if you want."

After the meal break, Kissre reflected on her encounter with Cevoka and decided maybe her view of Talents was prejudiced. Tired of self-examination, she decided to enjoy the ride.

The mountain passes drew her attention as her trust in Carillon's judgment grew. They were nearly always descending now, occasionally passing crystalline falls, which sprinkled cold mountain water on their sun-warmed skin. Carillon often brushed against shrubs that threw a pungent scent into the air. The ground crunched under Carillon's hooves as Kissre watched golden hawks hunt through the cloudless sky.

That night they camped on the riverbank. The men caught fish, and Cevoka set camp and cooked. They all insisted Kissre rest her healing limbs. Ignoring them, she limped between the animals, grooming Carillon and the ponies. Then she checked the tack for wear. She brushed Fudge, not that it brought order to his coat, and in general kept herself occupied. Often they forgot her status and half spoke, half-thought their comments. Used to isolation, she banked her annoyance.

After dinner Cevoka asked her to teach her the exercise. So, amid the men's quiet but amused attention, she began her pupil on the basic defense meditations, giving Cevoka a branch as a staff with which to practice. "Your mind will release you when you believe in yourself," she instructed as Cevoka fumbled through the movements. Over the next few days, Cevoka proved a capable student learning the movements with quick grace.

On their journey's last day, they emerged from the forest to look over a gentle downward slope toward the Geste River and Guerestu. The city spread from the river's banks into the surrounding foothills. Outside the city wall defenses, fields were divided into geometric blocks defining crops and the land's fertility. Her companions urged their mounts into gallops across the gentle slopes. With the route now clearly marked, and the challenge from the ponies, Kissre felt Carillon's eagerness and her own irrepressible desire. She urged her mount into a ground-eating gallop. Fudge's stretch and compress stride kept pace with Carillon. They soon caught and passed the racing ponies.

Carillon cleared the trunks of several downed trees and short ditches with equal ease, and plainly wanted more, even when Kissre slowed her to a prancing walk. The winded ponies caught up shortly.

"By the Holy One! Who would have guessed her so fast?" Jycel shouted, admiring Carillon as his pony abruptly dropped to an exhausted walk. "Can anyone ride her, or is she as nettlesome as that last behemoth you rode?"

"I would guess others might ride her, but Fudge might not let them," Kissre said.

"Mangy mutt." Jycel gave Fudge a displeased glance. Kissre laughed, knowing the dog had long ago won over both Jycel and his squad. Besides bestowing adulation on the owner of every caressing hand, and retrieving an endless number of tossed branches, on two different excursions he'd brought back large brown rabbits, their long back legs dangling from his mouth. His additions to the dinner pot enhanced their acceptance.

Within a candlemark of nearing the combined camp of Cygna's Northern and Eastern Armies north of Guerestu, a small band of mounted officers, including Dovel, joined them. For the remaining trip to the encampment, they talked. Kissre learned Marshal Ranor had already requested a meeting with her. Amid the greetings and jests with Jycel's squad, Dovel pulled his mount alongside Carillon. Smiling a greeting, he asked how she fared, his deep-set storm-colored eyes impersonal in his placid face. With a sigh of relief, Kissre answered him.

The small, mounted troop entered the camp. Marshal Ranor met them as she halted Carillon in the camp.

"Colonel Kissre," the Army's Marshal said as she dismounted. "I'm glad you agreed to Jycel's proposal. I've been most interested in the venture he is promoting and even more interested in the opportunity to talk with you."

Kissre looked over Ranor. If Dovel were a raven, this man was a hawk, tall, heavy, and short-necked. His short dark hair emphasized his stern, arrogant look of power. From the intense abstracted look in his eyes, Kissre realized he tried to read her. The look had become recognizable. Her eyes slid to Dovel, still mounted on his pony, whose very impassiveness seemed suspicious. She understood the signs there, too.

Ranor monopolized her time, ordering several troopers to see to Carillon and to settle her possessions into a tent. Dovel dismounted, and Fudge placed forefeet on his chest and stretched to greet Dovel face to face. Dovel permitted the whining, tail-wagging greeting, and the one lick of his chin. He returned the excited welcome with fond words and deep thumps on the dog's ribs. Frowning, Kissre called her dog to heel.

"Captain Dovel," Ranor said. "Gather the others I requested. We meet in a candlemark." During the interval Kissre was offered cider, bread, and cheese, but before she finished, found herself in a staff meeting. She fed the remains to Fudge who lay at her feet.

For a few interminable candlemarks, she described all her experiences with Pertelon's army, asked and answered endless questions about strategy and techniques, offensive and defensive, used by and against that army. Ranor had received and showed Kissre a communiqué from Duke Aurelias. When he asked about Pertelon's use of proscribed weapons, the silence grew profound.

Taking Aurelias's missive as permission to disclose information, Kissre replied. "They do have fuel or explosive propelled weapons, canon mostly, but I've also encountered small hand-held weapons capable of long-distance harm."

"Like arrows?"

"Yes, but without the bow. Just point and shoot. Distance thrice an arrow's."

He asked about the Battle of Anatole in Kaereya.

While answering, Kissre realized Ranor deftly tested her capability. She recognized that she represented not the mercenary Kissre, but Colonel Kissre Pierce of Aristo Aurelias' Army Battalion, and now King Warrick's Royal Guard of Kaereya.

"How does the Kaereyan Aegis work?" Marshal Ranor asked, turning the topic at last.

"I'm not a Talent. I cannot tell you how. Somehow, the land speaks to him. If an enemy approaches, he makes a riverbank or rock cliff or cave give way underfoot. He makes flocks of birds rise into the air, alarming invaders and giving away their position. This is what I saw. More, I can't tell you."

"It is enough. It gives us ideas. He does not tell your troops how to move?"

"No. The Kaereyan Army has a very strict command structure. Senior officers set plans. The troops do their best to achieve them. The standing army is very well trained. Secretary Corbin suggested if we are to combine forces, it would be useful for me to work with one of your platoons on patrol to discover how you work." It surprised her that several Captains, unknown to her, raised issues about her safety going into the fighting zone. "I'm trained as well, perhaps better, than most of your troops. It is my business."

The next day at her own insistence, she walked a border patrol with one of Jycel's Platoons. At departure, Marshal Ranor stood with Captain Jycel. Sergeant Oran, the platoon leader Jycel introduced, nodded and turned back to Jycel. The unit Oran selected to go with him consisted of five men. They stood with speculative gazes on Kissre, all were dressed in dull earth colors similar to herself.

She wore fighting gear and weapons of the House Aibhe, the short, eastern-style bow and arrows, toss blades, and the distinctive link cap. The only Cygnese style weapon was the short sword strapped to her side. She wore no other identifiers, no insignia or rank emblems. Her ensemble aroused interest.

"You are to check the border perimeters by the river for any signs of an incursion by Pertelon," Jycel told the men. He unfolded a map and showed the area. "Oran, the Squad will stay in frequent touch. I want you back before dark fall, so pace your unit accordingly."

"Colonel Kissre," Ranor said, eyeing her weapons. "You understand you are observing only?" He stood with Jycel's squad. Jycel didn't give orders but listened and allowed the other Captains to join him in his mental contact with his platoon. She saw general disapproval for herself. Dovel listened, holding Fudge on a thick leash.

"Yes, Marshal."

"Your dog is under control?"

All eyes turned to Fudge, who yipped under the scrutiny. "Yes. He is used to Captain Dovel and will obey him." She felt naked and edgy without him. He sensed trouble long before it arrived. Everyone else thought him an unpredictable distraction.

She knew Oran was a Receiver, so any other orders given remained a mystery. Oran nodded to Jycel, and they moved off. They walked a league before reaching the search perimeter. Oran ran a well-organized unit. The point man, two flankers, and a rear guard surrounded her and Oran. Once moving, her usual jittery uneasiness faded. She focused on her surroundings, and her senses turned hypersensitive to her local.

The land they walked was flat. Tall reeds reached above eye-level all around them, and the air reeked of muck and marsh. She heard the rustle of the wind-blown reeds, the spit and sputter of water flowing somewhere to their west, the sudden whoosh of flushed birds, and the quiet squelch of feet pulling from soft earth. The pull of the mud on her leg made it ache, but she ignored the distraction.

Tunnels broken into the reeds showed animal runs. Above the reeds, treetops outlined the river's edge. Beyond that, foothills rose on Cygna's side of the wide river valley. Kissre looked at the clouds scattered in the blue sky and watched the flight of small schools of birds. There was not much else to see.

Oran spoke orders in low tones to his men and navigated with knowledge evidently received from someone not blinded by the reed infested ground. She followed the squad's slow movements for the rest of the patrol, glad to reach firmer ground, exchanging reeds for tall grass. The strands undulated in the breeze with a soft whisper that allowed the sound of flying insects to penetrate the senses. Overhead, the intense summer sun reddened and burned breeze-dried skin and eyes.

A candlemark's walk brought them to the empty homes of an abandoned hamlet. Kissre's skin prickled, and her stomach tightened in suspicion and apprehension. The unit passed through the buildings, inspecting each as they came to it, but no hidden enemies lay ready for an ambush, and no fatal traps sprang. They swept through the small dwellings and surrounding crop fields to reach 'safe' territory. Then they headed back to camp.

Fudge greeted her as the patrol neared the camp. She talked quietly with the men while she petted Fudge. Afterward, she went directly to her tent and fell into her cot. She woke when Dovel entered her tent with food. Rising, she left the tent to sit on a campstool before accepting the plate from Dovel. "Thank you. I was hungry."

"You're pushing yourself too hard."

Kissre raised her eyes to Dovel. "I don't need a nursemaid." He said nothing, but discomfort shaded her body and mind.

"That was unkind, I'm sorry," she said. "The truth is, I do ache. It was a hard, tiring day. But I'm no longer acting of my own accord. You know that. The moment Marshal Ranor addressed me by rank, asked me questions about the Kaereyan army, and I answered, I became a representative of my country, of its army. Now I must carry out my duty."

He finally sat. "You are a native of Cygna." Fudge inserted his head in Dovel's lap. Kissre watched his long hand move over the shaggy brown head.

"And a citizen of Kaereya by choice." She ignored Dovel's concerned expression. "Marshal Ranor expects I'll report to the Kaereyan envoy on my findings here. Aurelias will expect that report. A curiosity-driven excursion has become a mission of some import."

"You knew it would." His hand continued its duty to Fudge. "It won't do any good if you can't finish it."

"I'll know what I need to know in two or three more patrols. I promise you not to overtax myself. All right?"

He nodded. "I have another request." A laugh erupted as he looked at her expression. "Don't look so wary. I want you to show me how you track."

"Really?" Several strong emotions hit Kissre at once, and she didn't know how to reply.

He nodded. "Think about it, please?"

Shortly he left. No one else visited her, probably on advice delivered from Dovel. She sighed and went back to bed.

On her third patrol, the squad covered the same ground in the same manner. Kissre, far beyond alarm, knew her actions spooked the men. Oran began urging her forward at her frequent halts. She listened for birds and animal movements, listened to the earth's sounds. The unnatural quiet made her edgy. "They're out there," she whispered to Oran. Her companions traveled without hesitation or undue concern.

"Can't be, squad would tell us."

"Even if they're nulls?"

"Yes, they recognize we're here. Hew will be watching the area around us."

"What if other voids hide there? Ask them if they pick up my presence, or if he knows I'm here by your assurance."

"Ma'am, you're only here to observe."

"I'm just asking you to take precautions."

"Everyone is, ma'am. Jycel says they sense nothing out of the ordinary nearby." Oran motioned his men forward.

They traversed a short stretch of reed-covered muck. Squelching steps measured the distance. Kissre knocked an arrow as they advanced. She fell behind Oran, and the rearguard caught up with her. Motioning him by, the man stopped. He shook his head no, obeying her hand motion for silence. He squatted next to her.

"Oran," the right flank man said with a hint of panic. Kissre readied her bow. "Oran," the man repeated. She heard the reeds rustle, heard an arrow's release, and heard the point hit. Responding quickly, she stood, aimed, and released her own. A strangled howl ascertained her accuracy.

Following her instincts and training, she scuttled into the reeds. The commotion of Oran's unit around their fallen man gave her a base point for direction. She made a wide arc, moving slowly and quietly with experience-honed skill.

In frozen moments she extended her hearing to the areas around her, let it take over her existence. Eventually, she heard her quarry. Several men moved, no longer following a trail but actively sought Cygnese—hunters searching for prey. Nock, shoot, nock, shoot, two arrows left her bow. One met its target.

At a noise behind her she swung, ready to shoot. It was the rearguard, following her. He aimed his bow. Kissre turned her attention back as a man erupted from the reeds and charged her. The rearguard's arrow took him in the chest. Two more men followed on the dead man's heels. Their arrows missed, her buckler deflecting one. An arrow from behind her took one lunging man in the throat. She drew her short sword. The last attacker swung his sword in a wild manner. Kissre came up under his swing with a lethal stroke, but he jumped back. They exchanged several clashing blade strikes.

She saw panic in the man's eyes, steeled her resolve and her stomach. As her shoulder brought her blade forward, she fell hard to the left, shoved. Pitched into the reeds, she fought to her feet and turned. Oran stood there with his bow aimed on her opponent's fleeing back.

Finished, he turned to her. "My apologies, Colonel Kissre, I acted under orders."

Spitting mud and reed bits she nodded and wondered if she had the strength left to rise. Accepting an extended hand, she pulled herself to her feet.

"Jycel sending another unit?"

"Yes, Ma'am, several, and Ranor ordered more."

"Is your man dead?"

"No, badly wounded." He spit his disgust into the reeds.

Kissre nodded and walked forward, following the track of the enemy. Both Oran and his rearguard clung to her like shadows. Beyond the furthest bodies, she pointed to the intersection of animal trails and the human tracks using them. "More than a few men used this path."

Oran nodded. "Where are they going? What are they doing?"

"My guess?" She squinted at the distant foothills. "I think they're infiltrating Cygna. Building a body of troops beyond the border."

When they returned to camp, Oran gave his report to Jycel, telling him the squad needed a Mapper Adept to sweep the borders for possible infiltration. They had found evidence of a trail into Cygna.

He and his men dispersed.

Kissre said nothing, but Marshal Ranor stared at her, his nostrils flaring in anger. He ordered her to his headquarters tent. Jycel and his squad followed her. Ranor didn't waste time, speaking even as other squad Captains entered the tent. "Your report, Colonel Kissre?" Sergeant Oran also entered, looking uncomfortable.

"Strategically, I think Pertelon is trying to infiltrate men into Cygna, probably to attack from within. When they are prepared for a battle, they will use a combined assault to take you by surprise from the back." Several laughs greeted her statement, and the Marshal looked unconvinced.

"They could be just reconnoitering the border," Jycel said.

"They could be," Kissre said, shrugging. "But I'd bet there are more trails. You won't know until the area is investigated. Doesn't matter. You have to stop access."

"Their best strategy is to amass troops just across the border from Guerestu," Jycel said.

"Is it?" Kissre said. "There are many strategic targets beside Guerestu. Every Talent along the border is a potential target."

"They cannot travel too far into Cygna without those same local Talents warning of their approach," Ranor said. "Rest assured, we would know if this were happening. So Guerestu remains the most logical target. Now, Colonel Kissre, can I ask what you will report to Kaereya?"

"I would not advise the Kaereyan command to place any troops under squad control with the present conditions."

The stunned silence formed a wall around her. Ranor moved to sit behind his camp desk, and Kissre turned to face him. The Marshal stared back. "Why?" His question broke the extended quiet.

"The platoon units depend too heavily on the squad's guidance. They do not use their own perception, do not investigate leads, they miss obvious clues." She stopped. "Excuse me, Marshal," Kissre said, suddenly aware of her state. "May I sit?" A chair was placed behind her, and she slowly lowered into it, trying not to sigh.

She looked at Jycel's furious face. "Captain Jycel, once I left the squad's presence, could you follow me?"

A mutinous line clamped his mouth. "No," he spat out. "I'd expected, depended, on a better result."

Returning her gaze to Ranor she noted the Marshal's anger. "Sir, you have an amazing tool. How amazing, I'm sure I cannot even guess, but it is fallible. There are means of circumventing your squads. Pertelon has learned how to escape your notice, and you cannot afford to rely on Talent alone. Each squad, from what I understand, varies in strengths and abilities, and their work is exhausting, even debilitating. Your army is less than a quarter the size of the army you face. If your platoons fail, Pertelon forces will push forward as far as your squad's locations and capture them. You cannot afford to waste either effort or men or the advantage this tool gives you. The men you put into the field are not expendable because they are null. They are the arms of your assaults, the backbone of your defenses. I assure you that Kaereya will never commit troops to leaders who find them expendable."

"I don't find my men expendable," Jycel yelled, stepping toward Kissre in anger.

"Then allow them the freedom to think for themselves, to make their own analysis of a situation. Trust them."

He glared at her so strangely it was like she spoke a foreign language.

"Colonel Kissre," Ranor said. He had risen and crossed his arms on his chest. Kissre noted his eyes twitched with the words he refused to say through his strained lips. An uneasy silence reigned in the tent for a moment. Picking up a letter knife, he jammed the point into his camp desk and exhaled a huge breath. "You're right."

Kissre wondered at the silent argument that must have flowed around her. Resuming his seat, the Marshal regarded her with a cool abstraction. "If Cygna wanted Kaereyan troops, under what circumstances could you see this happening?"

"I cannot speak for the envoy, only from my own viewpoint." Ranor nodded in acceptance, and she continued. "The pieces are here, the organization, just not the initiative. If I could take a platoon into the field without a squad's guidance? This would give me a better feel for what can be done for both sides."

"You've been wounded recently and very ill from it. Today, these last few days, have exhausted you."

"A hazard of my profession, but I made it through the mission. I will fulfill the next one, too. I improve daily. I would need a day to prepare."

"We cannot afford to lose a Kaereyan representative." Ranor rejected her offer, looking around at his captains.

One voice broke a lengthy silence.

"I can."

Kissre's swiveled her head to where Dovel stood.

"The bond is one way and not complete, but I can sense her presence. You need to speak aloud, sir. We all do."

Ranor looked at Kissre. "My apologies. I only asked if anyone could track you. All right, let's plan the details."

"Give me free rein over a platoon, Oran's if he will," Kissre said. It set off a firestorm of argument among the Captains. Kissre smiled over the outrage at hearing Oran say, "My platoon volunteers."

After the meeting, Kissre tracked Dovel down. It wasn't hard; she just followed Fudge. He did not look surprised as she burst through the flap of his tent following her furred tracker. "How long?"

His eyes rose from the book he was reading. "Since that first night."

"You didn't tell me."

"What point? You can't feel me. It's all one-sided."

"What else do you get from my mind? Thoughts?" She watched his eyes for evasion.

"No." He closed the book he held. "Emotions, sometimes, not often. How your body feels, even when you ignore it."

"Stay out of my mind."

"It's not a case of staying in or out of your mind."

"What then?"

"It's like seeing someone you know on a street, how you can pick them out from a crowd. You just know they're there."

She glared at him.

"Kissre, I've told no one else anything about you, not even Tyna."

"I thought you said I was a void, that you couldn't feel me."

"We touched. That changed things."

"A mistake."

"No, not a mistake."

"I am not a replacement for my sister!"

"I know. Even before I touched you, I knew that."

Unable to fathom him, believe him, or question him further, she stood silent, trying to measure the truth. Anger surfaced. Afraid of her rage and afraid of him, Kissre turned and stormed out of the tent. Jycel waited outside.

"How could you? You mocked our efforts before Ranor. We only showed you hospitality."

"I meant you no disrespect, but what I said needed saying."

"You could have discussed it with me first before humiliating my squad before its command."

Kissre looked at the angry squad Captain, aware of the fury already scalding her. She spoke in a dead calm. "You knew the chance you took when you asked me to work with your platoon." Somehow Jycel sensed her anger, and she saw his indecision, which inflamed her more. Her voice became even firmer in its quietness. "My duty to Kaereya required my speaking. Never expect me to do less than my duty. Goodnight, Captain Jycel."

~ * ~

Despite Jycel's continued pout, he allowed Oran's platoon to work with her. Tomel's squad volunteered also. Her inclination was to refuse Dovel's sergeant. On reflection, she realized Tomel's presence didn't matter. Dovel would follow her into the field anyway, so she agreed. After a long talk with the two sergeants, Kissre requested a Pathfinder. A man without a badge and an obvious local was brought.

He introduced himself as Cleat.

"How far does your knowledge of the land hereabouts extend?"

"Well, missus, was born in the Desolate Forest. Have traveled with my family group all over this part of Cygna from the cliffs of Seer Pass as far north as the Geste River's north branch. West as far as Sidih." He spoke in a heavy accent and mentioned her strange dialect. His covetous eyes fell on her jack and trews. Kissre noticed his own rough leather wear. Various pieces of fur, quilted work, and fang or bone buttons adorned the leather. Small bags were attached or hung from neck to waist, and she noted some were braided and woven grass pockets.

"You know the area intimately then?"

The man laughed at her wording. "Some places more than others."

"Do you hunt?"

At the affronted look, Kissre smiled.

"Must, missus. Trade and hunt."

She unrolled a map. Not sure he had ever seen one, she ran her fingers over areas as she talked. It was a tedious method to discover his knowledge, but sure enough, he soon corroborated her observations or added meaningful information of his own.

"My last question is this. Can you take orders from me without hesitation or question?"

Cleat rubbed his jaw several times while his glance skittered between her, Oran, Tomel, and the other platoon members where they stood to the side. "Don't know till the time comes, missus. Never listened to anybody but myself afore. We're notorious nulls."

"No more than myself. Good enough. Are you willing, then, to train with this platoon and complete one mission?"

A snort answered her. "For the right inducement." He rubbed his fingers together in an age-old sign.

~ * ~

As they prepared to leave the morning of the excursion, Kissre spoke with Jycel and Dovel. "We will be gone several nights. Is that a problem for your squads?" She glanced at Marshal Ranor. He nodded at her and glanced at Fudge standing next to her. Last night she spent arguing with him over the maneuvers she wished to carry out. Before leaving she gave Fudge's leash to Dovel. No matter how angry she was with the man, Fudge obeyed him.

Instead of heading down into the river border area, she headed her unit up along the ridge of foothills ranging the flood plain. Long candlemarks spent talking with Cleat had paid off. The pathfinder knew this section of land very well. Kissre told him what she looked for, and he told her where to find it. Enthralled with the map, he promptly learned to understand it, even if he couldn't read the words.

"It's not accurate, Ma'am," he said, picking up Oran and Tomel's formal address. Then he told her the layout and she marked it on the map. When he understood what she searched for, he helped select five sites for inspection.

During their travel, the men spoke only in whispers and hand signals to indicate their movements. Cleat, used to silent travel, had helped Kissre teach the others. The first two locations proved negative, with no signs of human habitation. At the third, they found indications of a camp incompletely concealed. Kissre and Cleat argued about the numbers involved and how long the camp had been abandoned.

She turned to Oran and Tomel. "Can you let the squads know of this?" They nodded. "Have they been giving you orders or information?"

"No, Ma'am," Tomel said. "But Oran says he knows they're visiting our minds often enough. My receiver agrees. Curiosity's got them caught tight." He sounded gleeful.

"Tell them to relay to Marshal Ranor the location of this site."

"Got a feeling, Ma'am, that Marshal Ranor's listening, as caught as any of them."

Kissre nodded. "We will continue and check the other two sites tonight. Remember, silence is imperative. Stay alert. If we run into the enemy, they won't be expecting night visitors. They've met no resistance, so their sentries might be slack, but don't expect it."

"Ma'am, why don't we split and check both camps at once? Cleat, go with one platoon, you with another?"

Kissre gave the suggestion some thought. "No. I don't want to divide the team. We have no means of communication except those capable of contacting the squads. If we should run into trouble, the enemy will have more than a platoon of men. We will stay together. Remind your men we are not here to engage. Our mission is to locate and relay enemy positions within Cygna's borders."

Before reaching the next site, they halted. Cleat held up a warning hand, and silence fell over the unit. Quiet reigned until they heard the faint sound of movement ahead, the clink of equipment, and the low murmur of voices. Men moving. Kissre crawled to Cleat's position signaling everyone to stay down and quiet. After the sound of the moving line diminished, Cleat whispered. "Let me follow them, Ma'am. I promise you they won't know I'm there."

"How many did you count?"

"I figured between fifteen and twenty men, three ponies, heavy laden."

"That's about what I got, too. Follow them. I'll take the unit to the next site and check it out. Return to this point and wait for our return."

"Yes, Ma'am." Cleat disappeared into the underbrush with a few faint crunches.

She crawled back to Oran. "Captain Jycel's Squad in touch with you?"

He nodded. "Worried."

"Tell them we have encountered Pertelon troops." Giving him the information, she raised her hand, signaling the unit together. When the men were close enough, she whispered, "We're going on to the next site. We know they are here. Are all of you certain of your ability to traverse this area in the dark soundlessly?" Each man nodded his assent. "Then let's go."

~ * ~

From the heights of the camp lookout, Dovel watched Kissre ride away. Kissre was not hard to spot among the Cygnese Pathfinders mounted on mountain ponies sent with her. He was glad to see her go.

At first, he was incensed Kissre would not consider his squad, then Tomel unexpectedly requested on his own. He had felt sure she would refuse. She hadn't. Never in his years as a squad Captain had he felt such apprehension over a platoon's welfare. Kissre wisely relayed most information through Jycel's Oran. Dovel knew he would have interfered, brought disciplinary action down on his squad. Reluctantly he had to admit she knew her business.

Two camps of Pertelon troops had been captured. They claimed they were in disputed territory and had the right to travel through it. It was currently causing a diplomatic disturbance, but Ranor felt they had nipped the action before it took hold. He still had Tracker Talents searching the area. No other incursions were found. Kissre doubted Ranor's assumption, but everyone else dismissed her suspicions.

Most of the squad captains worried more about repercussions among the platoons. Jycel finally basked in the triumph of his squad. All other Captains worried more about the platoons refusing to regard the squad's direction as imperative. Dovel could see how the two methods might fit together to form a stronger, safer, more effective force. Knew, in part, this was a reflection of Kissre's belief.

Kissre. In camp he could not fault her for her friendliness, or for her gestures of goodwill. They even played and sang together for the entertainment of the camp. If he tracked her down, she talked with him. If invited, she took walks with him or showed him Aibhe exercises in which Jycel's Cevoka often joined. But fault her he did. Except for her temper-driven visit to his tent, she never sought him out.

Their friendship was not enough, and now he knew it would never be enough. It was more than his Talent that reacted every time she neared him, although few realized this except Ulyss. His spirit lightened, the day seemed brighter, life more hopeful. Watching her caused a torturous longing he wanted to avoid—commitment. Although he knew his cause lost, he had still made a last attempt. He sent a letter explaining how he felt, unable to say the words aloud. She had not responded, refused to be caught alone with him, and remained adamantly civil.

Only Fudge visited, usually carrying a stick, wanting to play, sent when Kissre went on patrol. He watched the riders disappear down the road with the big dog loping alongside.

"You'll see her in Sidih."

Dovel turned from the road to look at Ulyss, who had come up next to him. There was no need to answer. Ulyss continued.

"Your Talent grows."

"Yes."

"I don't think your new abilities are due to my Catalyst influence."

"Have you mentioned it to anyone?"

"No. Not even Adele has noticed. The rest of the team just thinks I give you that kind of support. How did you follow her? I couldn't sense it."

"I felt her reflection on the earth."

"You felt...but that means she must have Earth Talent, and you bonded!" Ulyss said. "You didn't report this?"

"No. I imagine Ranor suspects."

At his Lieutenant's silence, Dovel regarded him. Ulyss looked worried. He justified his disregard of the law. "She is not a citizen of Cygna. There is no reason to report any suspicion or even, for that matter, certain knowledge."

"I doubt the powers in Sidih would agree with your assessment," Ulyss said, his concern became edged with skepticism. Whatever he was about to say changed. "This is a dangerous game—one that can only harm you. Marshal Ranor will report."

"Maybe not. He thinks it only my talent—that I slept with a null. I'm known for it. If he suspects anything, it is she has minuscule Talent. As Tyna's sister, it would be the most logical assumption."

"Dovel..." Ulyss swore and turned to walk with him as he returned to his tent. Dovel knew what he had been going to say and when

Ulyss changed his mind and offered, "What can I do to help you?"

Nine

Nine leagues northwest of the last Kaereyan Keep, at the mouth of Seer Pass, Kissre caught up with the Duke of Lambere's cavalcade. The journey led by Cleat had been both perilous in terrain and breathtaking in beauty.

"Not many know these routes and paths through the cliffs and foothills," he had told her, and she understood herself accepted into Pathfinder confidence. His last words to her on the banks of the North Thou River confirmed it. "Ma'am, in the coming conflict, me and my cousins would like to ride with you, you allowing."

"I'd be gratified, Cleat. I think you all have mercenary hearts."

He'd smiled and with a few farewells, the whole group turned and rode away.

The rest of her trek had just been long, hard riding. Carillon stood up to the task, but it clearly drained her. Even Fudge faded, so Kissre had dismounted and walked periodically to allow the animals to recover.

The sight before her was flagrant in its extravagance. Colorful banners and pennants, caparisoned horses, a contingent of blue-coated Royal Guards, and jewel-trimmed aristos of varying offices paraded through the desolate landscape. Her quick eyes scrutinized the banners as she rode past them. The more influential aristos would be part of the negotiation team. The rest were minor aristos, courtiers good for show but little else with a few probably holding anticipation for advancement. Even the out-of-favor Aristo Emory, the king's cousin, traveled with Aristo Aurelias.

Exhausted and aching with it, Kissre rode Carillon at a slow lope along the side of the column. She pulled the mare to a walk next to the ordinary-looking Aurelias and Quillon, his knight dressed in Kennetsurean fashion. Both men inspected her.

Quillon measured her in his usual perceptive manner. Her former taskmaster, Quillon acted as Aristo Aurelias' factotum. Wrinkles creased the corners of his observant hazel-gold eyes, seeming to glow in the bronze of his face. Kissre turned from his gaze.

"Colonel Kissre, glad you've arrived. You've had more experience traveling this route than any of us. It is a relief to have you." Aurelias, looking uncomfortable in the regalia of his rank, shifted on his own Novere bred horse. "Come ride with me. We have much to cover before we reach Cygna. You look good. Fully recovered?"

"Yes, thank you, Your Grace. I am glad to be of service, but with the size of your armed escort, you shouldn't have trouble traveling Seer Pass." Looking around, Kissre identified enough experienced guides and outriders to negate any need for her help.

Aristo Aurelias followed her gaze. "Corbin's dispatches said you would be of great assistance on the ride to Sidih. He said certain segments of the population identify with you, and your presence would alleviate suspicion. I trust his judgment. I understand this route is difficult for most travelers?"

Kissre looked at Aurelias' profile. His usual common brown-bird appearance differed, now feathered in silk, gold, and the garnets of state. "Yes, sir, much different. It's disputed status gives refuge to the worst vultures."

"Well, there's no sense in wasting time. You might as well start your report."

Dust coated, sweat-stained, and worn, Kissre felt unprepared but gathered her wits. They talked of Cygna's strengths and weaknesses, of her experiences in Sidih with Corbin, and her recent excursions with Cygna's army. Then Aurelias delved into the attack on her, her wounds, and the situation with her sister. Use to her employer's skillful inquiries, Kissre answered each question with a clear and detailed recall, quashing emotion.

For eight days the cavalcade crept forward at a walk until they finally entered Cygna through the Halli Road approach. Aristo Aurelias assigned Kissre to ride at his back and alongside Quillon.

At the ford into Cygna, Kissre sighed, observing a newly constructed bridge. A crowd similar to Aristo Aurelias' own waited on the far shore. Once across the bridge, diplomats, deans from the Governor's Cabinet, and adepts from the Adept Council joined them. Cygnese army captains, their squads, and platoons surrounded Aurelias' cavalcade to escort them to Sidih. Their pace slowed even further, and the road became lined with curious and silent Cygnese, indistinguishable in their conformity. Only Fudge seemed to raise interest. Fingers pointed, and heads bent one to another speaking in quiet tones.

The pace frustrated her, as did the endless restrictions of protocol. She found comfort only in continually shifting in the saddle. When she finally entered her sleep roll, her mind felt as wearied of boredom as the tedious travel. The duke and other important personages had rooms in taverns and homes in Halli. Quillon's arrangements for a unit of Royal Guards for His Grace's protection alleviated her of any duty. She slept hard.

Kissre woke to the feel of a knife blade creasing her throat. Just below her ear. It was dark, but a hint of light indicated pre-dawn. Her eyes flicked open, and she tensed.

"Up, Kissre," a well-known voice demanded in whispered tones. "Up, now."

"Quillon? There are at least three candlemarks before we leave."

"Quiet. You'll wake everyone. Up, laze-about. It's time to earn your keep. You need practice." He pushed her with a rough hand

and laid a practice shield and sword next to her sleep roll. Fudge stood next to him, head cocking side to side, looking down at Kissre in soundless interest.

Staggering as she rose, Kissre dressed and followed Quillon. In a field not far from the camp, he ordered her to put Fudge at stay. Then he started the session. After her time with the Cygnese army, she thought her body recovered. Quillon showed her the truth. Within a trice, he had found her weak spots and hammered mercilessly on them till she could no longer keep her guard up against his attack. Agility and timing failed at each assault. Quillon's wood practice blade pounded bruises onto her flesh. His buckler caught her, and she fell.

"You call yourself security? You sleep so soundly an assassin can get a knife to your throat. You're out of breath before starting practice. Your left side is so weak and stiff you can't hold a buckler properly. You limp like a crone and seem to have forgotten every defense you ever knew. How good are you at attack?"

Kissre didn't answer the gloating, taunting voice. She couldn't. Her burning lungs demanded air more than her pride needed to protest Quillon's denunciation.

"It's too late to get someone else, so I'll have to ensure you are capable of carrying out your duty."

Unable to move with his sword point held at her throat, Kissre groaned and collapsed. Quillon laughed. "Yes, you know what to expect. Put your weapons down. You need to build your strength. A short run would be a good beginning. If you can run."

Wearied by the time she mounted Carillon for the day's journey, Kissre felt the muscle quiver that would translate later into aching stiffness. Shivering from a quick bath in cold stream water and dressed in a formal blue uniform, she took her position. Aurelias, already mounted, gave her a puzzled look. Quillon sat impassively on his horse, but Kissre read his amusement all too clearly whenever her gaze fell on him. She was very willing to ride quietly. The morning set the tone and schedule for the rest of the journey. By the time she neared Sidih, she felt better, responded better, but the muscle ache never ceased. Quillon only intensified the sessions.

Once in Sidih, they paraded through the streets. Among the people lining the route, amid organized cheers of greeting for the emissary, shouts of 'Fudge' were nearly as numerous as 'that's her, that's the Blue Dragon, Captain Tyna's sister.' At each of the duke's occasional glances, she felt her face flame. Her embarrassment intensified as they passed a new tavern sign of a howling dog, obviously carved in Fudge's likeness. The cavalcade stopped before the Assembly House, and she dismounted. Corbin stood there, magnificent in color, size, and scale, waiting with Cygna's Governor Vitann.

Grooms appeared magically to lead mounts away, and the dignitaries were separated from the escorts. Soon only Aurelias, flanked by Kissre and Quillon, and a handful of Aristos remained.

During Corbin's introduction of the Right Honorable Governor Vitann to His Grace, Aristo Aurelias, the Duke of Lambere, Kissre felt the governor's fleeting glance and dismissal like a slap. An officer on duty, though, does not notice, let alone respond, to any personal slight.

From the courtyard all the way into the Assembly House, Vitann made formal introductions of members of the government. The lengthy exchange of greetings became involved and convoluted. Captain Tyna was introduced as one of the negotiators. Kissre refused to see the gaze cast at her. Eyes pierced her from the side, and she caught Quillon's offended regard. She ignored him. The party moved forward a few steps, and Vitann presented the next dignitary.

The next morning Quillon took her to the wooded park beyond their assigned residence. They fought with wooden swords that banged on metal bucklers with enough force to jar bones and bruise through leather padding. They fought until sweat blinded her, and her breath came in ragged, painful gasps. He trounced her, confusing her with his aggression. "Tomorrow," he said in parting, "dress in light armor, the weight will help build your endurance. Your duty is the morning watch."

He left before she could argue. Exhausted, she dragged herself to her room, a bath, and the ministrations of her maid, Fay, her only reward in returning to Sidih.

During the interminable meeting, she stood and listened, cursing Quillon. He probably took the afternoon watch to give himself time to recover from their exercise, unneeded she was sure. The preliminary talks began as speeches disguised as conversation. Each delegate on both sides laid out their position, from situations to desires to possibilities and necessities, back and forth.

A tedious sennight passed. During one break Captain Tyna, now rounded in pregnancy, approached her.

"I would like to talk to you Kissre."

"I am on duty, Captain Pierce." She watched outrage and annoyance cover the face in front of her. Tyna turned and walked away.

"You're very hard on your sister."

Kissre turned to Aristo Aurelias, unaware of his presence. "The connection has been severed. It would not do Captain Pierce any good to believe she can rekindle it."

"Intractable, Kissre? I'd always thought you open to compromise." His stare didn't break her resolve. "I've already heard all about it, Kissre. You'd do well to make peace. Everyone needs family. What happened wasn't her fault."

Burying her anger and blushing at the exposure of her past, Kissre remembered the time Aurelias had spent mourning lost family before finding his daughter. She amended her initial response. "It depends on the family, Your Grace."

"Well, tonight you stand in for my family. You will accompany me as an escort. I believe you were sent the appropriate dress?"

"A new duty, Aristo Aurelias?" Inwardly she groaned.

"A planned courtesy. I have no wife and need someone to be with me who can remember what is said, and judge responses."

Once relieved of duty, Kissre escaped to her room to get some peace but received none. Fay informed her she had a visitor. Captain

Pierce waited for her. Kissre entered the room slowly and kept a safe distance between them.

"I would prefer you say nothing. It is best to leave things as they are."

"Best for you. I know what you want, and after this, I will concede to your desires."

"But?"

"I must try, Kissre, to mend our rift. Let me apologize for our last meeting and our argument. I said things in anger that were wrong, meant to hurt."

"Tyna..." She stopped, hating this confrontation, and felt her anger build. Naomi had always sent letters filled with apologies. Messages that took months to find her. It never changed anything when they next met face to face. What Tyna wanted was impossible. Another day would come, an occasion where she either actually injured Tyna or she would be destroyed. The event should and could be avoided.

"The fault is not yours, but mine. What you said was perfectly true. You have no need to apologize. We are different people with different values and desires. I baited you, treated you and your squad with an antagonistic, ridiculing attitude. I know my faults. I have a grudge-holding, unforgiving nature tied to a long memory. What you said can't be taken back. It stands between us. Even without that reason, I want to sever our relationship for reasons of my own. Your squad was right to be afraid of me. There are times when I am afraid of me. The next time I might well kill you."

"I'm willing to chance that."

"I am not. I want you to leave."

She turned away and shortly heard the door close.

"You have time for a nap," Fay suggested as Kissre remained in the same position. "I'll have your clothing ready and wake you in time to prepare you for the banquet. They do not expect you as security, but as part of the envoy."

"Fay, do you have Talent brothers or sisters?" Kissre asked.

"Yes, ma'am."

"Do you get along with them?

"They are only minor Empaths, ma'am, and our mother didn't play favorites."

Kissre looked at her maid. "Is that commonly known?"

"Yes, ma'am. Little privacy is left to either Captain Tyna or you. All Sidih knows your story."

"And drew sides?"

"I'll wake you in a candlemark to get ready."

"It's not Captain Tyna's fault, Fay. It's mine."

~ * ~

Eldin rode, following Uilleam to a place the young man liked to hunt. Uilleam swore it was secluded, and for once, he was right.

Since swearing to his Aristo, Eldin had run interference on many of those who tormented Uilleam. Along with Uilleam, he was now a laughingstock. Clement sought to punish him through humiliation.

What Clement didn't realize and would never believe was that Eldin now embraced his given task.

"See?" Uilleam's eyes lit up as he stopped in a small glade. "No one comes here—too far to walk, too close for good hunting. Except rabbits. Good rabbit hunting."

"Is this where you shoot all your rabbits?" Eldin asked.

"Yes. Best spot, lots of rabbits." Uilleam gave him a wide-eyed smile. "My catches make King Clement laugh."

"Indeed, they do. Many know how well you catch rabbits."

"They laugh, too."

"Yes, but none can deny you are very good with your bow. Are you ready to start?"

"You're going to teach me here?"

"Yes, Uilleam, I am. Then no one will wonder about what we do. We will catch a few rabbits, and all is explained."

"Another secret?"

Something in the voice made Eldin look up from his inspection of the ground. Uilleam's guileless face looked at him with expectation. "Yes, another secret, another game. Take off your jerkin." Eldin pulling the cover back from his scabbard, withdrew the two wooden swords. He handed one to Uilleam.

"Show me what you have learned."

A very skilled former Royal Guardsman in Kaereya, Eldin critically watched Uilleam's moves. The boy possessed a natural athletic grace. Eldin corrected Uilleam's grip and his stance, along with the first stroke. "Show me the basic strokes you have learned."

Uilleam wasn't as far behind as he thought. In the next candlemark he drilled and re-drilled the boy on the basics until Uilleam whined he knew those moves.

"No, you don't." With one stroke he disarmed his opponent, whose surprise changed to awe. "You know the basic moves, but they are not done without thought. We will practice them until they are. I think I'll train you in hand-to-hand combat, too. You have the agility. Let's go now and catch a couple rabbits to explain our absence from court."

As they dismounted in the palace courtyard, Uilleam showed his rabbits to the grooms with delight. Smiling, Eldin took the rabbits from Uilleam and gave them to a groom. "See these get to the kitchen."

"But Eldin, I always take them."

"An Aristo always behaves in a courtly fashion, Uilleam. He does not run to the kitchen with rabbits."

"I did bad?" The brows over the brown eyes hooked with confusion.

"No. Not at all, but I told you I would teach you, did I not?"

"Can I go and tell Paddy how many rabbits I shot?"

"Yes. Why don't you do that?" Eldin watched as Uilleam turned with a laugh and ran away. Snickers came from the grooms, which he ignored. Returning to Uilleam's rooms, Eldin noticed King Clement, who walked with his cortege of war advisors and his witch. He stepped back and bowed his head as the king passed. The king's fine leather shoes stopped within his view.

"Sir Innes."

"Your Highness." Eldin did not look at Clement.

"I hear you were out hunting today with Aristo Leavold. How many rabbits did he catch?" Someone laughed.

"Five. You asked me, Your Highness, to make sure Aristo Leavold kept out of trouble."

"Yes. It is too bad you can't keep the younger brother in line. Unfortunately, he is not as simple as our Uilleam."

Eldin's skin prickled. "I had not heard, Your Highness, that Payden caused any trouble."

"Trouble comes in many forms, Sir Innes, but particularly with skill in arms."

"Yes, Your Highness."

Without another word, the king left.

Uilleam arrived at their rooms first. Payden usually stayed away as long as possible, so Eldin waited. The younger brother came in long after dark, emitting the strong scent of ale.

"What, waiting up?" Payden was not as tall as Uilleam, but well made. His looks were fair but not handsome, and the constant pout of his lips gave him a surly, sulking expression.

Uilleam had refused to sleep while Eldin remained awake. "Eldin wants to talk to you."

"Shut up, fool."

"That's no way to talk to Aristo Uilleam."

"Aristo Uilleam?" Payden laughed. "Aristo of nothing."

"It doesn't matter how he talks to me. I think it's funny."

"I don't," Eldin said. He felt for the boy, and perhaps Paden's constant awareness of his fall from power and glory made him bitter, but it gave him no right to mock his brother.

"So? You've no right to admonish me."

"No, I don't. But I am your brother's man, and it would be remiss of me not to warn you."

"My brother's man?" Payden laughed. "A nanny, you mean."

Eldin swallowed the insult. "This is important, Payden. I would not interfere otherwise." He stopped, unsure. "Listen, please."

Payden flopped into a chair, scowling. "All right, get it over. I want to sleep."

"Payden, I am going to urge you to not excel in your arms practice. I know how much it means to you. I know your talent."

"What? Are you crazy? How else can I improve my family's lot?" He jumped from his chair.

"You should listen to Eldin, Payden," Uilleam said, his face very serious. "He is a good man."

"Shut up! I don't have to listen to you or him! You both make my life miserable. I will not remain a joke all my life."

Eldin grabbed him by the arm as he headed for the door. The boy tried to break free, but Eldin, though shorter and more slender, was stronger. "The king notices Payden. Think! He cannot afford to have a Leavold rising among the ranks! You know how good you are, many know. Let that be enough. Your life may depend upon it. Don't bring notice to yourself!"

Payden made a scoffing noise, and his face turned threatening. "Let go!" He shook his arm from Eldin's hold. "How would you know how good I am? You're a foreigner and a traitor at that!" He left, slamming the door behind him.

"Is Payden in trouble?" Uilleam asked.

Eldin released his breath. "I hope not, Uilleam."

In the days that followed, Eldin tried to keep track of Payden. It wasn't too hard. The boy was always practicing or with a group of boys his age. He reflected on the calamitous position in which he found himself. Daily he took Uilleam into the woods for practice but began taking precautions that no one followed them.

~ * ~

"You looked beautiful last night, like a fine Aristo lady."

Kissre parried Quillon's thrusting advance and broke his guard long enough to deliver a loud blow deflected by his buckler. He grinned in his irritating manner. Their swords crossed as he renewed his attack. His power drove her back, and her buckler arm absorbed the violence of his attack. When he bore down on her like this, his advantage in weight and height told all. A dozen or so men stood watching, some from the envoy's escort and some from Cygna's foot soldiers. Somehow their morning matches had become cheap entertainment, an unwelcome audience to her daily trouncing.

"That is what, the fourth time you have acted the duke's escort? Romantic rumors will start in Kaereya."

She refused to give in to the taunting but focused on the job at hand. "Even dressed as an Aristo lady, I give the duke protection." With a heave of her buckler, she threw off his blade and made two quick thrusts at Quillon's chest. Each easily parried, but he moved backward to accomplish it, a small achievement.

A quick twist and a thrust from Quillon, and she not only lost her sword but also had to rub feeling back into her stinging wrist.

"Poor showing, Aibhe Master."

"Aibhe Masters come in different levels, like Zekarac Knights. Your level is higher than mine in sword work. I'm better with a bow." Her words broke with her gasps of breath, knowing she had not practiced Aibhe patterns in some time. She bent down and picked up her sword.

"Excuses? That is exactly your problem. Maybe I should fight your sister, Aibhe Master."

He had harped about Tyna...Captain Pierce...for days. Anger surged through her in a vicious but ill-planned attack. A foot pulled her legs out from under her, and she landed on her back with a practice sword at her throat pressing hard enough to bruise. Quillon's grinning face finished her humiliation.

"You should know better, Kissre, then to let anger guide your attack. But then, I've heard that you can't control anger and fear it will control you. What? Do your Aibhe practices fail you? I thought they taught you to fight through to calm?" The sword removed from her neck, and Quillon walked away.

If she could have found the strength, she'd have knifed him in the back. Weaponless, in Aibhe hand-to-hand, she could defeat him. Maybe. Knew with Aibhe weapons, she could destroy him. Just not with a heavy Kaereyan sword. She managed to rise to her elbows and throw a particularly nasty Kennetsure epithet at his back.

He only turned and smiled. "Tomorrow, with steel."

It was a promise; it meant wearing heavy chainmail. She groaned and threw her arms over her face. It was true. Her mental focus had evaporated. While not of Quillon's caliber, she should show better than she had. After a minute, she sighed and lowered her arms.

Sergeant Tomel stood above her. He offered a helping hand. Grasping it, she push-pulled herself to her feet. Tomel patted her on the back and left without a word. She looked at the gathered crowd. Others were already leaving, including Oran and several other platoon members who nodded a greeting before they left. Then she saw Zeba, standing small and shivering, her hands clasped together for warmth in the cold, early morning air. Her maid stood with her looking worried. Catching her breath, Kissre walked over to the tiny woman.

"So interesting, I had no idea!" Zeba said with a beaming smile, her blue eyes sparkling in delight. "So noisy. Is he of Kaereya's southern province? A Kennetsurean?"

"Quillon? Yes. It is nice to see you again, Zeba. What brings you out so early?" Looking at Zeba's blue hands, Kissre clasped them in hers. They were cold against her exercise-heated hands. "You should have dressed warmer. This early in the morning, it is cold."

"I'd heard about this and had to come and see. So much fury! So exciting."

"You noted, of course, I was thoroughly trounced."

"Well, that's why you are having him train you, isn't it? What good would you beating him be? This Quillon, could you introduce me, maybe tomorrow?"

"To what purpose?"

The blue eyes turned guileless and piercing at the same time. "You are a very suspicious woman, Kissre Pierce. For the same reason I met you, stories! Tales of Kennetsure! I want to hear what he knows. Go get yourself cleaned up. I know your duty starts soon."

Half laughing, she dropped Zeba's hands and dragged her sore body to her room, where Fay waited with a hot bath. A candlemark later, she assumed her position behind Aurelias. Today the talk commenced on how to put the two diverse armies together and if it were even possible. Tactics were brought up, who should be in command, and other problems, both strategic and organizational. She listened to Aristo Aurelias present Kaereya's position, all based on the information she had given him.

Captain Tyna presented Cygna's position and arguments against the Kaereyan stance. It was as if she argued with Tyna through an intermediary. She'd landed in purgatory.

~ * ~

The manservant showed Zeba into a large room to wait. Even retired, half-mad Oracles were accorded a great deal of respect. She and her maid took a seat and waited. Zeba inspected the room as she did so.

The room, strewn with beautiful objects, remained warm and cozy. Then she remembered—Tyna had been an itinerant merchant of artifacts, antiquities, and luxuries. One learned amazing things listening to the Maze or nulls if one were wise enough to listen. Zeba had known several city merchants with whom she used to trade when much younger. Now, on her infrequent jaunts to the shopping district, she purchased from their grandchildren. The young were less apt to gossip with an old lady. Luckily, a lifetime of well-developed eavesdropping skills helped her.

Dovel entered the room behind Kedriq and a very pregnant Tyna. "Dovel, you're here! You're back from Guerestu! What a surprise! Now you can introduce me." She turned to Tyna. "I'm Zeba. I've come without invitation or appointment."

"Tyna, my mentor, the Oracle Zeba, whom I've mentioned." Dovel's dry-toasted tones nearly made Zeba giggle.

"I know who you are, Oracle Zeba. Please, make yourself comfortable. I thank you for your service to Kissre."

The girl didn't turn a hair at Zeba's outright inspection. Where Kissre looked strong and bold, even defiant, her sister looked deliberate, delicate, and sharp. While Kissre showed precise military order with a flamboyant air, Tyna wore conservative dress with nonchalant certitude. Tyna exemplified fashion in her choice and control. Even her hair was more exact in tone. Naomi, while beautiful, had looked conflicted, moody, and reticent. Both girls bore her looks without her visceral moods.

"You look like your sister. And your mother."

"You knew my mother?"

"Years and years ago, before she left Cygna."

Refreshment came, an unexpected pleasure. "I don't mind if I do," Zeba told the servant, picking up a delicate tiny cake. A cup of tea was placed on the table next to her chair. "Is this tea? Such a rarity! You have a beautiful room, Captain Tyna. It is so kind of you to see me, too. Kissre, I must tell you, was not a service but my pleasure. She knows so many stories. I think we started a friendship. It seems to be something she is not very good at."

"Zeba, why are you here?" Dovel asked.

She could feel his agitation, a circumstance that surprised her. Dovel rarely gave off any emotion. Giving him the glare he deserved for such rudeness, she spoke to Tyna. "The Adept Council appointed me to facilitate reconciliation. Did Dovel tell you this? They felt Kissre's visit had an unfortunate effect on you." At Tyna's nod, Zeba smiled. "Of course, there is more. Besides my desire to help you and Kissre, I admit to curiosity and to the desire to reestablish an old acquaintanceship with Dovel and Kedriq."

"Yes, Dovel told me. I can't say you've been spectacularly successful in your appointed service."

"No, I haven't." Zeba took a sip from her cup. "Kissre can be purposefully vague, besides possessing stubbornness the size of Godhed Peak. She left before I could talk to you, and there can be no reconciliation without understanding on both sides. Since her return, well, she has been very elusive. Which is why I am visiting you." She smiled at Dovel, recognizing his half-smile of sardonic amusement. "Have you talked with her since her return?"

Tyna sighed. "I finally trapped her. She talked at me, but it did no good. Her anger is still so great she is afraid to come near me. She said she was afraid she might harm me."

Zeba felt Kedriq's apprehension at Tyna's words. *The girl had trouble controlling her inner shields. No wonder everyone bonded to her felt agitated and apprehensive.* Zeba looked at Kedriq. "You don't need to fear Kissre."

"Kissre has an ungovernable temper and is trained in violence. That makes her dangerous," Kedriq said in a belligerent voice.

"Ungovernable temper?" Zeba said, arching her eyebrows to convey her astonishment. "Kedriq, don't be ridiculous. Kissre has the tightest leashed temper of anyone I know."

"Exactly! Even she fears losing it. You don't know how badly she scared Tyna."

"A sibling argument, Kedriq. You and Larig haven't been together enough to have them. Larig is a dangerous Adept. Are you afraid of him or his temper?"

"Larig has no temper. Even if he did, he would never harm me."

Zeba sighed, exaggerating her frustration. "Naomi was at least right in her belief siblings should be raised together, with their parents. Kedriq, you do not know your brother at all! Larig owns a vile temper and hates what he does. He constantly worries about losing control and harming someone. What's more, he has." Zeba smiled at Kedriq's start. "I know a Probe who, in his age, visits where he shouldn't."

"Naomi caused all this," Tyna said, drawing Zeba's attention.

"Do you hate your mother?"

"No. I don't understand her. I'm angry with what she did, humiliated at her perversity, but I can't hate her."

"Did Kissre try to harm you?"

"I've explained over and over." Tyna arduously pushed herself from her seat. She waved her arms in the air with her frustration. "She hardly raised her voice. I was the one screaming."

Zeba raised her eyebrows. Tyna was near screaming now.

"It was her anger. It was...palpable." Her voice dropped. "I deserved it. I was angry at her reluctance to visit, mad that she didn't come sooner, jealous of her freedom, embarrassed at her appearance, angry at her continued rejection of Mama, and I said terrible things. I couldn't understand why she wouldn't talk about our mother, didn't mourn her. She even asked me to stop." Tyna rubbed her back as if in pain. "Naomi was sarcastic and petty in temper and constantly nagged, especially Kissre. I had all the temper tantrums. I don't remember Kissre ever getting angry. That's what scared me. I thought her so different."

"Did you believe her?"

"I don't know." She rolled her head to look at the ceiling. "Yes," she said, "I do. At first, I thought she must have misunderstood. That she had to be mistaken. I still can't believe my mother would do such a thing." When Tyna looked at Zeba, tears glistened on her face. "She cannot forgive me."

"Right now, Kissre is unyielding." Zeba took another cake from the tray on the table next to her. "Plus, she is very sensitive about people judging her, especially Talents. She was looking for trouble and found it." As Tyna's face crumbled in emotion, Zeba looked at Kedriq. "My mention of your brother is not without a purpose, for Kissre and Larig are very alike."

"In what way?" Kedriq asked, snorting in disbelief.

"Apply what you know of your brother to your wife's sister."

"Any words of wisdom for me?" Tyna asked.

"She cannot forgive your mother. Rightly so," Zeba said. "Poor Naomi. She took to heart all her Kernite teachings and kept all her Cygnese prejudices. You will have to wait. To recover your sister needs in part the patience to let her find her way to you."

Tyna snorted. "You don't know Kissre, then. That will never happen, for she won't even look for a way."

"I think I know her very well. She and I talked while she was ill. I came to quite like the young woman, and I wish to help her despite her many flaws." Zeba turned to Dovel, who sat studying the floor. He looked up at her mental poke.

"I've received much the same message as Tyna. We will be friends, nothing more."

"I could shake her until she relents." Tyna turned to pace the room. "If I could touch her mind, I'd wring her stupid stubbornness from it." She stopped. Her hand massaged her back. "Stop that, Dovel. I know how you'd like to end her stubbornness. I may be as big as her stupid horse, but I still...besides you are affecting Kedriq, and that's not fair."

Unrepentant, Dovel laughed. "Sorry, I ignored where my thoughts took me. And what you did to everybody was fair? If both of you suffer half the lust you inflicted, my transgression would only be called justified."

"I've developed inner shields, and at least she talks to you." She gave him a pointed look. "I've also learned how to detect shields."

"So you're reading me?" He sighed. "She hasn't talked to me, not in the last month."

"Well, she is tied up all day with her duty, and most evenings, too," Tyna said. "When she first came, she asked me to take her to see a play. Last night I found out she loves the theater. It was so strange. I thought I knew all about her. Last night, she looked like an elegant stranger. Someone I'd never met. Through Dovel, I've learned she loves music and is an accomplished vocalist. What a judgmental fool I've become. I see her every day, but it's like I don't exist for her."

"Her free time, like yours, is limited, plus she works out in the morning and has her animals to take care of," Zeba said, "but she notices you."

"She replaced me with a dog and a horse." Tyna wiped tears from her eyes.

"Yes she did. Luckily, the heart learns to accept many diverse individuals as family."

"You said she works out?" Tyna questioned.

"Combat practice with Quillon, Aristo Aurelias' knight," Dovel answered.

"It is, I guess, a null secret," Zeba said. "Most Talents are not interested in the comings and goings of a barbarian, especially one who confounds them so. Many of platoon leaders watch. You should go see for yourself. It is quite exciting."

"With Quillon? But he's a Knight of the Zekarac Order. One mistake and he could kill her!" Worry threaded Tyna's petulant voice.

"Zekarac Order?" Kedriq asked, looking interested.

"In Kaereya's southern province of Kennetsure, the Zekarac Order is the highest level a soldier can reach. They are reputedly taught superior ethics along with physical training and weapon skills. It's a very prestigious rank." Tyna sat easing into the chair with difficulty.

"Holy One, I hope this baby comes soon."

"You've only two more months," Kedriq reminded her.

"Two too many." She sat in silence a moment and looked at Zeba with interest. "How does she do?"

Dovel answered. "I've heard very well, even though she always loses. She can't match him for height, reach, or strength, but he doesn't hold back. Those who watch wouldn't go up against him even to spar. Most wouldn't challenge her, and some of them are reputed fine fighters. For a woman, the lower ranks hold her in high esteem."

"Why wouldn't they?" Tyna asked, her voice rising. "Proving Cygna's restriction against woman fighting is ridiculous."

"It is not," Kedriq said. "They become a liability on the field. Even your sister can't match her trainer and never will."

Zeba saw Dovel's cringe at the look and thought Tyna blasted at her mate.

"I watched her this morning," Zeba said. "It was a rather cold morning. Never have I witnessed a practice, let alone a battle. I'm afraid I would be too terrified to be of use."

"I don't want to give up," Tyna said. "How can we make her change her mind? Do you have any suggestions?"

"Ask Dovel."

At her look, Dovel said. "Water, with persistence, erodes rock."

Humor entered Zeba's thoughts. "Well, Kissre certainly puts a new definition on stubborn, but she is not rock."

"And have you any insights into this situation?" Dovel asked.

Zeba turned sober eyes to him. "I've seen many things, most of them unpleasant. Which is the right outcome, I can't say. Only to survive, Kissre will need help. Unfortunately, she must ask for it."

Dovel escorted Zeba and her maid back to the Assembly House. It was a long walk, but she wasn't tired.

"Are you sure you can do this?"

"I made it to Tyna's didn't I?" Zeba took several steps. "I am much improved." Her maid trailed them, Zeba having refused her arm for Dovel's.

"No one has said anything?"

"Only Sina," Zeba smiled at her maid. "And she'll say nothing. Everyone else, well, they see what they expect to see, what they are accustomed to seeing. If anyone says anything, it is how nice I look. Nice, ha. What an obsequious word. Although it is nice to walk again. I hadn't realized how much I missed it. Do you know, I think I couldn't walk because I didn't walk? You have not told Tyna." And at his expression, "Why not?"

"Because Kissre would see it as a betrayal. I told her I'd not tell anyone what I learn from her mind."

"You suspect more than what you learned from her mind."

He looked at Zeba from under his brows. "It would be a betrayal."

"To tell Tyna?"

His eyes searched the storefronts they passed, not seeing anything. She felt the wisps of his distraction. He hunted for something unavailable in Sidih. Zeba noted that for gray eyes, his were most intense. He spoke rather than mentally relay his response.

"Tyna must come to understand Kissre by herself."

"I'm glad we are in agreement on that."

As they neared the Assembly House, Zeba asked to sit down on one of the benches and sent her maid ahead. "Suspicions have been raised by Marshal Ranor. Don't look so surprised at my information. I have a few friends who are very well informed. Others have also reported strange occurrences, and now they have Tomel's testing results. He has moved to the level of Receiver. A near-null to that level! I understand the increase has not changed back. Neither has yours, nor mine. Not speaking of what you suspect won't change things."

She continued when he didn't answer. "Orrthu has suggested Kissre be tested. Vitann made a request, but the Duke of Lambere refused, on the principle it would be inappropriate contact for part of the envoy's staff. They may call me, or you, or Healer Bujyea. Don't think it, Dovel, and don't ask. I will tell the truth." He frowned at her, then looked away. She asked, "What do you want for Kissre?"

Dovel looked off into space for so long Zeba didn't think he would answer. "Choice. I want her to be able to choose."

Zeba patted his knee and smiled. "Few have that, especially in Cygna. We've an uphill climb and I've seen things...I worry for the future, Dovel. I begin to fear it."

Ten

It was late afternoon before Dovel found Kissre. From Carillon's back she pretended not to notice the attention that followed her. Children ran along yelling Fudge's name. The dog lope-walked next to the mare. He waved to gain her attention. Catching sight of him, she guided Carillon to the street side and stopped next to him. Fudge sat panting, but close enough for Dovel to run a hand over his head.

"They keep you busy. I thought you might have run away."

"It's been hard to find time to exercise Carillon and Fudge. They both get a little wild without exercise to calm them."

"You have time to share an ale with a friend?"

"What would I do with Fudge?"

Dovel gave the dog a couple friendly thumps. "Bring him with us."

"They won't…"

"…Of course they will. Come on, I'm buying." He waved to a young boy and flipped a coin. The lad quickly caught it. He asked to have Carillon watched.

Kissre seemed to relax as Fudge received a bigger welcome than either she or Dovel. "Has he eaten, Colonel Pierce? Can we give him something?" Fudge looked at Kissre with such a look of expectation, Dovel was sure he understood.

"If it's no trouble." A large bowl of water had already appeared. Every hand that went by on the way to the kitchen or tap patted the tangled fur back. Kissre spoke her hope that they washed well before serving.

Kissre accepted her tankard of ale, and they pulled benches out from one of the long tables. "Holy One!" she said. "They've given him a shank bone!"

Dovel twisted his head to look. "With meat, too."

"At least it is roasted."

He grinned, but Kissre still looked dismayed. "How is your training going?" he asked.

She groaned. "How'd you know about that? Never mind. Your maze, I expect."

"No, it has not been mentioned there. Actually it seems to be a null secret, except for Zeba, of course."

"And how did she know?"

He shrugged. "She's an Oracle, but it seems one who has cultivated many unlikely friendships. So?"

A grimace crossed her face. "I've been yelled at, bawled out, trounced on, beaten up, pounded down, and mashed in. In addition, I've been humiliated and called every despicable name known to man. Or woman."

"That good?"

"Shut up. I ache too bad to take any interest in quarreling. Even with you."

He laughed at her. "You're moving better."

"No choice." She smiled and waited. Her glance slid sideways while he sipped ale, and she commanded, "Fudge, here." Fudge came, carrying the bone. He dropped it at her feet. His tongue licked and re-licked his muzzle as he sat. With a huge yawn, he placed his head on the table. At a hand signal from Kissre, he groaned but lay down and renewed his interest in his bone.

Dovel spoke first. "No one seems to realize the reason they like him so much is because he is so well trained. That and his raw entertainment value."

"Thank you. He has a great personality but would be a menace without obedience."

He studied his ale. "As disciplined as his mistress." His gaze rose to hers. "I asked you before to teach me how you track what you look for when you go out on reconnaissance. I'm still hoping you might."

"Why?"

"So I can help my own platoons. So I can understand. You see things we can't or have forgotten how to observe."

"I don't think Marshal Ranor wants you placed in any danger."

"It's not dangerous in the countryside around Sidih."

She remained silent and finished her ale. Taking the hint, Dovel talked of Zeba, talked of musicians playing in Sidih, and talked of the inconsequential. Talked through another round of ale.

Fudge rose as the third round appeared. Kissre pulled out coins and paid the server. "My round, I think." The owner patted Fudge's head and pulled two biscuits out of his pocket.

"You spoil him," Kissre said.

"It is a pleasure, ma'am. It will bring me business. Everyone knows of Fudge and the Great Howling." He smiled and walked away.

Kissre took a long drink, and Dovel did the same. Putting her tankard down, she answered. "Yes."

He smiled.

"I have to get back." She rose as she spoke.

"I know. Let me know when and where. I'll be there. Thank you."

"What are friends for?" With a snap of her fingers, Fudge was at her heel, and they were both out the door.

~ * ~

"Tyna had a little boy." They stood at the edge of a wood where bushes and brambles thrived in the bit of extra light. He didn't need to feel her emotions. Over the months he had come to know Kissre very well.

163

"When?"

"Night before last."

Kissre didn't look at Dovel. "That's three sennight early."

"They are both fine." He expected he startled her. Otherwise, he doubted she would have made a comment.

"Mostly this is just a case of observation," Kissre said, "see the broken twigs? The way the grass is separated?"

"Hunters' tricks," he said, abiding by the change in subject.

"Exactly, but more. You've hunted?"

"Yes, long ago. Up in the hills around my home. Not since becoming a squad captain."

"Then you're halfway there. Can you always feel where I am?"

It was so casual. Her gaze wouldn't rise from her inspection of the tattoo on her wrist. He swallowed and looked away before speaking.

"Not when distance separates us, or when you are concentrating very hard, or when I am." He lowered himself to the ground and lay back with his hands under his head. The clouds today were very white and puffy, the sun hot. "Sometimes you just disappear, I'm not sure why, but maybe when you do your exercises. Most of the time, you're a shadow in my awareness, but that's all. When I think of you, I usually know where you are. If you are very close, I can feel your emotions. That's all, Kissre."

"You're a Probe."

Her implication disgusted him. "I don't enter your mind, I don't try to invade your privacy, and I don't try to manipulate you in any way. Besides, I doubt any Probe, including me, could enter your mind."

"You know how I feel right now?"

"No. Sometimes you are so self-contained nothing escapes."

"Then why explain so much?"

"I don't need to read your mind to know what you feel."

"That predictable?" She looked at him and grinned. "Thank you for telling me. Is there anyone else who can?"

"No. They can't even sense your mind to achieve recognition." He waited, watching the clouds floating by overhead, soaking up the sun's warmth between the coolness of the clouds' shadows. "Do you know how squads are trained? How mental bonds are made? Did Naomi ever tell you?"

"No. She just said the witches stole children. When I cried, she said they wouldn't want me, only Ty. Captain Pierce," she corrected herself.

He slid his gaze toward her. He knew she used the title as a wall, but she stood looking out over the mountainous land. "There are three methods. The hardest and the longest way is to establish a bond through training together."

"Like you do with your squad."

"Yes. How did you know?"

"Jycel mentioned it." She sat down next to him. "On the way to Guerestu. While I was teaching Cevoka Aibhe House exercises." She shrugged at his look. "We started moving in unison, and he said it was as boring as watching your squad practice." She swallowed a laugh. "Then he joined us."

"Other rituals like sharing meals, daily tasks, sports, games, or other entertainment, help establish a bond. The next way is to use drugs. It is most often used on children, especially if trainers run into resistance or blocks. If used too much, there are side effects. Some few never go through puberty. They are not pleasant to experience. It's basically raping the mind."

"Is that why so many squad members are so immature?"

He ignored her. "The last way is physical touch—sexual contact."

"Oh."

"Exactly."

"But you said I'm void."

"You are. That's why you can't feel me."

It was very quiet. Her mind was closed to him, but he didn't try to touch it.

"You've had sex with other nulls."

"If I tried, I could have felt their thoughts. I chose null partners because any minuscule Talent they possessed wouldn't lead to a bond formation."

"But not me?"

"You're touch void, not null."

She gave a skeptical half-laugh.

"It's true, Kiss. Ninety-nine percent of people have some measure of Touch Talent. It allows their discovery and training. You are completely void of Touch, but you must have some Earth Talent, or I couldn't follow you, couldn't sense you. Through that Talent, at some level, we've bonded." His eyes flicked to her face in the silence and remained caught at her pensive expression. She caught his regard, and her expression changed.

"You've been the hunter, now you must become the prey. Use your senses. Listen to what happens around you."

Just like Kissre. Change the subject. Drop the unwanted, the unacceptable into a pit and cover it. Dovel wielded his Earth Talent and floated over the ground, seeing its contours, the rocky slopes and slopes of scree, the growing fields, the coolness of the rivers, and the place where he lay. Kissre was there, at least her aura was apparent to his Talent. He felt time go by and felt so free, so at peace. There was no one around except the mind he wanted to touch but couldn't feel. Warm fingers touched the back of his hand, "Thank you for telling me."

He screamed as he fell. From floating above a green and blue world, he found himself suddenly dropped into the ground. Suffused in the earth's muted umbers, grays, rusts, and ochers, he fell deep through soil levels with increasing speed. His body sank through rock layers, water, and air pockets. Agonizing pressure sensitized every nerve ending. Each molecule, mineral, water, or air, bared itself to him as it drifted through his body, left its scent, and took part of him with it. It was impossible to stop. He felt the weight of the tons of rock and soil burying him. Heat built up around him and his body burned while pressure crushed him. It stopped his breath. Sensation beat upon sensation, overpowering his consciousness of self. His body dissolved. Skin, muscle, organ, and bone, atom-by-atom, dispersed within this underground universe. Somewhere within him, a spark of desperate desire flared.

Heat, energy, he could use that. Deftly he chained the energy and grounded himself, scraped and yanked his body back together, and barricaded his awareness. It was unbearable. He was suffocating, burning. He threw his Probe Talent out and searched and found a presence, wild and terrified. Tying himself to it, he pulled upward, up to Kissre.

Sudden cold wetness drenched him.

"Dovel!"

Opening his eyes, he looked at Kissre. She held a canteen above him. He took a deep breath.

"Sorry." Still stunned, he tried to sit. It was a struggle. When Kissre tried to help him, he flinched and warded her hand from his nettled skin.

She stopped, stunned. "What's the matter? Are you ill?"

"What happened?"

"You just had a spell or something. You yelled, then..." her hand waved in a helpless circle, "...you just fell silent and wouldn't respond. I was afraid to leave you. You want me to bring you a healer?"

"No. I'm fine." A spell taking him beyond his Talent's capacity, it made him shake, and his skin prickled in reaction. Why? He had been using his talent at Kissre's touch. *Kissre's touch.* An image of Ulyss entered his mind, and he swore. *It wasn't possible. Not that.*

"Like hell you are." Her worried face made him react as she moved.

He grabbed her leather-covered arm. "Settle down, I'm fine. My Talent got away from me for a minute, that's all."

She sat and looked out over the landscape, frowning.

"Kissre?" She looked at him not understanding.

"It might be better if you didn't touch any Adept. I was using my Talent when you touched me."

"And that drives an Adept crazy?"

"Sometimes...if you can't tell when Talent's in use, you shouldn't touch anyone. It's a disturbance."

"Anyone's touch, or my touch in particular?"

"Your touch," he spoke without thinking. With relief he felt her move away from him. *Holy One, don't let her touch anyone.* And how was he to prevent that? His breathing slowed, and his body felt chilled in the heavy silence. Who was safe to ask for advice?

He looked at Kissre's composed face. White lines edged her taut lips. Somehow, she had disappeared into herself and he cursed himself when she would not look at him.

"Use your senses. Sound, look, even scent, can tell you what is going on around you. That's how prey escape—they find where the hunter comes from and go in another direction." Her voice remained calm and impersonal.

He listened to her instruction. When he finally caught a glimpse of her shuttered eyes, he knew the depth of her hurt. Maybe the pit held too much to take more. What she hid behind the haunting green screens of her eyes alarmed him, but there was nothing he could do.

~ * ~

During the next month, Kissre dutifully kept her position by the door just inside the negotiation room. If anyone found her eccentricity of wearing dress gloves with her uniform strange, they didn't mention it.

It was impossible not to listen, and a hidden pride entered her at Tyna's participation. Tyna sometimes acted as a mediator between Cygnese conservatism and Kaereyan assertiveness. Sometimes she pressed for concessions from the Kaereyan delegation. Often she protected Cygna, the Talent squads, or the platoon men. Her thoughts were logical and well presented.

She had an intense desire to see Tyna's baby, going so far as to buy a gift. It sat like a sore in her room until she placed it in a saddlebag; even then, it itched like an old scab. She wanted free from this duty but wouldn't ask. Wanted desperately to return to Kaereya and her life before this visit.

If Tyna's eyes occasionally strayed in Kissre's direction, Kissre ignored her. She also didn't return Tyna's habitual greeting upon entering and leaving the room. Kissre gave reluctant responses to her frequent requests for information. His Grace, Aristo Aurelias had opened that door. On many occasions he had turned to his security officer and asked Colonel Kissre pertinent questions about military tactics and her experiences with Pertelon, Cygnese, and Kaereyan armies. Since then, Tyna did likewise.

"Kissre," she'd say in a polished, professional voice. "How do Pertelon troops act in such a situation?" Or worse. "Kiss, do you know…"

Someone's subdued snigger often accompanied the question. That everyone knew the situation between them, and watched the by-play during the long, often boring candlemarks, made Kissre cringe. That she invariably addressed her antagonist as 'Captain Pierce,' brought more titters and often a frown from Aristo Aurelias.

"Well, Kissre," Aurelias said while she walked with him back to his apartments after the military agreement was finally finished, "I think we've accomplished good work here. Just the beginning, of course. Is Quillon still keeping you busy in the mornings?"

"Yes, Your Grace."

"These interminable meetings have tied me up too much." He stretched his shoulders as if wringing them of trouble. "Once the agreement is signed, probably within the next sennight, I will be returning to Kaereyan with a small contingent. Quillon will be left in command here, and you will remain to handle security. I've heard there has been civil unrest, and not all agree with this alliance, so will not leave even a temporary Embassy unsecured."

"I will arrange for your trip." Kissre opened the door to his apartment, too upset with her continuance in Cygna to reply further.

At his nod, she turned and waited for Quillon to arrive for duty.

Eight days later, Aurelias left for Kaereya.

~ * ~

Kissre waited and watched, gently rubbing Fudge's head while Quillon drilled Kaereyan's Aristos in weapons' practice. In her other hand she held Carillon's reins. Finished with her own fight drill, she waited with her horse, dressed for their impending combat practice.

Aristo Emory Constantine, along with a few other showy Aristos, currently labored hard, sparring in wasted effort, listening but not hearing Quillon's instruction. A few of the Kaereyan soldiers stood watching, Quillon having already exhausted them.

Since he'd sparred with her long before these men assembled, Kissre stood excused from further public humiliation. Now she waited to endure a session on horseback. Quillon wanted to make sure she and Carillon worked together. Shortly after Aurelias' departure, Quillon requested that she teach him the hand-to-hand methods of the Aibhe. The request took her by surprise and still stunned her. After morning sessions, they now went through one of the prescribed movement routines of calm focus, directed focus, or inner and outer focus. They finished with hand-to-hand which Quillon excelled at, but she at least won sometimes.

The Aristos' session ended, and the reputation-plagued Aristo Emory came to stand next to her. Kissre hid her distaste. She knew his story, how he had left his cousin, the king, besieged by attackers. Since it had ended with Emory's brother's death, King Warrick had forgiven him, but Emory did not shine at court. His presence as part of the envoy's mission showed his position. With the near-certain advent of war, and Aurelias' departure with the treaty papers to Kaereya, redemptive possibilities loomed for the young man.

"You've received a gift of incredible value," Aristo Emory said, inspecting Carillon. He was disheveled, his red hair dust-coated. He panted from his exertions.

Kissre agreed, unsure whether his voice held envy or accusation.

"Do you plan on returning to Kaereya? I heard this was your homeland."

"Kaereya is my home now."

"With such patronage, you must feel your future assured."

"My future has always been in my hands," Kissre said. The Aristo smirked at her in disbelief, but Kissre was saved from answering.

Quillon walked over, not visibly tired from his daily routine. Brusquely he told Kissre to mount up while his own horse was led forward. After a sennight of sessions, word spread, and as Kissre slipped her foot into the stirrup, it seemed the number watching doubled. For the next candlemark she would forget their presence as Quillon drilled her in close contact weapons.

Kissre's pleasure in Carillon grew. Her mount held steady even through the clang of clashing weapons flailing over her head and the close contact of the opposing mount. Today, for once, Kissre felt a rhythm to her movements. Her body moved strong and free.

She stopped concentrating on mechanics and let her skill and instinct take over her movement. Time slowed, and she knew Quillon's moves before he executed them. An opportunity arose, and she answered. Her right leg urged Carillon to push into Quillon's mount. As Quillon's blade swung, she deflected it with her buckler, grunting with the strength needed to hold her arm in place. More leg pressure moved Carillon into his horse; Kissre rose to stand in her stirrups, caught the edge of his buckler with hers, jerked it forward, and thrust her blade down on his sword arm. Carillon kept moving, pushing now with her powerful haunches, forcing Quillon's mount back. The other animal stumbled and went down.

Kissre immediately disengaged, backing Carillon away. She saw Quillon fall with his mount. Sheathing her sword, she reached over and grabbed the other horse's reins under the jaw as the animal rose. Quillon rose from the ground. He dusted himself off and rubbed his arm where the wooden blade had hit it.

"Are you all right?"

Quillon nodded, showing his exhaustion. "You did not follow through."

"This is practice. I'm not trying to kill you. If my blade were real, you'd have no arm."

"Well, score to you for being the first to unhorse his opponent. It was a fair hit, Kissre. Well done and incredibly fast. Tonight I will wear the bruises, not you."

"I still carry enough black and blue to have not evened the score. Are we done for today?" She asked, trying to keep her smugness out of her voice.

Quillon's glare was her answer. "Go take care of your horse. Same time tomorrow."

Looking around at last, Kissre was appalled to see the numbers of men standing at the training field's edges. She recognized Cygnese squad captains scattered about, including Dovel, Jycel, and Kedriq, along with their squad members in one group.

Fudge bound to her side barking and ran several times around Carillon, who was too worn out to pay much heed. Kissre felt the sweat running down her back and sides and wanted nothing more than Fay's ministrations, but that had to wait on Carillon's care. She sighed and rode slowly off the field.

When she reached her apartment, Fay waited with a message to go to Corbin Napier's office. As she entered the envoy's office, a glance told her to expect the worse. Quillon waited there, still in his training gear.

Napier spoke as soon as she entered. "Word has come that Pertelon troops are marching on Sidih in massive numbers."

"How?" Kissre took a deep breath and closed her eyes for a brief moment, caught in the dread that incipient battle created. She opened them with Napier's next words.

"They infiltrated troops north of Guerestu."

"How did the Adepts not catch their movements? I was told this was impossible," Quillon asked, clearly disturbed.

"Marshal Ranor said it takes many Adepts and constant vigilance to protect the borders. During winter, they depend on the treacherous storms and snow to keep their enemies at bay. They eased up in their precautions at the end of the traditional raid season. Up until now, Cygna's battles have all been summer skirmishes and never against a full-blown army. The Cygnese Government, for all its Adepts, didn't expect a late-season attack. Marshal Ranor, when discussing this with Governor Vitann and me," Napier looked at Kissre, "mentioned that you told him, but he dismissed the possibility. They have determined the Pertelon army has weak Talents in their ranks. Trained differently from Cygna's Talents, but witches capable of hiding the presence of the troops with the help of null dissidents."

Swearing, Kissre asked, "Kaereyan troops?"

"At least two months away, and only if Warrick signs the treaty without spending much time debating the terms with his advisors."

"Which is unlikely," Kissre said.

"It's Ninth Month now. They cannot bring troops before First Month." Quillon said.

"Even if they do, they won't arrive in time. Pertelon hopes this is over before it begins," Kissre said.

Napier nodded. "Although the treaty is not signed," he said, "Governor Vitann has asked for the assistance of our soldiers here in Sidih. They would like your help in the coming fight, but I have no authority to commit our soldiers to hostilities."

"We haven't that many men," Quillon said, "but I suppose in the present circumstance everyone counts. Our priority must be to protect you and our mission here. Orders?"

"I have none," Corbin said. "Not until a messenger actually arrives will we know how to proceed. You and Quillon must decide how we can best serve. I do not think you need be too concerned for the safety of our embassy personnel. I expect we are protected unless Sidih is overrun with Pertelonese soldiers. From what Governor Vitann said a candlemark ago, Cygnese troops are already moving to engage the invaders."

Kissre refused to ask which squads. "Is there no way..." She stopped herself from saying more.

"Sidih's defenses are exceptional," Quillon said. "With the advent of a foreign army a sennight's march away, the population should support the Governor's efforts. Pertelon will find it hard to seize."

"Perhaps there is a way we can provide assistance to the Cygnese."

There was a short silence as both men looked at her.

"With no contravening orders, there is nothing to stop someone volunteering assistance, is there?"

Eleven

In the following days, Quillon insisted they continue their training sessions. She may have been the first to unhorse her opponent, but Quillon made up for that. A hard series of freezes had come early to this high country and Kissre found the sessions miserable. Not only was falling on the frozen ground painful but the cold also seeped through clothing.

Once begun, the exercise warmed her. By the time she finished, though, sweat dampened her clothes. The damp sucked body heat, cooling her to cold soon after her exertions ended. She shivered while riding Carillon back through the city from the training fields. To add to her discomfort today, sleeting rain fell and saturating everything.

Her and Quillon's offers of assistance had been rejected. It seemed Cygnese pride demanded they handle their own fights. Kissre wondered if the weather were an Adept trick and shivered. If so, it was effective. The extreme cold spell and the Northern Army succeeded in halting the invaders thirty leagues from Sidih. The army remained there, in the steep cliffs and hidden ravines of the surrounding terrain. Cygnese platoons excelled at this type of fighting.

Within the city, people talked with pride of the squads' defense. She imagined that at every tavern, wherever merchant met customer, at all church assemblies and dinner gatherings, in schoolrooms and work places, words, in whispered asides or confident gloats, spoke the Cygnese Adept's adage, 'Talent over body tallies'.

As a non-participant Kissre worried over her lack of knowledge. The Pertelonese seemed to be offering just the type of battle best suited to the Cygnese army, which was unlike King Clement.

As she made her way through the city, voices from those along the street yelled at her. "Hey, Kissre, not bad for so few!" and, "talents better than numbers!" and, "we've good fighters!" and, "Kissre, you hear? The Pertelon menace has fallen back without your help!" Kissre heard, smiled, and waved, or ignored as needed, but made no comment.

Her thoughts followed the repercussions if Pertelon failed to take Sidih. She halted Carillon in the middle of the street and caused some disruption in traffic with accompanying shouts and curses. Turning Carillon, she cantered the slippery streets back to the army camp.

At Ranor's headquarters she asked permission to see the Marshal. She waited in her bedraggled state, iced hair thawing, mud spattered, and tired. Fudge added the diverting scent of wet dog. An aide led her to a room where Marshal Ranor worked. Squad captain and lieutenants' faces turned to her, including Tyna and her squad. She didn't look for Dovel. She knew he helped at the front holding off the Pertelon's advance. Embarrassed, she begged Ranor's pardon for the interruption.

"Not at all, Colonel Kissre." Ranor waved her forward.

His complacent officers surrounded her, needling her back with their unspoken thoughts.

"We were going over squad reports and future strategy. What brings you?"

"I wished to see a map of troop locations, to look at what Pertelon does."

He spread his hand toward a topographical map with troop tags placed. Kissre approached the map taking in the land and tags. It was a wonderful map, delineating elevations and terrains. Drips of water fell from her hair to the paper she studied. She pushed her hair back with dirty fingers. Someone handed her a towel. She wiped her face and hair while voices talked around her of how they could continue to protect Sidih, drive the army back down the river they had followed into the highlands. Silence interspersed the dialogue.

"As you can see," Ranor interrupted the flow of voices around him, "Guerestu is protected by the entire Eastern Army. If the enemy turns and attacks, we will have them in a pincer action."

"Only if you abandon Guerestu to defend itself."

The Marshal's face flared with anger at her comment.

"How many troops are here?" she asked pointing to where the Pertelon tags rested. She accepted the answer, knowing they were far too low. "How did they advance so far without notice?" Silence broke through the soft background babble. "I know they have Talents shielding them. Plus you were not looking for them this late in the season. But where did they get Talents? How strong are their Talents?"

"We don't know where they got them. They're all very young and not that strong. Different in feeling."

"Pertelon or Cygna Talents?"

"What do you mean?"

"Is it possible they have stolen or turned young Cygnese Talents?"

"That is a possibility, or it might be a relatively new development in their country."

"Do they have the strength to hide more troops? Have your Talents checked all the land here?" She pointed to the large stretch of desolate forest between Sidih and Guerestu.

"No, not unless we track every inch of land. There are not enough Earth Talents to cover that much territory. We usually wait until locals report seeing something."

"So they don't need Talents to hide men? And no one has reported anything?" she asked, her eyes rose to study Ranor and held his gaze.

"No, it's doubtful an army hides there. That area is a particularly empty part of Cygna. The land barely supports anything other than the forest growing there, little game at this time of year. The terrain is rugged. They can't move an army through it." He sounded so sure. Kissre's soul shriveled, Pertelon's plan turned crystalline within her mind.

"I know. I've traveled through it. And yes, they can move an army through it, slowly, with supply lines. The attack on Sidih is a diversion; it kept your attention from their true objective. They have not committed enough troops to take Sidih if that was their intent."

A chorus of denial and dismissal ran through the room, then abruptly ceased. She knew the silence contained by an unheard order.

"What do you think Pertelon's true objective, Colonel Kissre?" The Marshal watched her with an expression of awakening perception.

"They are besieging Guerestu, surrounding it."

"How?"

"Building up troops here," she spread her hand over the desolate area. As she talked her fingers pointed on the map. "Kaereya information says Pertelon has five massive armies, each twice the size of any of yours. Their first two armies are in Kaereya along a very extended frontier. Another holds their eastern border, and the fourth, the Pertelon border outside Guerestu—controlling access to the Thou River. That army probably outnumbers your Eastern Army three or four to one."

"King Clement will not commit them to action unless it is clear Guerestu will fall," Ranor said. "Pertelon's fleet blockades the confluence of the Geste and Thou Rivers, so all river commerce to Guerestu has ceased, but we supply it from overland."

"Not for much longer. You must assume the fifth army is involved inside Cygna, entered by stealth, probably with the help of Cygnese dissidents and Pertelonese witches. Their goal has to be to isolate Guerestu and the Eastern Army. They can fight in winter because they've already built fortifications all through the summer.

"If you warn your Eastern Army in time, they can retreat behind the bulwarks of Guerestu. Perhaps, even get the outlying citizenry to safety." No one interrupted her, but Kissre's skin prickled with imagined messages thrown around the room. She continued her monologue. "Your army in Guerestu does not have any option but to close the city and defend it. The troops near Sidih will melt away to join those here," she pointed to the same spot on the map, "to finish encircling Guerestu. Have your talents check, but I think they will find massed armies here and here." She pointed to two spots.

Ranor broke in with a single word, "Tyna!" Kissre barely halted talking.

"Perhaps here, to secure supply lines from somewhere along the coast, and a second line somewhere here along the border." Finished, her gaze returned to Ranor. "Guerestu is to be starved into submission. If it is true that the Pertelon force has withdrawn from its march on Sidih, it might already be too late to stop. Pertelon will steal your richest prize, your eastern center of commerce, Guerestu, then destroy your economy. After that, they can conquer Sidih, Halli, and the rest of Cygna at their leisure, using Cygnese Talents against their own country."

"Tyna?" Ranor asked impatience in his voice.

"Kissre's right. We've found troops in one of the locations."

"How many?"

"Too many. They're fortified."

Ranor's eyes caught and held Kissre's gaze. She had only one solution for him. "Besiege the besiegers."

~ * ~

"You've worried my squad," Dovel said as Quillon slipped into a seat across from him in the Sidih tavern. "Why are you here and Kissre at the siege?"

The dark man gave a small shrug, his golden eyes flickering over Dovel. "I was sent by Kaereya to aid however I could until the Duke of Lambere returns with troops, so I help train your troops. Kissre volunteered to help in surveillance. She is more experienced in siege warfare, so I took the opportunity to seek you out. It is hard to hide from the many eyes that watch you but thank you for meeting me after receiving my message."

Dovel nodded his head once and raised a brow. "Why?" Already knowing the answer.

"Kissre."

"Again, why? You are closer to her than me. From what I've heard you pummeled her on a regular basis until she left for the front."

"As ordered." At Dovel's look, he said, "One of Kissre's friends told me to make sure she could protect herself."

"This person thought she'd need these skills?" Receiving no answer, Dovel studied the man while the Kennetsurean examined him in return. A man who probably knew Kissre as well as he did, maybe better. Quillon's steady eyes in his serene face seared into Dovel's with an intensity the squad leader found disquieting.

Dovel saw Quillon took everything in—the bar's slightly tawdry interior, the waitress who came and took their drink order, asking Dovel if he wanted his regular; another woman, a night lady, strolling by Dovel with a smile of familiarity.

"This was at your invitation," Dovel said, sipping his ale. "You've followed me around for days. Have I done something, or do you want something?"

"Both. Information." Quillon sipped his own drink. He put his tankard down. "I've heard you know what happened to Kissre here in Sidih."

"The attack?"

"Yes, and the events between her and her sister."

"Why come to me? And why expect I would tell?"

"I've also heard you had a relationship."

"As far as Kissre is concerned, it's finished. We're friends."

"Really?"

Dovel waited.

"What did you do to her?"

Dovel felt his face inflame with anger. "Noth..." He didn't finish the word. "When we first met, I knew her null. She looks a great deal like her sister."

"I've already heard about that. What did you do to cause her to wear gloves constantly and to retreat into so self-imposed an exile nothing can get in or out?"

Dovel swore. He looked into his half-empty tankard and downed the remaining ale. Done, he placed the Tankard down and waved to a maid. While waiting for the refill, he stared at the worn wood grain of the table. It reminded him of where Kissre's unharnessed power took him. After a minute he looked at Quillon. The man's observant, calm regard showed a mild but perceptible curiosity verging on hostility.

Dovel caught his breath; Talent came where you least expect it. "Has anyone told you that you have Talent?"

Quillon scoffed a smile. "No."

"It's true. I can feel it."

Shrugging, the man's expression didn't change. "So? It changes nothing for me. Can you read my mind?"

"Not without permission." He waited a breath. "Have you slept with Kissre?"

In the prolonged silence he guessed an answer. His jaw tightened so much his teeth hurt.

"What bearing does this have on Kissre's behavior in Cygna?"

"Think back. Afterward, do you remember feeling different?" He received no answer. Since honing his observation skills on Kissre, he had learned to pay attention to small movements in others. It came as a surprise that nulls used age-old communication tricks that Talents never developed. "You are familiar with our classes of Talent?"

"Since coming to Cygna. Yes."

"Kissre, like her sister Tyna, has a formidable Talent, but it is not noticed because no one can touch her mind. Sexual contact makes one Talent sensitive to another. In Kissre's case, just an inadvertent touch can increase someone's Talent."

"You think her a Catalyst?"

He looked at Quillon. "I know she is."

"You told her this and now she wears gloves?"

"No, I didn't tell her. I handled it poorly. My only excuse is at the time I was...I don't know." He looked at Quillon, half defiant, half guilty. "Kissre casually touched me while I was using Talent. It was a devastating experience."

"She injured you?"

"No. Yes." His mirthless laugh filled his ears. "She nearly killed me." He sighed and leaned back, his hands toying with his Tankard. "No Adept ever reaches full potential, seldom comes close." Even as he spoke, he wondered if it were right to do so. "During our previous contacts I was not exercising Talent, but found my Talent expanded almost immediately. My first reaction was she had some measure of Earth Talent. That explained the change. This time was different."

"When you were using your gift?"

"Yes. When she touched me while I used my Talent, I went so far beyond my capacity...I think I nearly died. The only Talent that causes that effect is a Catalyst...I know. I work with one constantly."

"But not on such a level?"

"No. It frightened Kissre, but she didn't know what had happened. I only told her not to touch anyone with Talent."

Quillon sat against his bench's tall wood back. "Kissre doesn't know about this Talent?"

Dovel watched Quillon consider the implications and draw a conclusion. "Kissre wouldn't believe it."

"Could this cause trouble?"

"It's a dangerous situation. If the Talent Review Board or Governor Vitann or any high-ranking Talent found out...I doubt she would be allowed to leave Cygna." Dovel swallowed, contemplating his punishment for his own defiant acts.

Placid eyes flared at him with defiance. "She is a citizen of Kaereya."

"It wouldn't matter. Once our mutual endeavor is over, maybe even before, Kissre will disappear. You won't find her."

"Is this why you tell me this?"

"Yes. I think too many people know."

"You're telling me this, if known, would it cause you trouble?"

"If known. Have I answered your questions?"

"Yes, I think you have."

~ * ~

"I've granted this interview because I think you both have been hiding information, contrary to the law. Before your request to speak with me, I received a report from Marshal Ranor," Vitann said, her hand tapped the envelope on her desk.

Her glare fell on Zeba like a hot coal, then moved to Healer Bujyea. They both sat before her desk, making Zeba feel like she and Bujyea were disobedient children. At her age that was quite a feat. In another situation it would have amused her.

Vitann continued after her brief pause. "He has suspicions about Kissre. They are not the first to come to my attention. You, at least, Healer Bujyea, came to the Adept Council at an earlier time. How long has this conspiracy been going on?" Vitann asked, her voice stiff in displeasure as she brushed her gray robes of state into orderly folds.

"It was not a conspiracy, Vitann." Healer Bujyea sat nearby, also very composed. "You know there were a lot of unsubstantiated suppositions, and a lot of shocked disbelief. There still is."

Zeba smiled, watching the Governor's tangible anger. Zeba felt small sitting in the oversized chair but kept her hands comfortably clasped in her lap.

Vitann inhaled until her nostrils pinched. Zeba felt she could almost read her mind without mental touch. Vitann, she knew, felt a small, ancient woman such as herself seemed more trouble than her worth. Her friends on the Maze told her that her recent coherence was seen as a sign and gift from the Holy One in the emerging time of crisis. The rumors must have reached Vitann, who obviously found it a mixed blessing.

"And the 'wait and see' is over? You've reached a conclusion?" Vitann Asked.

"Yes. That is why we asked to speak with you. I wish you to acquit Dovel, though. He came to me. I was just not cognizant enough to give him good counsel."

"You are now, though?" Vitann said, resting her hands on the chair's arms, in a formidable pose.

"Perhaps." Zeba put on her most angelic expression. Her observations had not been so clear for fifteen years or more. It felt good, like she had finally achieved control over her Talent, but not in this situation. Maybe living long enough contributed to that. She sighed. Living long enough to meet Kissre.

"Dovel knew your condition. His failure to come forward is not excused." Vitann dismissed her with soft words and looked at Bujyea who didn't look the least distressed. The Governor rose and took two steps to the casement window. It was clear her anger controlled her.

"Well, there is little you can afford to do about Dovel, anyway, what with Tyna's recent distress and with her baby only a few months old," Bujyea said. "You don't have that many high-level squad Captains as it is. Besides, I told the Talent Assessment Committee at about the same time, and they disregarded my information, told me it was impossible. Everyone sniggered when Oracle Zeba volunteered to investigate. Do you understand our reluctance to come with unsubstantiated allegations?"

Zeba suddenly stiffened, struck by a vision. They were wrong; Vitann could do something about Dovel. It scared her. Dovel had been recalled to Sidih. Vitann turned to look at Bujyea, suddenly calm and mollified, and Zeba cringed.

"Bujyea," Vitann said, giving the healer a frigid look. "You only reported suspicious Talent flourishes among those working with this patient. We all know stress and focus can cause such effects. Is it possible she is an Earth Talent as Marshal Ranor reported?"

"Certainly an Earth Talent," Bujyea said.

"Nothing more, surely?" Vitann asked in a smug, intolerable certainty.

Bujyea caught Vitann's gaze before he spoke. "A Catalyst." Zeba felt a chill over her skin and fell silent.

"Latent?"

"Most likely. Perhaps somewhat more," Bujyea answered.

Vitann froze a second. "A Mediator? Zeba! What do you know?"

"She cannot touch other minds, but her physical touch, even while she was ill, focused me." Zeba, feeling the weight of her reluctant admission, suffered a dizzying array of visions. She sighed, knowing her actions would now affect the future. Both she and Bujyea had agreed they would reveal the truth. "The effect has been long lasting. Bujyea placed her on Gregor's Mound. She healed herself but didn't drain the land. I know. I felt it."

Total and lengthy silence ensued. Zeba waited. Vitann's eyes widened and she remained silent a little longer. "You were wise to tell me this. If this is true…" She looked away. "We must take charge of this situation today. She cannot be allowed to leave Cygna."

"That may be both difficult and unwise, Vitann," Bujyea said. "She is a citizen of Kaereya, and part of their diplomatic mission. The two known Crucibles were not at all like Kissre. They were high-level Touch Adepts, but emotionally unstable and easily led."

"She was born in Cygna!" Vitann's voice burst through the room. She visibly calmed herself, containing a fury that frightened Zeba. "And what do you suggest?"

The healer sighed and uncrossed his legs to sit forward. "She is Touch void. Holds a resentment against Talents in general and is disinclined to remain in Cygna. Moreover, she is a trained soldier, capable of defending herself. I heard of training sessions, went, and saw for myself. Numerous platoon leaders watched. They were impressed, and speak of her as if she were her tattoo, calling her the Blue Dragon. She would be a formidable opponent with so much public support. Particularly among nulls."

"The public does not dictate policy." Vitann tapped her finger on her chair arm in thought, but it was clear the healer's oblique reference of the null resistance alarmed her. "But perhaps we should keep these suspicions quiet, see if there is a way to measure her talent. If there is talent." Vitann huffed.

"If the talent is trainable," the healer warned.

"Tyna won't help?"

"Don't even ask her," Zeba said. She felt she must remedy the situation but didn't know how. "You know the relations between them are bad. Tyna forgives easily, but Kissre does not. She clenches grudges close and bears one against her mother that she seems to have transferred to Tyna. She is part of the envoy's staff, held in esteem by Aristo Aurelias. If you doubt the regard in which the Kaereyan's hold her, look at that horse gifted her. It is a rare animal, gifted by the Aegis of Kaereya and his Seer wife. Hold your biases for now, or you could start a second war. You will have opportunity to come in contact with her, and time to draw your own conclusions."

"And you see nothing? Have no visions on how to develop the outcome desired?"

"My visions could be interpreted in any number of ways," Zeba said.

"What do you see, old woman? I demand that you tell me."

Zeba felt as if she shrunk in upon herself. "Every night, horrible dreams of savage, uncontrollable violence wake me. The associated feelings are unbearable. I cannot escape any of it. During daylight, at unpredictable moments, blood and entrails cover the reality of my day. Death, I see death everywhere, and Kissre is at its core."

"She is at the front," Vitann said. "Of course she would see violence. We must get her out of there."

"You can't. She is not ours to order," Zeba said. "I've thought of many permutations, thinking to affect my visions. I've done it in the past. Before, when I thought of the right circumstance, my visions changed. In this instance, no matter what I think of changing, Kissre here or there, the dreams stay the same."

~ * ~

Dovel stood before the Talent Review Board and Governor Vitann. They sat in a semi-circle around him.

"We've called you Captain Dovel, to explain yourself."

"I have nothing to explain."

"You have much to explain," Orrthu, head of Talent Testing, said. "Why you failed to report an unknown Talent. Why did you hide knowledge of a Talent? He is resisting entrance to his mind," she complained to Vitann. The testing Probe added, "You've changed since the last time I touched you, Captain Dovel."

Dean Alth turned to Vitann. "I pick up remarkable strength, beyond what he used to show."

"Did you know Tomel has been raised to Receiver level, Captain?" Vitann asked.

"Yes. He is one of my platoon sergeants, Governor Vitann."

"Marshal Ranor said you could track Kissre over land when none of the other Captains could feel her. A sure sign she has some aspect of Earth Talent, and that you've bonded with her."

"I think, Governor, the whole city seems to know I slept with Kissre, and a great deal more about Captain Tyna and her sister."

"You will submit to retesting."

"No."

"Then we'll pull Colonel Kissre in for testing."

"Colonel Kissre is a citizen of Kaereya, who is presently helping defend Cygna. I do not think the foreign envoy who is on his way with Kaereyan troops would agree to such proceedings."

"You dare threaten the Committee?" Orrthu asked, anger dressing her face and voice. "I can cause you interminable suffering. Your squad has been together how many years...seventeen if I remember right?" She smiled at him. "You've always tried to keep your distance, haven't you? Training bonds over sexual bonds, no drugs, ever. Not since they used them on you for your first testings. You were rather old to be brought in for education. A lax Talent in your area not following through on his duties."

"Orrthu." Dean Alth warned.

"No!" The angry Probe turned on the voice speaking to her more than just a vocal warning. "We cannot allow this defiance. We've already endured too much change! Dovel must be brought back to obedience." She turned to Dovel. "Despite your resistance, I'm sure you've witnessed at what cost the bonds might be broken. We can break those bonds, Dovel, easier than you might think."

"Dovel," Governor Vitann interrupted. "I've made plans for your future, as distinguished a future as someone with your rare Talent deserves. Don't throw that away. Allow yourself to be tested and tell us what you know of Kissre's Talent."

"Kissre deserves free choice. She has chosen another life and made her own way. My friendship and obligation to Kissre override my responsibility to you."

"If you take this track, I cannot help you, Dovel. Please help me help you." Vitann heard his reply and turned and left, as did most of the chairmen. Left alone with Orrthu, he slowly raised his eyes to her.

She smiled. "You know we will need to probe as well as test?" Her smile broadened as she saw his expression.

~ * ~

Candlemarks, maybe even days later, Dovel was led into Vitann's office. Shaky, ill, and disoriented, he needed his escort's help to walk.

"You should start feeling better as the drugs wear off," Vitann said as he was assisted into a chair before her desk. "You know your permission was not needed. The mandates of our society demanded this." At his look, "Yes, your shield has dissolved, and I can hear everything you think."

He forced voice to work. "Not everything I hope."

Her gaze rested on him. "Perhaps not everything. It is probably better I don't. Did Orrthu tell you the results? It is most impressive. You've jumped a level in almost every Talent. With that type of Talent, it is too bad Kissre didn't remain a prostitute. It would make things so much easier."

"Kissre was never a prostitute."

Vitann sighed. "Perhaps not. Jycel has tried hard enough to get into her bed."

"Do you know Kissre?" His voice cracked.

"No. I've seen her at various functions and during the negotiations. She has a challenging, disobliging look, appears to be a stubborn girl, and possesses either a head or Talent for strategy. We will find out which."

"Not a girl. Stubborn, yes; with a formidable will. You try to force her, coerce her into something she doesn't want, and you'll regret it. She will fight you every step of the way."

"Like you've done? You see the results. Kissre will be brought under control, and there is nothing you or she can do about it. We cannot let a Catalyst go."

He gave a weak laugh. "A touchy political situation for you."

"Yes. I would like your help."

"No."

"You still have a rapport with Kissre. You could talk her into voluntarily testing."

"No."

"It will happen, with or without your help. It might be better for Kissre if you did."

"Do you think nothing has changed? Do you think that everyone will accept your mandates and allow you to use whatever means necessary to carry them out? You said my shields were down. Do you think Tyna, and every other person tied to her, doesn't know what you've done? Do you think Tyna will allow her sister to be harmed in any way, with the guilt she already feels over Kissre? How bad do you want to prevail against Pertelon, Vitann? How well will you accept the mandates of King Clement?"

Vitann sat silent. "You may leave, Captain Dovel."

The door burst open and banged against the wall. Tyna, Ulyss, and Wyn entered. Tired beyond belief, Dovel welcomed his Lieutenants' aid. He heard Tyna speak in deadly calm words even as he reached the door.

"You leave Kissre alone, or I swear I'll cause such disruption the government will fail. And you know I can do it."

~ * ~

From the hallway, Zeba watched, her hands clutched tight together under her chin to stop their trembling. Dovel's mind had cleared some during his interview with Vitann, but now was a blazing agony, and Zeba wondered how Tyna and his squad endured it. She stopped outside the office door and looked at Larig's set, non-expression. Shaking her head, she damned Orrthu as she approached Vitann's desk. The Governor's eyes flicked to her and back to the papers in her hand, but her eyes were suspiciously red, her face blotched.

"Have you never learned you catch more flies with honey, Vitann?"

"Shut up, Zeba, or I'll give you to Orrthu, too."

"Arrogance will be our end, Vitann. Our society changes, and if we do not change with it, we cannot survive. Do you know how Adepts came to power in Cygna?"

"I don't need a history lesson, Zeba."

"Through acceptance of their differences by the general unmutated population. Now we hold all the power, call them nulls. We have become the persecutors, Vitann."

"I do not control language usage, Zeba. The fact remains that Talents came to power for the very reason that they have Talent." She sighed at Vitann's scoffing rebuttal. "I told you to be careful. You better hope Kissre doesn't learn of what you have done, for you do not know what she is."

Twelve

Even beneath her fur-lined coat and leather armor, Kissre felt the cold. It stole through every small opening with every movement. Shivers ran over Carillon's rough, winter-coated shoulder. Her horse stamped a foot, impatient to move, and Fudge moaned as he chewed at the ice clumps forming between the pads of his feet. Kissre flexed her fingers, switching the sight glass between hands to perform the action.

"It's too damn cold to be out watching them Pertelon brutes warm their asses in their barracks," her Pathfinder Cleat said. He had shown up one day shortly after her arrival, volunteering his service to her. As promised, he brought others with him. "They're burning down the forest to stay warm."

"And hard work it is." Kissre grinned at him. She did not mention renegade Pathfinders had helped the enemy, nor did Cleat. He sat on his gray, longhaired mountain pony, relaxed but attentive, wrapped in multiple wraps of fabric and fur, his sharp brown eyes peering out from under the edges of a fur hat and the stiff scarf that wrapped his face. Quillon sat beyond him, shivering in his saddle despite layer upon layer of heavy clothing. He'd arrived yesterday, orders from Aristo Aurelias having arrived at last.

She returned her attention to the view. The Pertelon army had cut a wide swath of trees. It took three men a day to cut each recalcitrant tree. Time could be marked in their progress. The trunk stubs and bare ground made a frontal attack suicide. One ray of fortune, Guerestu held firm, even under the tight grip surrounding it. Every day Kissre rode the line reconnoitering from the protection of the forest's low boughs and tall shrubs. Today Quillon had chosen to ride with her.

"How do you stand this every day? Are Cygna's Talents causing this wretched cold?" Quillon asked. The icy temperatures took Quillon to the edge of his temper. Unused to such conditions, the cold affected him more. "Do you think we could talk them into a warm spell? Even Fudge is freezing."

Kissre laughed, her breath turning into vaporous puffs. She lowered her distance glass. Her gloved fingers felt like icicles. "Worst ground I've ever seen, and they've certainly taken the advantage. Night sorties might be our only option. A small force could work through the barricades and past the sentries." She looked down. Fudge was shivering through an even shaggier winter coat. "We need to travel, build up body heat."

Quillon grunted, rearranging his cloak once more, this time stuffing the ends under his butt and thighs. "I dream both awake and asleep of a blistering Kennetsurean sun. At least Fay waits for you with warm food and drink. How did you talk her into coming to this unholy place to wait on you?"

"I didn't. She insisted. Says she works for the envoy and must go wherever I go. Tried to dissuade her." She glanced down at her dog. "Maybe I should leave Fudge in the tent with her."

"How hard did you try? I work for the envoy," Quillon pulled her back to his topic.

"Not much, I saw the advantage to me." She grinned. "Stop complaining. I know a servant waits for you. Pity the sentries. They stand in one place and have no one at all."

"He is not as good at massage. Besides, the sentries have fires."

"Ah-ha. The truth comes out. Fay has given you a back rub, and you're jealous over superior service for a subordinate officer. Did you try to hire her away?"

"Yes. She said she wished to continue serving the Blue Dragon."

Kissre frowned. "Don't encourage that."

"Encourage that? It's already ingrained among the Cygnese soldiers, no help needed. You got the tattoo. It's a little late to regret it."

Kissre ignored Quillon. "Fay tells me personal service is her family's calling. She takes pride in her work and feels an affinity for me because I'm null, too."

Quillon made a disgusted sound.

Dusk already edged the day as they walked their horses back through the camp to their tents. With a hand signal, Kissre released Fudge. He took off racing for her tent causing some minor mayhem along his route. Cleat crowed a laugh and shouted obscene encouragement as he watched Fudge's progress.

"You're cruel," Quillon said. "Did you see that? He nabbed that soldier's spitted fowl on the way."

"Not at all. He keeps the men prepared for a surprise attack. If they know a pony-sized creature is apt to catapult through the camp at any given moment, they should live in expectation. It's good training for when they are on patrol. I hope he didn't burn his mouth."

"Cruel and devious. Do you replace dinners or is the poor man to go hungry?"

Kissre ignored him, noting new arrivals in the Cygna camp as they wound through the compound. A skimming glance showed her Tyna's banner.

"Do you suppose she brought her baby?" Quillon asked, proving he had noted her wandering gaze. Kissre gave him a nasty look, which only caused him to laugh. "We have a combined debriefing this evening at Marshal Ranor's tent."

"That should make you happy. At least he keeps a warm tent."

Quillon smiled and performed a Kennetsurean act of obeisance. "I will walk with you at the appointed time." They dismounted, and soldiers led the horses away.

Fay waited with warm clothes and hot food on a glowing brazier. Initially against Fay coming, Kissre was now thankful. Fay knew how to combat cold and always made her life easier, an unfamiliar luxury she now loathed losing. After changing her clothes, Kissre squatted before the brazier and warmed her fingers in its radiant heat, trying to control her shivering.

"Drink this. It will help warm you."

She did. The beverage burned its way into her gut. Gasping, she caught her breath. "Holy One, Fay, I still have a debriefing to attend." Fay filled the empty cup with hot water, and Kissre held the container cupped in her hands, glad to feel the direct heat enter her skin.

"Captain Tyna was here asking after you."

Her eyes followed her maid. Fay knew the situation. "Is that a warning?"

"She said she would catch up with you later." Fay's soft voice, non-committal and placid, relayed the message.

Like hell she would. The last thing she needed was a face-to-face with Tyna. Forewarned was forearmed.

Through the next three days, Kissre slipped into debriefings, with either Quillon or Marshal Ranor, last to arrive and first to leave. She left camp before daybreak and often returned after nightfall. It was not avoidance, but duty.

Surveillance took all her time. She needed to find Pertelon's outposts, map their locations, and find their weaknesses. Of the latter, there weren't many. She and her Pathfinders watched as the trees behind the enemy were cut—for buildings, for roads, for fuel. The Cygnese did not cut the trees. Supply lines provided easier burning wood and charcoal. More often, soldiers picked up naturally felled timber. Not as arduous a task as cutting and chopping the stubborn, hard to ignite wood of trees.

"The forest protects the land," she heard one of Cleat's men say. "It takes three lifetimes for one to grow. It is considered a sin among us to destroy so much."

"Luckily, your people have an art for making a warm tent," Kissre said.

"Pony skin. Many do not make it through the winter."

Kissre did not like the look he gave Carillon, as if measuring her hide. Luckily, their supply lines were in no danger, and wagons of hay and grain arrived every few days.

Entering camp long after dark on the fourth day, Kissre reeled with cold and fatigue. She missed Fudge, left behind firmly staked in her tent. It was too cold, and the snow and ice jammed his cold-cracked footpads. He walked sore-footed leaving bloody tracks. She didn't jump from her perch on Carillon but carefully dismounted, only too aware of her numb feet. Although a soldier approached to take Carillon, she waved him off with a small request and unsaddled her mount in front of her tent, checking the mare's condition as she groomed her.

Carillon, dressed in the shaggy dull coat of winter, handled the cold better than her rider, but ate mountains of food. Kissre wondered if she'd be requested to send her back to Sidih. It would probably be better for both of her animals, but Kissre couldn't stand the thought.

A painful walk with needle-laced feet took Carillon to the picket line. Obtaining food, she watched contentedly as Carillon munched her way through her rations. The soldier returned with a pail of warmed water, and they talked in low voices as the mare drank. Finished, Kissre turned to go to her tent. Leaving the pickets, she found herself surrounded by Tyna and her squad.

"Let me pass," Kissre said. Deep within her, anger sparked at a trapped and forced confrontation.

"Not until we've talked." Tyna's posture insisted on a confrontation.

"We've nothing to talk about."

"You don't need to talk, but you are going to listen."

"No, Captain Tyna, I am not. I am too cold and tired. And I never talk when forced, particularly by ambush. Get out of my way."

"Too bad! There are some things you need to know."

Kissre sidestepped and took two steps to have the pale blonde Silvie step into her path. "You need to listen. People have tried to help you."

"I have already stated my objections at being detained in this manner, and with you, I have no restraining compunction against violence. Get out of my way, or I'll break you." Whatever her face held, Kissre saw with a flick of elated guilt, it frightened the woman.

Silvie stepped aside. Kissre was five steps beyond her when Tyna spoke.

"Does Dovel always have to pay the price for our family's follies? For our quarrels? Pray the Holy One save others from such a costly friendship."

Kissre stopped and closed her eyes. "Dovel and I are friends. I have put no cost on it."

"Others did it for you."

Cryptic messages were beyond her tolerance. Sweeping back, she grabbed Tyna by the arm and snarled at the squad, "Stay back and stay away. I won't harm her." She pulled Tyna along, talking as she moved. The squad followed but didn't approach too close.

"You give me even more than enough cause to fight Pertelon. If it not for King Clement and his land-grabbing war, I wouldn't be here or have to talk with you at all. Now, just what am I supposed to know about Dovel?" She pushed Tyna through her tent flap and released her, taking three steps to back up against her campaign trunk. "Fay, leave." Jerking off her fur-lined cloak, she handed it to the maid who rushed out of the tent.

"You're a stubborn bitch, Kissre," Tyna said, rubbing her arm. It was an act. Tyna's sleeve was too thick to permit injury.

Kissre remained silent, watched Tyna look around the interior, but read the Captain's agitation and resentment. She said nothing, just waited.

"The Talent Review Board subjected Dovel to retesting. They used drugs on him. Not a pleasant experience."

"What has that to do with me?"

"They did it because he wouldn't voluntarily reveal anything about you."

"There is nothing to reveal about me. I'm null, remember?"

"Some question that."

With a singularly repulsive curse, Kissre laughed. "I'm void. You've all told me so. Message delivered. Leave."

"Why?"

"Why what? Why leave? Because I don't want you here."

"Why this unforgivable attitude? I am not Naomi. Yes I said some mean, terrible things, thought worse things. Can you not at least allow me back into your society for the sake of kinship? Or must I pay for every misdeed or supposed slight of Naomi? Or is it because you're afraid to be near me? Afraid you can't handle that violent temper you leash so tight?"

Naomi's face rose before Kissre, enumerating her duties and responsibilities and her failures in carrying both out. Restraint gone, Kissre threw a saddle pack across the tent. "All those reasons, for which you can now feel grateful twice-over. Get out, Captain Pierce."

"You're unforgiving and stubborn, Kissre. Keep on, and you won't be on speaking terms with anyone but a dog and a horse."

"They, at least, do not judge."

Outside the tent, she heard Tyna rejoin her squad and heard another muttered invective against herself. When the sounds faded away, Kissre looked around. Fudge wasn't in the tent. Dovel must be back in camp. Expelling another vehement curse, she flung out of the tent.

Striding through the camp, she passed Dovel's squad seated around a fire, wrapped in blankets eating their dinner. They stared but didn't stop her. Without ceremony she flung aside the flap of Dovel's tent and entered. Fudge rose from next to the brazier and whined greeting as she approached. *Wretched dog.* She curtly ordered him to heel. At her tone, his ears crunched against his head. Dovel sat on the edge of a camp cot holding his head. Bloodshot and red-rimmed eyes rose to her as she entered.

"He came here when your maid allowed him out for a run. I didn't think you would mind."

Through clenched teeth, she asked, "Why?"

His eyes glazed and his expression turned vague. It was obvious Tyna touched his mind. Kissre felt her body react, felt a furious desire to strike anything.

"They want you tested."

"So what? Can their drugs get through a void? You let them do that to you? I don't need protection. Particularly from someone, anyone, already so vulnerable." By lowering her voice Kissre managed to control her rage, but she knew from his expression he felt it. She hated him for it.

"Kiss, I'm in no condition for this. I can't handle you. Not right now."

The pain of her anger was near unendurable. Unable to stop her inner shaking, unable to find an opponent, she left as she arrived, snapping her fingers for Fudge. Outside her tent Quillon stood armed, holding her weapons.

"Now?" she snapped.

"Yes. You are beyond calming meditations. Arm yourself."

Grabbing her sword and buckler from Quillon with a snarled curse, she followed him into a nearby field.

A three-quarter moon highlighted the silver crust lining the foot-trampled snow. The peaceful setting heightened her belligerence. Quillon didn't even allow her to set herself before he turned, his blade swinging in an arc toward her head. She reacted. For a quarter-mark, hard, unrestrained, temper-ridden fury echoed through the air.

"Enough," Kissre gasped, sucking frigid air. She backed several steps. When Quillon lowered his buckler, she slowly sank to her knees, then crumpled to her back feeling empty but calm at last.

Quillon staggered forward and collapsed next to her.

"Are you returned to tranquility?"

"No, you sword sadist, but I'm too damned tired to do anything about it." Her words came in gasps.

"I had just such a day, you spiny-assed war whore. By the Holy One, I wanted to pound an Aristo just so today and knew he couldn't withstand me. I'd have killed him. I'm glad you saved yourself for me."

She laughed. "Saved myself for you? As if I needed a zealous Zekarac Knight bent on hammering my cold-tortured body into bruised flesh. Next time, I'll save myself for when I'm not giving you every advantage."

His head twisted in her direction. "Not hammered, merely tenderized for your next match." He rose to lean back on the heels of his gloved palms. "I'm surprised they haven't called out the guard. We were loud enough to rouse the camp. No audience either. Your trip through the camp must have raised alarms."

"Damn Talents."

"You looked most ferocious. Even I felt qualms and nearly failed to challenge you. Tomorrow you will take the day off."

She swore and laughed at the same time. "No. It's better when I'm doing something."

"What's better?"

"Everything." She rolled to her hands and knees and used her sword to help push herself to her feet. Once up, she staggered in exhaustion. Quillon was already up and grabbed her arm as she stumbled. "You're freezing," he said.

Straightening, she pulled her elbow from his grasp. "I'm fine, just a bit cold. I don't need help."

Quillon sighed, reclaiming her elbow as she staggered on numb feet. "Stupid as well as stubborn. You need to get warm fast. I'll get Fay."

Fudge rose from where he lay on the edge of the field and waited for her to arrive. "I can take care of myself, thank you." His hand didn't leave her elbow. The walk back to her tent seemed to take forever. "Do I require handling?" she asked.

Quillon laughed. "Always. And with a delicate touch."

With a final obscenity, Kissre entered her tent. Thought had become a tenuous shadow. Remembering to wipe then sheath her sword in the scabbard and hang the buckler, she fell into bed, clad in leathers, hauberk, and boots.

~ * ~

The sound of hot food sizzling on a brazier and the smell of fresh bread roused her. Sour memory followed. Someone had laid blankets on her, with warming stones, recently replaced. It must have been Fay. Whoever removed her boots, had left the armor. It pinched and bruised skin with every small movement. At first her body wouldn't respond, but she forced herself to a sitting position and swung her legs off the bed. Four braziers burned within the tent. It was stifling hot. Fudge rose and whined, licking her hand. She roughed the fur on his head and rose to take him out and staggered. Surprised at her physical debility, she took a deep breath and steadied her steps.

Returning she found Fay heating a kettle of hot water. Fay handed her a bar of soap. Another kettle steamed on a second brazier and a basin of hot water sat next to several drying towels. Kissre smiled at the hint and removed her armor and clothes. Soaping herself and rinsing as she went, she relished feeling clean.

"Do your hair, too, and I will cut it. You look terrible. Your lips are all wind-dried and cracked, your eyes bloodshot. That's frostbite on your cheeks and fingers. Not bad, but you must now be extra careful. You need a healer Talent."

"No."

Fay didn't argue. "I'll put on salve, but it will need more."

"Thank you."

She clucked at Kissre's meek tone and made her stand in a larger basin, then poured pine-scented hot water over her lathered hair and body. The rivulets ran down Kissre's skin in warm caressing ribbons followed by cool shivers as the air touched her. Fay rubbed her body dry with rough toweling, then massaged in fragrant oils. Wrapped in yet another pre-warmed cloth, Kissre ate breakfast, sharing tidbits with Fudge.

Returned with clean clothes, Fay set them aside for Kissre to dress later. Before letting her mistress rise, she trimmed her hair and applied salve to the burning spots on Kissre's face. Fay provided coffee while she worked. Quillon had taught her to brew the beverage, but she didn't understand how Kissre and he could enjoy drinking it.

When Fay finished, Kissre handed her the empty cup, then slowly dressed, and put her armor back on despite Fay's protests. Her body was sated with exhaustion, and she found it hard to move at all but had thought of one urgent duty needing attention before she left camp.

She entered Tyna's spacious tent without ceremony. The large interior was partitioned in the middle. Her squad sat with Tyna in the forward partition sharing a noon meal. They looked at her with startled, wary expressions.

"They've no right to me." She spoke without greeting. "If they force a situation, if they attempt to use either friend or foe to get at me, they can start counting bodies. Tell them that. Tell them I will have my revenge." Without further word, she turned and left.

Once back in her tent, she sat on the bed feeling woozy. Quillon was right. She couldn't go out. In her state, it would put her men at risk. They could all rest today. Fay helped her undress, but she didn't remember finishing.

~ * ~

"Dovel?"

"Yes, Adele."

Dovel watched Kissre emerge from the Marshal's tent and mount Carillon. The mare stood a giant among a small contingent of Pathfinders' ponies. Kissre stopped to speak to her men. Over her armor, she wore a long fur-lined coat, its ankle-length flaps fanned out over Carillon's rump and forward to cover her legs as she mounted. Since Fudge didn't run at her side, he thought the dog would be along shortly. She had not curtailed Fudge's visits since the confrontation of three days ago. That night something had changed. He was just unsure of what.

"I have something to tell you."

He didn't take his gaze off Kissre.

"Personal, or duty?" He felt her guilt, her unease, and her desire.

"Personal." He finally looked at Adele. She appeared very serious, and her posture reinforced her mind's torment. He withdrew as far as he could to the edges of the bond between them. He still felt her resolution.

"Months ago, you sent Colonel Pierce a letter."

Kissre? His mind met Adele's. Briefly he saw himself last summer as he gave a letter to one of the camp pages. Then saw Adele take the letter back. As he watched the paper singe, the wax melt, boil and burn, he felt her satisfaction. Felt Adele's certainty that he would soon look her way. He withdrew from contact.

"I'm sorry." She said the words aloud.

Swallowing, Dovel looked away. "You know I never felt that way about you."

"I know." Her desolation was as strong as her remorse. "What are you going to do?"

He felt all he needed, all he wanted to feel. "Me? Nothing. I doubt that letter would have changed anything. You are the one who has to decide what to do."

"Decide what? You know I can't leave the squad."

"Not presently. This conflict won't last forever. Decide what you want afterward. Decide how you are going to work within the squad now."

"Do you forgive me?"

"Why? Because you thought you knew what was best for me? You caught me on a good day, Adele. If you need my forgiveness, you have it. Go forgive yourself and start finding your future."

He watched Adele walk away. Even with access to his mind, she didn't know him.

::You were easier on her than she deserved.:: Ulyss entered his mind.

::The squad heard?::

::You weren't broadcasting, but Adele couldn't keep her mind shut. She'll have a rough few days with anyone who heard.::

::Maybe; maybe not. Many do not like Kissre.:: Dovel raised his shields and returned to watching Kissre as the small troop rode through the camp and into the hillside trees skirting it.

Since his encounter with Orrthu, he had wallowed in a sty of self-pity and depression. Kissre, unaware of the power of the Talent Review Board, had not understood his obedience to their rule. She would have fought, according to a gleeful Tyna, would fight yet. Tyna described how fierce Kissre had looked, and wouldn't that surprise the malicious, stuffy, and formalistic Talents in Sidih.

Tyna obviously didn't know Kissre had slept the rest of the day away, ill with exhaustion and drugged by Fay. She would fight, though, right to the bloody end. A part of him wished to be present at such a confrontation. It might give even tradition-bound Orrthu a fright-filled pause. Tyna had danced about his tent just as elated with Kissre's response to herself. "She's breaking Dovel. She's breaking."

Ulyss came up to him, stamped his feet to try and ease the cold numbness. "That's because they can't feel her. It's good to see you up and about." He swiped the accumulation of the gently falling snow off his burlet.

"Thanks in good measure to my Lieutenants' support."

"Tyna's, too. Adele will be fine, Dovel. You needn't worry about her sensibilities. She insisted on misinterpreting you, misunderstanding your intentions to Kissre."

"Hopefully, this will be the last time." He smiled. His mind was not on either Adele or Ulyss. Although she hadn't given any sign, he knew Kissre had noticed his presence. Even with the fur-lined hat and the fur collar against her face, he'd seen, or felt, her eyes flick in his direction. This close, he could feel her responses, feel her movements.

"You should stop pining after her. No matter what Tyna has willed herself to believe, I don't think she'll come back, especially after her visit to your tent. Perhaps you should take your advice to Adele."

He finally looked at Ulyss. "I wasn't pining over Kissre, Ulyss. Just depressed at what we have become. Change can't happen soon enough for me."

"More philosophical meanderings today? You're still suffering the effects of those damn drugs." Ulyss swore and started ranting about what happened.

Dovel cut him short, hardly listening. "That, too."

"So what snapped you out of it? You've hardly been out of your tent since we arrived here."

Fudge loped up to Dovel, his tail wagging. The dog rose on his hind feet and made a few pirouetting jumps, his tongue dangling. Dovel grabbed the dog's head and rubbed his cheeks. From his pocket he took a ball and threw it. Fudge raced off. "Encouragement."

"From whom?"

Looking at his lieutenant, he noticed Ulyss had started a beard. The red face hair differed from his medium brown hair in a startling manner. Taking a deep, satisfied breath, he grinned at Ulyss. "Kissre. Lose your razor?"

"Thought my face would stay warmer. Well?"

"You can't tell?" Fudge bounded up and dropped the ball. Dovel continued their game.

"No, your shields have grown amazingly thick. Especially since you regained some control after your session with Adept Orrthu. Tyna had never experienced anything like your bout with the old hag. She's been on the offensive ever since."

"She shouldn't have gone to Kissre. There was no reason for her to know."

"Why in hell not? You acted in Kissre's interest."

"Because I don't want Kissre's pity or sense of obligation. Matter-of-fact, I'd like to be rid of it."

"Don't tell Tyna."

"No. I'm also gratified she did it, although Tyna was motivated by more than my crisis."

"Well, she has been trying to make amends with your intolerant barbarian," Ulyss said.

"You still think that?" He stopped his game with Fudge to look at Ulyss. "Don't you sense anything of Kissre through me?"

"No. She scares me, the way I can't feel her presence. It's unnerving. I've experienced some of your thoughts and feelings when in contact with her."

"Then you know? What the Talent Review Board wants?"

"No one believes she has Talent. It's too incredible."

"She's not a barbarian, you know. I think it's time I introduced you to her properly."

"Dovel, I don't think she'll be talking to you any time soon. We all heard the results of your last meeting. It woke the whole camp. I told you, forget her."

"That's funny. That dual gave me the first hope in ages."

~ * ~

"Ready to handle me?" Kissre asked Dovel as she dismounted before her tent. He and Fudge stood waiting. A soldier ran forward and grabbed the reins from Kissre. Interrupted, she gave the man some orders then turned to Dovel. Fudge walked forward and nudged her hand, his tail making slow loops behind him.

He gave her one of his tilt-corner smiles. "Somehow, above all else, I thought you wouldn't forgive me that comment."

"Then you've recovered from what they did to you?"

"Yes."

"I'm glad. Is that why you're here?" Standing still the cold infiltrated her anew.

"No. Marshal Ranor has called a debriefing for later tonight. He has ridden out with Quillon, and most of your contingent. They meet the Duke of Lambere and his troops to guide them to the camp." Uneasy silence enveloped them for a minute. "You've been outdoors all day. I thought I'd save you coming for Fudge and let you know what's going on. Can we talk?"

"Fay will have coffee ready. Would you like to come in?"

He nodded and lifted the flap to her tent. Kissre entered to embrace the welcoming fragrance of the brew. As expected, Fay bent over a brazier pouring coffee into cups. She either knew of Dovel's presence or had heard his voice. "Welcome, Captain Dovel. Mistress Kissre, take your outerwear off. I can feel the cold flowing from you. A heated robe lies on your bed."

"Just Kissre, Fay," Kissre said in her constantly repeated response, but she removed her long heavy coat, the hauberk, and arm and leg guards as Fay welcomed Dovel. Fudge sprawled next to the brazier.

"Have you had coffee?" Fay asked Dovel in her soft voice. At his negative headshake, she said, "It has a heavenly smell, but for first-time users, it possesses a bitter, nasty taste. Sir Quillon showed me how to make it and said the taste is acquired. Kissre enjoys it, but I find it more palatable with sweetener and cream."

"Goat's milk," Kissre corrected with a shudder. Sitting on a pillow next to the brazier, she gratefully accepted the cup Fay handed her. The maid's hands stayed on the cup, surrounding hers to make sure she didn't drop the cup, her eyes inspecting Kissre's face. Heat from the cup seeped into her cold stiff hands, but she found she still couldn't hold it.

"Your hands are freezing, but there is no frostbite. You were drawing maps without gloves?"

"It wasn't that cold."

"Only the amount of time you spent has chilled you too deeply. You will need warming."

"Just warm blankets will do," Kissre said.

"Where are they?" Dovel asked.

"Don't touch me," Kissre said as he approached.

"I'm not using," Dovel said, reaching for her hands and ignoring her physical retreat. When he kissed her curled fingers, Kissre felt a shock. Dovel saw her reaction. She pulled her hands from the welcoming warmth of his.

Shortly, Kissre found herself bootless, naked except for a robe, and ensconced in blankets with warming stones. She did not protest but sighed as the shivering lessened. She leaned back into a pillow propped against her campaign box. Fudge came and lay against her, resting his huge head in her lap. Drowsy, she closed her eyes.

"Is it like this every night? What do her men do? They must be as cold."

"Arrangements were made by Kissre for their care. They are all native Pathfinders anyhow and know how to take care of themselves. The temperature has dropped dramatically only within the last few candlemarks."

"I am here," Kissre snapped and opened her eyes. "You don't need to talk over me."

"The cold is nothing to dismiss," Dovel said.

Kissre was too tired to argue. What she really wanted was to sleep. "I don't. When is Aristo Aurelias to arrive?"

"He is already here," Aurelias said, entering with a blast of cold air. Kissre shivered as she stood, and the cold air swept up her robe and blanket. The duke waved both her and Dovel back to their seats. "I was told this tent would be warm, and there would be a good chance of coffee ready."

Behind him, Quillon entered with a smile and bow of obeisance to Fay, who blushed.

"My entourage is setting up camp. Hopefully, I will have a tent before dark, although a warm tent is doubtful. Hello, Kissre. Captain Dovel." Aurelias threw back his long cloak, removed his gloves, and reached toward the fire, as did Quillon. "Is there food?" Their entrance crowded the small tent.

"Yes, Your Grace," Fay said. "We were making Kissre warm. She had been on patrol all day and came in quite depleted. Let me get you warming stones, also." She curtseyed and left the tent.

"And we've been traveling all day," Quillon said, helping himself to coffee after handing Aurelias a cup. He settled onto a pillow with his cup. "But we were probably not out as long as Kissre, and we constantly moved or stopped by a fire every few candlemarks to warm. Having Talents broadcast your arrival is very helpful. I told Aristo Aurelias you would have a current report for him."

"You see me seated and ready," Kissre said, distrusting Quillon's genial manner.

"Too exhausted to do ought else, you mean?" Quillon said. He turned to Dovel and noted Dovel's smug smile and his gaze returned to her with a wide grin. "Or underdressed?"

Kissre returned his mockery with placid equanimity, aware the Kennetsurean was in a tweaking mood and she his target.

"Captain Dovel," Quillon continued in disengaging tones that masked his mockery. "Your presence surprises me. I thought you would have given up on such a poor friendship. After hearing you stood friend to Kissre at great cost to yourself, and she not only failed to thank you but also took umbrage at your effort, I imagined you done with this shrew. You must have a magnanimous nature, for you cannot expect an apology anytime soon."

"It would be a sad thing if I were forced to leave my own tent," Kissre said, equaling Quillon's serenity.

"You see what I mean—no forgiving, no apologizing, no thanking."

"You make me sound insufferable," Kissre said.

"Just prickly, but one gets used to it." Dovel smiled. He rose and helped Fay as she entered through the tent flap with a great tray of food. Two soldiers came behind her with more trays. Marshal Ranor followed on their heels, but Kissre didn't see him as she replied to Dovel.

"By all means, get used to it, if you can stand the spines." She rose, blushing, as she saw the Marshal.

"Good, everyone is here, wait, unless you could summon Ulyss?" Ranor asked Dovel as his gaze swiveled to each person. Dovel gave him his pillow, but Ranor refused. Yelling for his adjutant to bring more seating, he waited. "Is that coffee? I've heard about it. May I? How is it, Dovel?"

"Certainly," Aurelias said.

Quillon pulled another cup from Fay's tray as the maid handed plates of food to those gathered in the tent. Kissre took her plate, carefully arranged her blankets, and half-listened to the banter.

"Use sweetener and cream," Dovel advised. "Lots."

Fudge lay next to Kissre. She stroked his back as she watched with apathy, drained of any initiative. She picked at her food. Ulyss entered about the same time the extra pillow seats arrived, and everyone rearranged themselves as they found places around the brazier.

Ulyss looked as uncomfortable as Kissre felt. "You might as well relax as long as you're here." The only place left was a pillow next to her. At his tentative approach, she grinned. "My weapons are all sheathed. You will find me completely disarmed and too tired to bite."

Ulyss gave a soft laugh. "I've no fear of you, Colonel. You've never attacked anyone except on a battlefield."

As Ulyss spoke, Dovel sighed in relief and sank into a pillow. Aurelias and Ranor spoke in low tones. Quillon still ate.

"Kissre." She corrected. "And you've obviously forgotten my infamous encounter with Tyna and the equally well-known ignominy of my sessions with Quillon."

Ulyss's soft chuckle was covered by Quillon's retort, showing he listened. "You speak of me as an enemy? After the candlemarks I've spent training you? You miserable ingrate! I've even shown your maid how to brew coffee properly. You're incapable of thanking Dovel for his service, and you spit on mine."

"Cuss maybe, spit never."

"Kissre has no reason to thank me," Dovel said. "Tyna should not have informed her of what happened. It is a Cygnese matter."

"And this did not involve Kissre at all?" Aurelias asked, emerging from his exchange with Ranor. Surprise laced his voice.

"I think Kissre has already addressed any danger to herself," Ranor said. His compressed lips unsuccessfully hid a grin.

"It's ludicrous," Kissre said. Catching herself, she added, "Not what happened to you." She glanced at Dovel. "I should take a trip to Sidih to settle the matter. They must be very complacent to think I'd take no action against them."

"Please don't," Dovel said with a weak grin. "You've thrown enough threats their way already."

A side-glance showed Ulyss grinned into the coffee he pretended to drink. Mirth-lined eyes met hers. "Captain Tyna was pleased to pass your message on."

"Fay, some of our guests don't like the coffee," Kissre said. "Bring some hot cider, please." The maid nodded and left.

Aristo Aurelias spoke over Kissre's request. "Yes. Well, we will broach that subject in a minute. You have enough to do here without taking on Sidih. First, I should like to hear your report on the Pertelon fortifications and positions. Ranor has told me you've acted as tactical liaison here in camp."

Leaning back, Kissre grabbed her saddlebag, withdrew a sheaf of papers, and passed them to Aurelias. Marshal Ranor looked from his side.

"They're staying behind their fortifications, stripping the forest before and behind them," Kissre said. "This recent cold spell has stopped them as well as us, but they observe us. They are aware of us patrolling but don't muster unless there are forays into their zone." She shrugged. "Occasionally, they fire arrows, but we've been careful to stay out of range. The platoons that we have sent out can't reach their fortifications."

"Anything else?" Ranor asked. "What about prohibited weapons?"

"They have them. I've seen them. Fifteen cannons. They have not used them, though."

"How did you get the information?" Ranor asked.

"At night it is possible to work between their posts and through the barricades."

Aurelias looked up from his perusal of her maps. "You've done this?"

"Yes."

"When?" Quillon asked, interrupting. "You had no orders!"

"Once, four nights ago. I wanted to see how well-fortified their back door was and what weapons they concealed."

"And?" Aurelias asked.

"Minimal fortification, they don't need them. They have masses of troops. Think they might be planning an offensive. They've placed all their defenses westward, particularly along the lines indicated on the map. They're waiting on reinforcements but seem well supplied. We know they have a supply line coming from the sea. I think there is a second from the north. I'd like to take a small recon unit to see if it can be found and neutralized."

"I will send squad-led platoons to do that," Ranor said.

He and Aurelias talked over options, their own defense, and offensive avenues. Aurelias folded the papers and handed them to Ranor. "Now we move to your problem." He looked at her.

"I have no problem," Kissre said with a small huff of dismissal, pulling her blankets tighter.

"Ignoring it won't lessen its danger," Quillon said.

Aurelias looked at Quillon. "Tell me what you see as the problem."

"Kissre has a hidden Talent. Concealed from her as well. Some few here have discovered this Talent and know its value, Captain Dovel for one."

"I also reported suspicions of possible Talent," Ranor said. "When Dovel said he could track her, I and others knew she must have some Earth Talent. It's the only way he could track her."

At Aurelias' inquiring look, Ranor explained. "Kissre is void. Most Talents find her presence unnerving, seeing her but unable to feel her. If Captain Dovel can track her, it means they have bonded through a shared Earth Talent. Her behavior on the excursions with Captain Jycel's platoons also indicated this Talent. Since then, I've found her uncannily accurate in her assessment of land, enemy positions, and strategic maneuvers, which is another indicator."

"Or training," Kissre said.

"I was told this could cause Kissre danger," Quillon continued over her. "If her Talent became known, there are those in Sidih who would keep her here, willing or not. Since Captain Dovel was taken in for retesting, I believe they learned from him what Kissre is."

"She is an Earth Talent, then?" Aurelias asked.

"Yes, though she doesn't want to believe it," Dovel said. "But more importantly, she is a Catalyst."

"Which is why Ulyss is here," Ranor said. "He is a Latent Catalyst and can help verify Kissre's Talent."

All eyes turned to Kissre. "Even if I have Talent, no one has the right to detain me. Besides, since I can't control it, it's useless." Skepticism and determination filled her voice.

"I can't direct mine either," Ulyss said. "Sometimes I feel my only real Talent is as a low-level Empath and lucky to be in a squad at all."

"So how does your Talent work?" she asked.

"When I'm in bond with other Talents, my Talent enhances theirs."

Kissre shrugged. "There you have the crux of it. According to you," she said, looking at Dovel, "I can't bond with anyone."

Dovel grinned. "You can bond, you are only void in Touch Talent, but you don't even need to bond," he said. "And you don't need mental Touch. Any Talent you physically touch, skin to skin, is affected, and you know it."

"Nonsense," Kissre scoffed, but an unsettling silence fell around her. After an edgy stillness, Kissre looked at Ranor, who also looked disquieted about Dovel's revelation. "If you reported these suspicions, why are you here now? I assume you are not planning on taking me into custody?"

"Indeed not. You are too valuable to me where you are. I did what I was legally bound to do because others knew and watched. However, I am torn. It does not mean I wish you harm, to detain or even imprison you." He caught her eyes. "Yes, it might come to that. I also feel that if your touch could increase my squads' ability as much as I think it might, I'd be tempted to force you. Unfortunately, I know my officers and their squads, and this information might tear them apart. Word has spread about why Dovel was forcibly retested and about the results. Rumor claims they suspect an Earth Talent, but no word about a catalyst has leaked out."

At Kissre's expression, Ranor said, "He did not tell you? They did more than just retest him. They probed his mind while drugged. There are those here in camp who would help the Talent Review Board gain any of their goals."

"There are just as many, if not more, who would resist any attempt to coerce Kissre into service. Others would be just as glad to see the Board's abolishment," Ulyss said. Ranor nodded.

"Captain Dovel says your merely touching Ulyss should prove your Talent to you as well as to us," Quillon said. "You needn't look at him as if he suddenly turned into a snake. Just take his hand."

"I don't believe any of this." She pulled her blankets tighter. Everyone waited, watched her. She held out her hand. Ulyss's warm clasp closed around her fingers. She felt nothing and was too tired to care.

His reaction, though, was quite different. Kissre had never seen such an expression except on those dying from a sword thrust through their chest. She squeaked in warning as she pulled her hand back. Ulyss's paroxysm locked his hand on hers. She bolted upright as Dovel grabbed Ulyss and pulled his fingers open. Kissre sank back onto her pillow, shaken. Dovel attended his convulsing lieutenant.

"Catalyst to catalyst." Dovel said as Ulyss groaned, beginning to recover. "Heady mix."

Thirteen

"Are you all right?" Dovel asked Ulyss, feeling his lieutenant's disoriented mind settle with a familiar touch.

"Yeah, just shock. Feel a little strange, stupid. You told me not to reach for her, but I still tried, just habit. It's a natural reaction. Did you feel it? Like I could touch everyone, hear everyone? Do you think everyone heard me scream?" He gave a weak laugh. "And me only an Empath Level?"

"Yes," Dovel said, watching Kissre as he helped Ulyss. The others sat and watched as Quillon moved to wrap more blankets around Kissre. His strong arm circled her while he offered her hot coffee. Dovel felt a spike of jealousy. He sent a mental warning to Ranor not to approach her. If Ulyss was disoriented, Kissre was devastated. One of Marshal Ranor's staff entered the tent and informed his commander that all were gathering for his scheduled debriefing.

"Kissre, you need not attend. We already have your report," Aurelias said as he stood with Ranor and Quillon.

She lost her faraway look. "Your Grace, I'm still a soldier and expect to be employed as one. I will come."

"No, you will not," Ranor answered instead of Aurelias. "This does not impinge on your duties or honor, except that you are too tired to continue. Most of the army has done nothing during this siege except protect our position while you and your men scouted the enemy every day. We will talk more tomorrow about your duties."

Aurelias said with his command voice. "Kissre, believe or not as you choose, but I will not be robbed of your service. The Holy One knows I've run into your stubbornness before this, so this is a direct order. You are not to leave camp without a Kaereyan escort, nor to go off on unapproved excursions, particularly behind enemy lines. Allies or not, as a citizen and officer of the Kaereyan Army you have my protection. You will leave this country when I do, no matter what the Cygnese government declares." He nodded and left with Ranor and Quillon.

Fudge lay beside her. Arranging her blankets and dignity, she looked at Ulyss while she gathered her clothes to dress. The effort was too much, and she ended throwing them down. "Did I hurt you?"

"No. I was just unprepared for what I felt," Ulyss said. When Wyn appeared at Dovel's summons, he added, "I really don't need help." He turned to Kissre. "I want you to know that Dovel did not arrange this..."

"Ambush?" Kissre didn't look at Ulyss.

"Meeting. Marshal Ranor and Aristo Aurelias set it up. They felt it important to know."

Dovel put his hand on Ulyss's shoulder, Ulyss placed his on Dovel's. He smiled and then left with Wyn. Grabbing another blanket, Dovel threw it around his shoulders before sitting next to Kissre and drawing her into his arms. She didn't resist, and when he knew her asleep, he placed her on the bed.

~ * ~

The first sounds of the morning camp woke Kissre. She felt Dovel against her back with his arm around her waist. It was a warm and comforting presence.

She remembered waking the night before as he put her down and, feeling fear and panic overwhelm her, remembered saying, "Stay." The bed was small for two. She had rolled to her side, and he lay down next to her.

Listening, she knew him awake. His breathing had changed.

"Why, Kissre?" The whispered question brushed her ear.

"Because I was afraid." He didn't prod. She sighed. "I've lost so much. Last night I lost myself. Now I don't even know who I am. There is nothing left. I should not have...I used you, I'm sorry."

His hand stroked her shoulder and returned to rest on her waist. "I am here. I am glad you turned to me."

"Because you know I have some sort of Talent?"

"I ought to hit you for that." He remained silent a long time but didn't move his arm. "You are still you."

"Not like I was. I have something others want. Something I don't want, something of no use to me, and something I can't control."

"You don't know if all of that is true yet. Testing and training might change everything."

"Like you were tested? I don't think so." She twisted her head to look at him. "I've caused you nothing but trouble."

"Some. Are you feeling better?"

"Some." She hesitated a minute. "Will you make love to me?"

He groaned. "Kiss, do you know what you are asking?"

"Yes. No. I feel so lost." She turned onto her back so she could look him in the face. "Isn't it enough that I ask?"

He laughed. "Yes. No. Sleeping like this hasn't been easy. I've wanted you all night." He pushed the hair back off her forehead. "If we do this, there is no going back, understand? I can't be a lover one minute and a friend the next."

"Can't you be both?"

"Yes. I can be both. Or I can be a friend. If I become both, I can't return to being only a friend. Are you sure you want me or do you only want someone?"

"I've missed you."

"You've hidden it well."

"No, I haven't. I've been falling apart." She reached for him.

~ * ~

Later, he waited for her to finish dressing. Already clothed, he squatted before the brazier, rekindling the banked heat. Fay walked in, Kissre noticed, with breakfast for two. The maid placed the tray on a low table, smiled at Dovel, and left. Kissre sighed, between his squad's link with Dovel and Fay, their night's liaison would be all over the camp already.

"We need to talk." He looked up at her as she served herself.

"I know. Unless you can leave Cygna when this war is over, you know we're doomed to separation?"

"Until then?"

"Between the war and our duties? Whatever you want."

"I want us to share what free time we have."

She nodded. "Is your squad going to cause trouble? Do they already know?"

"Yes they know, but that won't cause a problem. You've not even met them all."

"Ulyss was enough. Am I now acceptable because they believe I have Talent?"

He ignored her surly remark. "You've apparently forgiven me for our initial encounter?"

"You thinking me a null Tyna? Yeah." She sighed. "I knew then. You had to have discovered the difference the first night, but you came back for more. It was hearing it from Tyna. Just don't ask me to make up with her. That's done and finished."

"She is your sister."

"Not anymore. It's better that way."

"Better for whom?"

She looked at Dovel. "For me. For Captain Pierce. Don't push."

"So why forgive me?"

Kissre looked up, panicked and surprised he asked. "Because you treated me like you cared, like what I felt mattered, even if you were wishing I were someone else. For most men, I've just been a convenience."

"I'd like to know I'm accepted for more than not treating you like a convenience. I'd like to know I'm not accepted out of obligation or charity."

Kissre didn't know how to explain what she felt. At her silence Dovel rose.

"Kiss, you're rotten at this." The tent flap fell behind him as he left. Fudge rolled to sitting and whined.

"Stay," she ordered, wondering how to fix what she broke. There was no time to ponder. Outside her tent, she recognized the noise of a camp mustering. Questioning a passing officer, she learned her predicted offensive had started. Pertelon troops had attacked their southern camp. She quickly donned her war gear.

~ * ~

"Where is Aristo Emory! His line is caving!" Kissre screamed. "Tell his Receiver he has to hold. Tell him we're bringing up reserves." Even as she spoke, she knew it too late. *Too damn late.* She swore every invective she knew as the line broke. Charging Pertelon troops breached the Kaereyan troop's line. More than expected. Emory's unit, her men, retreated in disorder. *Too late, too late.* Behind those lines, less than a furlong away, squads guided Cygnese troops. Kissre sent urgent orders to her troops, told her Sender to tell the squads to retreat.

The Sender stood dazed as Kissre mounted Carillon. "There are too many of them! Where are they coming from?" His voice rose with each word.

Kissre half-listened to the Sender's fear-laced cry. More enemy than the Cygnese army ever experienced surged against the failing defense.

Carillon twirled as Kissre screamed, "Did you send my message?" The young man looked blank. Kissre flicked him with her rein ends, and he flinched. "Answer me!"

"Sorry, ma'am. I'm sending now."

While assessing the situation, she made quick commands, "Tell the squads protecting this area to send up reserves immediately. Tell those on the field to retreat to a safer location along that ridge." She turned to her Royal Guard lieutenants and pointed to a defensible position. "Retreat and reassemble there until Aurelias sends orders." She left at a gallop, Fudge and six of her Pathfinders followed.

She pushed Carillon, rode her hard over very rough snow-covered terrain to meet her advancing reserve troops. She pulled to a sliding stop before the troop's captain, demanding, "Map!" He pulled out his copy. She pointed out her orders. "Take this route. I depend on you to stop the retreating troops at this point. Force them to hold a line."

"Yes, ma'am."

"You have any mounted?"

"Yes."

"Have them follow me."

His shouted orders followed her as she moved away. She headed to where the retreating troops would funnel. They ran into the company in disorderly retreat. Through threat and force, she rallied some of the units. Kissre realigned them in defensive locations and left some of the mounted to hold them until more foot reserves arrived. "Kill anyone who runs," she ordered as she left. Twice more she managed to reform the line.

"Ma'am." A Kaereyan soldier grabbed her stirrup. "There's a Cyg squad caught back there." He pointed in the direction. Dread clenched Kissre. Without further thought, she pushed Carillon through the retreating men and toward the collapsed line. Coming upon a Cygnese soldier, she demanded the location of the squad. He was a null but yelled he'd lead her there. Then Kissre realized all the troops around her were Cygnese, and all continued to hold their position.

She followed the man through the fighting troops, drawing her sword to help clear the way. Fringes of perception gave her awareness of Fudge lunging and fighting around and between Carillon's legs. Her Pathfinders were still with her along with a few of the Kaereyan mounted troops.

Spotting the squad, she advanced toward that hive of activity. Pertelonese troops nearly circled the spot and threatened to capture it. She started yelling orders as she passed, organizing the failing effort of the platoons protecting their squad. Slowly they formed a funnel of defense through the twisting needle-like line. They might be too late. Pertelon's forces seemed to know the prize they neared.

"Why aren't they retreating? They must know the danger!" She pressed Carillon harder and arrived in time to attack the first Pertelon troops to break the last Cygnese defenses.

Time slowed. She leaped from Carillon, slashed enemies, vaguely aware of the Cygnese troops' support and Fudge's vicious attacks. Thrusting her blade through a man, she pulled it free in time to slash another. Their opposition fell back.

She recognized the squad, recognized Jycel. He lay on the ground staring at nothing. The squad seemed uninjured but nearly unconscious as she lift-pushed them onto the laps of the mounted troops that had followed her. With one look, she realized the last was dead—Cevoka. Her likeness to Dovel filled Kissre with shock and dread. Time twisted between slow and fast, interspersed with flashes of the past with images of Cevoka on the trip to Guerestu, sharing meals and Aibhe rituals.

Kissre shook her head. *No time for this.* A couple Cygnese soldiers helped her lift and throw the body over Carillon. She tossed Carillon's reins to one of her Pathfinders. "Get them out of here!"

She turned to the troops still around her, newly aware of the sights and smells of carnage. She screamed her orders. "We will make an orderly retreat. Collapsing the line back on itself as we go. Check all bodies. We leave no living behind."

The Pertelon forces turned for another charge, but the retreat was already begun. Kissre kept the line close. They fought savagely. As they backed, the line strengthened. Jycel's troops held to their brutish task. Reinforcements arrived to help, and the line reformed. The Pertelonese troops stopped advancing. As more Kaereyan troops passed Kissre, they slowly started to push the enemy back. Lowering her aching arms, Kissre watched as the line moved forward. Troops, both Kaereyan and Cygnese, joined them, reinforced their strength. Behind them, she found the needed preparations and forces already forming to make the Pertelonese position untenable.

~ * ~

"It was a reckless act." Aurelias lambasted Kissre in his tent. She stood freshly cleaned from dirt and gore, neatly uniformed. "I realize

Aristo Emory did not show well. You had others at your disposal to rectify the situation."

"I did what I felt necessary. It was my line that broke and threatened Cygnese positions."

"Commanders give orders, staying out of the fray so they can continue to give orders! You endangered your position. You should have sent mounted troops to accomplish the task."

"I made the best choice available to me. The Aristos would not follow my orders. All I could do was leave them in command of their assigned positions. You will need to replace me. I am still a woman, and a commoner at that."

From Aurelias' silence, she knew she was right before Aurelias spoke. "Many of the Kaereyan officers and common soldiers are not prepared to take orders from a woman, no matter how competent. It would have made a difference if they had. This battle places Kaereya in an unfortunate light. I will not reduce you in rank, however." He looked at her over the small reading lenses through which he viewed papers. "Your battle instincts are too often accurate. I'm sorry, but putting you in charge of a mixed Cygnese and Kaereyan reconnaissance patrol will look like a demotion. It is a position you have held very successfully before this."

Leaving Aurelias' tent, Kissre snapped her fingers for Fudge and walked through the myriad camps to Jycel's tent. Among the Cygnese foot soldiers, she saw the platoon leader, Oran. He rose to his feet as she approached.

"Colonel, ma'am." Others around him also rose to their feet. She told them to sit, but all remained standing.

"How are your squad members?"

"Captain Tyna's with them, trying to hold them together."

Kissre looked at him hoping for more explanation without asking, conscious of all those listening. "Did you lose many men?"

"No, ma'am. Three dead. Six injured pretty bad. Two of the other platoons got hit hard, lost a quarter to half their men. Would have been a lot more if you hadn't come. We'd of all been dead."

"You held your positions." It was the highest tribute she could offer, and Oran understood. She saw Dovel emerge from a

tent, followed by Ulyss and the other members of his squad. ⹂ commanded Fudge to heel. He moaned. His tail whipped the groun⹁ as his head followed Dovel. "Are your men in the camp infirmary?"

"Yes, ma'am."

"Would you mind taking me to see them?"

A look of pleasure crossed Oran's tired face. "Be welcome to, ma'am."

"Give me one moment."

She approached Dovel, unsure of her welcome. He had not spoken to her since leaving her tent the previous day. "How is Jycel?"

He looked like he didn't want to speak to her but put out a hand to stroke Fudge as the dog's insistent nose poked at his palm. One of his team members looked at her with dislike, the others with curiosity. Ulyss gave her a dubious smile.

"With Tyna's help, he and the remaining squad will survive."

"What happened to them?"

Dovel sighed. "They were in bond, using their Talents together when Cevoka died. They shared her death."

"I see," Kissre said, though she didn't. She thought of all the men she had seen die. Those she had killed. She would not have liked to feel it, too. She looked away. "Can he have visitors?"

"Not yet."

She nodded. "Thank you for telling me."

Marshal Ranor, followed by a coterie of aides, walked up behind Dovel and Ulyss. His officers acknowledged him. Kissre saluted him in Kaereyan fashion, turned, and left. Fudge side-jumped and heeled next to her.

Dovel watched her halt by some of Jycel's platoon members, then walk off with them. As she passed, Cygnese soldiers rose in a wave of motion. Kissre remained oblivious to the tribute, her head bent, listening to the platoon leader.

"I've never seen them do that for anyone," Ulyss said. "What did she do?"

"I suggest we find out," Ranor said, stopping to watch his soldiers' tribute. He turned to Ulyss. "Since your initial meeting with

her, I have not had a chance to follow up." With a hand, he indicated they return to his headquarters. "Call in your platoon leaders."

~ * ~

"Never seen the like, sir."

Tomel had brought one of Jycel's platoon leaders. The man described the day's battle. "We'd have all died out there, no leadership, no direction. Blue Dragon just seemed to appear. And her the biggest target around, like she was immune to arrows. Jumped off that great horse and stood over the squad fighting off the enemy. Gave us all heart, sir. She fought with us side by side, yelling orders. Put Lieutenant Cevoka on her mount, got the squad out. But then, sir, she stayed. Made sure the rest of us got out, too. Oran is taking her to visit the wounded. Lots of soldiers alive today might not have been. They hold good respect for her, sir."

Ranor sat down and closed his eyes briefly. Dovel felt his mental anguish and retort. *::A Catalyst. We nearly lost a Catalyst.::* He spoke at the same time he dismissed the platoon leaders verbally, "Thank you for your report, that is all."

::We were so concerned about the squad, we assumed the platoons got them out,:: Ranor continued. *::Ulyss, how were you affected?::*

Ulyss answered aloud, projecting the images in his mind the stronger Talents would see. "I have never felt anything like it. Suddenly I could feel everyone in the room, saw their Talent, their strength, their thoughts. Except Kissre. Seeing her was the only way I knew her there. I knew Dovel could feel her and felt an urgent desire to touch her mind. That changed everything. Power surged around us, all of us, shimmering sheets of it with light and energy streaking through it. Saw fire patterns and earth patterns like they were one and the same. It was unbearable and tantalizing at the same time. I still have periods of disorientation."

::Any lasting effects?::

"Headache. For a while I thought I was burned out. I think I'm at a different level but feel afraid to try it out. Dovel says my Empath

Touch is much stronger. I noticed similar increases in him after his encounters with Kissre."

"What would you guess her Talent?"

"Can't say, but above my level. She's Catalyst undoubtedly. She increases other Talent's gifts most alarmingly but is as unaware of it as any Latent. Couldn't be a Mediator as she can't touch minds. I sensed more, something else I couldn't identify. Something I've never felt."

~ * ~

It took Kissre longer in the infirmary than she had planned. Oran introduced her to most of the wounded. As they finished, the exhausted-looking healer approached. Oran greeted him and offered an introduction.

"Healer Bujyea and I are acquainted, Sergeant Oran." She took Bujyea's hand and shook it. She did not release his grip and he gave no sign of wanting to free his hand. "How are you, sir?"

With a long look at her, he placed his other hand over their clasped hands. His drained expression eased. "You're looking much better than the last time I saw you. Are you here to visit the wounded?" he asked.

"Completely healed, thank you. Many of us briefly served together."

"Your dog is not with you?"

"Fudge is waiting at the door. Quietly." She grinned.

"Bring him in, Colonel Kissre. He might cheer some of the men."

He let go of her hand. "Thank you, Colonel Kissre."

She smiled. "Just Kissre to you, Healer Bujyea, thank you."

Afterward she went and checked Carillon. The mare had been freshly groomed and stood contentedly munching hay. Dovel approached while she fussed, talking to Carillon in reassuring nonsense. She watched him with wary eyes. "Hello."

Nodding, he patted Fudge's head and thumped his sides, but his face remained expressionless. "There's a meeting."

Kissre snorted in disgust. "With whom?"

"Ranor and Aurelias."

"You?"

"No. I'm out of it now, just the messenger. They want to see you. Now." He turned and started walking away.

"Dovel." She threw the brush she held in a bucket of horse grooming paraphernalia. He stopped but didn't turn. "I don't want you out of it." She took a step and stopped. "I can't say the words you want to hear, not because I don't want to, not because I don't feel them." She waited for any response. There was none. "You frighten me. What I feel for you frightens me."

He turned at last and looked at her, his inexpressive face unable or unwilling to show anything. "They want you now. Marshal Ranor's tent. Aurelias waits."

Kissre nodded and watched him walk away.

~ * ~

"I told you, I meant you no harm." Ranor's command voice sounded loud and pugnacious in the confines of his tent headquarters. Aristo Aurelias sat across from Ranor's camp desk, and Quillon stood behind the duke, listening through Ranor's harangue. Outside, a sudden and seething wind howled and blasted the camp with cold and snow. "But I am not prepared to see you harm yourself or waste your Talent, whatever it might be! You will not be allowed to endanger yourself on Cygnese land. Aristo Aurelias ordered you to keep a contingent of Kaereyan soldiers around you!"

"I rode with Kaereyan mounted archers."

"Colonel Kissre acted within the standards of her duty. To do less would have caused greater loss."

"I realize that! But I'm still a squad short. Jycel and his team won't work for months, if ever." Ranor paced. "And I am not prepared to lose a Catalyst on the field."

"It's where I belong," Kissre responded.

"The defeat was, in some measure, Kissre's failure."

Quillon made an unusual movement of protest at Aurelias' statement.

His liege continued, unaware. "She has been reassigned to reconnaissance and tactical command and will be with me during future battles."

Ranor settled, seeming to fluff feathers in calm, strengthening his hawk image to Kissre. "While many of my Talents hold you responsible for Cevoka's death, you've developed a certain reputation among my troops. On purpose?"

"No, sir. Your troops are more accustomed to women officers."

"Only in squads, not on the line."

"They've taken orders from women and don't find it offensive. It makes a difference."

"Kissre? Any questions?" Aurelias asked.

"A request. I want to lead my own reconnaissance patrols. It is the only way I can give you the information you need."

With some wrangling and prohibitions ordered as safeguards, she won her request. She figured because she had been so successful at it before. And Ranor didn't think she would become involved with Pertelonese troops with a Cygnese platoon added to her force.

She left headquarters in as great a fury as the approaching storm. Reaching her tent, she stood listening to the wind. She went to the adjacent partition where Fay stayed. "Move your belongings into my tent. I want Carillon in here tonight." Fay didn't even hesitate. By the time she retrieved Carillon from the picket line, Fay had emptied her section of the tent. Five more trips brought bedding, food, and water. Two soldiers helped her. During her trips she saw others leading horses and ponies away. Still, too many ponies stood tethered on the line. Cleat approached, the wind ruffling the fur of his long coat but otherwise not affecting him.

"If we take the rest of the ponies deep into the forest, they stand a better chance of survival. We know a site that is protected." He yelled to be heard, and Kissre yelled back.

"Do you have volunteers?"

"Yes, ma'am. My people know how to survive here. It would be a waste to let so many animals die."

"What extra will you need?" She led Cleat to the supply tents and left orders. It was another half-mark before Cleat and five of his men rode off leading the remaining ponies into a snow-laden gale. Kissre silently wished them well.

Back at her tent, fighting the frigid whipping air, she checked the tent supports and stakes before entering Carillon's new stable. Inside she brushed the snow off her shoulders. The mare stood uneasy but quiet, looking at Kissre with interest. Kissre spoke softly and rubbed her grey coat dry of melting snow. Her hands ran over another set and Kissre looked up in surprise. Dovel stood on the other side of the mare, wiping the hide on his side. His gaze caught hers in a level look.

"Fay left," he said as she ducked under Carillon's neck to face him. "She has a friend she wishes to spend the storm with and thought it might be crowded in here." He wiped something off her cheek. "You may lose your servant."

"Through the storm? What friend?"

"Yes. It's likely to be a long one. Quillon, I imagine."

Stunned, Kissre repeated, "Quillon?" Then laughed. When her humor ended, she asked, "Is that how long you'll be staying?"

"Much longer."

She slowly wiped Carillon's face. "We take this day by day?"

"Agreed." He watched her. "You tolerate my squad and my strange silences. I won't push my expectations on you."

"I don't interfere with your squad and duty. You don't interfere with mine?"

"Agreed."

Fourteen

For two days the gale rampaged through the camp, making existence hideous and duty near impossible. At the storm's end, the sun emerged for the first time in a sennight, and everyone set to digging out. Huge piles of snow soon accumulated everywhere. Ten tents had collapsed in camp, but no one was injured. After a long session of digging an area clear for the horses, Kissre returned to her tent. A little later, Dovel entered. Kissre sat sharpening her knives. She looked up to see what, for Dovel, was a broad smile, shown more in his eyes than with his mouth. "Good news?"

"Very. The Maze reports the storm destroyed Pertelon's fleet. They were standing off Guerestu and were blown into off-shore rocks."

"The re-supply ships?"

"Gone."

"So only the northern line remains. That is good news."

"It seems that one is gone, too." Kissre looked at him in inquiry.

"After the storm, a team of Tracker Talents scoured the land. Avalanches have closed the northern gate. Avalanches are always dangerous at this time of year. They did not choose good encampment sites."

Kissre sat in speculation. "Mountains should be left to those familiar with them. So, the besiegers are now besieged. Pertelon has left many stranded troops behind their fortifications. They will become more dangerous, more willing to take chances."

Dovel shrugged. "Ranor doesn't think much will happen over the next sennight or more while they still have food, and everyone is moving snow. They will ration it. If you can get leave for a sennight, I would like to leave camp."

"Travel will be difficult."

"Our supply lines have created a road. It is already open."

"Yes, then." She put away her weapons and rose. "I'm ready to leave this camp for a while."

"My squad will need to travel with us, and I expect if Ranor knows you are going, he will attach extra troops as protection."

"How about Cleat and his Pathfinders?" She started unbuckling the heavy cloak he still wore.

"I'll ask. You aren't curious about where I want to go?"

"Nope. It's enough you want to go. Besides, I'm bored." She removed the cloak and started on his other clothes. "Fudge needs exercise. He is in camp too much."

He stilled her hands. "Kiss, the storm's over, it's broad daylight, and anyone might enter."

Snapping her fingers, she took Fudge to the tent's outer flap.

"Fudge, guard." She turned to smile at Dovel. "Not now."

~ * ~

Kissre took her weapons and wore her armor, as did her Pathfinders. They appeared more like a guard for the traveling squad than anything. The Pathfinders were a blessing. They knew how to rough camp in the cold. One night they spent under the bent branches of one of the huge-girthed trees. Its snow-laden evergreen fronds touched the ground, but inside, the branches formed an enclosed shelter.

"This is how you saved the ponies?" She asked.

"Yeah, just like this," Cleat answered grinning. "The branches don't break, and the snow insulates. Smoke from fire travels up the trunk like a chimney. Trick's finding the right tree and making the right fire." He was right. With the insulating snow and pony hides thrown on the ground, the interior became warm enough to take off their heavy outerwear. It was almost comfortable.

Kissre watched Dovel's squad. They watched her in turn, making tentative attempts at conversation. It was clear they were uncomfortable, both with her and the situation in which they found themselves. Adele, the one Kissre liked least, helped her with meal chores and proved an able camp cook, but their conversation remained limited while working over the pots.

Dovel had brought her guith, and that night they played together. Cleat and his men enjoyed the music and often sang along with them, humming when they didn't know the words. Encouraged, Kissre sang them songs none of them had ever heard.

"How do you know so many?" Ulyss asked.

"I collect them."

"Collect them?" Cath asked in surprised tones, shoulder-length wispy straight hair swaying with her head movement.

"Some people collect objects, or art, or clothing, things to remember past travels. As a mercenary, my luggage and possessions are limited. There is always music in an army camp, and I noticed reoccurring themes. So, I started collecting songs."

"Did you write them down?" Cath asked.

"Some, but not all. I remember most without writing them down. Here, this one is from the Eastern Empire." She sang the foreign lyrics and unusual music. Then a contest began, a challenge to see if she could play all they named. Kissre insisted they sing any she didn't know until she learned them.

~ * ~

Four days passed in pleasant travel for the road and weather conditions. They did not go as far as Sidih. Dovel turned off the main road, and they traveled half a day to the south. After passing several hamlets, they turned down the lane to a farm, several barns with surrounding corrals and pastures.

The storm had not hit as hard west of the siege camp. The depth of snow on the ground steadily diminished. Here it was only a few fingers deep. Kissre glanced around at the fields filled with ponies, some newly foaled, cavorted in gangly exuberance. Her glance stopped, and she froze.

Carillon halted, sensing Kissre's distraction. Fudge barked and started running, taking the field's fence in a single leap. Out among the ponies stood a giant. Kissre slowly dismounted and climbed the fence, unaware of moving. She followed Fudge.

A buckskin head rose from a pile of hay in the field. The horse nickered a greeting and ambled toward her. She couldn't trust her vision, so she walked closer. As her arms closed around his neck, and she felt his warmth and inhaled his clean horse scent, belief came.

She heard others approach behind her. She turned, knowing her face tear drenched. "How? It's him! It can't be, but it is. You told me you put him down."

"No. I didn't. I said he didn't suffer. Well, he probably did, but there was a pony trainer there. I'll introduce you. This is his farm. Once we got Bother on his feet, he claimed Bother could be saved. I just couldn't do what you asked. I figured he deserved a fighting chance." He stroked Bother's neck. "I received word a while ago that Bother was eating the farm out of profit and to come get him." Looking around at the foals, Dovel added, "I imagine he might have been kept longer than necessary."

Kissre hugged Dovel. "Thank you." She cried harder, unable to stop the tears streaming down her face. "Thank you." He wrapped his arms around her. Fudge nipped at Bother's ankles and the big horse jumped, back kicked, and chased the dog around the field.

~ * ~

One look at the approaching page and Eldin realized disaster had fallen. "Aristo Uilleam." The page bowed. "King Clement asks for your presence. I am to take you to him."

"Prepare yourself. This cannot be good," Eldin whispered. They followed the page through a series of courtyards and hallways to an antechamber off the main courtroom.

Clement and his advisors, the senior Aristos and the arms master waited there. Eldin felt his soul freeze. Clement spoke before they had completely entered the room.

"My dear Aristo Leavold, I am so sorry. There has been an accident."

Eldin took Uilleam's arm, his fingers digging deep into the flesh. Uilleam looked at him, all huge eyes in his unnaturally pale face, then looked at the king. The courtiers parted. A body lay on the table behind them.

"It was something no one could have foreseen. His blade broke. His opponent could not stop his thrust in time. He did not suffer."

Eldin led Uilleam to Payden's body. Uilleam touched the cold and blue-white lifeless face. Uilleam's face remained vacant, looking at the blood-covered clothing with horror.

Uilleam's sudden scream and his explosion of grief startled all. Eldin placed his hand on Uilleam's shoulder as he bent over and cradled his brother in his arms. He raised his voice to overcome Uilleam's gasping sobs.

"Your Highness, Aristo Uilleam thanks you for this courtesy, but may he have some privacy?"

"Certainly, Sir Innes," Clement said. "We would not wish to impose ourself at such a grievous time."

Uilleam's unfettered emotion made Clement's lip curl, but the other Aristos looked nervous. They turned and filed out after the king. No one looked back.

The bereft weeping lasted some time. Uilleam interspersed his wails with a choked and sniveled discourse of sorrow and guilt with his brother's corpse. He fell silent at last, his face buried in his hands.

"Uilleam, they will send servants in soon to take care of Payden. Look at me!" Eldin could not pull the hands away. "Uilleam, you must get control of yourself."

"Why? All is ended."

"No, it isn't. You are still alive. If they learn your game, you won't be."

"It makes no difference. I want to die, too."

With tremendous effort, he pulled the hands down and looked into the grief-crazed eyes. "Payden demands that you don't. So do your parents and your grandfather. Only you can bring hope to this demented community."

A watery giggle escaped Uilleam. "Demented, demented, demented," he sang.

"Stop it!" Eldin slapped the pale face, and Uilleam's eyes filled with fury. The young man jumped to his feet, growling as he lifted Eldin and threw him.

Eldin picked himself up and rushed Uilleam. Though smaller, experience gave him an advantage. He wrestled Uilleam to the ground and held him in a fighter's hold. "Damn it, Uilleam, stop!" His whispered commands finally registered. He felt the urgent aggression leave the body he held. "Are you going to remain quiet?"

Uilleam nodded, and he helped him stand. Quiet tears ran down the grief-twisted face. "Listen, I know you've worked very hard to protect Payden, but nobody could save Payden without his cooperation. He wasn't as smart as you."

"He is all I tried to save."

"I am not trying to be cruel, Uilleam. He was your brother, and you loved him. I liked Payden. He was an attractive, bitter, yet talented boy who threatened King Clement's security. My sorrow could only be greater if Clement had killed you, too."

Their conversation, conducted in whispers, was broken when servants opened the doors. Eldin turned to them. "My apologies, Aristo Leavold's grief has caused some disruption to the room, but he is recovered now. I am taking him to his own apartment." He held out an arm to shepherd Uilleam out of the antechamber.

"Keep your head bowed, look at no one, and talk to no one," he whispered. Eldin, aware of the eyes on them, walked next to Uilleam. He deflected all those approaching with condolences with a shake of the head. Once the door to their apartment closed behind them, he leaned against it with a sigh of relief and closed his eyes.

"How did you know?" Uilleam's barely audible voice reached him from where he stood by the fireplace, hand grasping the mantle.

Eldin spoke loudly, overly loud, as he pointed at the door. "Aristo Uilleam, let me urge you to rest. This has been such a shock."

A quarter-mark passed. Eldin walked over to Uilleam, who had turned away. Uilleam spoke low, almost in a whisper. "How did you know?"

"Did you think I could train you in arms and learn nothing of you? A good fighter uses instinct and strategy. You showed both. How long have you played your game?"

"Since childhood." Tears started down his face. "I watched my father killed and then my grandfather." He gasped in a great breath and bent his head to his hands. "For long years I don't remember they say I didn't speak. Years. My nurse took care of both Payden and me. She taught me what she could. By the time I started speaking, I'd already been labeled stupid, somehow knew the label protected me from Clement. The other tormentors I was used to. Besides, it became a game to see how many I could fool for how long. Now I've killed Payden."

"No. Don't think it. Clement killed Payden. If not by his own hand, by his word."

"He killed my father and my grandfather. I saw him."

"And he allowed you to live?"

"He didn't know I was there. I had been playing a hiding game with my grandfather. I was under a heavily draped table."

"Does anyone else know of your deception?" Uilleam remained quiet. "Tell me, Uilleam."

"No. Any possible supporters have stayed away from court. they supplied Clement with the money he so desperately needs. I hate him so much. I'm surprised he can't feel it."

"Clement is no Adept, and his witches are weak ineffectual things. I know—I've encountered real witches. He only knows what he sees, and he saw Payden as a potential rival. A rallying point for any dissident noble who objected to his rule."

"Why did you do it? Why did you swear to me? It was the first hope I ever entertained of escaping this life. You must realize now I tested you. I was so surprised when you gave me the true words. I could not believe it."

"Because I hated what I had become, hated Clement. We will watch, Uilleam. Can you contact these Aristos you know? We might be able to build a group against Clement."

"How? It's useless, and there is always a possibility he knows."

"Payden's funeral will help show us the way, but you must keep up your pretense." Uilleam looked at the innocent eyes that hid a shrewd and wronged soul.

"Payden's death will seem a senseless killing to those who hate him. Watch. They will all come to good King Leavold's grandson's funeral. We will watch. Not everyone is as good at deception as yourself."

"I cannot do it." Uilleam sighed and walked away to flop in dejected despair into the only good chair. "It seems disrespectful to play the buffoon at my brother's funeral."

"No buffoon. You will be properly sober and quiet, and blank looking in grief, as directed by your man-nanny. Everyone knows of my pride. It is my besetting sin. Those who don't know you well will look to you as heir apparent."

Tears trickled down Uilleam's face. "Heir? Clement would never recognize me."

"Listen, Uilleam. There is a chance. I've thought of it ever since I learned your quality." Uilleam looked at him. "To hide in full view of an inimical court is no easy task. Clement is childless. He has not even sired any bastards. The king," sarcasm dripped off his tone, "is involved in a large strategy and is distracted by his desires for what is not his. He and his ministers have planned the defeat of Cygna and Kaereya for a long time. Years ago, they even stole witch children from Cygna, and a witch to train them. He keeps them hidden."

"I know."

Eldin paused. "You're very well informed."

"People ignore my presence. Don't think a dimwit would know what they talk about, anyway." He laughed. "I even heard the king wants the Cygnese witches to cure his inability to sire a child. There is a joke being passed. If he didn't conquer Cygna soon, he'd not only have to get a new and younger queen but also a man to do his business with her."

"He used similar tricks in Kaereya and failed. Let us hope the Cygnese witches also prevail against him. His overconfidence could defeat him. Now he fights along two very extended lines. Many of those most loyal to him are dead in battle or gone from Pertelon to the fronts. He is spreading the army thin. Those left at court are those he feels need watching."

"They would never help me."

"You are the last legitimate heir. Much can happen, and we need to be prepared for any number of contingencies. Now, you have me to act as an intermediary, but all is nothing unless you are determined to live."

"Becoming king means nothing to me, only his defeat." Uilleam's face lined with aggression, his jaw clenched forward. "That's all I want. That's why I try so hard with you. You are the only person I've trusted since my nurse left, since my mother died. But whatever the cost, I will have my revenge."

"I am your man. You already have my oath."

Fifteen

"Another pass we can't get through." Cleat followed his observation with a long string of profanities. "We're trapped."

Kissre continued to watch the Pertelon troops through the fading daylight. The heavily encumbered troops were starting to settle for the night. Unluckily, her complement arrived just in time to have their return route cut off. She lowered her sight glasses. "Not trapped, just cut off from safe retreat. Damn." Her reconnaissance mission had suddenly turned into a survival campaign. The starving and besieged Pertelon army had broken out and was moving in a ravine running below the ridge of forested hills she traveled.

She dismounted, loosening Bother's girth. She ran a hand over his neck both sorry and glad she had chosen to ride him. This occupied her hands while she considered options.

None of her Pathfinders nor the five platoon men had Talent. Early warning to Ranor was impossible. Her unit gathered around, and she kept her voice low. "We all know the Pertelon army is moving, and we're smack in the middle of it. The trail back to our camp is closed. I think they have two motives. One, certainly, is to re-establish a supply line. The second is to separate the two branches of the Kaereyan and Cygnese armies, trying to cut us in two. You've seen the numbers of men moving. They have probably split. Those blocking us are following this ravine west. They've left just as many in their fortifications. We need to move, to retrace our steps along this ridge, and to try and connect with Ranor's infantry. We will continue on a flanking course, moving at night. Cleat, you will take the point." She pointed to two other men, "You take his security. Keep quiet. Watch your mounts, keep them quiet."

A hand command reinforced Fudge's quiet discipline. She stared at Fudge. In a quick decision, she wrote a note, wrapped it in a cloth used to clean equipment, and tied it to Fudge's collar. "Find Dovel, Fudge. Go to Dovel." Fudge whined. She scrubbed a hand through his head fur. "Good boy, Fudge. Find Dovel." The dog jumped to his feet, and with one backward look, took off in a ground-eating trot. She watched him disappear into the undergrowth and the dark. "May the Holy One see you safe." *Dovel would be furious— sure she had planned to place herself in the main thrust of a Pertelon offensive.*

Throughout the night, they traveled slow, arduous leagues. They heard voices in the dark and halted until certain the direction to avoid became clear.

For two sleepless days, they traveled. While they rested near midmorning of the third day, Cleat sent a man to her. They heard fighting ahead. Kissre gave Bother's reins to one of her men. Crawling to a bluff overlooking a shallow valley, she joined Cleat. From the overlook she saw what lay before them and heard the sound of arms. By their colors, she recognized a Cygnese platoon in a desperate fight with overwhelming Pertelon forces. The doomed men fought in fierce action. More than half their number had already fallen. She recognized one man, Sergeant Tomel.

"Bring the men up and prepare."

Shortly the men gathered aroumd her. She gave her orders. One of the platoon men objected to endangering a Talent. It was his duty to protect Colonel Kissre.

"Then you best keep up with me," she said as she mounted Bother. He scrambled to his pony. She heard the rest of the men mount their ponies and prepare. Twice she touched her spurs to Bother's sides while curbing him back. The horse curved his neck and tucked his head close to his body as he tested the bit and tensed in anticipation. With a silent motion, she drew her sword and adjusted her buckler. "Now!" she said and urged Bother forward and down the bluff.

The impetus of the sudden cavalry assault worked, driving many of the Pertelon troops back, but not enough. Bother's hooves protected her back as the troop fractured into fighting groups. The enraged horse kicked, bit, and slashed at anyone approaching. Suddenly Kissre heard barking, and looking down, saw Fudge next to Bother's side. Bother heard Fudge, and the kicking stopped. Optimism surged, bringing renewed energy. If Fudge had gotten through, then the army was alerted to the invasion.

~ * ~

::Tomel's platoon has lost their receiver. We have lost contact. Tomel isn't trained enough to replace him.::

Adele's report infuriated Dovel. Since Fudge's letter delivery, and the dog's subsequent fight for release, his famed even-temper had vanished. Kissre was out there somewhere. Candlemarks had dragged on while the platoons advanced, then reports came of enemy engagement.

::Try and find them, Cath. Tomel is untrained but capable. They're in dangerous territory.:: Dovel touched Tyna's mind even while others touched his. *::We've lost a platoon behind enemy lines,::* he informed her.

::Have all squads and platoons retreat. Has anyone found Kissre?:: Tyna asked.

That was Dovel's agonized question, too.

Tyna established a link to Raynor. *::The fighting is especially heavy in that section. Pertelon's troops are advancing in force through the valley.::*

Ranor's anxiety poked through his preoccupation with the battle. *::We can't wait to find any lost platoon, others need our help. Kissre?::*

::No sign.::

Raynor's reply scalded through Tyna's mind to him. *::Dovel, you hunt. I need the others.::* The link closed.

::Stay linked to me.:: Dovel felt Tyna's mind join to him, expanding the territory their minds could search.

He could not feel Kissre.

::Found Tomel!:: Cath's mental send came as a shout. *::His platoon is in desperate need, they've lost too many men. They can't prevail. Help them!.::*

Dovel located Tomel through Cath's link, felt Tyna trailing him. Tomel, pressed with fighting, could not sense them.

::Adele, Ulyss, try to guide Tomel when he finishes this engagement. Wyn, Adele, keep track of the other platoons.:: Suddenly, he felt Tomel's desperation. The man was sending wildly, unaware of what he was doing. Praying for intervention, knowing there would be none.

"He sending," Adele shouted aloud, "that's not possible."

Dovel scanned the area knowing what he would find. With dread he felt her presence. Their one-way bond drew him, then kicked him with unexpected power. Tyna felt it through their bond and joined him. Suddenly the whole landscape became apparent, the desperate fight of those remaining in Tomel's platoon, the bloody bodies hacked and fallen, and the dog racing up a slope. Kaereyan led Pathfinders and five platoon men prepared to attack against impossible odds. He screamed her name, felt Tyna's gasp of denial.

Combined, they watched through Tomel's eyes as Bother burst through shrubbery cover and charged down a snow-covered embankment, watched as Kissre and her Pathfinders beat back Pertelon troops in a vicious assault.

~ * ~

Kissre scanned the vicinity, taking in details as her attention remained on the work at hand. Instant recognition of Bother in the mad rush rallied the Cygnese troops. Blending with her Kaereyan pathfinders, they fought with tenacity and prevented Pertelon's forward movement. A scream and motion near her offside caused Kissre a quick downward glance. Tomel, his feet sliding from under him, fell. The motion threw him under Bother's hooves. A hard check with the reins and Bother rose on his hind feet. Tomel scurried from under the looming hooves.

Another scream warned Kissre. Her eyes jerked back as a Pertelonese blade arced toward her. She parried, but too late. With detached acceptance she watched the blade's sweep toward her.

A brown flash across the man's chest bore her attacker back, robbing his blade of its goal. Its tip side-struck, sliced through her leather leg guard just beneath her hauberk but robbed of momentum. Fudge rose from the man with a blood-covered muzzle. Kissre resumed fighting.

Exhausting, indeterminate time passed. Maybe an instant, maybe candlemarks later, the Pertelon troops retreated in disorder. Kissre released a sigh-sob of relief. It worked, for now. She looked around the battlefield. They had losses, but most of her combined troop remained standing. Fudge jumped, placing his paws on the saddle leather on each side of her split legging, and barked. His muzzle mustache was clotted with blood, but he gave her his usual lolling tongue grin as he licked his muzzle clean.

Blood seeped from the sliced leg, stained her legging. She cursed. *Same damn leg.* Nausea struck. Kissre leaned over Bother's side and threw up, her vomit splashing on bodies and mixing with the snow, blood, and mud below her. Fighting the muzzy discord assailing her, she swayed backward, wiping her mouth on her gauntlet. Bother bucked and rose, but fell back on his forelegs with a jerk, throwing her forward. She glanced. Many hands held Bother down.

"Loosen his girth first." Voices circled her, and hands pulled her from Bother despite her protests, touched her leg, felt her face. She couldn't differentiate the voices.

"It's deep, but could'a been worse. Didn't take the leg or reach the bone." A burning pain in her thigh and a stinging beverage forced down her throat broke Kissre's muddle.

"We've got to move. They'll be back." She ordered, her eyes opening briefly on Cleat and Tomel's faces above her.

"Yes, Colonel," Tomel said, his hands covered with her blood. "Soon as we get you patched."

Speaking became a rocky effort. Thinking, too. "How many wounded?"

Cleat answered. "You and six others. Luckily Bother can carry you. Most can walk."

"Any unable to walk?"

"Two."

"How many horses?"

"Just Bother and one pony."

"We leave no one behind. Get a point patrol in place and find us a way out of here."

"Dovel says to move further south. Kaereyan troops are moving forward there. We should join them in fourteen candlemarks or so. His squad's checking land for the best route." She recognized Tomel's voice as her vision closed to pinpoints.

"Follow my orders."

"Hell, I'm following everyone's orders." The sergeant's words were the last she heard. Thoughts of things needing to be done reeled in her mind, but everything evaporated in silent darkness.

~ * ~

With Tomel's hands covered in Kissre's blood, Dovel felt a surge of power that didn't diminish even as Kissre passed out. It frightened him, and others, feeling that fright, joined him, including, of all people, Healer Bujyea.

His mental send touched Dovel. *::I've a bond, been covered in her blood on another occasion. I'll take care of Kissre, attend your own duties.::*

Reluctantly, Dovel turned his attention back to troop movements.

~ * ~

Kissre woke leaning on Bother's neck, a cold wet tongue licking her face. Her leg was numb with a throbbing undercurrent, but she felt moderately alert. Someone's hand brushed Fudge away from where he walked just below her face. She pushed herself up off Bother's neck in slow agonizing movement.

"Where are we?" She asked Tomel, who walked next to Fudge. They moved through heavy shrub cover. High over the surrounding peaks, a new day broke in a red-streaked sky, as if the sun mourned yesterday's losses.

"Two candlemarks and a lifetime from our lines."

"How long?"

"We've been traveling circuitously most of the night. We've re-established contact with Dovel's squad. They're guiding us. They report Pertelon's army is rallying for another strike. Most of the wounded, including yourself, have had some mending. One died. The Talents are drawing in a heavy fog to help us hide."

"Captain Dovel leading us?"

"And Captain Tyna."

"Tyna?"

"Yes, ma'am."

She swore in coarse mercenary slang, finishing with, "Tenacious bitch." Tomel's face became a study in horror, but he laughed, too. Bleak laughter croaked from her dry throat, and she felt better. Tomel offered her a canteen and after a long swig of stale water, she handed it back to him. Gathering her reins she ordered, "Get my Pathfinder; get me Cleat. I want a report. Get me one of your senders. Let's figure out how to get out of here."

"I'm Sending, now."

Kissre looked at him. "Now?"

"Yes, Ma'am."

"What's that, some kind of field promotion?"

"Colonel Kissre, Captain Dovel's squad is guiding us."

"All the more reason to reconnoiter. You know as well as I the squads can't do it all. We're not out of this yet."

Cleat ran up to her. "Colonel, we figure more than a thousand troops moving between us and the rest of the Cygnese army. Only have a small corridor of escape. We're following a ridge of the valley they're moving through. Mostly we've encountered smaller units trying to clear these hills."

"Which means they know we're here. What we need is time."

"More men, more like," Cleat said and spat.

She looked at her Pathfinder and Cygnese combined men. They stood intent and quiet. "The only way out is stealth and cunning. Stay quiet, stay alert."

~ * ~

Kissre regained consciousness. Dovel felt her waken; felt her mind. Her thoughts came through their bond. Dovel knew what she planned before she spoke her orders. Through him, to his squad, Tyna, other captains, and Ranor, the impact of Kissre's mind spread in an inexplicably constructed, binding maze.

A disorienting wave swept over him as others fell into the pattern. The maelstrom of linkage spread Talent to Talent throughout the army. He focused on Kissre and quickly suppressed the feeling but felt it ripple throughout the maze.

Somehow, her open mind became a wellspring of connectedness. She felt eerily similar to Tyna but knife precise and direct. The bond remained one-sided. It was strange to sit within a mind unaware of his presence, unable to communicate. A mind as battle savvy as any he had encountered, with years of skill and experience. His shock was nothing compared to Ranor's.

Even as plans and subterfuge, evasive moves, and backtracking evolved in her mind, squads throughout the army were ordered in expedient collateral measures. Dovel cursed the weather that failed to create easy energy for distracting the enemy. The land, his other Talent, lay useless, easy surface energies already exhausted.

Within Kissre's mind he felt things she caused and used unknowingly. The earth entered her mind like intuition, showing her the best route. Her thoughts mixed with his in a near inseparable manner. With Dovel acting as a conduit, Ranor ordered the rest of the army.

~ * ~

"There's more Perts ahead," Cleat reported. "Pestering some Kaereyans."

Kissre limped forward far enough to recognize the banners of the encumbered allies. "What are they doing so far south?" she asked.

"Don't know, ma'am."

"That was rhetorical, Cleat."

"We going to help them?"

"I know them. A stupid Aristo leads them. Now he's probably getting them killed." She hesitated. "Aristo Aurelias is moving troops, Cleat. That means all the armies are moving, Pertelon, Cygnese, and Kaereyan. It might be, yes. I think so."

"Think what?"

"I think the Pertelon commander made a mistake." A dangerous, absurd notion took hold. They could stop the Pertelon army here and now. The ground lay against the invaders. The key might be the stranded men. Cut through to them, get them to rally, together, confront and delay Pertelon's advance—even better, destroy this advance. Hold it until the combined Kaereyan and Cygnese armies converged here. *If that was Ranor and Aurelias' plan.* She backed up and motioned Cleat to follow. Back with the rest of the troop, she motioned them to listen.

"Our standing here might make a difference." Their wary expressions showed them unused to their commander explaining anything. "I will not order you, but I am requesting."

"You basing this on sighting a Kaereyan flag?"

"She's right," Tomel said. "Dovel says they are moving troops. He says we should hold tight."

"We're outnumbered, that's for sure," Cleat said. "Certain death lurks down there."

"That's why I am asking you. The time for action is now. Others die even as we speak. It's not a matter of safety. If we hold long enough, live or die, we will make all the difference. I want you to know this. Know what I'm asking you to do and why."

She looked at them, measuring their response. Death specters played in their tired, blood-shot eyes and dirt-streaked faces.

"Well, Colonel. I'm with you. Hate what them Perts done to my home," Cleat said and spat.

Other voices spoke their agreement. She told Tomel to tell Dovel what they planned. "We leave the mounts and the severely wounded here."

She chose their approach and gave the orders. One thing remained to do. She pulled a length of rope from her pack and tied Fudge to a fallen tree. With a final scuffing of his fury head, she said, "Quiet, Fudge. Stay. Wait for Dovel." He whined and pulled on the rope, barking as she walked away.

~ * ~

Coming upon a Pertelon troop blocking the way, Dovel felt Kissre's indecision. Worse, Kaereyan troops fought a losing battle below her. If they checked that access before the rest of Pertelon's army arrival, held them off, the momentum of the battle shifted. Without these added Pertelon troops in the fray, Aurelias had an opportunity to contain the troops pressing on his flank. Cygna had a chance to triumph. He felt her commitment with waves of disbelief echoing through the squads. Tomel's new Talent failed, his mind and body exhausted. He neither understood nor relayed Dovel's urgent message. Only the requirements of the coming battle registered in his tired mind.

Kissre's stranded troops charged, swift and deadly, surprise on their side. The assault took her troop through the barrier. As alarm, near panic, hit him from a hundred minds, Dovel worried about his concentration, then about Tyna's. Drawing on Ulyss, on Adele, Wyn, and Cath, he redirected his platoons, felt Tyna and others doing the same.

An idea, near instinctual, unfolded in Dovel's mind. Kissre needed help. Not thinking of consequences, he followed his impulse.

With an assist from Ulyss's Latent Talent, he stretched his Fire Talent outward across the sky. They touched and borrowed power from Kissre in intimate familiarity. This time fear and stupefaction didn't touch Ulyss. From the Kissre-centered maze, mind after mind helped buoy and propel Dovel. He rose through layers of clouds and air, higher and higher until he touched the sun-engendered energy encompassing all the land. Energy coursed through him in uncontrolled surges. Other Fire Talents quickly caught and stored it. He cut the bond, afraid of draining both Kissre and Ulyss. Back in his body, he reconnected to help those in the battle at hand. They had energy, but most squads were already too exhausted after two-days of non-stop battle and were unable to use it.

~ * ~

"Your Highness," Eldin said with a bow. He had been expecting the call for some days. Gossip, since the loss of the fleet outside Guerestu, burgeoned like leaks in the palace roof from the unending rain, seeping into everyone's knowledge. Rumor spread about the Cygnese witches' weather victory. Discontent spread through the surrounding city of Bhatar. The high taxes, the shortages, the families mourning dead members, all took their toll on the people's morale.

Dressed in formal regalia, the king and court assembled in the Ruby Throne Room, named for the cerise and sanguine marble covering the floors and walls. Ancient granite columns held ornate gilded capitals supporting a mural-clad ceiling. Gold glinted everywhere in the sunlight flooding throughout the vast clerestory windows. It accentuated the floors, revealing the veining in the stone that looked like roses twining through blood. Uilleam, when Eldin had first met him, had sing-songed about the floor. 'The court convenes in sanguine, makes peace in cerise, the king's great floral without one moral.'

"The dummy not with you?" King Clement asked, splendid in a purple velvet robe that dusted the floor behind him. His ministers backed him with provocative, supercilious smiles. The witch he adulated stood at his right hand, deeply spellbound while she worked her sorceress efforts.

Still dressed in black mourning, Eldin bowed. "Aristo Uilleam went to his apartment. Payden's burial has adversely affected him. I took him hunting to help restore his previous good humor." Titters of amusement circulated the room.

"That is sad, of course, but it proved most beneficial to the Kingdom. Look at how many diffident Aristos have visited my court for the funeral."

Many of those recalcitrant nobles stood in the throne room, forbidden to leave. Their unhappiness in their extended visit showed. Clement's left hand supported the hand of the oldest daughter of the most important of these men. Eldin saw that her elevated company made her nervous. Her eyes never rose from the floor. She wore orange harlot's colors that with her sallow skin turned her hair greenish. It was no doubt, a disparagement and a retaliation.

Eldin purposely kept his eyes off her. He puzzled at Clement's provocative behavior. In most instances the king was a canny and subversive man, not given to demonstrating his power. Whatever had happened, today Clement represented danger.

"And how many rabbits did the young man bag?"

"Three, sire."

"Indeed, such a proficient hunter." Clement laughed. "Pertelon has had a very successful hunt, too." His sly eyes slid over his company.

"I've called you for advice, Kaereyan."

"My aim has always been to serve, sire." Eldin bowed with a small flourish.

"Indeed. You even warned me about that witch entering Cygna."

"Colonel Kissre, Your Grace?" Eldin asked, after a surprised moment's thought.

"Yes. She is proving troublesome. I should have taken your failed attempt on her removal with greater concern. Our own witches seem unable to confound theirs. It is too bad, but we shall still prevail. We have superior weaponry." Clement's smile chilled Eldin as he sensed the ruler's malicious intent.

His blood seemed to congeal within him in icy streams, and he asked, "You are not afraid of the Protectors, sire?"

Clement laughed in scorn. "There are no Protectors. These are tried and true weapons, and they shall prevail in Cygna as they have elsewhere. Within candlemarks news shall arrive of our defeat of the Cygnese witches. Their power shall become my power. Before then this court will serve me."

"What service can I provide for you, sire?" Eldin asked.

"Since your arrival in my court, my plans have been subverted and destroyed. Do you act as a double agent for Kaereya?"

"No, Your Highness, I do not."

"What do you think of these nobles standing before you?"

"Your Highness, I can think nothing but that you are surrounded by your loyal subjects."

"Yes. Loyal. Do you know, some of them think Uilleam more than the idiot he is? Why do they refer to him as Prince Uilleam? Do you know why? Does that speak of loyalty? What could be more disloyal than avoiding my court, my presence? This has been my hunt—to find and root out the disloyal. Are you loyal, Kaereyan?"

The titters and rustles of a gathered crowd stopped in frightened silence. All noise ceased. "Sire, Uilleam is no threat to you."

"That was not my question. But then what would you know of loyalty?"

"I am loyal."

"Then I ask you to prove your loyalty."

"In what manner, sire?"

"Kill your charge."

~ * ~

They worked down the ridge. Once gathered on open ground, Kissre ordered them forward. They burst from concealing trees and engaged the enemy on its western flank. Fierce fighting engulfed them. Kissre, sword swinging, feet kicking, and buckler ramming, pushed her way to the Kaereyan troops. Time elongated, giving her a chance to plan her strokes, time to deflect blows. Screams and vile sounds rent the air. She saw Cleat take a blow. His assailant slit her Pathfinder's throat as he sank to his knees. Finishing her opponent, she twirled and with a single stroke slew the man who took Cleat. Turning, she resumed her battle to move forward.

It seemed forever before she reached the Kaereyans, and she felt her decreasing strength, her exhaustion. Two more of her Pathfinders went down. Through the tumult Tomel protected her back. Not breaking her strokes, she screamed at a Kaereyan sergeant as she fought her way toward him. "Help is coming. Hold them. Hold here." He nodded, never losing a stroke in his own urgent battle. The fighting went on. Slowly Kissre noticed her opponents thinned.

Unbelieving, she watched the Pertelon troops disengage. She sensed it before she saw it. The enemy retreated. Kissre halted, her breath rasping. To the south she saw Kaereyan Pennants advancing.

"They've arrived, Tomel, look!" She pointed. He wasn't behind her. Dovel's sergeant lay on the ground at her feet, blood seeping from multiple wounds. His eyes looked at her in anguish before awareness faded. "We finished it, Tomel. We stopped them."

Anger drove her to help finish any lingering enemy still engaged with her men. The space between them and the enemy widened as the Pertelonese withdrew. She looked around her. Less than twenty of her combined force remained. Thunder sounded. Confused, the men looked up at the blue sky, but Kissre turned to watch the Pertelonese lines. Puffs of smoke and rippling flashes warned her. Exhausted, she fell to her knees and yelled a warning.

The first blast fell short, sheering into departing Pertelon troops. Snow, mud, and body parts flew into the air. Movement nearby drew Kissre. Tomel moved. "Lay flat, give them no target," she yelled to those still standing.

She gathered Tomel beneath her and lay with her buckler over her head. The other soldiers followed her lead. The cannon's fire echoed through the valley, making it impossible to determine direction.

The roaring noise, the vibrating ground when the volley hit, and the flying debris deafened and blinded her. The bombardment went on endlessly, and with each passing moment, she knew one would soon land on or near her.

Overhead, a loud clap cracked, and a palpable, ripping tear rent the sky. The sky turned white with brilliant light that invaded her buckler's shelter. Kissre looked at the sky. Real thunder. Lightening. Bolt after bolt came from black clouds stacked on the horizon and hovering overhead. She felt her skin prickle as the bolts hit.

Slowly the unearthly sounds deadened as the ringing in her ears muffled outside sound. Beneath her, the ground continued shaking with each canon's blast, with each burst of light.

Something touched her cheek. She looked down but couldn't hear what Tomel screamed. He looked up at her in question. She read his lips. "The Protectors?"

"I don't know, maybe Protectors, maybe Talents. They're hitting the Pertelon cannon." It occurred to her to tell him the Talents were the Protectors, but Tomel had passed out. She knew him bleeding to death but knew soon they would all die. Whether from cannon blast or lightning bolt, they were still vulnerable targets.

~ * ~

"Sire!" Eldin protested. Expectation hushed the Ruby Throne Room. Movement stilled, and those present fell silent and watchful, waiting for blood to flow.

"You will not be the only one asked to prove your loyalty this day." He ran his hand along the ill-looking young cheek next to him. The girl closed her eyes tight but did not flinch. Eldin saw tears sparkle below her lashes.

"Why don't you ask me about my loyalty, Your Highness-minus?"

An insolent voice spoke from the back of the room, and Eldin silently cursed. His heart congealed.

"Here he is," Clement said. "Aristo Uilleam, showing his trademark idiocy. Do you make fun of your king? Payden's cleverness cost him. What shall your dim-wittedness cost you, boy?"

"You cost me Payden," Uilleam accused. His flat but exquisitely controlled voice raised the unease filling the hall. "It didn't take Eldin long to discover who murdered Payden, or who ordered it." He strolled casually through the exquisite courtiers and nobles. His grey breeches were splashed with dark splotches of blood, and a collar of office dangled from one hand. A sober grey and black leaf design intertwined on his jack, emphasizing his pale color and the over brightness of his blue eyes. Eldin saw the determination lining Uilleam's features. "Your Master of Arms is dead. I just killed him."

Clement's eyes widened at Uilleam's articulate phrasing. He turned to Eldin. "The traitor is ever inventive." His attention returned to Uilleam. "I misjudged you, but that is nothing to the mistake you've made, Uilleam. You have to be smarter than to walk unarmed into a room filled with my guards."

Uilleam stopped next to Eldin and threw the arms master's emblem on the floor before Clement. "It depends on your goals. Mine has never been to claim the crown."

Clement laughed. "Tonight, my goal is to remove all dross from my path. My witch tells me Cygna will fall today." He waved a hand at the enthralled woman. "Even now she stays in contact with others at the front. My troops are moving, my future conquests insured. Too bad you will not live to see my victory."

"You should not have come down," Eldin said. "He will kill you."

"I know," Uilleam said in dull acceptance.

Eldin watched the gathered nobles push their wives behind them and back away from the king, looking for any of Clement's defenders.

"I know he will kill me, but not how he killed my grandfather, choking the old man with his hands. Or how he killed my father that same night, stabbing him with King Theobald's knife, making it look like the son strangled the father, his king." His eyes never left Clement. "Your supporters stood guard outside the door, allowing your evil."

"You can't know that! It's a lie. A lie, I say!"

"No lie, King Usurper. I was there, I saw. You wore dark clothing, having snuck into the palace. Shall I describe my father's clothing? My grandfather's? Or how the old man fought you until you grabbed a candlestick and struck him? Then you twisted the Signet Regal from his finger, but it wouldn't loosen, so you cut off his finger. In trying to slip it on, you dropped it and had to scrabble on the floor and under the bed to find it." Uilleam's voice lowered as he approached King Clement. "Don't back up, royal-boil! Everyone knows me harmless. Look, I'm unarmed, not even an eating knife. You want me dead? Now is a good time to perform the feat."

The king waved his armed guards forward with a hand movement. He stood supremely self-confidant, arrogant in his assurance. "Your loyal man is mine. He will kill you. I have no fear."

With a laugh, Uilleam asked, "Will you kill me, Eldin? Will you stab me in the back?" His gaze remained on Clement.

A circle of nobles stopped the advance of the guards. Without Clement's permission to kill, the guards halted. Sensing danger, the king's ministers stepped back, easing as far as possible from Clement.

"No, Uilleam. I swore to you. I am your man." Eldin pulled a knife and his light sword from its scabbard.

"Then you will die, too," Clement said.

"I expect to. You would have killed me anyway. Unfortunately for you, Your Highness, those who supported you in the murder of your predecessor are also dead, or warring for you in Kaereya or Cygna."

"Guards!"

"I think, sire," Duke Chaim said, stepping forward, dragging a man wearing priest's vestments. "That you must answer to these allegations. They've been made before the Abbot and before the Body Noblesse."

"You have not gutted all justice or all honorable men in Pertelon." Uilleam was not quite within striking distance of Clement. "You needed them, didn't you? Their seats produced the profits you needed. So you drained them as dry as you dared while preventing a general uprising. They could wait for degradation and forfeiture until you achieved your greater goals."

"Which is now. The fleet meant nothing." Clement sneered. "There are enough troops in Cygna to destroy their army. With Cygna, with their witches, I conquer Kaereya." He pulled the young woman on his arm before him as cover between himself and Uilleam. "Even if I killed you before all these witnesses, no one will touch me. They're cowards. Afraid to lose anything, let alone everything."

"You were in your prime when you killed the king, but not young. Twenty years you've ruled." Uilleam slowly circled the king and girl he held.

"They've been years of good rule."

Uilleam, fast as a striking snake, put out his hand and pulled the young woman free. Clement reacted as Uilleam stepped forward, pulling his knife and slicing into Uilleam. The girl fell from the force of Uilleam's pull, but a man caught her, and she stood safe out of reach.

"Payden was your last victim."

Amid the gasps and shouts, Eldin advanced to Uilleam's back. Uilleam stood holding his right side. Uilleam's glance flew to him then back to Clement. He put a bloody hand out, stopping Eldin's advance. "No, he is mine."

Clement smiled and swung the knife in his hand, threatening, forcing Uilleam and Eldin to take defensive steps away. The king held his arm ready to throw the blade, but an orange-clad body stepped into the blade as he threw, covering Uilleam's body. Clement's blade entered all the way to the hilt. A scream rent the room. Uilleam caught the girl as she fell.

Her father ran to her as the king stepped back in the face of Eldin's sword. Uilleam relinquished his place to the father. She looked at her sire. "He swore he would have you killed if I did not go with him willingly. I am so sorry."

With another backward step, the king turned and drew a sword from the scabbard of a nobleman near the crowd's edge. He advanced, threatening with the weapon. Eldin stepped in front of Uilleam. A hard push shoved him out of the way. Eldin fell heavily next to the whore-clad girl's body and her kneeling father. Uilleam sidestepped as the king harried him, the crowd shifting as the drama's participants moved. Only the witch remained immobile, lost in her casting.

"You bastard." Clement smiled. "You might think you've ruined my plans, but I am greater than that. You think this worm didn't know what happened to his daughter?" He waved a hand at the kneeling man. "Too bad you die now and won't see my ultimate achievement." He thrust and cut Uilleam's arm.

Eldin turned and pulled the knife from the girl. It came with a sickening snick. A hand grasped his arm, but Eldin twisted, rolled, and rose, tossing the blade with trained accuracy. Clement screamed and dropped the sword. His hand grasped the blade's handle, and he pulled it from his arm. In that instant, Uilleam struck. With a quick dive, Eldin claimed the dropped sword and stopped anyone from interfering.

The king and Uilleam grappled on the floor. One of Clement's ministers ran forward to help the king. He kicked Uilleam but retreated, screaming, as Eldin's sword sliced his arm. Clement grasped the knife the man had offered.

Uilleam, his usual placid face distorted with the twenty years of anger, appeared inhuman, frightening. His quick hands deflected the knife Clement still grasped. Handhold and counter handhold, they wrestled. Eldin knew Uilleam played with the king, toyed with his prey, unafraid because he didn't care for any outcome but one.

The witch suddenly awoke and screamed, "No, no, impossible, no!" Her outburst broke Clement's concentration. Her eyes widened to unholy circles of horror in her stricken face.

"Guards, guards!" Clement screamed in panic seeing his witch's tormented expression. Several of the King's Guard advanced on him, swords in hand. Eldin fought them off, but in turning, his eye caught the flicker of a blade flying from the Aristo still kneeling by his daughter. "Uilleam," he screamed in warning.

"Die! Spawn of evil!" The distraught words echoed through the chamber.

Everyone stopped. Uilleam screamed and fell with the king.

"No! You won't cheat me!" His hands closed on Clement's neck. They squeezed, changed grip, and squeezed again until the man below him went limp. Everyone else stood, shocked, watching. Uilleam didn't stop his constricting hands even after the face turned blue and the body flaccid.

Taking a deep breath, Eldin pulled Uilleam off the body. "He's dead, Uilleam. You have your wish."

Blood pooled in an expanding lake on the red marble floor, looking more innocuous than its presence indicated. Uilleam got to his feet looking crazed, ferocious, and bereft. Eldin speculated on the possibility of escape. His calculations came up as insignificant, so he took the only possible avenue. "Uilleam did not kill him. The knife did. You saw it. He did not throw the knife."

Duke Chaim knelt by Clement's body. "Clement is dead." The Abbott stepped forward. His hand rent the air with the motions of Holy rites. Chaim removed the chain of office and the Signet Regal. With slow movements, he stepped to Uilleam and placed the heavy chain over the boy's head. Uilleam looked bewildered. Chaim lifted the boy's hand and placed the ring on the rule finger, before kneeling to kiss the ringed hand.

"Long live King Uilleam."

A chorus of voices repeated the call, "Long live King Uilleam." Around them Aristos and the guardsmen kneeled in obeisance. Eldin dropped to one knee and bent his head. "Long live King Uilleam."

~ * ~

Dovel sank to the ground where his squad already lay, his legs unable to support him any longer. Aides surrounded them with warm blankets, drinks, care, and comfort. He knew Kissre lived, but his mind refused to relay more. With the energy he pulled from the sky, Tyna had formed lightning and set up strong storm fronts. Their strength reflected her wrath strengthened by the anger of numerous squad captains. She had to be exhausted.

It would rain within candlemarks, probably downpour for days. He had drawn on Kissre's Talent and wondered how it affected her. There was nothing to feel, even if he had the strength. Her mind was closed to him, her presence a mere mist of sensation. Was she as weak as all the other Talents involved in this combined effort? He had felt squad after squad drop from the maze. Only Tyna had stayed with him to the end, both driven by sheer obstinacy. Someone needed to get to Kissre.

Sixteen

The canons resonated in her ears, though she knew them stopped. She rose to her knees, unable to believe she lived. Debris shifted off her buckler, falling to the rent ground. There was nothing left inside her. No feeling or thought as she walked the body-strewn landscape. There was nothing to be done for Tomel. He was either dead or dying. Muted groans and cries penetrated the ringing in her ears. They rose from all around her, competing with the hollow hum in her head. Shaky with fatigue, she pushed herself, willed her feet to move, stupefied to the sights, sounds, and smells of death teeming around her. *What had happened?* Other confused figures milled about in the mayhem.

Too distraught, too stunned, to comprehend the spectacle, she wandered through the thick, dead-still air. *Bother. Fudge. Had they survived?* She twirled to find the direction, but she was lost, everything so changed. *That hill, that was it, wasn't it? No. That one.* She walked. It was. It must be. Three times she stopped to rest while climbing the hill. Her heart sank. A shell had struck nearby. No buckskin horse, no shaggy brown dog waited. The wounded men were gone, the earth torn asunder.

A dead pony lay on the ground; his neck stretched forward, tongue extended in a comic, grotesque way. Its back end was missing, entrails spilling on the ground. She backed away from the grizzly sight. Kissre swallowed hard. *It wasn't Bother. Not Bother. Not again.* She spun, searching the ground. Nothing. The land lay clutched in a creeping yellow blanket of fog. She shouted, whistled, shouted some more, and staggered the length of hill and back. Nothing but bodies appeared through the grisly clouds. She sank to her knees.

A shadow moved slowly beyond some ghostly bones of shrubbery. The form walked toward her out of the amber haze enveloping the hilltop. An errant breeze exploded the acrid and discolored air with a strong whipping gust. A faint roll of thunder echoed through the hills.

She walked forward and fell on Bother's neck, half-hearing her own sobbing relief, her apologies, and her babbling encouragement. She felt him realign his weight and looked down. Blood rolled down his left foreleg. Frantic, she inspected the wound and sighed with relief. It was a minor gash. Slowly and methodically she searched his body for wounds. She found a few raw patches, a few more small gashes, none threatening, but attesting to his nearness to death. He needed care.

A low whimper broke her inane chatter. "Fudge?" Another low whine answered her. She renewed her search. It took an eternity to find him. He lay under the pony carcass. Trapped. She tried to pull him free. He yipped and bit at her hands. Grabbing the dead horse's front legs, she pulled. Only half the animal was still too heavy. What did half a pony weigh? She had to do it, so kept trying.

Fudge whined in weak bouts. Inspecting how the dog lay below, she pulled her sword and hacked through the carcass's neck. Done with the decapitation, she thrust her sword into the soil. It swung back and forth with her thrust's force. Once more, she pulled on the carcass's legs. With harsh grunts, sobs, obscenities, and sheer will, she pulled. It moved an inch, then two.

Maddened to frenzied desperation, she kept trying. As if in concert, the wind picked up, throwing debris in her face and eyes, causing tears to run down her cheeks. Inch by inch, through exhausting effort, the carcass moved. Fudge quieted long before she finished uncovering his body. He lay in a depression with more debris still covering him.

She grabbed Fudge under his shoulders and lifted him. His body remained entrenched. Grabbing her boot knife, she dug the soil away, pulled once more, then dug and pulled again in endless repetition. She gasped and stumbled backward when a final tug pulled him free. His front legs were broken. He made no sound, and his head lolled against her arm. An ear placed over his heart proved a thread of life held, but not for long. With gentle fingers, she caressed his rough fur, pulled his great body into her lap, and stroked his long face. He didn't move, didn't whine or whimper. His eyes lay half closed and glazed.

"No, no. No!" Her voice rose in a howl of protest that twined in constricting bands around her chest. Her sword hilt floated above her, a testament to the day's violence. "I can't bear it. Please, please, by the Holy One, please!"

She answered her own plea. *What did the Holy One have to do with such carnage, such hell, such human-induced devastation, as she had witnessed?* Burying her face against Fudge, she cried until depleted. Oddly, sudden quiet fell as she calmed. Even the reverberation in her ears ended. She looked at her sword standing on its tip end. From where she looked, it seemed to hover among the puffy clouds, reminding her of the spire on the cathedral in Sidih. Thunder reverberated once more through the heavy air, even though the overhead sky was a pale cerulean.

She rose to her knees and stopped, tongue-tied. How did one, who hadn't believed in years, pray?

"I know it's wrong to ask for help when I've neglected prayer and ignored you for so many years. Please hear me. I ask for Fudge."

She halted. Words clogged in her throat refusing to emerge. Even squeezing her lids tight shut would not stop the new tears blurring her vision and stinging her eyes.

Fudge's life, that's all she wanted. She would beg for it if she could but had been effectively silenced. What could she ask for?

So much blood, so much loss, it was unbearable. Closing her eyes only produced more horror, enactments of the last day's desperate efforts, the paralyzing fear of the canon, the lightning barrages, and the slaughter of friends. She stared around the death-burdened valley below her.

She saw all the men lying in the field, in as bad a shape, or worse, than Fudge. They deserved comfort and healing. This poor, tired land lay sapped of strength at the very inception of the growing season. She felt it, sensed it below her, as wounded as those bleeding on it. She sighed, feeling so tired. Exhaustion trapped her in deep lassitude, and she felt herself fall somewhere between reality and dream.

~ * ~

A gray mist came off the hilltops, preventing all but the closest vision. Wraith images formed in that murk, mocking her weakness.

Down deep, that's where strength lay. It would be so easy to draw it up, trap it where it was needed. Where the witches could use it. Healer Bujyea would know how to use it. Pull it up, twist it, lock it in place for his use; it could be done—if one knew how.

Almost outside herself, Kissre heard her mumbled words, unable to stop, doubting she spoke yet hearing the words. "I could pray to you, Holy One. If I did, I would plead that you heal the land, give succor to all those lying in this death-bier valley. The Holy One would say, with what right do you ask, hypocrite? I'd say, with no right to any appeal, but I beg it. So much lost, so much wasted. He would say, but for you? For a dog? Yes, but not for me; I deserve naught of your aid. For a loyal friend, for a comrade in arms, for any life not yet finished." A sense of hopelessness overcame her. There is always a collection, a demand for sacrifice, and she had nothing to offer. "My life, my spirit, is blood-tainted."

"Is there nothing you could give to those who touched you in life?" a voice asked.

"Nothing. I have been governed by anger and jealousy, afraid to give any of myself. Afraid if I did, my anger would escape. Without anger, there would be nothing left."

"*Give over your hatred.*"

"Hatred?"

"*Yes.*"

It took her a moment. "My mother? I didn't hate her. I was angry. I wanted her to love me."

"*You hated her. Admit it.*"

"It's wrong."

"*As wrong as hating your sister because your mother loved her more?*"

"Help him, help them."

"*You help them. The means are within your reach.*"

"What means?" she asked. Her eyes snapped open on a discordant world.

"What means?" she screamed.

Disturbed, the cloud-lined gray sky churned, a stiff wind stirring it. Thunder cracked overhead as she shrieked,

"What means?" She looked at her hands, mud and the rust of dried blood coated them.

Before her eyes, reality turned gossamer. *She faded until her body turned transparent. Her essence floated a few fingers in height over the see-through land, and she spread like a wide flat sheet floating from a wash line. She followed the land's contours, through mud, snow, ice, branches, through dead bodies and those still living.*

The land's smells and tastes filled her. She felt pain from those injured and dying in the cold, among multitudes but alone. Her dream moved faster, absorbing the men, their individual histories and ancestries leading back in time, and incredibly, the future void made by their absence. She whirled in a storm of sensation while shriveling inside, and knew death came for her. It didn't matter. Let Fudge live, Carillon and Bother, Tomel, her family. Her family. Tyna. Please forgive me; I tried to do what was best.

Her words fell from her mouth in small iridescent spheres. The spheres floated in dancing motions before becoming wind riven. They sped outward then coalesced into an arrow that flew skyward

before arcing. The curve sharpened, bringing the dart back toward her. There was no escape. She cried as it pierced her chest, her heart, felt that pumping organ shudder, its beat captured in an agonizing rhythm that slowly stopped. All noise and distraction ceased. The world turned dull, as veil upon veil slowly fell over her.

"That's what I said."

She turned around with the smell of fresh-baked bread and the evening stew permeating the room. "Naomi?" *Kissre said to the familiar blue-clad figure standing in the kitchen of her childhood house. Her father sat at the kitchen table, his head in his hands, half-sleeping, tired from a long day spent harvesting.*

"You never forgave me; always held that quiet anger. There was no living with your expectations, your condemnation." *Her mother looked at her with Tyna's hazel eyes, and like Tyna, a golden woman in skin, hair, and eyes. She peeled apples.* "There was nothing I could say. Every apology was deemed inadequate. As long as you hate me, none of us can go forward."

"Why? I only wanted you to love me, too."

"Why is anything the way it is? I did what I thought best, Kissre. You can't keep crying for what I couldn't give you."

Like loose sand, Naomi's image shifted. "Momma!" *she shrieked, but her words were blown back into her mouth by the blast of wind that came from nowhere.* "Come back. I forgive you! I don't care why. I wanted you to love me. Please, just come back."

"She won't." *Gervan, her mercenary mentor, stood next to her. This had been her first real battle. He had saved her life five times over. Stupid mistakes. Tears ran down her face, and she was unable to stop them. She had killed; the befouling work made her ill. She yearned to wash herself. Would always crave it, knowing she would never feel clean again and would always carry the smell of slaughter in her nose.*

Blood and bits of gore coated Gervan from the breastplate down; splashes sprinkled his face. Soon he would hand her his weapons and armor and tell her to cleanse them. Kissre gritted her teeth as he ran the back of bloody fingers down her cheek and neck. "Not now, not then. She's dead."

"You're dead."

"And you'll die. Decide your fate. Never knew you to be fainthearted. What do you want?"

"I want no more death today, not here."

"For a dog?"

"For everyone."

Gervan laughed in scoffing mockery. "Death is necessary." The sounds changed into flickering, unreal colors that revealed the battlefield. Lightning struck the earth close to where she stood. She felt its power tingle over her skin, tasted the mordant smell of it. Energy. She followed it into the earth, felt it spread out underneath the soil, and placed a hand on the grainy surface. Energy trapped, held there by the sheer massiveness of the land. Through her fingers, she felt the weak pulse of life under the soil. It was full of water, full of air, a separate world of potential. Without a thought, she dove into the land as if into water, fell as if through air.

Energy. Deep inside it filled the ground with sound, so much energy it would flood the surface if it could reach. She needed to change potential to practical, needed the energy to weave broken bones and tissues together.

~ * ~

The aides were moving other squads to their tents. Trying to get them to cover before the storm broke. Dovel refused to move. Wanted to stay close, touching the earth, starring at the storm-strewn sky. He watched the massive thunderheads, so white and imposing, slowly roll away, pushed by whirls of grey. Because he refused to move, his squad remained. They made no plea for him to move, just waited.

Beneath him the earth surged. Not with motion, but energy. He felt the flow. Dizzy, disoriented, he closed his eyes. "Kissre." His numb heart expanded unbearably.

"Where is she?" Ulyss asked.

"You felt it?" Dovel asked.

His squad stirred on the ground with renewed strength but unaware of any change. They looked at him with fatigue-dulled eyes.

"Can't you feel it?" He held out his hands and rose. Energy from below tingled on his palms even held at waist height. He looked at them. None held a speck of Earth Talent. Ulyss's eyes widened.

"Yes. By the Holy One..." Ulyss rose in sluggish effort. A surge of power invigorated Dovel as his Catalyst reacted.

Other Talents emerged from hastily erected tents, and Dovel knew them all Earth Talents. They sensed and sought the unusual power.

"What is happening?" Cath asked, her eyes searching the landscape. Dovel felt her fear.

"Dovel?" Tyna walked up to them. "What are you doing?"

"It's not him," Ulyss said, and Dovel felt the bond between the two Catalysts.

Dovel said nothing but started to walk, then jogged toward the battlefield. He felt Tyna follow him.

"Where are you going?" Adele yelled as he left.

"To Kissre," Ulyss said, rising to follow.

"But we're all exhausted," she said, her petulance and dismay sounding alike. "Ranor has the reserve troops scouring the fields for survivors. They will bring her back."

He heard them, felt them scramble to come after him, felt Tyna's squad following. He looked at Tyna, her face showing her beginning attempts to recognize Kissre.

"What is happening?" she asked him.

~ * ~

"What are you doing Zeba?" Vitann asked as she passed the Governor. Zeba stopped in the main entry corridor of the Assembly House. Her maid did not stop but seemed lost in a trance, leaving Zeba behind her. Zeba saw the distrust in Vitann's face as she raised mild eyes to the Governor. Vitann obviously expected a witticism at her expense.

"Why, Vitann, can't you feel it?"

"Feel what?"

"Come outdoors, Vitann." She linked a hand around Vitann's arm and pulled her, sure curiosity would make the Governor follow.

Larig, at the Governor's back, looked ready to jump out of his skin. Zeba clearly felt his conflict between duty and desire. "Look at your Shield, Vitann. Take mercy on him."

"Larig?" Vitann looked at the young man as if he were a stranger. By then, they were out the door. Vitann's eyes grew large, and her face slackened in shock. "What is it?"

Zeba watched others gathering around Gregor's Mound. Once there, they settled into meditative poses, either kneeling or standing. Others stood around with surprised, questioning expressions. She trusted Vitann could sort them as easily as she did. Earth Talents converged at the mound; Fire Talents wondered what transpired.

When her feet touched the soil, Zeba felt the shock. Subtle vibrations entered the soles of her feet and crawled up her spine to ignite a spark at the back of her head. Vitann's gasp showed she felt the energy. An urgent compulsion sent them to the mound, and Zeba sank to her knees, her hands braced against the grass. A glance showed a number of enthralled people with no Talent patch on their sleeve settle into uneasy postures by the mound. Others spread themselves, stretching on the ground, getting as close to the soil as possible.

She heard the hiss as Larig withdrew his blade and flinched as the sword sank into the mound with one strong thrust. The hilt swung on its axis. Before it stopped, Larig knelt, his hands full of soil, held out to his sides, head bowed.

"What is it?" Vitann asked Zeba when she knelt next to her.

"An Earth calling. The first since Gregor gathered energy here two hundred years ago. It resonates in harmony with this new calling, pulling energy."

"But...no one is here."

"No. The Crucible is on a battlefield outside Guerestu. We assist."

"Gregor needed no assistance."

"Gregor was a trained Talent who worked one specific calling. I can't talk anymore, Vitann. Listen to the Earth. Tie into the Maze. Feel the Crucible draw energy from deep underground. Hope that Dovel gets to her soon."

"Why is she doing it?"

"For her dog. Listen to what is going on around you, Vitann!"

Zeba watched Vitann as awareness struck and a look of near ecstasy took over the harsh features. Zeba smiled. Such untrained generosity.

~ * ~

"Kissre."

The words were so soft she didn't think she had heard them, but she looked over her shoulder. "Dovel! What are you doing here?" He looked solid and comforting, a reassuring presence.

"You brought me."

"Me, how?"

"I felt your distress and came. What are you doing?"

She grinned. "Look at all the energy. It's so easy to tie it where it can do some good. I don't seem able to carry enough, though. Every bundle just slips away before I can get it to the wounded. Fudge needs it, too."

"Let me help."

"You will? Thanks!" She picked up an armload of bundles and passed them to Dovel; picked up some for herself. Standing up, she turned around. Dovel stood there empty handed. She didn't question his delivering the energy; he was a Talent, after all. Occasionally he didn't stand there so she tossed the energy into the soil, staking it in place, but by the next armload he was back, and she gave it to him. Armload by armload, candlemark by candlemark, eon by eon, she handed Dovel energy.

No hands reached to take the bundle. She looked for Dovel. Cevoka performed Aibhe drills surrounded by towering trees, their enormous girth thinning into branches far above her head. Kissre didn't dare drop her bundle. She stood in the forest as it had been last summer, pine-scented, with a green canopy far overhead. Old branches emerged in broken spirals from massive red, orange and brown splotched trunks. The sun streamed down in discernible ribbons of light. Quiet and peace reigned.

"You died before I could get to you, I'm sorry."

"I know. It hurt. I was glad to go, but I saw you arrive. Saw you save Jycel and the others. We were too far forward." Cevoka shrugged but didn't stop her movement. "I told you where I would be. I like it here, don't you? I am so glad you taught me this." She performed the motions of the focus ritual.

Kissre looked at the trees, listened to the silence. "It looks lonely."

"You've been alone most of your life. Listen...hear the earth?"

She did and frowned. "Am I dead, too?"

"You don't know?"

"No."

Cevoka laughed and continued her graceful dance. "You always seem so self-assured. I think we could have been friends."

"I thought we were."

"Almost. You never trusted me. There is no friendship without trust."

"Kissre." Dovel spoke.

She turned back to him and blinked her eyes several times. They were deep in the bowels of the earth. Rock melted around them.

Strange sounds, bass grindings, high soprano pressure pulses, alto and tenor voices mingling with the sounds of matter and energy in flux. Earth music.

"Do you hear it, Dovel?"

"It's time to go, Kissre."

"Do you hear it?"

"Yes. We have to leave. You've been here too long."

"I want to hear it. Let me listen."

"Fudge waits."

"Fudge?" She looked at him blankly. "He's dying. He'll be here with me soon."

"You're not dead. Nor is Fudge. Help him. Please come, Kissre."

"But the music..."

"There is new music on the surface, Kissre. You will like it."

"New music? But..." She was drawn by the sounds, "...this hasn't finished."

"It doesn't end. It goes on and on. You can put the energy down. Please come. He held out a hand.

"No, this is for Fudge. This is for the wounded."

"It isn't needed anymore."

"I can't put it down." She floated behind Dovel and wondered how he saw her, how he found her, insubstantial as she seemed. Then she felt-saw Fudge. Surprised, she saw her own body cradled in Dovel's arms. They sat amid a circle of others who stood or kneeled in the carnage of the battlefield. Memory came. She couldn't go there. Not yet. One more thing remained. She had to do it.

This time she welcomed the dream, formed and used it. She heard Dovel scream, but she was already whirling and moving outward in all directions at such a speed no one could stop her. Once more, she accelerated to an alarming velocity through the field. She sensed the new feeling in the land but ignored it. Only when passed through human flesh, energy flickered from her fingertips. Tomel! She felt his slight presence with joy. It took so little to make so much difference. It was a sweet dream.

Looking into her non-existent hands, she saw only one small bundle left. She gasped in agony and felt herself collapsing, falling backward. Pellets of icy water pummeled her face. The smell of earth and carnage filled her senses, and her ears still drummed with the muffled hammering of canon and underground anvils. It took an effort to open her eyes. Dovel filled her vision. His face was wet, too, bent down, watching her.

Heaviness in her lap drew her attention. Fudge's head lay there. Her hand, where it lay on Fudge's shoulder, weighed much more than it should. She willed her fingers of her other hand open. A small bluish-white spark snapped between her palm and Fudge's fur. Leaden weight closed her eyes.

~ * ~

Dovel looked around him. His squad stood nearby, hovering over a still enraptured Ulyss. Tyna and her squad knelt there, and Jycel's Hew looked bereft. Other Earth Talents stood or knelt in the blood and mud covering the ground. Hew's defection had drawn the rest of Jycel's squad, like he had drawn his, and Tyna her squad, as all Earth Talents present drew their squads. A crowd of Talents gathered around them. Sometime during the Drawing, Cygnese platoons had surrounded them. He felt Marshal Ranor approach with long, fast strides trailed by a coterie of adjuncts and officers.

"The Catalyst?" Ranor asked those standing near Dovel.

"The Crucible." Dovel stopped, choked, and gasped. "Exhausted. Alive." Dovel held her tighter.

Ranor's mouth firmed. "She looks dead. None of you looks much better."

Beyond him, Dovel saw squads of men moving back onto the battlefield to sort the living and dead. Many led ponies hitched to carts. He watched. Never had he, nor any other Captain, nor any squad, been this close to a battle's aftermath. A constant buzz of voices hovered over the field consisting of groans, pleas for help, for water. Voices talked to wives, to mothers, or rambled talking to no one. Most of his squad and those that came with him were ill from the intense sights and smells. Their faces carried the same horror he knew covered his. He looked at Kissre. She was covered in the battle's effluent.

"You've all broken a cardinal rule. Talents are not allowed on a battlefield." Ranor regarded the battlefield. Dovel followed his gaze. The misting rain was melting the remaining snow at an alarming rate. The blood-dyed mounds would make a quagmire of the field.

"We'll discuss it later. The weather is worsening." Ranor gazed at the sky. "I hope we can clear the field before it hits, or many will die of exposure." Even as he spoke, men rose, weak, staggering, and dazed. At a motion from Ranor's hand, a line of pony carts pulled near them. Aides jumped from the carts and started moving among the Talent Officers, urging them onto the conveyances.

They took Kissre from his arms. He tried to gently pick up Fudge, but the dog weighed too much for his exhaustion to overcome. Others helped lift Fudge into the Cart, placing the dog next to his mistress. Fudge lay, head bent in a lifeless manner.

"Captain Dovel, you must come. We have orders," an aide warned.

He nodded. "One minute." With weary steps he walked to where the great buckskin horse stood. Bother nickered softly as Dovel touched his neck. He ran his hand down the horse's rough, winter-coated neck, now wet with rain and mired with mud. The horse's ribs showed the last days' hard usage. Taking up the reins, he tied them to the back of the cart. For a moment, he looked at the sword standing hilt end up from the ground. He even put a hand on it. Energy surged through his fingers and crackled like painful fire. He let go. As he watched, it changed states, thickening, crusting in iron, copper, and nickel drawn from deep within the earth. It became only a vague resemblance of itself.

Someone called. Rousing, he returned to the cart. Hands pulled him in the cart. He closed his eyes. Tyna's mind touched his. *::We lost you while you touched Kissre. What happened?::*

"I lost her, too. She faded in and out. It was difficult following her. If I didn't have a touch of Chronos Talent, I would never have found her." He didn't realize he had spoken aloud. "I thought it was Earth Talent that bound us."

Tyna nudged him. He opened his eyes and saw everyone looking at him, including the aides. "It doesn't matter. This incident won't be anyone's secret."

::Dovel.:: Tyna mentally admonished him.

::She went through time, Tyna, kept losing herself in it. She changed it. In some way, she changed time.::

Seventeen

Kissre woke feeling hung-over, thirsty, and queasy. A headache pounded in her temples. Looking around, she recognized her surroundings as an infirmary. A building. She couldn't recall how she got there. She didn't call out but lay quiet. Sadness enveloped her.

A low moan-whine drew her attention. At the bed's edge, Fudge lay on a thick pallet of folded blankets, chewing on bandages covering his front legs. She rolled off the bed and threw an arm over him. Fudged eagerly licked her face. He tried to get up, but with stiff front legs, he flopped around. She bade him to be still, yet his tail thumped the floor and nearly knocked over a nearby tripod table. She laughed at him.

"You're awake."

Kissre looked up at Healer Bujyea. "How?" She rose, slowly. Bujyea steadied her with a hand under her elbow. He ordered her to sit. And she did, gratefully, on the bed's edge. Fudge also tried to stand, but fell back into a sitting position, then slid to a surprised, splay-legged supine.

"What am I doing here?" she asked.

"You were wounded earlier. The wound needed further treatment. It is healing well." Bujyea knelt. He fussed over Fudge as he would any of his patients. "He is doing much better. He needs care. You were exhausted. It was decided to keep you with the wounded while the camp was moved."

"The camp was moved? How long have I been asleep? A year?

Bujyea laughed. "Not quite, but several days. You woke up several times but were not quite lucid. Your presence also made Fudge more amenable, didn't it Fudge?" He gave the dog an enthusiastic head rub, and Fudge licked him.

"His legs?"

"Healing, but he'll need casts until they heal fully. You understand the healers' services had to go to the wounded men first?"

"I'm surprised to find him here at all."

"How much do you remember after the battle?" Bujyea asked, rising.

"By the time I found Fudge things were getting muddled. I remember pulling him free, knew he was dying. A storm was approaching. I could feel it. From then on, I don't remember much, but experienced some really horrendous dreams."

"After such exertion, I'm not surprised."

"Could you find out if a Sergeant Tomel lived?"

"I already know. He does. It was a near thing."

"Do you know anything about the others who were with me?"

"Two of your Pathfinders live. Three of Tomel's platoon and seven of the Kaereyan troop you joined."

"Not many." She sighed, feeling tired.

"More than anyone expected."

It was no consolation. "Can they have visitors?"

Bujyea gave her a strange look. "If you want."

She heard sounds around her and realized she was in a large building. "We're in Guerestu? What happened to the siege?"

"Yes, we're in Guerestu. The siege...ended. The storm caused havoc. With all those trees the Pertelon army cut down, a dangerous situation developed. The ground had been slowly thawing. Before the battle even started, small slides had begun."

"Talent warming or natural?"

Bujyea snorted. "This is Cygna. The rain triggered a devastating slide. Everyone left in the siege camp died under a wall of mud. We are still digging, hoping to find survivors, but it is dangerous work."

Another voice spoke. "There is more."

Quillon stood in the doorway. His arm was bandaged, and he walked with a limp, proving others had faced harsh odds. He nodded to the healer and inspected her room. "Private? How luxurious." Seeing Fudge, the stoic Zekarac Knight started talking to the dog in a falsetto voice. He lowered himself with obvious difficulty and pain to the floor. "Poor Fudge, poor boy!" Fudge whined in greeting, tail thumping and twisting to nose Quillon. Quillon, while talking childish jabber to the dog, pulled the huge chocolate shoulders onto his lap and stroked the shaggy fur. From a pocket, Quillon pulled biscuits that Fudge gobbled whole.

"What more?" Kissre asked exasperated.

"There is a new king in Pertelon. King Uilleam, grandson of the previous king. The war is over."

"Oh." She tried to absorb the information. "The Pertelon army is removing from Kaereya?"

"We don't know yet. Those who survived this battle are withdrawing."

"Then...Aristo Aurelias must be planning for a withdrawal of the Kaereyan forces?"

"Some of them, yes. Others remain as part of the treaty. I will take some back to Kaereya when the time comes. He has already withdrawn troops to Guerestu for security, at least until a location for a peace negotiation is determined. The land is very unstable near the campsites. Later Aristo Aurelias will go to Sidih for more trade negotiations with Governor Vitann."

"I must report."

"I'm afraid not," Bujyea said.

Kissre's head turned to look at the healer. "Why not?"

"Governor Vitann gave orders that you are to be kept here. I'm afraid she had Cygnese guards posted to prevent your leaving."

"You might look again, Healer Bujyea." Quillon bestowed one of his wide, soft smiles on the man. "You will find Kaereyan guards posted also. To prevent any unwilling form of travel." His gaze moved to Kissre. "Aristo Aurelias will be here presently. You will leave with him."

"For the Holy One's sake, why?"

Bujyea looked at Quillon. "There was an incident. Either you will remember, or those involved will tell you."

"Who's involved?"

"Captain Dovel."

Kissre found her feet, ignored the twinge of pain, and turned on the healer. "Remember what? Where is Dovel? Tyna is all right?"

"Tyna is fine. Captain Dovel is busy working for Marshal Ranor. There is much work needing completion."

"Tell her the truth," Quillon said.

Bujyea sighed. "You performed an Earth Calling."

"A what?" Kissre shook her head in denial. "Couldn't have. Suffered battle fatigue."

"Yes to both—a calling of quite magnificent proportions. From the Maze, we learned it extended to the furthest reaches of Cygna and probably beyond. A Calling that involved everyone with even an inkling of Earth Talent. You are not the only one suffering from headache overload. The whole country knows what you are, knows you saved troops from dying for Fudge's sake. The energy you delivered allowed a rare synergism. Within ten furlongs of your presence, even minor Earth Talents came. They performed healing right there on the battlefield. Even the Talents of Pertelon felt what you did. You showed no partiality to army allegiance in whom you saved."

Bujyea pushed her back onto the bed. There was no resistance in her body.

"You feel tired? Surprised you slept so long? You were lucky. You were more than exhausted after the battle. Extending yourself with such a Calling nearly killed you."

Eighteen

Dovel had felt her coming, expected her. He watched Kissre approach through the comfortable salon allotted squad officers at the Guerestu hotel where they were quartered. He had not seen her since the Calling, so he studied her now. Her doubt of any welcome was clear, and she worked to hide a returned limp.

Tyna was upstairs. She and her squad shared this lodging, as did Jycel and several other captains tied to Tyna. Tyna would not let Jycel or his team out of her sight for long as she deemed their recovery still fragile. Jycel sat at a table now, watching, as did everyone in the room, the Crucible's entry. From negation as a null to near reverence among Talents would inflate most heads, but not Kissre. As always, she seemed blind to every tribute given her. Inside, he knew she found it embarrassing and irksome.

Aurelias had ordered her to stay in his apartments with her Cygnese maid, Fay, who seemed more loyal to Kissre than Cygna. It was far too late to protect Kissre from notoriety, also too late for Vitann to threaten her. Stories traveled with alarming dispatch. If her Calling already hovered as legend, her visit to the wounded had cemented her position among the populace. He knew nulls still held her in esteem, even if she proved to have Talent.

Knowledge of his relationship with her seemed widespread. With Kissre out of reach, he bore the brunt of public attention. People approached him with messages for her. "No matter what her Talent, without Touch, she remains as null as the rest of us." A strange greeting and the unexpected attention earned him restrictions and his own set of guards from Vitann.

Today, two Royal Guardsmen and two Cygnese guards came with Kissre. All took a position at the door's entrance. With her arrival came a whiff of spring flowers. An abundant and early spring claimed southern Cygna.

Dovel felt an immediate surge of energy, allowing touch with all about him. It was unwelcome but unavoidable this close to Kissre. She stopped at the table where Jycel and his remaining squad sat. They were changed, thinner, vulnerable looking. Jycel, his assured, assertive air gone, somehow looked more reliant. She greeted each squad member. Hew stared at Kissre, his mind filled with awe she couldn't feel.

"I have not had the opportunity to talk with you before, to express my sympathy...I am so very sorry about Cevoka...She was a good person."

Jycel looked uncertain as to what to say. "Thank you." He stood, went to put out his hand, and then withdrew it. "I know you saved us. We, I know, seemed ungrateful at the time."

"Your platoons held their positions. They saved you, not me. It was my fault my men failed to hold their line."

"It was my fault we were so close to the front. We had been warned to move back. I didn't because it was easier to work closer. I was arrogant in thinking nothing could touch us."

She picked up Jycel's hand where it hung at his side and place her other over their joined hands. Dovel heard the drawn breath throughout the room, but no one could prevent her. "Many mistakes were made. Cevoka was one of those who paid. She and all the others are at peace now. We are left to make our own as best we may." Jycel pulled his hand from hers. His head swam with a disorientation that affected his squad and seeped through the Talents in the room.

She turned and looked at Dovel saying nothing.

"I'm glad you came," he said at last. "My room's upstairs. We can have privacy there."

A crooked grin crossed her face. "As nice as that sounds," she nodded to her guards. "It's difficult with observers. I've earned the unique position of simultaneously being in everyone's good grace while remaining on their wrong side. Yes, I want to talk with you, but I expect publicly will have to do. You're my one tie to memory. Healer Bujyea said you had information. I also need to talk to Captain Pierce. Is she here?"

"I'll get her."

Kissre's head turned to the woman who spoke. "Silvie? Thank you." Silvie rushed from the room.

"Are you escaped or freed?" Dovel asked. "No one has been allowed to come near. Two Cygnese and two Kaereyan guards?"

"Leashed." She looked at her guards. "Two to prevent my leaving and two to prevent my staying. My exact situation is somewhat ambiguous. Unfortunately, no one bargained on how well obstinacy and obnoxiousness work." At his look, she added, "Since Aristo Aurelias broke me out of the infirmary, I have been kept rather secluded. Today I have permission for a brief visit."

"Fudge?"

"Getting around better. Thank you for taking care that he, Bother, and Carillon got back safely. It seems you are developing a habit of rescuing my animals."

"I think you did that. Believe me, the whole army would fight to save your animals."

Red mottled Kissre's cheeks. "It's a bitch, though. I lost my sword. It'll cost me to replace it. A friend gifted me with it, and I treasured it."

"It was left on the field, Kissre."

"Hell, some scavenger got it then."

"No one took it."

She gave him a strange look. "No one took it? It's damaged? Things were muddled there at the end. I thought I'd dropped it."

Tyna entered, and Kissre turned, a new flush mounting her neck and cheeks.

"Would you like privacy?" Dovel asked.

She gave him another mocking look. "To what purpose? Nothing between us has been private." She turned to face her sister as she approached. "Hello, Tyna."

Tyna looked both worried and expectant. "Kissre." Hesitancy tinged her voice. "Silvie said you wanted to see me." Kedriq, Silvie, and the rest of her squad stood behind Tyna.

"Yes. Well." Kissre took an audible inhalation, her neck and face now deep red. "I came to apologize...for my behavior these past months. Everyone seems to know what has passed between us, so there's no use rehashing it, except to tell you I am sorry."

Whatever Kissre had expected, it wasn't Tyna's response. Her face showed her astonishment, her shock. As Tyna squealed, she launched herself into a dance, wrapping her arms around her sister. Her elation twirled both women as Tyna sang, "Kiss, Kissy, Kiss. I knew you'd return to me."

Kissre looked mortified, and Ulyss stepped forward to keep her from falling as she staggered on her bad leg. "Ty, I only apologized, didn't say I'd change. And don't bring up Naomi, because I'm not sure how I feel."

"You talking to me is enough. Oh, Kiss, I'm sorry, too. Come to my room, please, come and talk to me."

"I think, perhaps Kissre might feel more comfortable, Tyna, if we all settle here to talk."

Tyna gave Dovel a mutinous look, but his other message, unheard by Kissre, made her smile.

"You are right. I tend to go overboard. I won't rush you, Kiss."

"Ma'am," one of Kissre's guards interrupted, opening the door. A tapping sound triggered Kissre's temper, and she flung off Tyna and took angry steps toward the door. Fudge entered, head low and sheepish, tail wagging from between his hind legs. His stiff front legs took each step in a slow wooden gait.

"You escaped! You bad dog." Arms akimbo, she watched as Fudge limped forward. "Who let him loose? Has no one any common sense?" she demanded of the guard. "This is too far for him to walk."

"Ma'am, I don't know, but no one would harm him."

"Don't talk to that poor dog like that!" Tyna cried. "He followed you here limping on both legs. How can you? Poor Fudge." Her last words were crooning encouragement to the dog, and Dovel grinned with sardonic humor.

Tyna continued talking to Fudge as if he was a baby. Several others joined her in petting and making a fuss over Fudge, who licked up the adoration and managed to look pathetic and deserving. Kissre turned an indignant and burdened look on Dovel, her eyes rolling in disgust. "They have no idea how hard it is to carry a hundred-weight dog home. Ty," she said, raising her voice. "Let me remind you—you don't like Fudge. You're afraid of him."

"Don't like him?" Tyna looked at Kissre as if she had taken leave of her wits. "Don't be absurd. Fudge is a wonderful dog." She returned to cooing to Fudge, who licked her face with furious intensity while she laughed.

Dovel took a step closer to Kissre. "You could stay here."

"Can't, under orders. You haven't visited." She watched the group around Fudge. "They obviously haven't seen him bite."

"He won't attack anyone. You know it. Was that an invitation?"

She gave him a strange look. "You needed one? I wanted to talk to you."

He lifted his hands in an invitation to the chairs behind him. "I wanted to talk to you, too. But, as you said, there is no privacy here."

"I thought there was between you and me."

"Not much left."

"You can read my thoughts?"

"Only when we're both using our respective Talents. That's what I needed to talk to you about."

Kissre sat with a drop, favoring her sore leg and her humor twisted out of shape. Others, even Jycel and his squad, pulled up chairs. Fudge lumbered over, sat, and placed his head in her lap.

Dovel watched as Kissre unconsciously stroked the dog's head. He looked down to hide his smile.

"Healer Bujyea said you don't remember what happened after the battle," Tyna said.

"Yeah." Her glance fell on Dovel. "I remember seeing you once," she said. "I think. That's about it. He said you knew what happened. I need to know."

"What about your dreams?" Dovel asked.

She stiffened. "What about them?"

"Did Healer Bujyea tell you they weren't dreams?" Tyna asked.

"You saw them?"

"No, she didn't, not the dreams, at least." Dovel placed a hand on her sleeve. "Through the last battle, I had contact with your mind."

"How?"

"You sent Fudge to me with a message. I couldn't feel you, so knew there was trouble. When threatened, you somehow encase yourself in invisibility. Afterward, when we tried to tie him, he turned wild and escaped. I knew he would return to you and tracked him. The warning was enough to start the army moving. Through Fudge, I found you, but by then you were wounded. When Tomel touched you, when your blood covered him, he literally jumped a Talent level." He hesitated. "Did you know you use Earth Talent when under battle stress?"

Kissre gave him an unbelieving look. "How is Tomel?"

"We have him here. You can visit him in a while," Dovel said and returned to the previous topic. Kissre couldn't sidestep this issue. "It's true. The minute you used, I heard your thoughts. It was one of the strangest experiences of my life. As you sought ways to get your men out of harm's way, we coordinated the combined armies to assist."

"I didn't feel you."

"I know."

"Who else?"

"While we were in bond...everyone tied in any way to me."

"Your squad?"

"Yes, and Tyna's."

"We did, too," Jycel said. "Even though not involved in the battle. There are fifteen Captains tied to Tyna, and they are bonded to others."

The obscenity she uttered shocked everyone. Dovel's smile widened. "There is more. After the battle, you weren't exactly dreaming."

"Everyone in on that, too?" Kissre's chin jutted in defiant anger.

"No. Not even me, partly, but not entirely. Kissre, you did an Earth Calling. Every Earth Talent in Cygna felt it and participated."

"Yeah. Bujyea said that. I still don't understand."

"Your desire to save Fudge, your desire to help the wounded left on the field, had unexpected results. Do you remember telling me the energy just dissipated?"

"That was really you?" She looked bewildered. "But what about Naomi, Gervan, and Cevoka? Were they real, too?"

His "I don't know," coincided with Jycel's, "Cevoka?" And Tyna's, "Naomi?"

He looked at the others, and both their mouths snapped shut. "I wasn't with you all the time. So you remember the incident?" She nodded but did not respond. "Kiss, the surface was accepting the energy because, being untrained, you were feeding all of Cygna. Talents from all over Cygna felt it. They pulled the energy from me as you handed it off, but you locked even more into the earth."

"That's why you were so quick. I wondered."

Her comments didn't make much sense. Until a trained Talent analyst talked with her, it would probably remain unexplained. "Yes. No one expected your last act. It was generous to madness. No one has ever done anything like that."

"I don't remember."

"You delivered life energy to the wounded. It saved hundreds of lives others had given up on. No one can explain how you did it. That's why Governor Vitann won't let you go."

"They have no choice if I choose to leave."

"Far warning—it won't be easy."

She started laughing. He thought her a little hysterical. "Why tell me this?"

"If it is your desire, we will help you get out of Cygna," Jycel said.

Dovel knew her reply before she spoke.

"That is a kind offer, but Aristo Aurelias will make sure I get out of Cygna. Even if he couldn't, I know how to leave without his help. You all are too vulnerable to extend such support."

As Tyna started arguing, Dovel sighed.

~ * ~

"You've been quiet. Was your visit productive?" Quillon entered the drawing room of the apartments given the Duke of Lambere. Aristo Aurelias entered right behind him, returned from speaking with the governor's representative. Kissre, who had been looking through the illustrated pages of a manuscript with apathy, looked up as he entered.

Short of screaming in frustration, there is not much but quiet. "I made peace with Tyna."

"Good, about time. Family is important," Aurelias said.

She felt his eyes on her. She huffed softly. "I'm trying."

Quillon snorted, waited while Aurelias gave him some orders, then left, closing the door behind him.

"I've good news. Pertelon is sending a peace emissary. A combined escort of Cygnese and Kaereyan armies will accompany their delegation to Sidih. I expect the negotiations to conclude in an expedient fashion. From Sidih, Quillon will take Kaereya's troops home. You will travel with him. The sooner you are out of this country, the better."

"Thank you."

"You sound very melancholy. That is what you want, isn't it?"

"What? Yes. Of course it is."

"Sit down," Aurelias ordered as she rose to leave. He took a chair opposite her as she seated herself. "Kissre, you need to think about what you want before much longer. You cannot remain a mercenary, not with what we've learned about your abilities. On a battlefield, you have become a liability. If you didn't have an aptitude for strategy, this last encounter would have been disastrous. The Cygnese army was ready to destroy itself to save you." He let his words penetrate. "No one on a battlefield can be indispensable. You know that."

"Are you saying you no longer need my services?"

"No, I am not. There will always be a place for you in Kaereya, just not the position you have previously held. Your Talent now separates you from your employment. Kaereya also develops Talents. You will be accepted there."

"There are other countries. They don't have Talents, don't know about me."

"You know better than that. News travels through armies as if through the Talents' maze, and yours is a secret already disclosed. The mercenaries in both armies will carry the story, much embellished, to their next employment."

"It is what I am."

"No. It is what you were. It is time to change. I'm advising you to know what you are discarding before you do so."

"I don't have that many options. Stay in Cygna and become a puppet or leave and sell my services as a mercenary. Cygna is one of the few countries that accept women as leaders, yet I can't fit into their type of command structure. You know I cannot become more than I am in Kaereya. The Aristos would not have it," she said, forgetting she talked to one. "It is the same in the Eastern Empire, and I do not care for the constant political bickering and maneuvering of Sunderlune." She sighed. "And frankly, I am too old to start a new career."

"You sell yourself short. You are an excellent trainer of dogs, horses, and men. You analyze situations and give strategic counsel. You are levelheaded and astute. You transform energy for the use of others. There are other options."

"What? Wife and mother?"

He gave her an odd look. "Certainly, if you wanted it."

"Most men are wary of me, and truth, I think I am too set in my ways to submit to a husband's expectations."

Aurelias grinned. "Most husbands and wives seldom have all their expectations met. A good marriage is give and take. Forgive me for what I'm going to tell you, but you are not the most intuitive woman when it comes to men. Matter-of-fact, you seem void in that talent, too." He raised a hand to ward off her retort. "I know you can take the measure of an enemy in a glance, most men, too, enemy or not. What you have never been able to judge is their commitment to you."

"Excuse me, Your Grace, but experience has taught me of men's commitment."

He did not rebuke her tart tone but continued relentlessly. "You've suspected Dovel's motives, ignored Quillon's overtures, and been blind to mine."

Kissre said nothing, so astounded she was sure her mouth fell open. Aurelias laughed.

"Just so. Decide your future, Kissre. You have Talents that help people. Do you want to control them, use them? Or do you want them used by the wrong type of people and put to evil uses?"

"You're advising me to stay here? I can't exist as a caged bird, and most Cygnese won't even touch me."

"They're afraid, Kissre. Knowing what you know about yourself, would you trust anyone who extended their hand to you?" He sighed. "You've stood through long days and endless candlemarks of negotiation and compromise. Have you learned nothing?"

~ * ~

Dovel visited, finally. Kissre read in the library with Fudge sleeping at her feet. She said the first thing that entered her mind.

"I don't suppose I can bustle you off to my bed for the afternoon?"

His corner smile flitted on his lips. "Certainly a unique greeting and a new standard for hospitality." He bent and stroked Fudge's side.

"What? You expected Kennetsurean coffee and sweet cakes?"

"That would be acceptable, but hearing your dulcet tones, probably not forthcoming. Has no one argued with you lately?"

"Every day, three times a day. I don't know why everyone is so obstinate!" She threw the book aside. "I'm not allowed to take a ride or even care for my horses—"

"They're fine. Even Bother. The army just delivered a second load of grain and hay just for him and Carillon. They have their own platoon of grooms. Your two remaining Pathfinders seem to have adopted the animals. I've ridden Carillon, but you must teach Bother to accept another rider."

"Ride him bareback...I can't leave the premises, and everyone feels they have the right to make decisions on my behalf. Even Fay!"

"Bareback? That is all it takes?"

"Yes! You're not listening!" She snapped.

"Are you practicing your Aibhe routines?"

She picked up a flagon and threw it against the opposite wall. "Yes!"

Fudge woke startled. He moaned in complaint, sighed, and put his head back down with grumbling sounds. Dovel started laughing, his immobile face breaking into a broad grin. The door burst open, and one of the Kaereyan guards asked if everything was all right.

"I dropped my drink," Kissre said, ignoring the liquid seeping down the wainscoting. The guard withdrew with a warning look at Dovel, who only marginally managed a sober deportment.

She glanced at him. "They are not working. The harder I exercise inside, the more my body craves the outside."

"They've put you in quite a state. So much for Vitann's plan to safely box a dragon. You'd eat anyone on the premises. I think you need to get out of here."

"I am not a dragon," she said, her body tensing with her correction. "They won't let me. Quillon knows all my escape tricks, and the minute I'm out of sight, Fudge starts howling."

"Perhaps with me? If I promise your safe return?"

Something in his manner made her stop and stare. She approached closer, eyes narrowed, hands on her hips. "They asked you, didn't they?"

"It was suggested some time away might benefit everyone."

His indulgent tone tightened her lips. He startled her by grabbing and kissing her hard. "Don't waste time arguing. Yes, we'll have an escort, but let me show you Guerestu. We'll take Fudge."

"Just as I was thinking the bedroom started sounding better and better."

~ * ~

Dovel found the afternoon unseasonably warm. Neither he nor Kissre wore bulky outerwear. That small freedom was a welcome harbinger of summer. Once out of her confinement, Kissre's mood lightened.

Quillon had sought him out, told him Kissre needed diversion. He had known but had been forbidden visiting. His squad had been just as frustrated with him. With the Duke of Lambere's interference in Cygnese prohibitions, he found himself invited where he most wanted to go.

Fewer superiors regulated Kissre's actions, but her visit to the squad's lodgings had been highly restricted for her own safety. Vitann had also forbidden Tyna from visiting her sister, afraid of another quarrel between the two. Tyna blunted her frustration on him. He knew her teasing showed her annoyance and maybe the humbling realization that her own magnificent gifts resulted from her sister's touch as much as natural capability. The presence of an unfettered Crucible unsettled every Talent and every null, with strong emotions ranging from outraged aversion to tormented desire. It created a volatile situation that affected everyone.

He found himself the butt of much humor. Kissre's effect on his Talents became both a gift and a curse. It became so bad, even looking at a person brought their thoughts—usually with a crude joke circulating about hunting Talent among nulls. His unpredictable displays of temper startled many, including himself, but brought some relief in the simple expedient that people avoided him.

"Come back."

"What?"

"You were thinking or involved in another conversation. It's not polite."

"I was reflecting that this outing has soothed my temper."

"You had a temper? I don't believe it."

He grinned. "As bad as yours. My squad was eager to see my back."

"So they put us together to let us wear ourselves out on each other rather than those around us?"

"Something like that."

Fudge's leg splints were gone, but he still walked slowly. Stares and smiles followed everywhere they went. Everyone wanted to babble and coo over Fudge, though her guards kept anyone from approaching too close to Kissre. Storeowners offered Fudge biscuits and other tidbits at every stop. After a candlemark, Dovel noticed the dog tiring.

"Probably all those treats lying heavy in your gut," Kissre accused when Fudge laid down and refused to move. Fudge only whined and looked up at them from the top of his eyes.

Dovel laughed. "We should stop and let him rest." Daylight lingered in the late afternoon even as the air began cooling enough to become uncomfortable. Across the street, Tyna waved, beckoning them as she and Kedriq entered a tavern.

"Can you stand company?" he asked.

"Was this part of the plan?"

"No. We don't have to go if you would rather not. There are a few other places. But since the siege, not much palatable is put on any table."

"No. It's all right. I suppose I should start acting like a sister. I might even pick a quarrel."

That sobered Dovel, but only for a second. He grinned. "Please, don't. The last one nearly tore Cygna apart. Besides, Vitann has kept Tyna from visiting, fearing that very thing."

Kissre returned his grin, and he sensed something give inside her. She relaxed. "Up, Fudge. Come on, boy." Fudge groaned and rose in an ungainly fashion but didn't move. He looked at Kissre with a lowered head and sheepish eyes. Dovel picked him up with a grunt of his own and walked across the street.

~ * ~

Inside, the tavern was spacious and crowded with patrons, although their entrance brought an abrupt silence. Only the desultory strains of a guith emanated from the far reaches of the dark interior.

Kissre observed Dovel's bland expression and guessed he took the brunt of the silence. His smile was strained, and she laughed. "I didn't ask you to carry him."

Fudge whined, and the owner responded with overtones of concern as normal tavern noise returned. Tyna came over and started directing the staff. An impromptu bed for the dog was prepared at Tyna's table. Dovel gratefully lowered his burden. Kissre refused a meal for him. "He's already eaten too much." She knelt, scratched Fudge behind the ears, and checked he was comfortable.

"It's not too drafty on the floor for him, is it?"

She identified the soft voice and closed her eyes briefly. *Polite. Remember polite*, she adjured herself before raising her gaze to Silvie. "He still has his winter coat. He'll be more comfortable where it is a little cooler."

"May I pet him?"

She nodded. "Fudge enjoys attention."

Silvie knelt as Kissre rose, and she watched as Fudge gently received the woman's timid overtures. After a few tentative touches, he just as gently licked Silvie's nose. Prepared for horrified rejection, Silvie surprised Kissre and laughed.

Tyna asked her a question, and Kissre turned her attention to the rest of the company. "First time I've been allowed out," Kissre answered.

She took a seat next to Dovel. As Silvie took her seat, Kissre turned to check Fudge. He gnawed a bone. Her temper flared, and she looked at Dovel but said nothing. Reading the message in his expression, she calmed and tried to enjoy herself. The difficulty was getting everyone else to relax. Conversation became strained, although there were no long silences.

By the time they had shared a meal, the semblance of privacy evaporated. Kissre smirked to herself at the results. All around her squad captains and lieutenants gathered at nearby tables. Tyna attracted Talents like Fudge attracted tidbits. Most Kissre had never met. Dovel's squad arrived. Jycel and company came. Rounds of ale kept arriving, but she still nursed her first.

"You think they came because of Tyna, don't you?" Dovel asked.

"Stay out of my mind," she whispered back.

"Not in there. Don't have to be. They came to see you."

"Whatever for?"

"Irresistible draw—because all of us were with you during the last battle. We experienced everything you did. They felt something they have never felt before, and now, none of them can feel you at all."

She wished he hadn't told her that. They inspected her with unreadable but avid expressions. Kissre gave Dovel a brief glance that said she was glad, at least, she couldn't hear them. She swallowed a laugh at his expression and quickly took another sip of ale, aware now of the gazes following her tattoo.

She rose. "Excuse me."

Within three steps Dovel caught up with her. Fudge at his heels. "You and Fudge are becoming indistinguishable. Afraid I'm headed for the back door?"

"Pull back your fangs, dragon. I promised to see you home. Besides, I felt you might be on a mission to do something about the lamentable music."

Kissre laughed. "I thought they were prickly spines. Fudge owns the fangs. Let's face down this player and show him what atrocious music should sound like. You know any good drinking songs?"

"Only bad ones."

"Bet I know worse. May I borrow your instrument?" Kissre asked the young man who looked at her as is if she held her sword over his head. He quickly relinquished his guith and abandoned his stage for a stool in a somewhat dark corner. Fudge snuffled around, investigating the area. She turned to Dovel, the prize grasped in her capable hands. "You think there is another in the place?"

He looked back through the tavern. "The owner is already bringing another. He knows opportunity when he sees it. What forfeit do we play for?"

Kissre re-tuned the mishandled instrument, disregarding the interest and curiosity fluttering around her that she knew impinged on Dovel's perception. The noise of people moving, chairs, benches, and stools scraped across the wood floor. The sound drew her attention, and she looked out on the movement. "I win, I choose where you sleep tonight."

Dovel laughed outright. She saw the surprised looks his action drew from his friends who gathered around but knew the surrounding noise drowned their private conversation.

His eyes sparkled in the candlelight. "Trying to ensure your bet? If I win, you must entertain me for a sennight. You may take the stage."

"That sounds like a hedged bet." She snapped her fingers, and Fudge returned from sniffing the gathering audience.

"I was going to say I would choose when you slept, but a sense of inadequacy bettered my judgment."

Kissre laughed and ordered Fudge down. He grumbled but stretched out, resting his head on his forelegs. Waiters brought lamps, their steps skirting the dog. More stools arrived, and Dovel snagged one from nearby. He sat, and she watched him tune the instrument.

"You going to listen?" Kissre asked those drawing near her. The gathered faces nodded or gave vocal assent. From their sleeves, she saw they were a mix of curious Talents and eager nulls. "Then you're going to have to sing." Nervous laughs met her as she played a few soft chords. "All right. Repeat after me." Soon everyone sang the bawdy lyrics she taught, turning the evening into a tribute to bad taste. Long past the tavern's normal closing time, Kissre played and sang, some solo, some duet with Dovel, and sometimes they led a sing-along.

The delighted owner kept them well supplied with ale, and Kissre shook hands with him and his staff as she left, ignoring their reaction. With a wave of her hand she motioned Fudge out. Dovel followed her. Once outside, she found her four guards waited. For so late a candlemark, many people milled around, both Talents and nulls. Tyna and many of her companions had left without waiting for Dovel.

Regarding her guards, he seemed indecisive.

"Aurelias leaves tomorrow," she said.

"I've heard. I have to stay here until the army returns to Sidih."

"This might be our last time together. You coming?"

"I'm wondering if you are allowed guests."

"Don't know," she admitted, then grinned. "But, I believe I won the forfeit."

Nineteen

A wild windflower landed on Kissre's already petal-lined lap. With a self-conscious side-glance at Duke Aurelias' face, she picked it up and placed it with other spring flowers overflowing from her opened saddlebags. As she did, dried rose petals fell from her sleeves to float to the road. More petals decorated Bother's mane.

The floral tribute began when the wives and camp followers of Cygna's Second and Third Armies threw the dried petals and spring flowers on her as the Envoy and the Kaereyan Army marched out of Guerestu. It was not the last time for the floral shower.

More disconcerting than the flowers, men lined their route, nodding in respect from the roadside, and children ran out to touch her boot. A few of them even kissed it. Kissre, worried about her footgear's cleanliness, was at a loss on how to end the embarrassing behavior. Worse, the Cygnese squad captains escorting them witnessed it all. As did Quillon, who rode behind Aristo Aurelias wearing a smug smile she could feel.

Thank the Holy One, Bother's calm strides never faltered. Kissre glanced down frequently, keeping an eye on Fudge as he walked. His tongue hung in an even pant, and every so often, he licked his muzzle.

"He's fine." Duke Aurelias assured her from Fudge's other side. Despite his amused look, his tone was distracted and gruff. "Although, I suspect your spectators would prefer to see him on the outside rather than between our mounts."

"Maybe, but I think at our next rest, I'll have him ride in one of the carts. Those splints haven't been off that long."

Only a huffed, sour, "As you please," answered her—little amused Aurelias since the Pertelon Peace Emissary had arrived in Guerestu.

"King Uilleam didn't send a traitor to negotiate peace."

"He betrayed Kaereya!"

"And Pertelon was an enemy a few sennights ago."

Aurelias snorted and stared straight ahead.

Whatever he had once been, Kissre sensed a quiet and thoughtfulness in the Emissary, Pertelon's First Minister. He insisted she call him Eldin. "My rank is new," he had said with a gracious bow, not offering her the customary handclasp, so someone had spoken to him. "And I am more used to informality." He was attractive, courtly, austere in dress, and a little shorter than herself. Yet an essence of toughness underlaid his image.

The man rode with them, well protected by his own contingent of Pertelon troops, and surrounded by Cygnese and Kaereyan troops.

Aristo Aurelias' Novere stallion tossed his head and pranced as his rider gathered him from a small disobedience. White foam gathered around the horse's bit as the animal worried it. The crowds tried the stallion's temper, a taller horse, darker and taupe rather than Carillon's lavender.

As a gesture of goodwill, Kissre offered Carillon to Marshal Ranor for the ride to Sidih. Political prudence suggested the Marshal should ride abreast and at an equal level with the Kaereyan duke. Ranor eagerly accepted her invitation and rode next to Aurelias radiating pleasure.

Aurelias had thanked her for the gesture. "Such details sometimes become problems," he said, looking overwrought. She noticed Quillon also aided in subtle ways as duty engulfed the envoy and Commander of the Kaereyan Army.

His words described her dilemma. What was she to do with two such animals? An embarrassment of riches and Kissre knew she could not part with either one. She sighed.

Bother and the two Novere horses made an impressive lead for the long caravan. Kaereyan Aristos and Cygnese squads followed, leading the foot troops. Aurelias had ordered Kissre to accompany him back to Sidih for completion of his diplomatic mission. He dashed her hopes of returning to the emotional safety of Kaereya. She never expected Cygnese citizens would line the road to watch the cavalcade along the route from Guerestu, It slowly sank into Kissre that leaving Cygna might not be easy.

Turning in the saddle, she addressed the duke's aide riding behind her and next to Quillon. She asked that Captain Jycel ride forward.

"Can you stop this?" Kissre asked as Jycel brought his pony alongside Bother. "It's dangerous for these children to run beneath Bother's hooves."

His expression became disconnected for a minute. "Senders are putting a message out, but I doubt it will help much. Nulls can't hear, and the Talents won't stop as long as the nulls continue." He smiled at her and fell back to ride next to Quillon. He was right. Children continued to run to her with flowers, their arms and hands covered with painted-on dragons. She cursed.

"They are trying," Jycel said from behind where he rode with Quillon.

She turned in her saddle to look at him. "Not that. If the paint on these children turns into tattoos, I'll be brought up on charges."

"You set new styles," Jycel laughed.

"No, don't put your gloves on," Quillon said. "Let them see it."

Kissre swore as Quillon continued conversing with Jycel, ignoring her problem. The duke's horse jumped, and the skittish animal bumped Bother, who sidestepped. Fudge loped out of the way between Bother's legs. He stayed to Bother's offside to the gratified shouts of the onlookers. Aurelias apologized.

"No matter what you think of him, he aided both Cygna and Kaereya by restoring the rightful heir to Pertelon."

Aurelias' brows lowered as he turned to her. "I thought you Touch void."

Laughing, she said, "It doesn't take a divining gift to know you are a better horseman than this."

"The man's a traitor."

"Not in Pertelon or Cygna. King Uilleam gave him full authority to negotiate. That bespeaks a broad trust. As Your Grace has frequently told me, people change. The Holy One knows there are a few Kaereyan Aristos who could drive me into Pertelonese arms."

Narrowed eyes inspected her, and Aurelias emitted a grunted snort. "It was a surprise that is all."

"Yeah," Kissre said as another flower fell in her lap. "For me, too."

It was worse in Sidih. People lined the streets, chanting her name, screaming when they saw Bother.

Quillon's voice floated forward. "The next rumor will be you brought him back to life."

Kissre swiveled her head to regard his gloating face. She cursed him. He only smiled wider.

~ * ~

The Shield showed up two days later. Already set upon by guards that made her back itch, Kissre's temper whipped everyone indiscriminately, even with three calming meditations and an exercise routine that exhausted her. Aurelias swore as he stormed from her that it would be a prime goal of his negotiations to get Dovel to Sidih.

She wished Dovel present to relieve her boredom, but he and the rest of the army remained at Guerestu until the treaty was signed, maybe longer. Both Quillon and Duke Aurelias, tied up in the peace negotiations, had admonished her about her temper. It did no good. She had no outlet for her restlessness. Sitting, remaining still, became impossible.

Quillon, acting as sole security for the duke. He also trained two Royal Guards to take over her previous position, so he didn't have time to practice with her. They wouldn't permit her any duty that put her before the Cygnese statesmen and discouraged her appearance among the general populace. When Quillon, driven by her sarcasm, practiced with her, they attracted such a crowd, the city's peacekeepers were called.

The Shield Larig was announced as a man looking like Kedriq entered the room where she read. Kissre stared. "What are you doing here? Did Tyna and Dovel return, too?"

"I am not Kedriq. I am Larig, a gift from Cygna, your Shield."

"You look like Kedriq."

"He is my brother."

It took a minute's thought, but she knew she had seen him at the negotiations but had mistaken him for Kedriq.

"You were at the negotiations."

"I was Governor Vitann's Shield, her bodyguard."

The explanation infuriated Kissre. "You're Vitann's spy?" Her voice spit acid, giving Larig the welcome the governor's representative deserved.

"More like a watchdog."

She had not expected humor or calm in the voice of the unsmiling replica of Tyna's husband.

"Why were you sent?" Aurelias asked from the open door, having obviously heard. Both he and Quillon walked into the room and insisted on remaining for the interview. Kissre damned servants who reported her every moment.

"I protect the Crucible Kissre."

The comment ignited Kissre's temper. "I don't need another protector or guardian. The Holy One knows I have enough."

"Governor Vitann said Cygna owed you." The blond man bowed his head before regarding her with unwavering intensity. "I am a tangible payment."

"So she threatens me with imprisonment?"

"Kissre!" Quillon said. "Hear him out."

She glared at Quillon as she spoke. "Just detainment, then?"

"Governor Vitann's decrees are no longer my concern. My oath is to the Crucible."

Kissre stopped her full invective as she turned her head toward Larig. She heard Quillon's laugh. Tired of being caught unaware, her teeth clicked with the forceful closing of her jaw. In a more mollified tone, she asked, "You swore to Vitann? You were her Shield?"

"Vitann annulled the oath."

Kissre smiled. "Then let me annul this one."

"Impossible."

"If Vitann nullified your vow to her, so can I."

"I swore to Vitann, personally. For you, I swore to the Holy One before the altar at the Cathedral Celestyn. It cannot be undone."

"Even if Governor Vitann, or another official, wants information about me?"

"I am sworn to you, the Crucible Kissre."

"And when I leave Cygna?"

"I am sworn to you."

After two days of alternately ignoring Larig, insulting, provoking, or screaming at him in temper, he showed her to an enclosed arena. "You need to vent your ill-humor," he said, smiling. He threw her a wooden blade as he picked up one for himself.

Catching the blade, she said, "Use steel."

"You may use steel if you wish. I cannot draw steel against you."

"You will if you continue to spar with me." She started a pre-battle Aibhe exercise. "I need to get a new sword, anyway. Some rules. We agree here and now, or you leave."

"I will do my duty."

"Good, that makes you more open to negotiation. You will not address me as 'the Crucible.' I am Kissre Pierce. You may call me Kissre. You will not bow your head every time you come into my presence."

"Kissre in private, the Crucible in public."

"Kissre Pierce or even Colonel Pierce in public." She swung the practice blade, loosening her tight shoulders. "You realize I'm fairly competent at protecting myself?"

"I watch your back and watch when you can't. You have held my position. You know how it works. Your life is different now. Mistress Pierce..."

"Kissre."

"...The day of the battle, you became a legend in Cygna, and soon outlanders will know. Eminence brings vulnerability."

"You will not interfere with my duties, whatever they may become. You will not follow in my footsteps. You will not hover. You will be invisible and stay out of my way." She exercised with the blade, stepping through the Aibhe practice. "I'm sure the list will lengthen."

"You will advise me when you plan to leave protected premises. I will travel with you. I will judge the danger of any situation, and I will follow my own views of how to best protect you. You will listen and obey my advice."

Provoked, Kissre attacked. Their blades repeatedly cracked in the silence of the arena. After several skirmishes where Larig ignored obvious opportunities, she battered him with an offense that took him to the wall.

"You will not let me win!" Her fury echoed off the walls. "You want to protect me? Then make sure I keep an edge, with a weapon or without. You pull back on a fair hit, and I'll show no mercy. A few bruises or cuts protect me more than an unearned win." She snarled, "Or a guardsman with no arm."

The man grinned in evil pleasure, pushed her off, and renewed the fight. He was skilled, nearly as good as Quillon, but not as tall, heavy, or with as long a reach. It was fair. Kissre lost only because a twice-wounded leg gave way, upsetting her balance.

Larig would not touch her extended hand to help her rise, but stepped back, leaving her to gain her own feet. They stood, their breath labored, looking at each other. Kissre extended her hand in the traditional peace salute at the end of practice. "Afraid?"

"Undeserving."

"I will not be treated as an untouchable. Let the Holy One separate the rest."

With reluctance, Larig took her hand in the salute. Once he dropped his hand, she attacked him in hand to hand combat and beat him. She extended her hand to help him rise from the arena's sand floor. This time he did not hesitate to take the offered help.

"You will teach me this, and the thing you did before we fought."

"Are you asking or commanding?"

"Both. As your Shield, I need to know all forms of fighting. This is new, and I must learn it."

Kissre laughed. "If you must." It made her think of Aurelias' words about other things she could do. *Training and teaching.* If ever a country needed to train its foot soldiers, it was Cygna. Pausing, she realized she would not be here, so it didn't matter, but maybe in Kaereya.

~ * ~

Larig stopped his attack and stepped back. "You have a visitor."

Zeba heard his winded words and smiled as both opponents looked to where she stood. She had waited until she had been noticed and was sorry the pleasure of watching their battle was over. Larig's last aggressive sally was powerful, but Kissre's counterattack was as strong, taking precise dance-like movements.

Kissre looked to the side of the arena where she stood. The Crucible nodded to Larig. He returned her salute and walked away. It was odd to sense Larig's presence and only see Kissre move. Kissre's inaccessibility always struck Zeba afresh. It would take many Talents a long time to accept such an odd condition. Through the maze, she knew those with her in the last battle were changed afterward. Caught in an inexplicable bond to someone they couldn't comprehend in any other way than as a null. This new, most-important member of the Talent community, generated conflicting, forceful emotions.

"Where is your maid?"

"I don't need someone to watch my every movement, Kissre."

"Sorry, just not accustomed to seeing you without her."

"Well, I wanted to talk to you privately. I can wait until your practice is over, although others may try to break your privacy now that I have. For that, I apologize. Is he beating you?"

"Actually, no. We are evenly matched. He has a slightly longer reach. I am faster and more flexible. More skillful." She grinned.

"In certain methods, only," Larig said.

Zeba chuckled. Clearly hearing Larig's mental quip *::Anyone might have difficulty coping with all the Crucible's undoubted attributes. I do.::*

Something in her face afforded Kissre recognition. "Talk aloud! Both of you!"

"We've been very rude," Zeba apologized with her disarming smile. "Larig picked up some unguarded thoughts from my mind and answered them. Yes, about you. I was thinking of how some of my compatriots might have difficulty dealing with you."

"I doubt they'll get the chance unless they go to Kaereya."

"You still plan on leaving?"

"Yes."

"What about Dovel?"

"Is that what brought you here?"

"No. I needed to speak with you."

"Something to convince me to remain?"

"No, more than likely to make you bolt for Kaereya."

Kissre started removing her practice gear. Larig unstrapped his as he walked over. "Oracle Zeba."

"Shield Larig, your mind is much lighter of late."

A snorting sound erupted from Kissre with a curse. "The fool gave up a cushy job just to get his brains bashed out."

"I find my new Entrusted less amenable, but my conditioning much improved."

"It is true, Kissre tries the patience of many, but she has a few small merits."

"Yes, Oracle Zeba. Have you dismissed your guardian?"

"Guardian? Her maid is a guardian?" Astonishment washed Kissre's face.

"But of course," Larig's laugh sounded indulgent. "You don't think the Adept Council allows Oracles out alone, do you? Zeba?"

Zeba felt it time to look a little sheepish. "She thinks me resting, which is why I couldn't wait until after your practice."

"Larig, Zeba and I need to be private. I'll see you back at the Embassy."

"I will wait outside the entrance." Larig picked up the equipment and left.

"What is so important that you escaped your guardian?" Kissre swore afresh and shook her head. Zeba felt sure she envisioned ways to escape such a fate.

"Yes, it is reprehensible that some Talents are regarded as needing such. In my case, I must admit, it has been a wise precaution. There have been times when I...well, never mind."

"Zeba, I don't have much time."

"Did you know I knew your mother? Not well, not as a friend, but as much as you think you stumble over Talents here, there are not that many."

"I don't want to talk of Naomi." Kissre started picking up her equipment.

"Tyna is only your half-sister."

She couldn't feel Kissre's shock, but the woman straightened and turned slowly to Zeba, her face guarded.

"I knew your mother's mentor. He was not the most understanding of men, especially for a girl taken from a Kernite Sect. He selected a temporary mate he felt would help her develop her Talent and possibly produce a viable Talent."

"They bred her?"

"Not quite, Naomi had some latitude to accept or decline. No place is perfect, Kissre, not even Kaereya. You've seen much of the world and already know that. Through the past centuries, the Adept Council's power had grown without anyone to question its motives. It proved disastrous in Naomi's case."

"She must not have been the only one."

"No. There were many damaged in countless ways. Reform came, but too late for Naomi."

"What? They don't use coercion *now*? Or do they just twist minds into believing that's what they want?" Kissre was silent a moment. "So she gave birth to a null daughter the Adept Council didn't want, so she was stuck with it. With me."

"No. Naomi could have given you in adoption. She kept you, more Kernite training. Family is family. Later she met Tyna's father."

"He loved her. I always wondered why he never interfered between Naomi and me."

"When Naomi fled, both her talent and his were so meager the Review Board did not think it necessary to hunt them, to bring them back. Most minor Talents are often considered null."

"She sensed Tyna's Talent. That's why she fled."

"Perhaps. She might have sensed your effect on Tyna's Talent. Naomi was never measured after her pregnancy with you. Considering what you are, you might have affected your mother's Talent. No one will ever know now."

"My father?"

"He is still living. I imagine he knows who you are."

"Does Tyna know?"

"I don't believe so. If she learns, it must come from you."

"So I was basically a child of rape. No wonder she didn't want me." She sighed and looked at her feet. "Why did you decide to tell me this?"

Zeba sighed. "Not rape, Kissre. A loveless union perhaps, but your father was not a monster. I think she wanted you. I believe she loved you. Her relationship with your father permanently distorted her view of you, filled her with conflict. I tell you this because I would like you to stay in Cygna."

Kissre laughed. "You can't believe this story would encourage me."

"I know, but you needed to know the truth before you decide. Cygna needs people like you. You could do great good here. Help meld those with Talent and those without back into a cohesive population."

"Is that what you see?" The green eyes stared into Zeba as if she could fathom her visions.

"Your touch has not only made my visions clearer but it has also increased them. I see so many different timelines, they cannot be sorted out."

"I don't believe you."

"Whom do you trust or believe? Dovel? Quillon? Aristo Aurelias?"

Kissre did not answer at first but blanched then blushed. "I trust different people in different ways."

"But no one completely?"

"I don't know. I have never stayed anywhere long enough to worry about it. May I ask you a question?"

"Certainly. That you still talk to me is a credit to your civility."

"Would Dovel be allowed to leave Cygna?"

"No."

"Not even for short trips?"

"I can't answer that. No policy has been made about Talents leaving Cygna."

"Cygna has sent envoys to other countries. Kedriq was sent to Kaereya."

"Not often, and never major Talents. Vitann had a specific reason to send Kedriq away. Another Oracle had predicted his former squad captain's death. Vitann knew it would affect Larig if Kedriq died, so she wanted to see how Kedriq handled separation. Very well, it turned out, but he loathed his Captain. Otherwise, the Adept Council protects Cygna's Talents. What are you thinking?"

"Something stupid."

"You want Dovel? In a long-term sense? A Talent?"

"Yeah. I keep asking that myself. It doesn't seem possible to achieve, anyway."

The door to the arena opened, and Larig entered with Zeba's maid. The woman bowed to Kissre, then gently scolded Zeba. Zeba raised her eyebrows at Kissre and made a few words of placation to her guardian and friend. She turned back to the Crucible.

"Kissre, you've come to a turning point in your life. I see possibilities and successes in Kaereya. I also see them in Cygna, and even in other places. None of them is a perfect choice. No choice comes without its conflicts and troubles. I also see disasters. I can tell you this. The one constant throughout is you must learn to use and control your Talent. You can only do that in Cygna."

"And if I don't?"

"If you don't, others will do it for you."

~ * ~

With the conclusion of the peace negotiations, Kissre watched two squads and their platoons leave on the journey to escort Aristo Innes and his company to the border. In two days Quillon would leave for Kaereya with the majority of the Kaereyan forces.

"Well, Kissre, come to a decision, yet?" Aristo Aurelias asked as those involved in the formal departure ceremony dispersed. Dovel had not returned from Guerestu. She was surprised. Governor Vitann had brandished every other inducement to remain, and dire predictions if she left.

"If you plan to leave, go with Quillon." Aurelias' gaze had not left her. "The Cygnese are at their most altruistic, but you've rejected all their offers. Things will change the longer you stay. You should expect opposition to your departure and not just from the government."

"I know. It's not only the Adept Council but also the citizenry."

"They are in an uproar at rumors of your leaving, Kissre. They think of you as their own. If you leave, it must be soon."

She snorted. "They don't know me very well. But I don't wish to cause you more trouble. I'll travel with Quillon."

"Before you leave, I want to talk with you." Her chin rose at his tone.

"Well, you have lost your mercenary's subservience to a superior." He laughed at her expression. "We need to talk about your future employment. I told you, you cannot remain a mercenary or soldier. There are several other positions you could fill."

Kissre nodded and followed him to his office where they talked. Two days later she joined the procession taking the western route to the Seer Pass with only one defection. Before leaving, Fay came to her with her younger sister.

"I wish to leave your service."

"You've never been in my service, Fay. I am not the one who pays you. But I'd gladly hire you if my own position were not so uncertain."

"You were put into my care. My sister, Marisse, wishes to serve you now, if you have no other you wish. I have instructed her in your preferences and how you like things done."

Kissre swallowed at the last bit, images of Zeba's guardian springing to mind. "Fay, you know I am leaving Cygna. Besides not knowing how I could pay her. I don't know if your sister is willing to travel."

"Oh, yes. I am willing," Marisse said, eager to please.

"You now have Larig with you, and Quillon assures me you will have a good income. I am going too, but with Quillon. He and I will marry, which is why I can no longer serve you."

The news stopped Kissre's progress in her repair and cleaning of equipment. It was true Duke Aurelias had increased her pay, told her Kaereya's King Warrick would approve. But she wasn't sure yet what her position was, or if she was ready for a retinue. With two horses and four retainers, since the Pathfinders remained, determined to care for Bother and Carillon, it seemed she already possessed one. "I'm speechless, Fay. I had no idea. I wish you happiness."

"Thank you. We did not try to keep it secret, but you have been preoccupied with other things."

"Let me serve you, ma'am, until you are at Cygna's borders, and if you decide I will please, I will leave with you."

Kissre gave an inner sigh and looked at Marisse. She was a younger version of Fay. "That is no way to treat any employee. You are very young, but I shall gladly hire you here and now at your sister's recommendation. Thank you." Both women looked ecstatic. A nagging question came to Kissre. "Fay, since you've touched me..."

"Yes, Crucible Kissre. I have changed, not enough to become a great Talent, but I've been tested and there has been an inner awakening. My Touch Talent is now evident, and even a little Fire Talent has been detected."

"It was nothing I did, Fay, it was already within you."

"If you say so, Crucible Kissre, then I believe you."

Swallowing her tart reply, Kissre gave Fay leave to show Marisse her duties.

Twenty

At the Duke of Lambere's request, Zeba sat in on the day's negotiations on commerce. It was an unusual request and excited Zeba, even though she knew it involved a lot of sitting. "I've become very proficient at that skill over the years," she told her maid. For herself, she knew timelines were sorting out. She arrived early and took her seat at the far left end of the table out of the negotiator's cross-table positions.

For a third day, early summer storms converged on Cygna. Along with strong gusting winds, the continually misting rain was interspersed with drowning cloudbursts that made being outdoors miserable. She had been unable to walk in the gardens. With the Fountains of Power working again, the gardens had become a new pleasure. Without the exercise, she found herself antsy with boredom.

Vitann entered first, trailed by Secretary Egwent. She took the center of her delegation's side of the table. A new Shield, much older than her last, took his position behind her. Adept Orrthu came in and sat to Vitann's right. Dean Alth sat next to her. Egwent sat on Vitann's left, and Dean Ferran came in last to sit next to him. Zeba's gaze followed His Grace as he entered. A small entourage of a secretary and a fellow delegate followed him. A Kaereyan Royal Guard entered last. They all sorted themselves into seats on the opposite side of the table. The guard stood behind Aristo Aurelias' chair, facing Vitann's Shield. Zeba observed Aurelias. He was undoubtedly an unpretentious man for a Kaereyan Aristo, almost Cygnese looking in his conservative appearance.

Visions of him had played in her head for days. She smiled in expectation of a rousing confrontation. It would balance the smug satisfaction emanating from the Talents in the room. They never planned to release Kissre, even as she left. Vitann felt sure public pressure, even confrontation, would force the Crucible to stay. The recent continued bad weather would enforce the public's foreboding and gloom at Kissre's departure.

Zeba grinned at how little they understood. Her own sources told her the people sorrowed at the Crucible's leaving but wouldn't stop her. Nulls seemed to understand her desire to escape the Talent Board's Control, even made them feel better about being null themselves. Zeba had already seen the effect their somber departure accolade would have on Kissre.

The meeting started.

"Today, Governor," Aurelias said, "with the treaty completed, I believe we are to begin talks on a trade agreement. We've talked of an exchange of craftsmen already. You've expressed interest in our scholars, in our silk and spice production, and Kaereya in your glassworks."

For several candlemarks the delegations spoke of crafts and trade exchanges. Zeba waited for the coming confrontation, feeling the Talent's tension rise as the meeting continued. Aurelias broached the subject first.

"King Warrick would like some Talents to help teach in Kaereya. A request has been made for the Oracle Zeba."

"Why an Oracle?" Orrthu asked. "You request too much. Talents never leave Cygna."

"I have felt an unrelenting promise of travel recently." Zeba felt Orrthu's disgust at her interruption.

"You are too old to travel and too inconsistent to be of any help teaching anyone."

"My mission has been advised Zeba would be the most logical to help train a seeress." The duke looked down at the papers in his hand.

"The seeress is your daughter, is she not?" Vitann asked.

"Yes, she is, but the request was forwarded from King Warrick. Her husband, the Aegis of Kaereya, made the request. He also asked that an Earth Talent might be beneficial for himself."

"You wish two high-ranking Talents from us? Let your Talents come here for training," Dean Alth said.

"That is not possible. The Aegis cannot leave Kaereya, and my daughter won't leave him."

"Then give us something in return...there is Kissre," the Dean said.

"Kissre is non-negotiable. She has already made her choice. It was to return to Kaereya."

"Everything is negotiable, Your Grace." Vitann remained unperturbed.

"Kissre has turned down every offer you've made her. As a Kaereyan citizen, she is free to make her own choice. Even the Oracle Zeba or any other Talent requested by Kaereya must come willingly and by choice."

"And I do agree, most eagerly." Zeba bestowed a gracious smile on everyone.

The doors to the room opened with a draft that cooled the heated atmosphere. Everyone turned at the interruption. Both Shield and Royal Guard drew weapons. Orrthu gasped as the Crucible Kissre stood with her hands on the door latches. No guard outside dared touch her. She entered looking robust and vital, rain droplets covering her hair and jack. Fudge followed, smelling of wet dog. Water dripped from his soaked coat, and his nails clicked on the stone floor. His tongue hung from his long muzzle, and his sides still heaved from exertion.

Zeba grinned. No Talent had sensed the Crucible's approach, and their shock reverberated through the room. Vitann rose in a stiff movement. Hiding her amusement, Zeba held a hand out to Fudge, who obligingly approached for a scratch under his ear. He was very wet and smelled stronger up close, but Zeba found a dry spot below the ear.

"Crucible Kissre," Governor Vitann said, clearly shocked. "I understood you accepted Larig as a Shield. Where is he?" The Governor waved her Shield to ease, and he sheathed his weapon. Aurelias' Guardsman also relaxed.

"He was detained with Quillon for a few candlemarks after I left. I expect he shall arrive presently."

Elation lined Kissre's smile. A game, Zeba thought, with a sworn Shield. She cringed. Larig would be frantic and frustrated with his new Entrusted. Zeba smiled, wondering what countermoves the Shield would employ, not knowing for whom she felt sorry. She knew the other Talents missed all of the nuances in Kissre's behavior. Dovel would not have, and she could envision his stiff lips twitching in droll humor. She felt each Talent trying to reach the mind behind the sparkling green eyes, ignoring all else.

Running footsteps sounded in the hall behind Kissre's back. Larig appeared long after his unchecked fury slapped the mind.

"You made good time." Kissre smiled at her Shield. "Your pony must be faster than I imagined."

He gave Kissre an angry, offended look before falling into the calmness of his training. It gave Zeba pause. Who would save Kissre from her Shield, or vice-versa?

"You traveled the countryside without protection?" It was clear Vitann placed extreme control on herself as her alarm reached everyone's mind. "You allowed the Crucible to travel alone?"

"Am I too late?" Kissre asked, addressing Aristo Aurelias.

"No, I believe your name had just come into the proceedings."

"Would you help me?"

Aurelias smiled. "It would be my pleasure."

The Governor gave Kissre a serpent's smile, containing her anger. "You've met, I think, everyone here..." Vitann continued her introductions as her long arm swept Kissre toward a chair at the table. She walked with Kissre, towering over her by as much as Dovel.

Kissre stopped next to Zeba and picked up her hand from where it lay on the table. Kissre had not touched her at their last meeting. Zeba felt the change. Before, not much fed through the touch. Now, it was like a conduit to earth strength. "It has been a while since I last saw you. I am glad to see you looking so well." She spoke as though the meeting in the arena never happened.

More aware than Vitann of the Crucible's purposely wrought havoc, Zeba smiled at the mischief. "I survived a frigid winter in fine fettle. I understand you endured the cold in less comfort."

Vitann interrupted. "We heard Quillon left with the Kaereyan army. The last news said you traveled with them."

"I decided to follow up on another option offered by His Grace, Aristo Aurelias. I hope it remains viable?"

"It does." His eyes shifted to the Governor. "I proposed a position with the Kaereyan Embassy."

"And you have decided to accept his offer?" Vitann took her seat and motioned others to do the same.

"I haven't decided."

"What then, brings you to us, Crucible?" Vitann asked.

"Colonel Kissre," she corrected. "I wanted to negotiate some details before I accepted such a position." An extended silence met her statement. Kissre looked around the elegant room. "Talk aloud." Her sharp voice startled the Talents. Zeba noticed the secretary, a null, hid his smile.

Zeba smiled. The girl was very observant. Talents always assumed nulls didn't know when they communicated. The shocked minds around her reminded Zeba of opening a long-unused linen closet. The fresh air helped mitigate musty odors.

"Negotiate?" Vitann asked, resting her hands on her chair's arms. "With Cygna? You are, I assume, talking of mutual benefit?"

"I'm willing to let His Grace negotiate for me."

"Certainly, an interesting idea. What terms would be most attractive to you?"

"Terms giving me the right to travel when and where I want, in or out of Cygna, without hindrance or having to constantly watch my back. Terms that acknowledged my Kaereyan citizenship."

Zeba's gaze went to Larig's face. Relaxed in her knowledge that she was unimportant to the negotiations, she felt his turmoil. His mind still rolled with outraged pride, but humor tickled its corners, and a firm resolution that Kissre would not trick him again. She silently spoke to the affronted Shield. ::You are not dealing with a sedate middle-aged woman now. Did you get the excitement you craved?::

His eyes swiveled to her as his mind touched her. ::My new duty may stretch my capabilities, both physical and mentally, but I will not lament having gotten what I wanted.::

"What benefit would Cygna derive from your presence?" Vitann asked Kissre. Zeba returned her attention to the conversation.

"I thought Cygna had already benefited?" Aurelias said. His comment brought startled silence. It was, for Zeba, a precious moment.

"She should be taken into custody right now," Orrthu said in a grating voice followed by a mental message the ambassador could not hear. ::She is a formidable Talent with dangerous personal tendencies, as shown all too clearly today.::

A subtle movement from Larig drew Adept Orrthu's eyes. ::You, at least, still belong to Cygna. Watch your step.::

"I am sworn to the Crucible." Larig's voice broke the silence in the room, startling some.

"By the Governor's permission," Orrthu answered.

"By oath to the Holy One at the Sacred Altar of the Cathedral Celestyn."

::You did not!:: Vitann said.

Larig bowed his head and spoke his answer. "It is recorded."

Zeba caught his beatific smile aimed at the floor. The devilish pleasure of it never entered his mind. Holy One, Kissre's influence?

"Another example of how these outlanders' infectious, antagonistic attitudes harm our traditions," Orrthu's voice rose with her grating accusation, her anger stifling her Talent.

"You may rest assured, Adept Orrthu, that none of my outlander attitudes will ever touch you," Kissre said.

The statement hung over the table. The Talents were clearly shocked at the implication.

"Is that a threat?" Orrthu asked.

"I would not wish to infect you."

"Enough!" Vitann said. "How does any benefit come to Cygna from your proposition?

"It has been my understanding that I have a gift that might benefit Cygna. It would be easier for your Talents to access it in Cygna than it would in Kaereya."

"You would use your talents for Cygna's benefit?"

"If we came to mutual agreement."

"Enough, Vitann. She is here. Take her. Do not allow her to dictate to you."

"Quiet, Orrthu!" Vitann demanded.

"That's right, Orrthu. Even without Larig, I could inflict enough harm that you wouldn't worry about tomorrow. Ask Larig of my skills with weapons, and I'll tell you I am better without." Behind the Crucible, Zeba saw the Shield smile at Orrthu in affirmation and a clear violation of duty.

Aurelias cleared his throat and, in a curt tone, interrupted. "Colonel Kissre, permit me to handle the negotiations."

Orrthu's screech drowned him out. "You are making a dangerous adversary, miss!"

"You chose the path." The utter calm of the voice carried more menace than Orrthu's outburst. Zeba felt the inherent danger and noticed Vitann, for once, didn't miss it.

Zeba shivered but realized Orrthu, relying on Touch alone, missed the deadly promise in Kissre's flat tones.

"I told you not to test Dovel against his will," Zeba inserted the reminder, enjoying Orrthu's dismay. "You've refused all my advice. But, as you've already pointed out, I am an Oracle."

"Shut-up, old woman!"

"Orrthu!" Vitann said, demanding order. She turned back to Kissre. "Are you speaking of a contractual obligation between us?"

"I'm sure His Grace will work out the details. I think, if you leave me to my own devices, I might offer help when you need it."

Only Zeba laughed.

"In other words, you chose when and if to help us?"

"I would work for the Kaereyan Embassy. I would like to live in peace, civility...and safety."

"Cygna is your country!" Orrthu said.

Vitann held up a restraining hand. "Would you help increase a person's Talent?"

"Colonel Pierce," the authority in Aurelias' interruption brought quiet. "Would you now allow me to proceed with these negotiations you have so rudely interrupted?"

"I beg pardon, Your Grace." Kissre smiled, and faint contrition touched her face.

"Not another word, hear?"

Kissre nodded her acceptance. Vitann immediately transferred her attention to the Duke of Lambere.

"What do you need from Kissre?" Aurelias asked.

"Her touch."

"Her body," Orrthu said. "We need her bonded to as many Talents as possible."

"That is impossible. The touch, perhaps, with proper safeguards for Kissre. Her body, absolutely not, if you suggest what I think you do."

"What if we offered Kissre a position in Cygna with the same benefits?" Vitann said.

"Such as?"

"Training our troops. A position in the army."

"Not likely, but I'll consider the proposal. I feel Kissre, as a citizen of Kaereya, would be safest employed in the Embassy as a consultant."

"It won't be that way," Zeba said, with a flat sigh. "I see Kissre in Kaereya."

"Zeba, I remind you that you are not part of these proceedings." Vitann's concentration remained unbroken by the interruption.

"My daughter sees the same," Aurelias said. "She wrote to me as much. Kissre will return to Kaereya eventually."

Catching Vitann's gaze drop to the table, Zeba said, "You might consider dividing her." Even as she spoke, images formed at the back of her mind. She closed her eyes and saw shifting possibilities.

Orrthu made a disgusted noise.

"How?" Aurelias asked.

Zeba opened her eyes. "You said you needed teachers in Kaereya. Kissre likes to travel, considers Kaereya her home. Her Talent is needed in Cygna, and her remaining family resides here. Yet, I see she will be needed in Kaereya. She also requires training to prevent her from harming anyone unintentionally or receiving harm herself."

"She cannot do that in Kaereya," Vitann replied. "It would take several very specialized Talents to accomplish her training. Dovel would have been a logical choice, but with their intimacy, that becomes difficult."

"She could do it in Kaereya," Zeba said.

"How?" Aristo Aurelias asked.

"You asked for an exchange of personnel. Let her act as a liaison between our countries. Let her take a chosen group of Talent Adepts with her to Kaereya to teach your Talents. No one could protect Talents better than Kissre and Larig as a team. At a prearranged time, she comes back to Cygna. Perhaps spend six months in each country. She has a world view that could benefit both countries."

"Is that what you see?" Vitann asked.

"I see many possibilities. I mention a compromise that causes the most benefit and the least harm."

"Impossible! She belongs to Cygna. Here, she can be protected," Orrthu said.

"From whom?" The duke's voice turned as frigid as his expression.

"I suggest we table these talks until tomorrow. We can meet without the distraction of the Crucible." Vitann glanced at Aurelias looking inordinately pleased about something. "Cygna needs Kissre, but we are open to compromise. We would like her to be tested and trained to wear Talent's markings, and we want her to help increase certain Talents' abilities. This might involve touching, but from what I am experiencing today, her presence might be enough. Of course, our people desire Kissre's presence. They see her as a symbol of their safety and protection."

"I have your guarantee Kissre will be left unharmed and unfettered while in Cygna?" Aurelias asked.

"Of course. We would never harm the Crucible."

A snorted laugh, muffled at the outset, broke the brief silence. Zeba glanced at Kissre, but the Crucible only regarded the tabletop.

Within a half-candlemark the Kaereyan delegation left, Larig dogging the Crucible, waiting and eager to explode in chastisement. Zeba felt the suppressed emotion about to fall on Kissre's unrepentant head and Aurelias' knowledge and humor at the situation. Zeba envisioned their next weapon's practice.

Vitann made a silent comment to Zeba before the delegation left. ::*Since her Calling she has changed.* I can feel the power within her. The ground around her, even this interior floor, thrummed with it. How could such Talent have escaped notice?::

"Because the land was drained, and she had not yet sought its strength. Larig is with them, Vitann. He hears us." Zeba felt Larig's oath run through the minds of the Cygnese delegates.

"He cannot be trusted." Orrthu still simmered at the Shield's defiance.

"She doesn't know, doesn't feel it." Vitann's mind remained on Kissre.

"No."

"Anybody touching her…"

"Would have to be careful. Even Dovel said some of his experiences bordered dangerous territory. She won't have her actions interfered with. A self-imposed limitation is the only answer."

"She will have to be supervised," Orrthu said.

"Anyone under hire, under contract, has less than free will. Who could train her?"

"She needs testing," Orrthu said. "She can no longer lead sorties and carry on like she's a null."

"Not your type of testing, Orrthu," Vitann said, half lost in thought.

"She increased Dovel's already formidable Talent. She made nulls into Talents. Probably made Tyna's Talent what it is. Her service is owed!" Orrthu scowled at Vitann.

"Unfortunately, it was thrown away. I'm afraid she won't forgive either you or me for Dovel's testing."

"Her forgiveness is unnecessary."

"A warning, Orrthu," Zeba sighed, breaking into the conversation, already knowing her advice would go unheeded. "Kissre is just coming to accept her Talent. If you turn her away with threats and without proper training, there is a great chance for her to twist it."

"All the more reason to impose limits."

"Certainly not with drugs," Vitann said in a level voice. "We must always remember what she is and how most Cygnese view her. She could become a great asset, link our divided population, and return all Cygna to a peaceful accord."

"She won't be dictated to, Vitann," Zeba said. "She will touch those you don't choose, just to provoke. She avoided a Shield just to prove she could. She would never give up trying to escape an imposed confinement of any sort. She would see it as imprisonment, or worse, an act of war."

"We must take advantage while she is here," Orrthu said. "Find a way to keep her, master her. Travel is out of the question. What if she fell into enemy hands? What if she decided to travel outside of Kaereya or Cygna? She must conform to traditional Talent deportment. With proper conditioning, she would not continue to embarrass us. Such training would benefit Tyna, for that matter."

"For the Holy One's sake, Orrthu, think about what you're saying," Zeba said, her tolerance ended.

"Shut up, Zeba, or I'll pull you in for retraining."

"Enough, Orrthu," Vitann faced Orrthu. "You will not approach either Tyna or Kissre! Or Zeba," she added as an afterthought.

"Although her appearance first strikes one as outlandish, her fashion is only different, exotic; although, it looks comfortable. I saw nothing amiss when she attended formal functions. I expect by this time next year, most young Cygnese will be wearing earrings and outlander garb. We might look into forbidding tattooing."

Zeba laughed at Vitann's unstated repugnance. "You are planning too much, Vitann. I repeat, she won't be dictated to. She will choose her own way, her own mate. Force her, and you will lose her. We may be able to guide, but never coerce."

"What do you see, Zeba?"

"I see many threads, all probabilities, some advantageous, but always disastrous when Kissre felt imprisoned. In fighting for her freedom, either she destroys us or we her. Only one time will become a reality. Let her go to Kaereya where she feels safe among friends. She needs training. Kaereya Talents need training. Let her learn to accept us there. It is not just the Catalyst Talent. That endangers her more than anything."

"Would you really go with her? Leave Cygna?"

"I look forward to it."

Vitann shivered and looked at Zeba as though her desire was unnatural.

"And take responsibility for your own actions?" Orrthu asked in a dismissive voice. "Or must we pull you from your own time rambles?"

"Well, certainly you couldn't help," Vitann said. "The girl despises you."

"Uncouth barbarian! Bringing that filthy dog into the building and into the Governor's presence!"

Vitann continued ignoring Orrthu's sputtering. "Even with her Talent, not many could be pressured into bedding her, let alone marrying her. Her appearance and reputation frighten many, her Talent, even more. It's hard to imagine Dovel."

Orrthu sniffed. "He always showed undisciplined tendencies."

"A Crucible, on the other hand, must keep to a certain standard." Vitann shouted for her secretary. "Tomorrow at first business mark,

I want these people." She dictated a quick but extensive list. "Zeba, I will want you, too. We will plan our best strategy. We will ask for permanent residence with dual citizenship and permitted leaves for travel to Kaereya. We select the Talents to work with her. Surround her with them. Touching is inevitable if enough situations are encountered. Her self-imposed discipline will serve us."

"Discipline will only go so far," Orrthu warned Vitann.

Vitann laughed. "Far enough. A trained mercenary of Kissre's caliber survives on discipline, always honors a contract, and knows how to obey orders. You will not mention anything you've learned about Kissre, Orrthu." She glared at the woman. "Is that clear?" Her gaze turned to Zeba. "Is it that way between them? Are you sure? I thought it only a temporary thing. Curiosity. Propinquity."

Orrthu looked at the other two women. "You both are acting in a dangerously incompetent manner. She has a Shield protecting her, but no one to protect us from her! You will regret this day's work."

"Change comes, Orrthu, ready or not, and we must accept it as best we may," Vitann said. "How can she harm Cygna? She has already returned the land to vitality, and everyone knows it. She made new strengths available to every Earth Talent. If she harms either me or you in anger, it will be counted as part of the cost."

Orrthu made a scoffing sound, but Zeba sensed the fright that hid behind her vehement front.

Vitann took off on a new tack. "Such a crippled power without Touch. She constitutes a puzzle. One I am glad to accept. There are already stories circulating about her. They say all the nulls who listened to her sing at that tavern in Guerestu developed Talent. My sources say most were already known Talents. It's nonsense, but people want to believe it. She will find her way restricted with little interference from us. Plus Dovel. We can use that susceptibility." Vitann said. "Altogether, I look forward to this negotiation." She looked at Orrthu. "You will not be present tomorrow."

"Judging new Talents is part of my duty."

"Not this time. You will hinder us."

"And testing?"

"Do you value your life? Kissre is more than you can handle, Orrthu. She won't be intimidated by your Probe Talent or respect your position. And those Talents capable of opposing her won't help you because they already either respect or fear her. You and I, Orrthu, didn't experience the battlefield at Guerestu, those who did—"

"There are other means."

Vitann's full attention fell on Orrthu. "Which you will not use. I've already decided."

"I'll take this to the Adept's Council."

"Take it to the Deans' Cabinet, too." Vitann shrugged dismissal and watched Orrthu's infuriated exit. She continued as if nothing happened. "She wastes her time. Neither the Deans nor the ranking adepts will do a thing. They are as much in awe as everyone else. Besides, anyone with a speck of political sense knows what will happen if either Chamber orders Kissre harmed in any way. We must not estrange the general populace again or incite the null rebels...and Orrthu's handling of Dovel upset more than a few Talents. Dovel..."

"...I expect Dovel will provide Kissre all the incentive you need. Vitann, you must handle her with extreme care."

A strange smile grew on Vitann's face. "He will surely provide a distracting influence. It's funny how sometimes two opposites find the perfect fit. Do you have any predictions on the number of children? Holy One, what we should see."

"Be careful, Vitann. Things rarely go how you might wish."

"You sense another danger?"

"She has Chronos Talent. Did you not feel it during the Calling?"

"I'm unsure of what I felt. My Earth Talent isn't that strong."

"Good, then most other Talents probably didn't either. She nudged time, Vitann. Pushed us into a more peaceful probability just because she desired it." An uncomfortable silence grew. "Dovel knows. I expect most Chronos Talents do. That's why he told Aristo Aurelias to ask for my help, not only for the duke's daughter but also for Kissre."

"A Channel?" Vitann's complexion turned pasty. "It is only a predicted Talent. Who could train her?"

"I think it might require a team. Dovel has reached Factor level, and his Chronos Talent has developed to Veil. Consider Adepts Elvia or Awley, perhaps even Bujyea. They are all older and stable in themselves, and they have studied how Talent works. The carnage of this war has depressed the healer, and I think this assignment would cheer him. We must not overlook Larig, either."

"Larig? A Shield? How could he possibly help?"

"Larig practices arms with Kissre daily."

"You think through these exercises, he might gain entry into her mind, like Dovel?"

"It would not hurt to have two who know how Kissre feels. More importantly, Larig's Talent grows."

"A Channel," Vitann repeated. "Why can't she choose her own future then?"

"Because all her Talent is used instinctively, she doesn't even know she has it," Zeba said.

"Can you help her?" Vitann repeated.

"With the Adept Council's permission, I would like to try. It will be difficult."

"Do you think she plans on children?"

Zeba smiled. "Right now, I don't think she is planning further than supper. Kissre and Larig should provide some small entertainment in the following months." Zeba considered the Governor. "A loss for you, Vitann."

Vitann sighed and then smiled. "Worth it. An older Shield suits me better. I knew the boy was dissatisfied. I'm too old and set in my ways, too conservative and quiet. He craved adventure and challenge." She laughed. "A Crucible and a possible Channel, and Larig personally swearing to her. I think his wish answered, rot him. He will be an even better Shield for it. She must be tested, but how? Who else knows?"

It was apparent to Zeba Vitann wasn't listening.

"Training is more important than testing. How do you plan to test a void, Vitann? The whole nation knows she is a Crucible," Zeba said, sighing. Visions already shifted, reformed. "Dovel knows about the Time Talent. Perhaps Tyna, although siblings invariably overlook each other."

"Her mother inadvertently trained her well with mercenary training. It will not be like our last Crucible."

"No. Kissre is very stable, but set in her ways, coming late into her gifts. She likes her privacy. She hasn't any idea what she is or how her Talent works."

"And that might work well for us, too."

Zeba frowned at Vitann. "Be careful of overconfidence, Vitann. She has not yet agreed, and you don't know all her demands."

"She will agree to whatever Aristo Aurelias negotiates." Her hand swept over the contract. "And I will sweetly sing his refrain. She will get what she wants and find it is what we desire. We will make sure the Maze is full of the justice of letting Kissre go to Kaereya. Smooth her path. Talents out of Cygna. This change thing, perhaps it is not so bad. We cannot treat her like Gregor, cannot keep her safely caged like a pet bird. It will be hard, but we must let this dragon fly and call her to hand with lures. When Cygna becomes a place of welcome, security, and understanding, she will seek it. After all, it is her heritage. If we must learn change, she must learn acceptance. It will work both ways, you will see. Besides, like her sister, we will cast other webs to ensnare her."

~ * ~

After candlemarks of wandering Sidih in the light rain, rejecting offers of night comfort, and ignoring the entertainment beckoning from open tavern doors, Dovel decided he couldn't keep his squad waiting any longer. He owed them. They owned him. Even if the squad disbanded, they would be tied for life. At this point, disbanding seemed best. Adele needed to be away from him. Let her find the affection she craved in Wyn. He raised his face to the cold rain and stood a moment before starting home.

A short walk took him home. Following Tyna's example, he and several other Captains had purchased their own retreats. His was on the opposite side of town from Tyna's and outside the city walls, set in a beautiful, wooded grove surrounded by large clear fields of grass with a mountain cliff at the building's back. It sat on high, sloping ground, overlooking most of Sidih, with spectacular views of the southern ranges.

Last winter, he envisioned a Novere mare and a Buckskin stallion grazing in the pasture, perhaps with a colt romping the field. Now he didn't care, hadn't even gone there since the previous summer.

The rain ended while he walked and the smell of burning wood hung heavy in the air, a reminder spring had just ended, and the nights were cold. The barn doors stood open. Several stout men pulled bales of hay into the upper level; the late afternoon sun caught them in half-sun and half-shadow. He returned their greeting, then walked into the horse scented, stable-lined corridor of the interior.

A large buckskin head emerged from one door with a soft nicker. Kissre had asked if she might leave Bother, let him gain weight before taking the journey back with the Duke of Lambere. He stopped and stroked the soft silky muzzle that nibbled at his fingers. "So, she's left us, old man." A crush of loneliness descended like a sudden kick in the gut.

By emptying his mind of thought and sensation, he could recover. It took time, and he leaned his head against the stall door and closed his eyes while he waited.

A snuffling nose worked its way up his leg, and Dovel's hand fell in instinctive response. A rough tongue licked it with a low, rough whine. He gazed down. "Fudge?"

Another head emerged from the next stall. The lavender gray nose ended with hay trailing from munching jaws. The soft crunching sound pulled him into reality. "Carillon?" His voice was a whisper.

He placed a hand on the smooth, warm neck.

"Is something wrong with her?"

Hearing the voice, Dovel turned in a swift spin. "Kissre? Kiss!" His brows rose in surprise. Two steps let him trap her in his arms, his lips fell on her in rough greeting, and he spun her around, pinning her body against the stall partition. He held her shorter length there by the pressure of his. Fudge wormed around his legs, thumped him with his robust tail. Kissre helped. Her arms fastened around his neck, and she nibbled at his lower lip throughout.

"You're here?" he asked, and without answer, "I thought you left with Quillon! By the Holy One!" He twirled, and she clutched him, shouting at the indignity. Fudge barked his enthusiasm. He let her slide down into a prolonged kiss that only ended as he became aware of an audience. His squad stood there, grinning and watching, as did Larig.

"Shield Larig?" he asked, in his duty voice.

"I am sworn to the Crucible," the man said. "Be careful how you handle her."

Kissre's brows rose in ire. She bent and brushed the debris from her trews. "It's all part of my being here." She smiled offhandedly. "Aristo Aurelias negotiates my stay."

"They are negotiating you?"

"Yeah. I took a job with the embassy. I think. The details get worked out tomorrow. I'll explain it all later, but I'd like to change." She indicated the damp riding clothes she still wore. "I rode long and hard today." Her eyes flicked to the Shield while she felt his damp hair and shirt. "You need to change, too. And I'm hungry."

Dovel exchanged looks with Ulyss, who shrugged. Obviously, his Kiss had no idea what Larig represented.

"You're staying." It was not a question.

"Yes."

"For me?"

"Mostly, but not all. Aristo Aurelias advised me to change careers. I know you will be retiring in a few years. How do you feel about breeding horses? Ulyss showed me around." She did not touch him as they walked toward his house. "I like your house. Ah...he put me in your room, hope you don't mind."

"I've always treasured Ulyss's innate intelligence."

Kissre smiled. A snap of her fingers brought Fudge from his inspection of the yard to her heel. While his squad waited below, Dovel followed Kissre upstairs.

He leaned against his bedroom door as she searched through a satchel. Ulyss touched his mind with images of platoons descending on his home and setting up camp, and he sighed in regret. A Crucible's presence demanded certain precautions. "Do you want me to inform Tyna?"

"She'll find out soon enough, probably already knows. No, Ty can wait. Let's forget her for a while." She swore. "All my luggage is still with Quillon. I have very few clothes with me. I wonder if Marisse will quit when she learns of the size of the household awaiting her ministrations?"

Some of her conversation would need further explanation, but that he dismissed for now. Smiling, he helped her remove her tunic. His hands ran over her smooth skin. "We'll buy you more tomorrow." Another thought interrupted him, his hands stilled. "This isn't only because of Bother is it?"

"How can you ask?" A wayward smile crooked her lips. "It's a case of performance, pure and simple. At least I know you won't be using any Talent."

"I beg to differ," he said and enjoyed her laugh.

It was a candlemark before they came down for a delayed dinner. By then, Dovel not only felt but also heard Tyna and her squad, plus Jycel and his squad, waiting for them. A groan from Kissre proved her superb hearing. Leaving his room, they ran into Larig's solid presence. Kissre turned red, then exploded. "Enough. You know the rules."

Stepping aside, Larig spoke. "You broke them."

Dovel felt surprised at the un-Shield like insolence reflected in Larig's satisfied mind and his open devotion. The Shield followed them, causing a shifting stir and rustle among the waiting crowd. Dovel felt a wry smile. Life seemed full of surprises. His squad had said nothing.

"Kiss?" Tyna asked, staring at Larig, as did Kedriq. To the Talents present, Larig exuded relief, satisfaction, and happiness. He smiled as he exchanged glances with Kedriq.

"I'm staying," Kiss said, taking her nephew from her sister's arms and holding him up for inspection. "For a while, anyway. Maybe."

"You have to hold him..."

Kissre made a rude noise and lowered the baby to rest on her shoulder. "I know how to hold a baby. I held you." She looked at the crowded room. "Holy One! You expect Dov to feed all of you?"

"Kiss!" Dovel rebuked her inhospitality.

"Yeah. Well, it's a good thing I'm employed. I think."

Ulyss snorted a laugh at Dovel's retort and turned to the group. "Don't worry," he advised his Captain. "It looks like anyone here not already used to her humor will quickly learn. We have a lot to celebrate. I warned the kitchen when Kissre first arrived to expect guests for dinner. Just didn't think we'd have to wait so long." He laughed as Kissre's face reddened. Even Adele, who had remained quiet, laughed.

"Serves you right," Tyna said. "Now, you know how it feels."

"Well, this is another of those rules I mentioned." She turned to Larig. "You will not stand outside my bedroom door, ever."

Larig's unruffled expression answered Kissre's angry glare calmly, although his chin firmed fractionally. "Better than in it. When you follow the rules, I will. I expect the list to grow lengthy."

Tyna laughed. "You are at war with him, too?" She glanced at Dovel. "This will be a happy house. My sympathies, Dovel, I think you've lost your famed serenity at last."

Kissre growled and received a knock on the chin from her nephew's flailing hands. Fudge snuffed around Larig's legs and the Shield put out a hand to pet the shaggy head. Fudge's tail waved in amiable circles.

"Traitor," Kissre said, then returned to her baby talk. Shortly they were called to dinner.

"Sit," she ordered pointing to a chair down the side of the table when Larig moved behind her.

The Shield took it with reluctance. Dovel looked at the plates of roasted bird sided with beans and sighed. His first taste told Dovel he needed a different cook, and from Kissre's expression, she agreed with him.

During dinner, Kissre explained her meeting with Aurelias and the Governor to absolute silence.

"Kaereya has requested Zeba to help train their seer, and the Aegis has requested an Earth Talent to help him. It seems the emergence of Talent in Kaereya has drawn our nations closer."

"It might forge alliances with Pertelon, too, if their Talents are their own," Tyna said.

"Maybe. It has been suggested that I become an agent for both Cygna and Kaereya." She laughed and looked at Dovel. "Vitann thinks she can control me. Zeba thinks I need training." Dead silence met her remark.

"You do," Dovel said, stating what everyone in the room knew, felt. Once unleashed, subtle energy enveloped her presence. "Is Zeba going to train you?"

"Don't know. If allowed, I suppose."

"Did they mention levels?" Tyna asked.

"I wasn't paying much attention by then. They started arguing, and I got a little bored. That Orrthu is a dervish." She grinned. "Having had time to think things over, I might just change my mind about working with Orrthu."

Stunned silence, then a vocal group negation met her idea.

"I think your threat worked well enough," Larig said. Once settled, he ate with enthusiasm.

"You threatened Orrthu?" Dovel asked.

"Again?" Tyna asked.

"Yeah." She took a bite of her dinner. "Just by way of an opening foray."

"Foray? A rout you mean. You will not act so precipitously or without warning me ahead of time," Larig said. "You are not a free agent in these matters."

"I think," Kissre said with a thoughtful look at Larig, "we are going to need a written contract."

"Would you follow its terms?"

Dovel grinned as Kissre abruptly changed the subject. "Anyway, Aurelias agreed to negotiate for me. All these stupid Talent levels are hard to keep straight. Besides, I'd made clear what I wanted, freedom of person, freedom to travel, basically—a life. I remain a

Kaereyan citizen working at the Embassy. Zeba suggested another solution that I spend time in each country. She kept seeing me in Kaereya."

"Did they ask to test you?" Tyna asked.

"Yeah, but that hasn't been settled." Her voice revealed Vitann's uphill battle.

"But Larig is a Shield," Adele said.

Kissre shrugged. "He's been with me a fortnight. We are working out our own negotiations."

"It is an arduous process," Larig said. "The Crucible's protection is my sworn duty, no matter whether I protect her from others or her own rash actions." He gave her back her own angry glare. "You will not trick me in such a manner again."

Kissre grinned at the challenge. "It'll keep you on your toes. Good training tactic."

Tyna asked for the particulars, and while Larig talked, Dovel listened with a prick of jealousy. He quelled it, remembering feeling himself planted firmly in her mind. She remained distrustful, often disrespectful, but loyal.

He needed to tell her how he felt. The situation of speaking of his emotions had never occurred before now. If he did not know hers ahead of time, he would never summon the courage to speak. It gave him a new respect for nulls. His eyes fell on Larig. Practicing together might make it possible for a Probe of Larig's ability to break through Kissre's impervious void. The future loomed with a difference he never expected, with unexpected opportunities and diversions...and uncertainties.

"Governor Vitann guaranteed Kissre freedom while the contract is negotiated," Larig said. "I think they will come to an accord. The Governor and Adept Council want Kissre at any cost."

"Why was Vitann so upset you swore to me? She sent you to me."

A satisfied smile covered the Shield's face. "She sent me to use against you. Once she released me from my vow, she could not dictate how I accepted my next one."

"Off with the old permanently?" Kissre shrugged when Larig did not answer her. She looked around her. "Damn it. You'll talk words when I'm about, or I'll start throwing things. Sharp things."

"Sorry," several voices said in unison. They were still distracted, looking not at her, but Larig, then Dovel.

"Everyone in Cygna knows Kiss is a Crucible—that alone required Larig." He hesitated before adding, "I expect only a few very strong Chronos Talents suspect she might be a Channel." He looked at Cath, both a weak Earth and Chronos Talent. She nodded.

"The only one, ever," Cath said. "I didn't know what I had felt, but looking back, I know it to be time disorientation. I didn't know how it happened."

"Being Touch void," Dovel continued, "they aren't sure how to measure her or even control...to train her Talent. It is considered a dangerous situation."

The information didn't faze Kissre. She laughed at their expressions in the dead silence. "Control, they can't. I can't. Means nothing."

Dovel felt the emotions flow around the table, felt Kissre's response to their silence. Then felt her emotions and read her body. He knew she did not want to belong; to become part of this group. It terrified her. He picked up her hand, and with the touch, her thoughts came to him. *How could she possibly stay? Only hurt could come.* She put that away to deal with when he no longer wanted her. Talent, testing, and training, all worried her.

"You will learn. Ask Zeba to help you. She'd be a good mentor for you," Dovel said. "And I will be there, no matter how many spines you sprout."

Tyna placed a hand on Kissre's "Change is frightening, and I know trust is hard for you." .

"You read my mind?"

"No, your face. It's all right, Kiss, we'll make them accept you as you are, as we are. Your freedom will mean the freedom for every Talent to choose, for every null to excel."

"For everyone, Tyna, to do both," Dovel corrected.

Twenty-one

Late in the afternoon, after two worry-filled days, Kissre glanced up from her concentration on a tricky maneuver she was teaching Carillon and saw Aurelias stood next to Dovel at the paddock's gate. Carillon snorted, feeling her rider stiffen in the saddle and inadvertently cause the bit to bite. Taking a breath, Kissre released her tight fingers and relaxed into the saddle, relieving the mare's anxiety.

She could not read Aurelias expression as she guided Carillon to the standing men to dismount. Every nerve begged for an immediate answer, but her mind didn't want to acknowledge any limitation, restriction, or supervision placed on her. A quick glance showed Larig standing a few paces away roughly petting Fudge. Some bodyguard, waylaid by a dog, she huffed to herself. *You're a mercenary, a for-hire-to-whomever. You've always had limitations and supervision. Why quibble now?* An irritating inner voice argued.

Because this was different, it would change her life in ways unimaginable. Anxiety, anger, anticipation, and dread jumbled inside her mind and stomach. *Show some deportment!* She glanced at Dovel and her qualms eased. She took another deep breath and smiled at Aurelias.

Everyone waited for her to speak first. "Your mouth must be dry from arguing. Let's go inside and have a glass or two of wine while you tell me my future."

"I am rather dry," Aurelias agreed in his maddeningly well-bred voice. *Damn him, he was testing her!* She smiled what must have been a grimace because Aurelias grinned.

Kissre passed Carillon's reins off to a groom and followed Dovel and Aurelias through the exercise and stable yards to the front of Dovel's home. Larig trailed her, his presence acceptable but no less aggravating. As if nothing out of the ordinary happened, as if no life-altering decisions needed to be made, her love and her boss engaged in small talk on the brief walk. *Nattering nuts, they were going to drive her crazy.* Shortly they stood in the entrance hall, joined by Dovel's squad.

Anger and frustration seethed through her lips. "Won't you..."

A mousy-haired person took a step from behind Ulyss, her hands holding one of Kissre's traveling bags. *Marisse.* Guilt whipped Kissre. Without a word, she had abandoned her maid with all their luggage on the road with Quillon. The maid bowed her head to Kissre, and she returned the acknowledgment. The girl looked altogether self-satisfied and smug with it.

"I thought I left you with Quillon?"

"You did, mistress, but as the maid to the Catalyst Kissre, I have some small measure of respect, and I have forever been known for my persistence...and persuasiveness." Marisse smiled. Kissre judged it a sly, subtle challenge. She dropped her eyes in a demure pose. "And Quillon standing fully armed behind me while I requested transport surely assisted my request."

"Good, like Larig, just the sort of person to keep up with Kissre and help keep her in order." Aurelias smiled broadly at Marisse while he bestowed his approval.

Marisse smiled in genuine pleasure at being compared to a Shield.

"Well, then," Kissre drawled, "why don't we all adjourn to the sitting room and let His Grace tell us of the results of his negotiations?"

"If you would prefer privacy, we would understand," Adele offered. Everyone's stunned look told Kissre this was no small offering. She just prevented a sigh from escaping but could not prevent the wry twist to her smile when she glanced at Dovel. "No, come in and listen. What affects me, affects you."

Marisse turned to go into the servant's quarters. "Marisse, please join us."

"But, mistress..."

"...Kissre."

"I am only your maid."

"So you'll be going where I do. Come." She turned and entered the sitting room. They had gathered chairs in a large circle, leaving one for her directly across from Aurelias and next to Dovel. Even Larig slouched in one, but he rose at her entrance. Ready to rebuke him, she found he rose only to pull another chair forward for Melisse who entered right behind her.

Kissre huffed and took her seat. "I hope you have something good to report after two days without a word."

Aurelias smiled briefly at her jab. "That is for you to determine. Nothing has been decided and will not be decided without your approval."

Dovel's fingers wrapped her hand where it lay on the armrest. "Together, here or in Kaereya, whatever you decide." She knew how huge an offering he made. Without looking, she knew his squad agreed. Foolish. Make the wrong choice and she would not only be smuggling a Talent squad out of Cygna but also starting another war. She threw Aurelias a glare. He better have good options.

The man in question huffed in annoyance. "Negotiate from calm, Kissre. You were doing fine."

"Then tell me my choices."

He hesitated a slivering, knife-edged pause before beginning. "If you choose to renounce your Kaereyan citizenship and take a position in the Cygnese army as one of Marshal Ranor's senior officers, you will be given a restriction-free life in Cygna and the mate of your choice...as long as you remain in Cygna."

"They're bargaining with Dovel? Meaning I could not return home?" Kissre made no further comment. Dovel's fingers tightened on her hand in reassurance.

"No. Remember, these are only offers made by Governor Vitann."

Kissre noted Aurelias' regard and wiped the frown from her face.

"If you choose to remain as a Royal Guardsman to King Warrick, and take a position as head of security and advisor to the Kaereyan ambassador, you would be assured personal safety. But as a foreign representative, your movements outside the embassy would be limited by the Cygnese government. You would need permission for any travel when not journeying with the Embassy personnel to Kaereya."

"Meaning a Talent escort everywhere you wish to go, at the very least. Don't accept that." Cath frowned and shook her head.

"Or only to places where there was a chance to run into and possibly touch Talents," Ulyss agreed.

It became unnaturally silent, but Kissre didn't think anyone answered some unheard question and contained her grin. They had all been conscientious about speaking aloud in her presence.

"Or be seduced by one," Adele added, the thought etched on her face.

Kissre laughed a single sharp sound. "I'd like to see someone try."

"They'd use drugs," Dovel told her.

"No, they will not, to any of it," Larig said. Another silence ensued as those in the room looked at her Shield's formidable expression. His gaze fell on Kissre. "You will touch only those whom you want to touch. I promise it."

"Besides, any such action would drive me out of Cygna, which would be the reverse of what they want," Kissre replied. She looked at Larig. "I would be safe enough, but the thought of never being able to ride anywhere, travel when I wished...I'd feel trapped. Any other choices?"

"Yes. The last proposal seems the most promising. With the promise that you will resign from the Kaereyan Army, never seek a mercenary's position, remain out of all combat situations other than maneuvers, training, or in an advisory position, the Cygnese government is willing to acknowledge your citizenship with Kaereya. For this concession, you will be allowed to travel to Kaereya for four months of every year accompanied by an appropriate number of platoons for your safety. During your time in Cygna, you will accept an advisory position within the Cygnese government." Aurelias paused. "With any of the choices, you will be required to be tested and trained by appointed Talents and provide services to enhance Talent's capabilities whenever requested."

Kissre watched Aurelias' face and slowly smiled. "These were Vitann's offers? What did you wrangle in concession?"

"Actually, I think Zeba mentioned it. The embellishments are the Governors. I said I would talk to you first, but I doubted either the first or second options are viable. The last was marginally acceptable, but you would choose the length of time you spent in each country. With the condition that along with those platoons sent to escort you in Kaereya, they sent Talents to help train you and other Kaereyans needing help." At her glance, he swiftly inserted, "I know, not an altogether altruistic condition, considering my daughter's needs." At her nod, he continued. "And that when in Cygna you would be attached to the Embassy as an advisor. While in Cygna, Kaereyan troops would be posted to protect you from any aggression."

Appalled, Kissre jumped up and shouted, "I'd always be traveling with a damn army at my heels?" Noticing Dovel's squad didn't even cringe at her outburst, Kissre resumed her seat and contained her ire.

"That item is a negotiation trade-off. They threw their demand down to see what concessions they get back, so I countered with an equally disagreeable offer to them."

Kissre huffed at having risen to Aurelias' lure.

The duke calmly continued. "Finally, that if you agreed to be tested it must be conducted without the use of drugs and in the presence of your Shield, and that you be presented a number of possible training Talents and allowed to choose from those instructors."

"Accept it. Tell them I will spend as long as you need to finish negotiations here in Cygna. Afterward, I will travel with you to Kaereya. Dovel and his squad will come with us, along with Zeba and whomever you think will best serve in Kaereya."

"You're sure?"

Kissre looked at the faces surrounding her, willing to uproot their lives for Dovel, and he for her. "There are few I trust as much as you, Your Grace. Make the best deal you can, but make sure it includes Dovel."

~ * ~

Sharing a bed every night was a new experience—satisfying, comforting but still unfamiliar and unusual. Kissre lay on her side with an arm thrown over Dovel's chest. From his breathing, she knew he was still awake.

"Will you be satisfied?" he asked.

"What? You ask after that performance?" His chest moved in subtle laughter. "Are you prepared for what would happen if I reneged on Aurelias' negotiations?"

"Probably not, and I'm sure my squad isn't, but whatever it takes to make you happy and content, I am willing to do. If that means disappearing into the night and a life on the run, so be it."

"You would go with me?" Her eyes teared at Dovel's admission. He rolled to face her, grasping her hand and holding it next to his chest.

He kissed her brow. "Yes. Kissre, I love you. I will stay with you until you tell me to go."

"You want to marry me?"

"Yes, I want you for my wife, but doubt the Talent Council will give us that permission. They want to use me as a bargaining chip to gain your compliance."

"They gave permission to Tyna."

"It was different. She wanted to stay in Cygna. They have two reasons to refuse your marriage. The first being that marriage ostensibly would put you off bounds to sexual contact with other Talents. Then, they know if you leave, you will take Larig and me with you, and possibly my squad. It would be a huge loss of Talent."

"You're willing to risk the Talent Board's wrath?"

"Just say the word." His face was close enough that his breath warmed her skin.

"If you want to marry, we can marry in Kaereya whenever we get there." She kissed him, and his lips returned her salute in a hard, urgent promise. "Besides, I'm taking you with me no matter what the Council wants."

"You don't want to get married?"

"I don't need anything legal to tell me I love you and will stay as long as you want me in return."

"You love me?"

She laughed. "You know I do. Don't sound so surprised."

"What about children?"

She threw her arms around him. "Yes, yes, yes. Three, I think. We will raise them, just you and me, not the Talent Board. You will breed horses in Cygna, and I will train them. In Kaereya, you will train Talents, and I will protect you. In between, we will train soldiers and squads both here and in Kaereya."

"Even if you must journey with an army at your heels?"

"As long as you travel with it, I won't care."

"Is that why you told His Grace to accept the offer? He was testing you, you know."

"Aurelias heard what he wanted me to tell him. And yes, I know he tested me, so I will accept his challenge and take his offer with a few adjustments. I will accept dual citizenship. While in Cygna, I will be an advisor to the Kaereyan Embassy, and in Kaereya, an advisor to the Cygnese Embassy. They will both need one. And Aurelias can teach me how to both advise and negotiate. I'm sure he already has plans to that effect."

"It would be wise to have a more sedentary employment if you plan on getting pregnant."

"I think so, too. So I will resign from my military position."

"And what about helping Talents develop their gift?"

She smiled to herself. "You mean by touching them? Oh, don't worry. If they want my touch, they'll have to learn to wield weapons other than their minds to earn it."

Dovel started laughing. "You are cruel."

"No, just practical. Eventually, they're bound to need the experience. I'm sure my foresight in these matters is what attracted you."

He leaned into another kiss. "Among other things."

Meet Rhobin Lee Courtright

Born and raised in Michigan, Rhobin spent one year in Colorado and twenty years in Missouri raising her family and working as a business writer. She now lives back in Michigan on twenty acres near the small village. Always interested in science, history, nature, and art, her overactive imagination led her to speculate on life beyond Earth, and the 'what-ifs' of changes to humanity that soon turned into fantasy and science fiction novels. She writes about writing and her quirks of mind on her blog at www.rhobincourtright.com

Other Novels By Rhobin Lee Courtright

Aegis Series:

Magic Aegis - Centuries ago, the witch Chloe cast the Aegis spell, binding four men and their descendants to protect Kaereya. Now, when needed most, magic is lost.

Change - Her mother demanded two things of Tyna...that she never expose her true nature and that she never enter Cygna, the land of witches. Now, her mother is dead, and her sister has abandoned her.

Acceptance - Responsibility and duty drove mercenary Kissre to find her estranged sister in Cygna, the land of witches.

Legend's Cipher - What Bertok had not related when the bishop gave him this mission was his most buried secret—he possessed an unnatural ability.

Black Angel Series:

Rogue's Rules - Traitor, mutineer, deserter—slanderous words fixed to Ensign Jezlynn Chambers' name.

Loser's Game - Jezlynn has plied the pirates' trade but won't let anyone use the signature of the Black Angel to hide their crimes.

Devil's Due - Command ordered Jezlynn into the Space Service Corp, yet it is one thing to think you can accomplish a goal, another to achieve it.

Angels Thread - Just when Jezlynn believes she has overcome her past it returns to haunt her

Home World Series:

Home World Aginfeld - On technically advanced but feudal Aginfeld, Alix Risseu is held for theft...the sentence is death. Only Alix is innocent.

Nanite Warrior - Hearing herself claimed as wife, Xandra gave a weak laugh. "Bad luck just won't end, but this time, I'm sure yours is worse than mine, husband."

Dragoons' Journey - Brigit has moved constantly for years, now a message offers her freedom on Aginfeld, a place her enemy, the Colonial Pact, desperately wants.

Home World Reax - Maera escaped the future planned for her on Reax, so what could make her return? Learning of her home planet's devastation.

The Carolingians:

Constantine's Legacy - Leonard must learn to be the Frankish warrior his father Radulf, the Dux Provinciae, demands. His difficult training is nothing compared to the dangerous deceptions he discovers.

Letter to Our Readers

Enjoy this book?

You can make a difference.

As an independent publisher, Wings ePress, Inc. does not have the financial clout of the large New York publishers. We can't afford large magazine spreads or subway posters to tell people about our quality books.

But we do have something much more effective and powerful than ads. We have a large base of loyal readers.

Honest reviews help bring the attention of new readers to our books.

If you enjoyed this book, we would appreciate it if you would spend a few minutes posting a review on the site where you purchased this book or on the Wings ePress, Inc. webpages at: https://wingsepress. com/

Thank You